BOOKS BY LANDIS WADE

<u>The Indie Retirement Mystery Series</u>

Deadly Declarations

Deadly Gold Rush

Death by Podcasting with co-author Sarah Archer

<u>The Write Quotes Series</u>

The Writing Life

Learning to Write

Writing Process & Tools

Storytelling, Inspiration, & Research

Writing Techniques & Characters

Writing Community, Revision, & Editors

The Emotional Writing Journey

Publishing and Book Marketing

<u>The Christmas Courtroom Trilogy</u>

The Christmas Heist

The Legally Binding Christmas

The Christmas Redemption

The Write Quotes series is available in print and ebook.

All other books are available in print, ebook, and audiobook.

Learn more at www.landiswade.com

PRAISE FOR DEADLY GOLD RUSH

"A fascinating history wrapped in an intriguing mystery. *Deadly Gold Rush* strikes pay-dirt with a story of murder and betrayal that proves the age-old allure of gold is still as deadly as ever."

—**Mark de Castrique**, Edgar nominated author of twenty-four mystery novels, including the Secret Lives Mystery Series

Landis Wade's writing style is as vivid as a film reel: Each scene is layered with atmosphere, tension, and rich Southern detail. Charlotte sleeps. A gunshot echoes. And by morning, the trap is set. In *Deadly Gold Rush*, Harriet Keaton, Craig Travail, and Yeager Alexander face an old enemy who knows exactly where to strike. Taut, immersive, and impossible to put down.

—**Molly Grantham**, 4x-Emmy winner, 3x-author, and global speaker

Deadly Gold Rush takes us on a twist-filled ride through Charlotte's hidden gold rush history with a group of lively retirees who seek the bright side in their golden years. The perfect mix of history, mystery, humor, and heart.

—**Sarah Archer**, screenwriter and author of *The Plus One*

Craig Travail, Harriet Keaton, and Yeager Alexander are on another thrilling adventure through Charlotte's history, this time the gold rush. *Deadly Gold Rush* hooks you with mysteries and secrets from page one and entertains you throughout with the comings and goings of the Independence Retirement Community. This is an engaging mystery, one that will keep you guessing until the very end.

—**Halli Gomez**, award-winning author of *List of Ten*

Deadly Gold Rush brings back the feisty trio of retirees at the Independence Retirement Community. Their penchant for solving crimes and their love of North Carolina history gets them caught up in a fast-moving case where what happened in the past has present-day reverberations: a dangerous treasure hunt for missing 1830s gold coins and a murder trial, with a touch of romance. *Deadly Gold Rush* is an entertaining mystery as well as a fascinating look into Charlotte's history as the epicenter for the United States's first gold rush.

—**Mark West**, award-winning author and UNC Charlotte English professor

Deadly Gold Rush hooked me from the very first page. Fans of Wade's previous novel, *Deadly Declarations*, will be pleased to join the motley crew from the Indie Retirement Community once again as they find themselves tangled in another compelling mystery. Elegantly written and gripping, Wade expertly weaves together a tale that is dramatic and thrilling, romantic and heartwarming, while shining a light on Charlotte's enthralling gold rush history buried for nearly two centuries beneath the city's skyscrapers. I absolutely loved it. *Deadly Gold Rush* will most certainly be a must-read of 2026.

—**Joy Callaway**, international bestselling author of *The Star of Camp Greene*

Can a legal thriller spiced with murder and mayhem be charming and funny? *Deadly Gold Rush* by Landis Wade – who pairs retirees with treasure hunts and Charlotte gold rush history with salsa dancing – proves that it can. All that glitters in the second Indie Retirement mystery isn't gold, though. Residents Harriet Keaton, Craig Travail, and Yeager Alexander team up again to save the Indie from foreclosure and to find out who has framed Harriet's brother for murder. *Deadly Gold Rush*, part caper and all heart, strikes gold.

—**Sara E. Johnson**, author of the Alexa Glock Forensics Mysteries, NYT's Readers' Pick, and Claymore Award Best Mystery Finalist

In Memory of Mom & Dad

COPYRIGHT

Publisher: Lystra Books & Literary Services, LLC 391 Lystra Estates Drive, Chapel Hill, NC 27517

Printed in the United States of America

DEADLY GOLD RUSH

AN INDIE RETIREMENT MYSTERY

LANDIS WADE

All that glisters is not gold; Often have you heard that told
–William Shakespeare, *The Merchant of Venice*

During the gold rush, it's a good time to be in the pick and shovel business
–Mark Twain

The idols of the heathen are silver and gold
–Psalm 135:15

PART I

DAY ONE - THE GOLDEN YEARS

CHAPTER 1

DEATH IN THE PASSAGE

The narrow alleyway walls muffled the gunshot as uptown Charlotte slept. It was one thirty in the morning on Tuesday, April 1.

The phone call didn't last long.

"It's me," the caller said. "I need your help."

"I'm listening."

"I have a body."

"Whose?"

"Chance Landry."

"Where are you?"

"Lincoln Street. Inside the Rivafinoli Passage in South End. Next to the Queen Charlotte mural."

"Anyone with you?"

The caller explained who else was still there.

"You leave. Tell them to stay with the body and wait for my call. I need to think."

Three minutes later, the call was made to the only living person remaining in the passage who could help.

"I am going to text you an address." Next, they explained what to do with Landry's body when they got to the address.

"Are you kidding? He's already dead."

But the person giving instructions had no sense of humor. "Just do it."

A text message followed with the address.

The person who received the message knew how to follow directions and did as they were told.

CHAPTER 2

VENGEANCE IS SWEET

The 11:15 p.m. email on Craig Travail's phone read: *Your friends are about to suffer financial ruin, untold heartbreak, and trials and tribulations. You have only yourself to blame.*

What?

Travail read the email again, slower this time. He read it twice more. There was no author name. Just an unknown *vengeanceissweet* email address.

Travail exhaled. His email checking practice was a bad habit, a routine held over from his career when clients expected their lawyers to be available 24/7.

Nothing good ever came of his itch to scratch his email in-box for late-night messages, like now, when it would be twice as difficult to sleep after watching the late-night local news—with its smorgasbord of crimes, collisions, and natural disasters—and reading this email.

One news story was about elder fraud, a reminder of how susceptible retirees are to financial fraud schemes. Was that what was coming for his friends at the Independence Retirement Community, which everyone called the Indie? Were the residents about to suffer financial ruin because of risky investments? If so, he'd be angry at the perpetrators for their heartless guile and frustrated with his friends for being so gullible.

The television show made the point, though, and he agreed, that adults spend most of their lives collecting assets to make retirement possible and the rest of their days worried if their accumulated treasure will last as long as they do, leading some retirees to make risky and uninformed choices with their nest eggs. Was that what his friends had done? Made bad choices with their money? Is that what the emailer taunted him about?

Travail's instinct was to fire off a harsh response to the email with some choice lawyer-like words and warnings, but he ignored the bait—he suspected they wouldn't respond anyway—and he punched the remote control instead.

The television screen faded to black, and his den fell silent, save for Blue's rhythmic snores and his jerking legs. Travail's black and tan coonhound must be dreaming, chasing ducks along the lake behind Travail's cottage, as he was apt to do in real life, and as usual, failing to catch the waterfowl before they darted back into the water. Travail leaned over his club chair's arm and let his free hand graze on Blue's back until his pet stopped running in his sleep.

Maybe the email was a prank. Maybe, like him, a friend had become bored with life at the Indie. And yet, the email bothered him.

Whose lives—which friends' lives—were about to be shattered? And how? And for that matter, why? And what did he have to do with it?

Since moving a year earlier into the Independence Retirement Community, Travail had made two best friends, Harriet Keaton and Yeager Alexander, and several other good friends. He'd met many other retirees, some whose company he tolerated and some whose company he could do without. Either way, he didn't want to see anyone hurt. He certainly didn't want his close friends to suffer, and he didn't want to be the person responsible for their pain.

The flame on the candle he'd lit this morning was down to the base of the wick. He turned away from it, detesting the severe loneliness of March 31.

There was no logic for feeling so alone—what with all the crimes, court cases, and historic mysteries Harriet, Yeager, and he navigated since he arrived at the Indie and the time they spent together—but it was hard to control his feelings, especially the feeling of being by himself. A Jewish resident told him about the tradition of lighting a candle on the anniversary of a loved one's death. It felt loving to strike the match in Rachael's honor, but as day became night, Travail's mood shifted. It had been three years to the day.

The flickering light had a strobe-like effect on the things that reminded him of Rachael: her furniture, her quilts, her artwork, her pictures. Travail missed Rachael's kindness, her playfulness, her creativity, and the rituals they shared. The flicker made the past too present, making him long for another night and morning and day together. She was here, there, and everywhere, but nowhere at all.

Assertive is what he'd needed to be in the moment that changed everything. He and Rachael were in the mountains at a high-elevation rental for a getaway when a freak storm rolled in and dumped six inches of snow on the ground. Rachael decided to drive to the local general store to stock the pantry for their cozy weekend together. He had a work call and offered to go with her after he finished.

"It's just snow," she'd said.

"Okay, but be careful," he'd responded.

"Always, dear." Then she kissed him on the mouth, patted his bottom, and walked out of his life forever.

The news came in a phone call from the local police. First came the shock, then the grief, and then the Monday-morning quarterbacking. He should have insisted Rachael let him drive her. He should have done more to protect her. If he had, maybe she would still be here. Maybe the out-of-control delivery truck that hit the black ice would have killed him instead of her, or maybe Travail could have prevented the accident.

Spring in North Carolina was supposed to be about new beginnings, not endings, with the dogwoods and azaleas in bloom, but his eyes grew wet from the memories, and he felt a sudden heaviness in his body.

He looked at the email again and became resolute. For sure, he would not make the same mistake twice with the people he cared about. He would protect them.

But who was behind the email?

Whoever wanted sweet vengeance against his friends wanted vengeance against him too, because their pain would be his pain. The question for his lawyer brain—used to solving riddles for years—was: who despised them and him that much?

Like an unexpected electric shock, the answer startled him. This email was exactly the kind of plot his nemesis, Robert Elkin, would conjure. If Elkin hurt Harriet, Yeager, and his other close friends, he would hurt Travail worse.

But wasn't Elkin no longer a threat? They'd exposed his concealment of the truth about the Mecklenburg Declaration of Independence, avoided death at the hands of his father, pushed him out of his Big Law leadership position, and seen to it that the state bar took his law license. Elkin no longer had big-time lawyer power. The only thing he had was anger, resentment, and a low-paying job as a paralegal with a former client, though Travail didn't know the client's name or their business. It was a sharp drop from the level of influence that had made the man dangerous, and yet, there was reason to be cautious. Elkin was cunning and would hold a grudge till death do they part.

Travail leaned his head back in his chair, looked up at the ceiling, and pondered the text again: *financial ruin, untold heartbreak, and trials and tribulations.*

Harriet was too smart to get caught up in a financial scam. Not so with Yeager. He was impulsive, likely to jump at the chance to possess something shiny because it might become shinier.

Travail pulled an olive-colored sweatshirt over his t-shirt, woke Blue, and took him into the backyard to do his business under the stars. While he waited, Travail glanced across Lost Cove Lake to Harriet's cottage. He inhaled the fresh night air, and he marveled at the main building's reflection on the lake's surface. Harriet's lights were out. She, an early riser, must be asleep.

Seeing Harriet's peaceful cottage raised a question he'd been pondering. Should he ask her on a date? Carrie Roberts, the Indie Gossip Queen, thought so and often shared her opinion.

Most days, it seemed like the right decision not to ask Harriet—or anyone else, for that matter—on a date. Three years wasn't that long, really, since Rachael died. And yet, here he was, caught in a web he'd spun for himself, trapped somewhere between what he no longer had and the companionship he wanted but resisted. Harriet was his friend. Should he keep it that way?

Harriet would most likely turn him down anyway. He was a project, and he knew it, starting with the lesson she'd had to teach him last year that retirement living is not life's dead end but a fresh path forward. And now, with him being a sixty-six-year-old widower afraid to address his feelings, she'd be quick to beg off.

Blue finished up, and the two headed inside. His watch told him it was a new day. He blew out the dwindling flame on the candle and headed to his bedroom, where Blue was already curled up on the end of Travail's queen-size bed. Wearing only striped boxers and a white cotton t-shirt, Travail pulled the covers up to his chin. With a good night's sleep, he'd be fresh in the morning to put his effort into stopping Elkin. He still had his law license, after all, and as Yeager would tell him from time to time, "You ain't dead yet."

He closed his eyes and imagined tying a dry fly rig with two nymphs on a dropper line, the key to catching river trout on and below the surface at the same time. This falling-asleep system was better than counting backward from three hundred by threes. It worked its charm in less than five minutes.

Travail didn't know when he dozed off that the murder train had left the station. He didn't know when he began to snore that someone had already set the trap for his friends. And he didn't know when he fell into a deep sleep that when the sun came up, he would ponder, and not for the first time, how he could have been so wrong to believe retirement living would ever be boring or lonely.

CHAPTER 3

STRANGE PLACE FOR A BODY

"Get up, Craig Travail."

Get up from what?

And why was Chuck Yeager Alexander standing alongside a Tennessee leg of the Watauga River yelling at him to get up?

Yeager stepped off the riverbank and walked across the smooth surface in Travail's direction. The man normally swam to retrieve trout. But walking on water? Unbelievable.

Again, with the booming voice. "Wake up, Craig Travail. Harriet needs our help."

Strong hands clasped Travail's shoulders and yanked him from a river with the prettiest trout he'd ever seen to a dark room where a gigantic figure hovered over him. Blue growled.

Travail let his feet fall to the floor and put one hand on Blue's head to calm his pet. The illuminated bedside clock said it was 3:15 in the morning, Tuesday, April 1.

Was this an April Fool's joke?

But then, that voice again. "Thought I'd never get you to wake up, Craig Travail."

Yeager tossed Travail the khaki pants he'd left on the chair beside his bed.

Travail was sure he'd locked the doors. With dead bolts, in fact. "How'd you get in?"

Yeager waved his hand at Travail as if getting into Travail's cottage was the easiest thing he'd ever done. "Put your pants on. We need to get to Harriet's house. There's trouble with her brother."

What brother? And what trouble?

Yeager left the room before Travail could quiz him, but even in his sleepy state, the word *heartbreak* came to mind.

Travail tripped as he tried to put one leg into his pants. With both legs in, he went to the bathroom, splashed water on his face, and rubbed deodorant under his arms.

Dressed in khaki pants and the olive-colored sweatshirt he wore the night before, Travail found Yeager in the kitchen wearing blue jeans and a light flannel shirt, unbuttoned and loose to reveal a white t-shirt that said in black letters, "I act before I think."

Yeager handed Travail a thermal cup of steaming black coffee and tugged at his sleeve. The sound of a motor running and Yeager's impatience were Travail's clues that if he was going to learn what trouble Harriet had with her brother, he'd better move.

But when Yeager's truck approached Harriet's cottage, Yeager didn't slow down.

"I thought you said we were going to Harriet's house."

"We are. The one uptown."

First, Harriet had a brother he didn't know about. Next, she had an uptown house. He'd wait for the trifecta.

"Bet you didn't know Harriet's brother just got out of prison."

Bingo.

A deer crossed the road, and Yeager swerved to avoid a collision, causing hot coffee to spill in Travail's lap. The liquid soaked through his pants and left him wet and irritable.

After they passed through the Indie's front gates and onto the main road, Travail looked at Yeager. "Tell me about the trouble."

Yeager leaned forward as he ran a red light and kept his eyes on the road. "Joey is her twin, but he's nothing like Harriet."

That was not an answer to Travail's question, but it got him thinking about a person who was nothing like Harriet Keaton. He must be irresponsible, uneducated, unattractive, unorganized, shy, and unwilling to be helpful or encouraging to others. And he was 99-percent sure Harriet had never been to prison. There was that difference too.

But a twin brother? She'd never said a word about him. He wanted to know why, but he shouldn't press the matter. Yeager might give him the lecture about how he needed to pay more attention to the world around him, because "if you did, you'd know what the heck was going on in your friends' lives, Craig Travail."

It was true. He wasn't intuitive about personal matters.

Yeager read his mind. "Harriet's got secrets too."

"Apparently not from you." Travail's tone was sharper than he intended.

Maybe he reacted the way he did because Yeager woke him up before what Yeager called the "butt crack of dawn." Or maybe it was because Harriet confided in Yeager before him, even though that would make sense since she and Yeager had been friends for twenty years, and he'd been at the Indie for only one year. Still, Harriet and he had become close friends—was that the right way to describe their relationship?—after they'd almost lost their lives on Yeager's quest to solve the mystery of the Mecklenburg Declaration of Independence. If Harriet had a brother, why hadn't she told him?

"It's a long story. Best to let Harriet fill you in."

Travail wasn't awake enough to argue. "At least tell me why we're in such a hurry."

"Did you know the tobacco chewing judge you and Harriet faced in court last year moved into the Indie?"

Travail turned his head to Yeager. "Roscoe Brady?"

"They call him 'Chaw,' but yes, that's the one. Been here about a week. He's our judge in the new Indie People's Court."

"The new what?"

Yeager hit a pothole and bounced Travail off the bench seat.

"Read your bulletin. Holding court in the chapel was my idea. Hard to lie staring God in the face."

"Excuse me?"

"We've got a fun case at four thirty today, one hour before dinner. Court draws a good crowd because it doubles as happy hour. You should drop by. My role is—"

Travail cut Yeager off. "What does this have to do with Harriet and her brother?"

Yeager crossed a double yellow line to pass a garbage truck, throwing Travail against the passenger-side door. When Yeager swerved back toward his lane, Travail fell toward Yeager and Yeager pushed him back in his place. "By the way, how do you think the women-folk will like Chaw's habit? He can hold his spit for at least thirty minutes."

Travail wasn't thinking about anyone's habit other than Yeager's of not getting to the point, when Charlotte's uptown skyline came into view.

They crossed Independence Boulevard and zipped past Central Piedmont Community College, where a reminder of their previous investigation appeared. A statue of a colonial man in a tricorn hat leaning forward on a horse was in a race as fast as theirs, only his race took place 250 years earlier when he delivered the Mecklenburg Declaration of Independence five hundred miles to the Second Continental Congress in Philadelphia. The statue evoked a memory of how troublemaker Robert Elkin's entanglement with a secret Virginia society almost got Travail and his good friends killed last year.

Yeager acknowledged Captain James Jack's statue with a "Huzzah!" as he ran another red light and then turned right on Morehead Street. He continued to exceed the speed limit and veer off topic. "We solved the mystery about the mink coats."

Travail didn't care. The gossipy Indie residents had been abuzz about the thefts, but he didn't think a missing mink coat in the South was that big a crisis.

"It was Lena Rand, poor thing. She's in memory care now. When they cleaned out her unit, they found fifteen mink coats in her closet. She'd been wearing them home from dinner. Thought they were hers. Sometimes, the answer to a mystery is not that complicated."

Travail didn't respond. His focus was on Harriet as he sipped the remainder of his coffee Yeager's reckless ride hadn't spilled. Perhaps this morning's mystery would be as uncomplicated as the mink coat caper. He hoped so, for Harriet's sake.

Yeager made a sharp turn and entered the district in South End where successful gold mines prospered in the early nineteenth century, though there was nothing to remind the public of that history but a few historic signs. There were no houses in sight. Yet.

"Almost there, Craig Travail. Harriet's house backs up to the Gold District, near where the Rudisill Mine used to operate."

Travail knew nothing about the Rudisill Mine, other than the name, but it was good to know they were getting close. Curiosity and his concern for Harriet made the perilous drive feel slow. And it was the middle of the night.

They swerved through several streets and crested a hill—Yeager said it used to be called Rudisill Hill—where, off to the right, South End stood up to be noticed.

There were several office towers under construction, with mixed-use developments spread out before them. Uptown businesses—law firms included—hurried to make the move to the shimmery new business and entertainment district under continuous construction. Perhaps this was why someone on the historic planning commission said the city logo should be the picture of a bulldozer.

A few quick turns later, Yeager stopped his truck behind two police cars and a firetruck parked in front of a one-story house, narrow across the front, with cream siding. The yard had Harriet's gardener's touch, with staggered flower beds, waiting on the spring bloom, a contrast to the junkyard next door guarded by a chain-link fence.

Yeager killed the engine as his Jitterbug phone—the one with the retiree-sized buttons, as he liked to remind Travail and Harriet—rang. He answered, listened, and didn't say much, a rarity in the one year Travail had known Yeager.

"Righto. I will let you know what I find," he said, before he closed the flip phone and turned to Travail. "The police arrested Harriet's brother, but he's still in the house. Time to hurry, Craig Travail. His name is Joey Penman."

They stepped out of Yeager's truck, and to Travail's surprise, Yeager whispered, "See you soon." He then slipped around the house's corner closest to the junkyard, unnoticed by the crowd of people on Harriet's property. Where was he going?

Two firefighters carrying axes approached, and Travail stepped aside to let them pass. Why the axes? And why had the police arrested Harriet's brother?

A person dressed in white coveralls—perhaps a forensic examiner —sat on the porch steps removing crime scene protective gloves. As if someone had died.

Harriet sat on the porch swing near a uniformed police officer taking instruction from a man in a dark brown suit. By the man's clothes and demeanor, he looked like he might be a detective.

Travail and Harriet locked eyes. She quick-stepped it down the porch steps, and met him on her sidewalk halfway between the street and the house. She wore sage-green knit pants and a matching long-sleeved top. Her outfit, complete with tennis shoes, looked comfortable, unlike her facial expression. Not prone to fluster under pressure, this morning was the exception. Her voice caught. "Thank you for—"

Travail felt on edge as he opened his arms and gave Harriet a hug, feeling the tension in her body. "How can I help?"

With her red curls wilder than usual, she turned her head from side to side as if to see whether anyone could hear them. "Just act like a lawyer. My brother Joey is in big trouble."

Before Travail could ask Harriet any questions about her brother's trouble, the man in the brown suit—a suit that upon closer inspection had seen better days—stood before them holding an unlit cigar, reminding Travail of a '70s television detective.

"I'm Detective Sizemore. I assume you're the lawyer Ms. Keaton said was coming. We've got quite a situation here."

What was the situation? The detective didn't elaborate, and Harriet couldn't say with the detective hovering. "I'm Craig Travail here to represent Ms. Keaton's brother. May I see him?"

"Absolutely. He's inside. Don't worry. He hasn't said a word."

Travail looked at Harriet as they walked toward the house. She was stoic, offering no clues as to what he was about to encounter.

The uniformed police officer on the porch moved aside for them to enter the house. Harriet led the way as they stepped into a small living area.

A man sat on a couch with his arms behind his back, presumably in handcuffs, with another uniformed police officer looking over him. The man's beard showed he hadn't shaved in a few days, and his short red hair mixed with gray was unbrushed. He wore torn blue jeans and a maroon sweatshirt. He kept his eyes lowered. Harriet didn't look at him, and he didn't look at her.

Travail broke the awkward silence. "You must be Joey Penman. I'm Craig Travail, a lawyer. Your lawyer, if you'd like me to be. I am Harriet's friend."

Joey didn't look up and didn't respond.

The screen door opened and shut behind them. The detective spoke to Joey. "Time to go."

Travail blinked. "You said I could talk with my client."

Detective Sizemore laughed. "No. I said you could see him."

"Where are you taking him? And why?"

The detective examined his phone. "It says here that William Joseph Penman, who I gather from your conversation goes by Joey, violated his post-release supervision obligations when he missed his recent meeting with his parole officer. We're taking him in to keep him comfortable for his video conference hearing today at 4 p.m. Nice we ran into him. What's the word? Fortuitous? Now he can attend his hearing."

Harriet whispered to Travail. "Can he do that?"

Travail wasn't sure. His limited experience in criminal law didn't extend to post-release supervision and its violation process. He could research it, but that wouldn't help them now. He affected an official tone. "My client has a constitutional right to speak with his lawyer."

The detective shrugged. "We have to process him first. You can speak to him at the jail. Let's say three o'clock. You can have a chat before his hearing."

The detective nodded at the police officer, who pulled Harriet's brother from the sofa and pushed him out the front door, allowing the detective to focus his full attention on Harriet. "Do you mind telling me why your brother was in your house and a dead man is in your basement?"

Travail felt that heightened sense of nervousness he got when his clients spoke in court, worried about how they would fare, but at least in those situations, they had time to prepare. A dead body in Harriet's basement was something he suspected Harriet was unprepared to address.

Travail whispered in Harriet's ear. "Don't say a word." With a corpse in her basement, Harriet could be a suspect too.

She ignored him.

"After my brother went to prison—a fact you seem to know, Detective—my father died, leaving this house to me. I haven't talked with Joey in years, and I didn't know he was going to drop by for a visit. I also don't know how the parole officer lost contact with him." Harriet said it like it was the parole officer's fault and finished with, "I have no clue who is under my house, but I have a question for you."

The detective waited.

"How do you explain my collapsed kitchen floor?"

Surprised, Travail looked through a door to the kitchen to see the destruction. So focused on Joey, he hadn't noticed the mess when he came in the house. And now, he was as interested as Harriet in the detective's answer to her question. Why had the kitchen floor collapsed?

But the detective ignored the question. "The business card we found in the dead man's wallet says he was a real estate developer named Chance Landry."

Harriet flinched, and the detective picked up on it. "I see you recognize the name. Didn't he testify against your brother in the trial that sent him to prison?"

Harriet regained her composure and fired back. "You think my brother killed his accuser in a twenty-year-old trial, placed him under my house, and after the floor collapsed on the corpse, he waited for the fire department to arrive, knowing they would find the evidence and call you?"

"The floor collapse made significant noise. Neighbors heard it and called 911." The detective rubbed his chin. "Maybe he stayed to protect you. To take the fall."

At that, Harriet did something unexpected, even for her. She held out her wrists. "I can't take it anymore. I confess. After I deposited my Social Security check yesterday, I killed Landry, placed his body under my house, and danced to my success on my kitchen floor until it collapsed on him. I tricked my twin brother into coming here, knowing he would take the blame as an ex-convict."

Detective Sizemore shrugged before he called to the woman in the white suit to "bring the knife." She handed him a baggie he held up for Harriet to see. "Do you recognize this?"

She opened her mouth but didn't speak, causing Travail to step forward and shield her. "Was the man under the house killed with that knife?"

The detective grinned. "He took a bullet between the eyes, but seeing as how this knife was stuck in his back when we found him, I'd say the knife helped."

"Where's the gun?" Travail was all business now, angling to shift attention from Harriet.

"Good question, Counselor." The detective shifted his gaze to Harriet. "The knife came from your kitchen set. Care to tell us where we can find the gun?"

Harriet pushed the detective aside and walked toward the door. Travail took out his business card—the one Yeager insisted he have for his solo, almost non-existent law practice—and gave it to the detective. The card did not say, "100-percent money-back guarantee" or "we win all our cases," as Yeager had suggested—"because you're so good at law stuff, Craig Travail"—but it had his mobile phone number and email address. If the detective arrested Joey or Harriet for Chance Landry's murder, he wanted to be the first person the detective called.

"One more thing, Ms. Keaton."

Harriet stopped and turned as the detective held up a bowling-ball-sized clear plastic bag that looked like it contained coins.

"Any idea why these nineteenth-century gold coins were scattered in your basement and on the victim? Do you and your brother collect coins?"

Harriet didn't answer. She tugged Travail's arm, and he followed her out of the house.

The screen door slammed behind them, and they walked in silence to the street.

Travail couldn't help but think about the email he'd received hours earlier. Was this the untold heartbreak for Harriet, the fact her twin brother—or she, or both of them—might face trial for murder? He could sense tension in Harriet's stiff posture.

"Your kitchen knife?"

"I didn't kill Landry, Craig."

"I didn't think—"

The detective's voice rang out. "As they say on television, Ms. Keaton, don't leave town."

CHAPTER 4

REDISCOVERING THE RUDISILL MINE

Standing at the curb beside Harriet's Toyota hybrid, Travail waited for her to direct their next move when something caught his attention. A shadow-like figure advanced toward the street beyond the junkyard's chain-link fence.

Harriet whispered in his ear. "He's out. Tell him to follow me."

By "him," Travail presumed she meant Yeager, who was behind the steering wheel by the time Travail climbed in his truck. Dirt covered Yeager's shirt and pants.

"Where to, Craig Travail?"

Travail pointed to Harriet's vehicle—"wherever Harriet goes"—and Yeager followed her. They took the first right on Mint Street, made a right on Summit Avenue, and stopped alongside a historical marker that read:

Largest and most productive of all the gold mines in the Charlotte gold mining region was the Rudisill. Gold was first discovered at this mine in 1826. The great wealth produced at the Rudisill made the fortunes of many and played a key role in the development and growth of Charlotte. The mine had numerous shafts and was worked to a depth of more than 350 feet. Mining operations existed at this site for more than a century, with all operations coming to an end by 1937.

Yeager was right. Harriet's house backed up to the old Rudisill Mine. But why stop here? Was this location just a place to talk without being overheard by the police, or did Harriet think the historic gold mine played a part in today's drama?

Harriet led the way to the rear of the dirt lot, separated from her backyard by thick foliage and overgrown weeds. They gathered around a flat ground level concrete slab while the emergency vehicles' lights flashed through the trees and scrub.

Harriet knelt and placed both hands on the slab. "This is the cover to the Rudisill Mine's pump shaft. It's how they removed underground water from the mine so miners could do their work. There are deep underground mine shafts in this area." She addressed Yeager. "What did you see under the house?"

"Half your kitchen fell into and across a deep hole in the ground."

"Has to be a collapsed mine shaft. When I was a child in the early '60s, my dad read in the *Charlotte News* about a bulldozer that fell into a mine shaft three blocks from here at Junk City Auto Parts, which is now an auto repair shop."

She pointed in the direction of the Carolina Panthers' professional football stadium. "When he took our family to see the bulldozer, Joey and I got too close to the hole, my mother said. It looked like a bottomless pit."

Travail looked toward the stadium and back toward Harriet's house. "Bad luck all around. Structural damage insurance won't cover, with a dead man—presumably thanks to pre-meditated murder—to make matters worse. Complicated." He sighed.

Yeager slapped Travail on the back. "Sun ain't even up yet, Craig Travail, and you're spouting legalese good as usual. You've still got it."

Harriet forced Yeager to refocus. "Where, exactly, did you find Landry when you crawled in my basement?"

So that's where Yeager went. Under the house.

Yeager glanced toward the house and rubbed his beard. "It was a tight fit, but I crawled in far enough to find him entangled in the debris that fell into the hole."

Travail didn't want to sound like a smart-ass lawyer again so early in the morning, but he had a theory. "How hard would it have been for somebody to push the body into that deep hole?"

"Easy-peasy."

Travail looked toward Harriet's house. "Maybe the killer never intended the victim to be hidden for long. Maybe the killer planned to tip off the police to the body under the house, but when the kitchen collapsed, the killer fled, and the neighbors made the call for him. Or for her."

"You must have been reading your detective books, Craig Travail."

Travail didn't say aloud what else might be possible. Harriet's brother could have hidden the body under the house and stayed at the scene to protect Harriet after the shaft caved in.

"What are you thinking, Craig?" Harriet asked.

"I'm thinking we will know more after I speak with your brother today."

"No need. He can fend for himself. Been doing it for twenty years in prison."

This wasn't like Harriet to turn her back on someone close to her, especially a twin brother, but then again, Travail knew nothing about Harriet's relationship with her brother.

"I thought you wanted me to be his lawyer."

"I said act like a lawyer, like you're doing now."

"Then I should talk with him. For your sake."

Harriet's shoulders drew back, and her eyes narrowed. "You think you know what's best 'for my sake.' The answer is no, Craig."

Travail wouldn't let it go. "A dead man was found in your house, with your knife in his back. You could be implicated. And you don't want me to talk with Joey? Be his lawyer?"

"No. I don't."

Yeager edged his way into the argument with a question, and for once, Travail appreciated Yeager's ability to build a tangent into every conversation. "What do you know about gold coins, Harriet? I found several under your house." He handed one to Harriet.

Harriet used the flashlight on her phone to illuminate the brilliant yellow shine on the coin. Everyone leaned close to have a look.

The date 1838 appeared on the coin's face with a small "C" stamped above it. Above the "C" was a woman's head with wavy hair. She wore a crown that said "Liberty." Stars surrounded her head.

Harriet flipped the coin over to reveal an eagle clutching a shield and arrows. "United States of America" formed a circle around the edge. Below the eagle were the numbers and letter: 2 1/2 D.

Yeager pointed at the coin in Harriet's palm. "They're all like that."

Harriet turned off the light on her phone and handed the coin back to Yeager. "The letter 'C' means the coin was made at the US Mint's Charlotte branch. This is a quarter eagle, worth two dollars and fifty cents in 1838."

"How do you know that?" Travail's coin knowledge was nonexistent.

"From my father, but don't ask me why, Craig. I don't want to talk about his obsession." Then to Yeager: "Where did you find the coins? The police showed us a bag of coins they said they had collected near and on the body."

"Found two in the dirt next to Landry's feet and one near his right elbow."

Yeager returned the coin to his pocket. "I'll speak with Brian Tartly to see if the coins are legit. He's an Indie resident. Expert in rare coins. He and his son own a coin-collecting store off Highway 51, but Brian is retired. He takes his Indie dates to the store to impress them."

Travail sighed. "Is there any resident at the Indie who is not an expert in something and who is not dating someone else at the Indie?"

Harriet's face softened. "Retirement communities are the best place to find an expert on anything you need to know, Craig. Lots of life's experiences there. They're also the best place to find a date with the opposite sex, if you're a man." She paused. "You two are the only Indie men who aren't dating anyone. Imagine that."

Travail pretended not to hear her. He shifted his thoughts to what the coins had to do with Landry's death. The answer might make a difference in Joey's or Harriet's defense if either were arrested. "Any idea what one of those coins is worth?"

Harriet did. "If they're real, Craig, they're worth a lot more than two dollars and fifty cents. A whole lot more."

CHAPTER 5

GOSSIP AS HEALTHCARE

With only a one-hour catnap to take her edge off before the sun was up, Harriet dressed in a calf-length cornflower-blue shirtdress and low wedge shoes for her breakfast meeting. Because it was still early, she threw on a light sweater. Her short night's sleep was no reason to let herself go, especially when paying a visit to her best friend.

She left her Indie cottage's backyard, making her way along the gravel path that fronted Lost Cove Lake. Fog rose from the glassy surface and blocked her view of Craig's cottage, but it did not hide the movement of a person's bulky silhouette on Craig's side of the lake.

The mystery man had to be Yeager, making his morning rounds to ensure the community was crime-free and its residents were well-protected, doing his unasked-for volunteer work as a one-man security service. Boy did she love his loyalty and his energy, but she didn't need it now. She kept her head down, and picked up her pace to be on time.

Harriet's conscience nagged her as she thought about her family history she'd kept hidden from Craig. The shame of her brother-turned-criminal and her father's obsession with gold coins held her back. Worse than the secrets she hid from Craig were the secrets her family hid from her, forcing her to ponder for the last twenty years what drove

Joey to commit the crime that sent him to prison. And why her father did not defend her brother.

Craig was kind to offer to represent her brother at his parole video hearing—and Yeager was all Yeager saying, "I smell a rat, and it ain't your brother"—but Craig's offer was a waste of time. She doubted Joey would accept his help.

Harriet stopped before her destination and read the sign above the door. The Indie named the Collins Center in honor of deceased professor Matthew Collins, whose research led to the truth about the Mecklenburg Declaration of Independence. His granddaughter, Lori Collins, had supplied a generous contribution for the construction.

Like most residents, Harriet disliked the feel of the place. It wasn't because the center was unclean, or lacked excellent healthcare. It was the unmistakable nursing-home scent—the disinfectants and air fresheners fighting to mask the odor of bodily fluids—and seeing their friends bound to a space they might never leave until the undertaker carried them out feet first.

Harriet sucked in a breath and stepped into the lobby. She approached the counter and identified the friend she was there to see. Her friend's diagnosis had been a slap in the face, a reminder cancer could happen to anyone, even the strongest and the loudest, as with the one Indie resident Harriet could talk to about her brother and her father.

"She's in the dining room." The receptionist handed Harriet the temporary name tag, her ticket to the place most residents tried to avoid visiting.

Being early for the breakfast crowd, the dining room was empty, except for her friend, who spotted Harriet and waved her over.

"Morning, Harriet. Hope you're hungry. I ordered for you."

Harriet came around the table, leaned over the wheelchair's edge, and gave her friend a hug before settling into the seat next to her.

Carrie Roberts was dressed in a loose-fitting floral-print top with elbow-length sleeves and elastic-waist white capri pants. She was the only person who knew Harriet's family history and who, despite her penchant for gossip, kept that history to herself.

It had to be hard on Carrie, the Indie Gossip Queen, to stay mum for Harriet, but despite the temptation to tell Harriet's family tales to her gossip-craving audience, Carrie had kept quiet for all the years they'd known each other. Harriet loved that about her, and loved her vibrant spirit, despite a cancer diagnosis for which there was no cure.

"Let's not make this visit about my health today. I'm talked-out about scans and treatments, and the fact my legs don't work anymore."

Harriet couldn't help herself. "How are you feeling?"

A staff member politely interrupted their conversation to set plates covered with eggs, bacon, toast, and pancakes before Carrie and Harriet.

Carrie smiled, thanked the server, and pointed at the food. "Thanks to good steroids, that's how I feel today. Eat up."

Harriet didn't rush the conversation and let Carrie take the lead. While they ate, she learned the latest Indie gossip, listening without interest to the girlfriend-boyfriend dramas and the complaints about the staff and restaurant food, while waiting patiently for any non-tabloid-like facts.

Harriet's ears perked up when Carrie mentioned a ten-million-dollar addition to the Indie bank accounts made possible by the Standish Company and the Indie's newest resident, Celia Standish. The Standish name dredged up her brother's twenty-year-old trial for a second time in one day. Celia's son, Junior, had testified against Joey in his trial.

"Celia's a tough old bird, or they wouldn't have moved her up the wait list and admitted her after she turned ninety. Remember, Harriet, you gotta wait your turn and walk into this place. They don't like to see a nonagenarian shuffle in with a walker, not that she needs one."

Harriet knew the length of their wait list and the walk-in rule, but the Indie would have admitted Celia on a stretcher at the front of the line given the Standish Company's generous ten million dollar cash infusion.

Carrie laughed. "You're thinking money talks."

"Ten million dollars to our bank accounts is a lot of talk, Carrie."

"Well, it's money Celia made for the Standish Company. After her husband died, she became an independent woman, like you, Harriet."

"Spare me."

Carrie stabbed a piece of bacon with her fork. "I won't apologize for calling you an independent woman, but if you don't want me to talk about the Standish family, I'll—"

"That was twenty years ago. Her son, Junior, not Celia, testified against Joey."

Carrie swallowed. "Junior's death was hard on Celia. A son should not die before his mother."

Harriet nodded as she reflected on Junior's death. It happened shortly after her brother's trial. An accident, they said. Fell and hit his head. She'd never thought much about the specifics. Harriet let Carrie do what she did best: talk.

Carrie forked some eggs, swallowed again, and continued. "When Celia's husband died, she took over the Standish Company as board chair, and she made her son Junior president. They made good money together developing commercial properties."

Carrie drank some juice. "After her Junior died, Celia ran the company until she retired this year. She chose her grandson, Lester Sterling Standish the Third, who attended a prestigious business school, as her successor. He's got big plans to develop property in South End. He signed the check to the Indie for the ten million dollars."

Thinking the man's name made Harriet nauseous, as if Lester Sterling Standish the Third were a privileged lord of the manor who hadn't earned his way except through lineage luck. "Should we call him The Third?"

"Have some respect. Our ten-million-dollar money man goes by Sterling. A pretty boy, to be sure, and not your type, I'll admit. Tall, athletic. Wears shirts with alligator logos. He's won a few tennis tournaments and keeps his golf clubs in his trunk just in case the sun shines. Oh, and he loves to make and spend money. You can tell by his Tesla and his Rolex watch."

Carrie waved at a resident and continued with a question. "Don't you find it odd Junior died so soon after your brother's trial, especially since he testified against Joey?"

Harriet never thought much about Junior's death, but now that Chance Landry was dead, maybe she should. After all, despite their age differences, Junior and her father were good friends and did business together, and Landry worked for the Standish Company. And now the Standish clan had returned and put money in the Indie accounts.

"Carrie, I don't like the idea of us being beholden to a Standish."

Carrie wiped her mouth with her napkin. "You're right to have questions. The ten million dollars was not a gift. It was a loan, and everything at the Indie except our individual units is collateral for the loan. Plus, the Standish Company got two Indie board seats in the deal, an executive board seat for Sterling's wife, Bailey, with the requirement that our bookkeeper, Jenny Montgomery, report directly to her, or should I say, Mrs. Lester Sterling Standish the Third. They also got a regular board seat for Celia."

"Why the loan? Is the Indie in trouble?"

"Ask Jenny. She'll tell you everything."

Harriet smiled. "You're in a wheelchair at the Collins Center now. How do you keep up?"

"Ain't dead yet, as Yeager would say. I operate like a mafia boss in prison."

"Is that how it feels here? Like a prison?"

Spooning her last piece of pancake, Carrie chewed before she answered. "Figure of speech. The point is, I've got my communication lines open. If you want to know what's up, I'm still your gal."

Having lost their privacy with the appearance of other wheelchair users, Carrie pushed back from the table. "Roll me to the back porch, and we'll talk about why you're here."

"Yeager said he made you a sign."

"He's a good man, despite his quirks, and handsome in a weathered way—don't you think?—like an aging cowboy movie star." Carrie didn't wait for Harriet to disagree. "We have ten minutes before my invalid friends gather for my morning news report. Let's roll."

With Harriet pushing and Carrie sharing more facts about the Standish clan, they made their way down one hall, past two nursing stations, through the game room, and onto the back covered deck that overlooked Freedom Lake. In the porch's corner stood a wooden sign with the words "Carrie's Corner." Carrie applied her brakes, and Harriet took the rocker beside her. "It's a beautiful view," Harriet said.

"Except for that." Carrie pointed down the slope.

A male figure near Freedom Lake's far end aimed what looked like a small rifle at the water. They heard a pop and a shout before Yeager —it had to be Yeager—undressed and threw himself into the lake.

"Not again," Harriet said.

"You haven't trained Yeager very well."

"He's untrainable."

"Get your boyfriend to do it. They're good pals, aren't they?"

Harriet wagged her finger at Carrie. "Number one, Craig is not my boyfriend. Number two, Yeager is untrainable."

"But he is loyal."

Harriet couldn't argue with that statement, but she wasn't here to talk about Yeager. Carrie pressed ahead anyway. "How do you feel about him?"

"He vacillates between manic and double-manic and will want us to dig for buried treasure before the week is out."

"Not Yeager. Craig. Don't you think he looks like Tom Hanks?"

Harriet was determined to stop this conversation in its tracks. "I raised one husband. I don't need to raise another."

Carrie grinned. "Already thinking about marriage, are we?"

Harriet exhaled and shook her head. "Let me rephrase. I don't need a man, period."

"Who said anything about what you need? I am trying to find out what you want. I know you like him."

Confused was a better way to think about her feelings for Craig. It started a year ago when he moved into the Indie, when, within days, they were allies to discover why Matthew Collins died, why Matthew cut his granddaughter Lori out of his will, and how the Mecklenburg Declaration of Independence fit into the answers to those questions. She and Craig had developed a bond, a heat-of-the-battle match that drew them close. They grew closer still after men tried to kill them.

At the Indie ceremony last May 20, when Yeager revealed the truth about the Meck Dec, Harriet had taken Craig's hand in a spur-of-the-moment gesture, grateful for their survival. Since then, neither she nor Craig touched hands or mentioned they ever had, dancing around feelings they had for each other.

"I like him, sure, but I like you too. Can we move on, please?"

Carrie shifted the conversation to Harriet's brother. "Isn't it time for Joey to be out of prison?"

Harriet huffed. "He got out a few weeks ago. But he's back in today."

"What do you mean?"

Harriet set her rocker in motion and relayed to Carrie the details of the morning's events and Joey's arrest.

"That doesn't sound good, but I have faith in Joey."

Harriet didn't, but she held her tongue. All she had were questions about her brother and no good answers.

Carrie paused before she spoke again, as if she searched for the right words. Finally, she said, "Your brother was innocent twenty years ago. I believe he is again."

Harriet slowed her rocker to a stop. "If he was innocent, why didn't my father testify on his behalf?"

"Your father was a complicated man, God rest his soul."

"Which does nothing to prove Joey's innocence."

Carrie shifted in her chair and grimaced. She offered a gentle smile and placed her hands in Harriet's. "Dear, I have little time left. Do you want me to talk about your brother and your father, and what really happened, or do you want me to tell you a salacious yarn of local importance? Either works for me."

Harriet didn't know whether to spit or cry. Seeing her twin brother today for the first time in twenty years, his arrest today, and the dredged-up twenty-year-old trial had taken its toll. She'd held off displaying any emotion for as long as she could. She slumped forward and put her head in her hands.

Twenty years of built-up tears escaped Harriet. Her best friend rested a hand on Harriet's back, rubbed in a circular motion, and did the thing she was best known for at the Indie.

"I heard Mamie Snyder left her pocketbook in the art room on Tuesday, and when she went back after hours to retrieve it, she found Maximiliano Esposito—you know him as the Godfather—displaying his full Monty for Becky Trainer while Becky praised the Lord for his attentive care. Needless to say…"

CHAPTER 6

RETIREE GOLD FEVER

Travail stood at the back of the filled-to-capacity community hall, waiting on Harriet and Yeager for the mid-morning breakfast lecture. Once they joined him, they headed to the buffet line as Peaches, the activities director, dressed in a bedazzled sweater that fought to hold back her buxom bosom, pulled a mic from the podium and banged it on her hand three times.

When the feedback subsided, Peaches giggled her thanks to everyone for coming to the monthly lecture, told everyone to keep eating, and reminded them "not to forget about the dating-over-65 discussion tomorrow afternoon." She stood on her toes. "That means you, too, Craig. The single ladies would like to get on your dance card."

Harriet poked him in the side. "Didn't know you had a dance card, Craig. Should I be jealous?"

Jealous? No. She didn't need to be jealous.

What did she mean, anyway?

Yeager pointed at the man next to Peaches and nudged Travail. "Have you met Mike Peterson, a resident historian? He's my client today in the People's Court."

Again with the People's Court. Twice in one morning. "I don't understand."

But Yeager didn't answer. He was busy dishing up food in the buffet line.

Travail kept his focus on the podium as Peaches introduced Mike Peterson and handed him the microphone. His wire-frame glasses offered a scholarly touch to his lean build, but he might as well have been dressed for a Jimmy Buffet concert rather than the classroom. His cream linen drawstring pants, his floral-print Hawaiian shirt—untucked, to be sure—and his slip-on boat shoes matched his carefree expression. The speaker committee must have saved good money with this selection.

Mike started off his presentation with a question. "Does anyone know what people mean when they say Charlotte's streets were paved with gold?"

Yeager knew the answer, but he couldn't raise his hand because his hands were full, with orange juice in one and a plate filled with eggs, bacon, grits, white toast, and fruit in the other. The fruit was courtesy of Harriet, who transferred what she called "healthy items" from her plate to Yeager's because she had already eaten.

A resident who Yeager nicknamed "Dirt Man Dan"—because of his real estate career "buying, selling, developing, and playing in dirt for a living"—raised his hand and correctly answered the speaker's question.

"Exactly," the speaker said. "During the gold rush period, the town spread crushed ore remains from the gold mines on the streets, as if they were paved with gold."

Yeager mumbled, "teacher's pet" in Dan's direction as they took seats in the back of the room, far enough away to carry on a conversation without disrupting the lecture.

Yeager dug into his meal, food being his first obsession. Second on his obsession list was his latest infatuation with Charlotte's gold history. He had texted Travail and Harriet to join him for this lecture, and they agreed, if only to see if they could learn anything helpful to explain the mystery of the gold coins found with the dead body in Harriet's basement.

"In 1799," the speaker said, "a young boy named Conrad Reed fished in a small creek on his father's farm forty miles outside Charlotte, where he found a seventeen-pound gold nugget. They didn't know what they'd found. The property is now a state historical site known as Reed Gold Mine."

Yeager leaned over. "Did you know, Craig Travail, the Reeds used that gold nugget as a door stop for three years before selling it to a Fayetteville jeweler for three dollars and fifty cents, and it was worth more than three thousand dollars at the time?"

No, he didn't know that, but he found it interesting and disappointing how gold scams had been around for over two hundred years.

Yeager placed one gold coin he'd found under Harriet's uptown house on the table. Harriet pushed the coin back. "Put that away," she whispered. "You didn't tell anyone about the coins, did you?"

Yeager paused long enough to reveal he had.

Harriet huffed. "Have you ever kept a secret in your life?"

"I didn't say a word about your brother's arrest, Harriet, or where we found the coins."

Travail swallowed some of his ham-and-cheese biscuit. "That's two out of three secrets, Harriet. Like winning the lottery for Yeager."

"Why thank you, Craig Travail. Now, I've got a secret for y'all that won't be a secret much longer. The investment club—"

A timeline on the big screen distracted Yeager. He turned to look as the speaker used a laser pointer. "In 1825, Charlotte was a small village, but by 1830, the population grew with an influx of mining experts and European miners. The most interesting character was the Count Chevalier Vincent de Rivafinoli."

Though the name was unusual, Travail had seen or heard the name somewhere before, perhaps in a local newspaper or on the news. He picked up a copy of the speaker's handout and read an excerpt in it from *The Miners' and Farmers' Journal* in 1831.

The Chevalier de Rivafinoli who has purchased several mines in the vicinity of Charlotte, Mecklenburg County, lately arrived at his mines from the North, bringing with him some of the most learned and practical miners of England, Germany, Wales, Scotland, Ireland, Switzerland, Italy, and France, with seventy or eighty working hands. We have authority for saying that a considerable number of laborers might find employment in his mines. Charlotte is rapidly improving, and in the lapse of time, may rival any town in the State. A spirit of enterprise has been created among some of the people of the town and county which must rapidly extend itself as the speculation increases.

Travail used his phone to Google the name Rivafinoli and learned that one of the mines he worked was the Rudisill Mine next to Harriet's house. Interesting.

The speaker pointed to another year on the timeline. "By 1835, Charlotte had become the US gold capital, causing President Andrew Jackson to sign the law to construct the first branch of the US Mint in Charlotte."

A photo of the Charlotte Mint appeared on the screen. "On March 27, 1838, the Charlotte Mint manufactured gold coins for the first time, stamping a "C" on each coin to show its origin."

The next slide showed a gold coin like the one Yeager found. Harriet had been right about the coins' origin.

"What secret?" Harriet asked Yeager.

"What?"

"You said you had something to tell us that would not be a secret much longer."

"Righto. The Indie investment club is in trouble."

Two women in the row ahead shushed them. Harriet whispered to Travail and Yeager to follow her. They grabbed their plates and did as they were told.

Travail caught up with Harriet and Yeager at a table in a secluded alcove where they could hear the amplified lecture and see the presentation but carry on their conversation without being overheard.

"What do you mean, the investment club is in trouble?" Harriet's disdain for the Indie investment club was common knowledge to residents.

Before Travail arrived at the Indie, thirty residents formed the club to share information about how to invest their assets, which was acceptable to Harriet until the foolish club president, as Harriet called him, convinced club members to invest in unique and risky ventures.

The first terrible investment, in Harriet's opinion, was their decision to fund a romance film by a first-time screenwriter set in the North Carolina foothills. "Way too risky," Harriet had told Travail, "to put your money on romance."

But the club members liked romance, and everyone else in the club except Yeager—who deferred to Harriet to stay on her good side—bought in to the "love fund," as it came to be known, and wouldn't you know it, they tripled their money when Netflix purchased *Love in the Appalachian Foothills* for its holiday lineup. It was a fortunate break the club never let Harriet live down, kidding her for being "love averse."

Is that what Travail was? Love averse? Were he and Harriet alike in that way?

Yeager explained the investment club's problem. "Scams. The residents could use a talented lawyer, Craig Travail."

Travail finished his biscuit and wiped his hands on his napkin. He'd wait for Harriet to suss out the facts and see if he could help.

"What scams?" Harriet asked.

"Most fell into the category of 'boy, how dumb could I be' scams."

"Like what?"

"One good friend who will remain nameless because he swore me to secrecy—see, I can keep a secret, Harriet—fell for an email sweetheart scam. He was heartbroken to learn his soon-to-be-soulmate—the woman he'd wired ten thousand dollars for emergency surgery, car repairs, and a plane ticket to come live with him at the Indie—had disappeared from his email inbox.

"Unfortunate, but not surprising. What else?"

"Six people fell for the lottery scam where they were told to deposit a twenty-thousand-dollar winning check in their bank, with instructions to wire back a two-thousand-dollar processing fee. Seemed simple enough, except after they parted with their two thousand dollars, the twenty-thousand-dollar checks bounced."

Travail was sympathetic. "I watched a report on elder fraud on the local news last night. It is becoming a real problem in this country. The criminals are good. They say—"

Harriet cut Travail off. "What else, Yeager?"

"Let's see. There was—" Yeager stroked his beard, and then counted with the fingers and thumb on his right hand. "There was an electronic-money-mule scam, a grandma-I-need-money scam, a guaranteed-government-grant scam, a secret-shopper scam, and an IRS scam."

When he ran out of digits on his right hand to use as props, he used his left. "There was also a blackmail scam in which they had to pay a ransom or the scammer would reveal their web-surfing history." Yeager laughed. "Half the club got caught up in that one, and not all were men."

Harriet pushed her drink aside. "What's the most anyone lost?"

"Around fifteen thousand dollars, except the president. He was greedy enough to fall for the Nigerian email scam, even though it looked like a preschooler typed the email. They promised him a two-million-dollar commission if the Nigerian government could temporarily park twenty million dollars in his account for safekeeping. The bad guys used his account information to deplete his accounts. Yesterday, he moved in with his kids."

"Who's in charge of the club now?"

"Nobody. They want you to be president, Harriet. They say you were right to be careful."

Harriet shook her head. "Not interested."

Yeager paused, looked at the speaker, and continued. "It's not just the scams that have them worried about their future. The club members —we—invested in gold."

"And that's a problem why?"

"Some residents are having second thoughts, and while I like the idea of investing in gold, I found out after the fact the investments were Dirt Man Dan's idea. And as you know, I don't trust him."

What Travail knew about Dan Barnard was sparse. They'd met once at an Indie rummage sale to raise money for Alzheimer's disease, at which they were the volunteer muscle to move resident donations from their homes to the staging area. Dan worked hard and was polite. He had deep-set eyes and a long face. Along with his pleasant but melancholy attitude, he had a head of gray hair that suggested he'd seen a lot of life in his life.

Travail was curious. "Why don't you trust Dan?"

"He testified against Joey in his criminal case. Made him out to be a criminal when he wasn't."

Travail was losing his lawyerly edge. Perhaps it was the lack of sleep from being roused so early or the shock of what they found under Harriet's uptown house, but Travail hadn't asked Harriet and Yeager the question that needed to be asked.

"What, exactly, was Joey convicted of twenty years ago?"

Harriet hesitated, so Yeager stepped in. "Appraisal fraud."

"What did he do, specifically?"

Yeager looked at Harriet first, then continued. "Joey was a licensed real estate appraiser who worked with his father. According to Chance Landry and Dan Barnard, and the jury who decided the case, Joey committed criminal fraud in the preparation of appraisals on property in South End."

Travail looked to Harriet. Surely, she could share more. She must have been at the trial.

"Craig, I don't want to talk about Joey's fraud trial. It's too painful. I have the trial materials you can pour over to your heart's content. Transcripts. Exhibits. The whole nine yards."

Harriet turned to Yeager and redirected the conversation. "Tell us about the investment club's gold investments and Dan's role."

"About six months ago, the club president—it was really Dirt Man Dan who arranged it—had a financial expert speak to the club on Zoom about an imminent stock market crash. Her solution was to invest in gold.

"Three ways to do it. We could convert our retirement assets to gold bullion coins. We could invest in gold futures—admittedly more risky and hard to predict the outcome, she said. And we could invest our money in an actual gold mine, which sounded cool to me.

"As the expert told it, the IRS and the federal government would confiscate our IRAs and take away our Social Security when the crash happens. She predicted the price per ounce of gold bullion was going to skyrocket and gold mining operations were a solid investment. She and her team phoned residents and spoke with us one-on-one."

Travail was concerned about the expert's misleading sales tactic, but this didn't explain why Yeager didn't trust Dan's involvement, so Travail pressed him. "Apart from Dan's testimony against Joey, why don't you trust him?"

"He's slippery. Majors in half-truths."

That didn't fit with what Travail knew about Dan. He'd only spent one day with Dan, but he'd seemed like an honest guy. They'd shared their stories, and nothing about Dan's story felt false. Like Travail, Dan was single, having lost his wife a few years ago, and he had difficulties adjusting to Indie life. The women who ran the rummage sale appreciated Dan's help and never spoke a bad word against him. Maybe Yeager had overreacted about Dan. "Harriet, I'd like to take you up on your offer to review Joey's trial materials."

Harriet said "fine" but returned to the gold investment inquiry. "How did you invest your money, Yeager?"

Yeager scratched his beard. "Number one, I didn't know Dan was behind this. Number two, I liked the fact the gold mining company was local."

The speaker asked for raised hands from the audience of anyone who'd ever swapped their assets for gold bullion coins. The room quieted as practically every hand in the room went up. Yeager eased his hand into the air too.

"Oh my," the speaker said.

Oh my, was right, Travail thought. This could be a problem. Commercials and social media were rampant with teasers that encouraged retirees to buy gold bullion. It sounded good. After all, gold was gold. But unscrupulous characters in that industry preyed on the uninformed.

Travail got Yeager's attention. "How much did you and others invest?"

"The gold mine stock was five hundred thousand dollars a person. Along with Nelli, Becky, and me, seven others bought the stock. Fifty people paid a hundred thousand dollars for their gold bullion coins, including me."

Harriet gave Yeager a *have-you-lost-your-mind* look. "Let me get this straight. You and nine other residents invested five million dollars in a gold mine, and you and forty-nine other residents bought five million dollars' worth of gold bullion coins?"

"Yup. The mining company investment came with gold bars as security in case things didn't pan out." Yeager smiled, either at his stupid pun or because he believed he'd protected himself well.

The email Travail received last night popped into his head: *Your friends are about to suffer financial ruin.* "Did you get a second opinion from a finance expert?"

"Don't worry, Craig Travail. Gold is a hedge against the upcoming depression."

Harriet expressed her frustration to Yeager. "Has everyone here gone gold crazy?"

"Let's put it this way, Harriet. If you took a gigantic metal detector and waved it over the Indie, the gold pinging sound would bust your eardrums. We have more gold bullion on site than you'd find at a coin-collector convention."

"Any paperwork for your investments?" Travail hoped he could find a loophole in the fine print and get his friend out of this mess, not that Yeager even knew he was in one.

"Good lawyerly question. We received coin authentication certificates and stock subscription paperwork." Then: "The thing is, if I had known Dirt Man Dan was involved, I would have done more research. I may be overinvested in gold."

Harriet grunted. "Ya think? What do you know about gold mining?"

"I know the mining company is local. We can keep an eye on them." Yeager scrolled through his picture library on his phone until he found a stock certificate image. He enlarged the image and read the words aloud: "The South End Mining Company, a subsidiary of the Standish Company."

Harriet looked stricken. "You invested your savings in the Standish Company, of all companies?"

"They're going to build an underground mining museum too. That's in the deal."

Travail held his tongue but worried nonetheless. This venture didn't sound plausible with what was sure to be massive red tape, environmental hurdles, and construction challenges, just to consider a few obstacles, but he kept those thoughts to himself. There was no reason to pile on. Better to get all the facts, something Yeager had failed to do.

Yeager appealed to Harriet. "This is what your father worked to achieve, and now it's possible. The Standish Company owns the underground land rights needed to harvest the gold and build the museum, and now I own a piece. Thought you'd be happy."

Harriet did not look happy. Nor did Travail have a clue what her father had worked to achieve, but it appeared to have something to do with underground property in South End that her brother appraised for the Standish Company.

Travail needed more information on the gold mine investment. "Did they make any other promises?"

"Underground development was their pitch. You ever go to Underground Atlanta? City beneath a city? I saw it when it was in its prime in the early '70s. They plan to build apartments, stores, bars, and entertainment spots underneath South End and connect them to the underground gold mine museum."

Travail wanted to point out that Underground Atlanta went bust, but the speaker interrupted their conversation again. "Mr. Alexander, please come up. I understand you have an interesting story to tell about some gold coins."

Harriet stood. "I've had enough."

Yeager leaned into Travail. "She's in a mood, Craig Travail. I don't blame her after what happened this morning. You look after her now."

Travail would do just that. But first, a request. "Email me the documents so I can look them over. I'd like to check the fine print."

"Will do. But don't forget about my championship croquet match today at one thirty sharp in this room. I expect you and Harriet to be there."

Yeager jogged to the podium, dodging tables and chairs as he went. He accepted the mic from Mike Peterson, surveyed the crowd, and held up a gold coin. "I can't tell you where I found this because I might start another Charlotte gold rush." He laughed along with several others at his lame joke. "I can tell you this though: this will not be the only gold to be found in Charlotte, because—"

Travail's phone buzzed as he left the community hall.

It was a text.

From the detective.

It read: "Your client Joey Penman's fingerprints are on the knife we found in the victim's back. Just thought you'd want to know."

CHAPTER 7

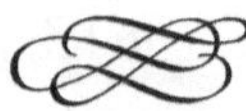

NEW SHERIFF IN TOWN

Travail hurried to catch up to Harriet after she bolted from the building. She was halfway down the gravel path to her cottage before he caught up to her, breathless.

Harriet stood with her arms folded across her shirt dress. "You skipped exercise for the last two months, didn't you?"

Travail gulped air. "How did you know?"

"Lucky guess."

Travail took a moment to steady his breath and work up the courage to ask what he'd wanted to ask all morning. "Are you okay? Sorry. I know you're not okay. What I mean is—"

"I know what you mean. You want to be supportive, but if this is about my brother, I don't think there is anything to be done about him. He is who he is." Her tone was diffident.

This wasn't like Harriet, who took off down the path as Travail did his best to keep up. He followed her to her cottage and onto her back deck, where she turned and faced him, arms crossed, again, in that familiar, stubborn position.

"Are you following me?"

"Would you like to talk?"

"No."

Travail glanced across the lake and spied his cottage, where he'd arrived one year earlier after his law firm—Robert Elkin, to be more precise—wrongfully fired him after his long, loyal career. At his adult children's encouragement, he'd moved into the Indie to get a fresh start, but at the time, it felt like his story's end. The view prompted him to remember how bereft he'd felt, and more than that, how there was nothing in the whole wide world he could do about his situation.

Had it not been for Harriet, and Yeager as supporting cast member, Travail might have wallowed away his life in isolation and without purpose, but Harriet was the spear's point. She poked him and gave him a reason to keep going.

As Harriet tightened the grip on her crossed arms, Travail recalled how he'd pushed Harriet away at every opportunity—like she was doing to him now—and how, despite Travail being surly, she continued to encourage him.

To be sure, Harriet's bedside manner was not for the fainthearted. She was about doing, not brooding. She turned his extra bedroom into a law office, became his paralegal, and shamed him into taking the legal case that blew the lid off the long-kept secret of the Mecklenburg Declaration of Independence. She ran interference for Travail, while Yeager made them laugh and did everything else that needed to be done. She distracted him from his misery and gave him the time he needed to turn himself around.

Now, he wanted to help her, to return the favor, and she was reluctant.

Harriet's voice was soft but firm, almost like her message was a mixed signal. "You don't have to represent my brother. You'd be in over your head anyway in criminal court. Help Yeager find his buried treasure instead."

Travail was going to help her, whether she liked it or not, but he'd prefer to win her over. "Let's talk tonight. Dinner at my place. Six thirty. Let Yeager know. Homemade pizza."

Harriet unfolded her arms. "By homemade pizza, you mean you will pick up a pizza and take it to your home?"

Travail refused to admit the obvious. "Don't forget about Yeager's croquet match today. He is counting on us. I may be late because I've got to go to the Indie board meeting first."

Harriet mumbled something unintelligible as her phone rang. She answered and listened. "Hold on." She put her hand over the phone. "The detective wants to ask me a few questions."

"Put him on speaker."

She did as suggested.

"Detective, I am here with Craig Travail." She looked up. "He's my lawyer."

The detective said, "Fine. This won't take long."

They heard papers rustle on the other end before the detective asked his first question. "Had you been in touch with your brother since they released him from prison?"

"Not until I saw him early this morning."

The paper rustling got louder. "How did that happen?"

"I got a call from the neighbor about the noise at the house. When I got there, Joey and the fire department were there. And then you showed up. Joey and I didn't have time to talk.."

Travail interjected. "Is Harriet a suspect?"

More papers shuffled. "Too early to say."

Travail mouthed to Harriet. "We can stop this conversation."

She waved him off.

"Ms. Keaton, did you give your brother a key to the house?"

"The key has been hidden in the same place for seventy years."

"So you're saying you did nothing to help your brother?"

Harriet's face narrowed, and her brow tightened. Travail reached for the phone, but Harriet pushed him away. "My brother and I aren't on good terms, but he did not murder that man, and I didn't help him. Do your job, Detective." She ended the call.

To Travail, she said, "How'd I do?"

"About like you always do when you believe you've run into a fool."

Travail looked at his watch and realized he only had five minutes to make it to the Indie board meeting. When their friend Sue Ellen Parker died, he'd reluctantly agreed to take her place on the board. He hustled to the main building.

As he hurried to his meeting, he had three things on his mind. One, he needed to get back to his regular exercise routine. Two, he needed to conspire with Yeager—after all, Yeager loved conspiracies—to get Harriet to open up and allow them to help her by helping Joey. And three, he needed to assess the gold investment risks to Yeager and the community.

He could do without any more surprises today.

Travail opened the door to the administrative wing, where he ran into Jenny Montgomery, the Indie's bookkeeper, knocking her back and spilling her papers to the floor.

At six feet four, she was a tall woman with an even taller opinion of herself. Her attitude, combined with her height, led Yeager to give her the nickname High Brow.

Travail had seen that cocksureness in Jenny when she attended the Indie board meetings to report on finances. She did not believe all questions were good questions. And yet, despite her impatience with stupidity—she was like Harriet in that way—she was competent at her job. She kept a tight set of books.

"Sorry." He offered to help Jenny up, but she swatted his hand away and got up on her own. She wore a taupe blazer with pants to match. All business.

Travail bent down and picked up a document with the words *NOTICE OF EMPLOYMENT TERMINATION* across the top, but before he could read more, Jenny snatched it from his hand and pushed him aside.

As she walked out the door, she said, "This is not over, Craig."

Travail did not know who had been fired or why Jenny was upset, but she was going in the wrong direction. As the bookkeeper, she was a regular attendee at Indie board meetings. He looked at his watch, decided he had no time to follow her, and continued to the meeting room.

When he arrived, he found three unexpected people present and only one regular attendee, Becky Trainer. When he'd first met Becky right after he moved to the Indie, she was the board president who presided over the battle Harriet fought about bird feeders at the Indie. Harriet wanted them. Sue Ellen Parker, now deceased, hadn't. And Becky, being Sue Ellen's ally, backed Sue Ellen.

While Sue Ellen won the bird feeder war, Harriet had the last word, telling everyone the birds Sue Ellen had outlawed would make it a point to crap on her porch. Travail smiled as he remembered the scene, his first clue Harriet would be an unstoppable force.

Becky looked different from when Travail first met her one year earlier, when her thin physique, 1950s bouffant hairstyle, and bland attire had reminded him of a Number 2 pencil topped with an oversized brown eraser. Today, she was dressed in slim black pants cropped to the ankle, a knit white top, and a cardigan. She wore flats and simple jewelry. Her hair was cut in a neat bob.

Travail had wrongly judged Becky at first, mistaking her for Sue Ellen's pawn. Instead, Becky had used her forensic banking experience to help Travail in a court case, and while she missed her friend Sue Ellen, she, like so many strong women he'd met at the Indie, kept putting one foot in front of the other.

Unlike Travail, Becky began dating in the last year. She became sweet on Max Esposito, the man who'd rescued Harriet, Yeager, and Travail from death at the hand of Robert Elkin's father one year ago. According to Carrie Roberts, the romance was the reason for the new clothes and hairdo.

Becky had done a fine job leading the Indie board, but today, she didn't sit in the president's seat. She turned her eyes away when she saw him look at her for an explanation.

"Sit," the woman in the president's seat said to him.

Travail didn't sit. "I must be in the wrong room."

"You're in the right place," the pretender-in-charge said. "My name is Mrs. Lester Sterling Standish the Third." She said her name, with a stress on *the Third*, like the name had power and prominence, though Travail had never heard the name. "You can call me Bailey. I am the new Indie president and board chair."

Bailey wore a bold-patterned long shirtdress with yellow flowers on a black background that shouted for attention. Travail imagined some female residents might complain her dress was unbuttoned three too many times, revealing way too much cleavage. But her dress didn't explain her superior attitude or her possession of the president's chair.

"I don't understand."

"All in good time." She pointed to her left, to the person seated next to Becky. "I believe you know Dan Barnard." Travail nodded to Dan, who wore a golden yellow golf shirt, tan slacks, and breathable lace-up sneakers.

"I appointed Dan as a board member to take Mamie Snyder's place after she stepped down. Mamie had a recent shock that caused her heart to race when she witnessed a naked coupling in the art room." The new president smirked as she looked at Becky, but Becky didn't return her gaze.

Dan didn't say a word. He was never overly talkative with Travail, but perhaps today he needed Bailey's permission to speak. Or perhaps this was the unpleasant version Yeager made him out to be. Either way, Dan's presence solidified his allegiance to the Standish family, who he knew nothing about.

"Next to you, if you will be so kind as to sit, Mr. Travail, is my grandmother-in-law, Celia Standish, your newest resident. She won't tell you how old she is, but they don't make ninety-year-old tacks as sharp as her."

Celia smiled, turned in her chair, and nodded to Travail. "Nice to meet you." A petite woman who displayed no obvious physical weaknesses, she was dressed in a short blue jacket over a white blouse and navy tailored slacks with low-heeled shoes. Diamond earrings, a gold link bracelet, and a diamond-ringed watch blended well with her platinum bob. Her posture was perfect, but her face was lined to reflect her age.

Bailey was her opposite, a brunette with light streaks in her hair, who wore a thick make-up mask and looked like a jewelry-store mannequin draped in gold and silver decor. With rings on her fingers, bangles and bracelets on her wrists, earrings—big gold hoops—and several necklaces, she oozed spendthrift. She and Harriet would not get along well, and part of Travail looked forward to putting them in the same room together.

Bailey pointed at the empty chair again, and Travail slid into it, figuring the answer to the board member shuffle was about to be revealed.

"At Celia's request, my husband's real estate company loaned ten million dollars to the Indie—a loan necessary to avoid state regulatory oversight—and in return, and in order to be sure the Indie manages its finances properly, Celia and I took board seats in place of two residents who were glad to be done with their jobs. Don't let our gender deceive you, Mr. Travail. We have experience running a business."

Travail didn't think of the Indie so much as a business as he did a residential community with bills to pay. He didn't like this woman's attitude, and he felt himself go into lawyer mode.

"Why the ten million dollar loan? At our last meeting, the finances were in good shape."

Bailey sniffed. "Right to the point, I see." She opened a folder, turned it around, and slid it across the table in Travail's direction. "A lot can change in thirty days, Mr. Travail."

He glanced at the balance sheet. It showed one million dollars in the operating account and nine million dollars in the reserve account. It also showed a loan to the Indie by the Standish Company for ten million dollars. "Were the loan funds deposited into these two accounts?"

"They were," Bailey said.

Travail was confused. At the last board meeting, the accounts held similar balances, but the Indie was not in debt for ten million dollars. Something happened to the money in the last thirty days, something that necessitated a loan. Why wasn't the full board consulted? He wished High Brow were here to clear this up. "Why is Jenny Mont-gomery not here?"

"I fired her," Bailey said.

Dirt Man Dan spoke up for the first time. "Malfeasance."

Was Jenny responsible for losing ten million dollars? That charge didn't fit the person with fifteen years of accounting experience and stellar reviews. "I don't understand."

Bailey tapped the table with her knuckles. "Today is not the time to go into the details of what happened to the money. It is time for the board to plan our next steps. Celia here—my dear grandmother-in-law —had her heart set on living her final years at the Indie, only to find out after she purchased her place you were broke."

Travail knew from experience what needed to happen in financial fraud cases. "Have you contacted the police?"

"No, and we don't plan to. The money is gone. It is irretrievable. We didn't want to worry the residents, so we made the loan and we're here to fix the problem."

"We should report the loss." Travail's voice was firm.

Bailey laughed as she looked around the table at the board members other than Travail. "Mr. Travail has a motion for us to vote on. All in favor of calling the police, scaring the residents, depressing property values, and discouraging future residents from buying here, raise your hand."

Travail and Becky raised their hands.

"All opposed."

Bailey, Celia, and Dan raised their hands, and their collaboration made Travail suspicious. He turned to Bailey and asked his point-blank question. "What is it you really want?"

Mrs. Lester Sterling Standish the Third let out a high-pitched laugh. "Come now, Mr. Travail. My grandmother-in-law lives here. We want the best for her and for all the residents."

The answer felt like whitewash, and he fell back into lawyer mode. "What's the name of your husband's real estate company?"

"My, my, Mr. Travail, you are full of questions today." Bailey's wrist bangles and bracelets clinked as she pointed to Celia. "Would you like to tell him?"

Celia's voice was gentle, but there was something more behind her polite veneer he couldn't put his finger on. "My grandson Sterling, Bailey's husband, bought the Standish Company from me. We—I mean, he—is in the commercial real estate business now focused on developing South End. In particular, land within the Gold District."

It was the second time in one day circumstances required Travail to think about the Gold District, the land adjacent to Harriet's family home. Why was the Standish Company interested in that land? And why did it have an interest in running a retirement community? Surely, a for-profit real estate company wasn't involved at the Indie solely to make grandma's stay pleasant.

Bailey leaned toward Travail. "We want two more things, Mr. Travail, which I am sure you will find reasonable."

Time for the next two shoes to drop.

"The ten-million-dollar loan needs to be paid off on time."

"I want to see the loan documents."

"They are in your board packet." She pointed to a folder on the table.

Travail picked up the folder and glanced through it. Inside was the note for ten million dollars, signed by former treasurer Mamie Snyder and witnessed by former bookkeeper Jenny Montgomery. The loan was due to be repaid four months from now. Attached to the loan was a mortgage on the Indie's common elements, all the land and buildings other than the actual units and cottages themselves.

He didn't know how the Indie could repay such a significant debt within 120 days. It made him reconsider his opinion about a for-profit real estate company wanting to have nothing to do with the Indie property. If the Indie couldn't repay the loan, the Standish Company would foreclose and own most of the land. Was that their plan?

And what was Dan Barnard's role? Did his influence on the Indie investment club have anything to do with this Indie board takeover? Experience taught him to be wary.

Bailey looked at Becky, and then at Travail. "If you don't want to serve on the board, we can find replacements."

"I am not going anywhere." Becky's voice was firm. Good for her.

"How about you, Mr. Travail? With Joey Penman's arrest, you have your hands full."

How did Bailey Standish know about Joey's arrest? It was another coincidence he didn't like. "You can call me Craig. I am sure I can make myself available to do my board duty."

"Fine then. Do you have any more questions, Craig?" Bailey tapped her blue painted fingernails on the boardroom table.

"You said there were two more things for today. What's the second?"

"Financial security, of course. We need to improve how we manage our finances." She made a motion she handle the bookkeeping until they could hire someone new. Bailey raised her hand in favor and Dan and Celia did the same. Before Travail or Becky could object or ask any questions, Mrs. Lester Sterling Standish the Third, slapped her right hand on the table. "Motion passes. The books will be in excellent hands."

Bailey's face glowed. "The next item is a monthly dues increase and a lump-sum assessment on every resident, payable in four months when the loan is due. We've got to raise capital to pay off the debt owed to my husband's company."

CHAPTER 8

CROQUET SMACKDOWN

Harriet found two seats in the community room and saved one for Craig. When he arrived with one minute to spare before the croquet match started, she patted the open seat beside her, and Craig took it.

What had served as a lecture hall this morning was now a proper indoor croquet court. The staff had removed the furniture and installed wickets in their pre-drilled holes in the fast-rolling carpet.

Craig pointed at Yeager. "What's he wearing?"

Harriet leaned in close. "That, Craig, is what happens when Clorox comes in contact with a flannel shirt and blue jeans. All whites."

Lafontaine Creech, the silver-haired, scarlet-cheeked commissioner of the IICO—the Indie Indoor Croquet Organization—went over the rules for the Indie championship match with the four contestants. The league players who didn't make the finals wore their true whites and sat silent in one long row.

Harriet fought her fatigue. Other than the catnap, she'd been up since 2:30 am. "It's been a long day."

"Longer than you think," Craig said.

Several residents in their true whites gave Harriet and Craig side eyes for their conversation. She looked over her shoulder, then whispered: "Let's move to the back where we can talk."

They resettled in the back corner, where Craig shared the bad news about the Indie board. "They voted to raise monthly dues by $2,500 and to assess each resident $50,000, payable in four months to repay a ten-million-dollar loan from the Standish Company."

"That's ridiculous. Most residents are on a fixed income. Others have their money tied up in gold bullion coins and mining stock."

Craig didn't have any comforting words. "The board will be aggressive to foreclose on residents' homes if they fall behind on their dues or don't pay their assessment at the end of four months."

Harriet rubbed her hands together. "Do you trust Bailey Standish?"

"No. I plan to talk with Jenny Montgomery about what happened."

Craig looked at his watch, which made Harriet notice his blue sport coat and red tie. "Going to the prom, Craig?"

Commissioner Creech blew his whistle, and the four players started play on wicket number one.

"Is that Nelli?"

"Don't change the subject, Craig, but yes, that's Nelli. She's Yeager's partner."

"In her motorized wheelchair?"

"What else would she play in?"

Really, how had it escaped Craig that Nelli, known as NASCAR Nelli for her wheelchair speed in the Indie hallways, was Yeager's croquet partner? For a lawyer who was detail-oriented, he sometimes missed what was right in front of him when it came to his friends' lives. "She likes to think croquet is like polo and her wheelchair is like her horse."

Harriet slid closer to Craig. "Back to the coat and tie, Craig. You're going to see my brother, aren't you?"

As croquet balls clinked off wooden mallets in the cavernous room, Craig ignored her question with a question. "When was the last time you and your brother talked?"

"Twenty years ago, but it doesn't matter."

"As his lawyer, it does to me. I'd like to know what you can tell me so I can help him."

Harriet fixed her eyes on the contestants to resist the urge to rebuke Craig.

Yeager stood spread-eagled over a ball with his mallet between his legs. He drew back and made contact, causing his ball to careen off another ball and through a wicket.

Nelli yelled "hell yeah" and pumped her fist in the air, causing Commissioner Creech to demand decorum. Yeager laughed, and their competitors scowled.

Craig looked at his watch again. "I have ten minutes before I need to leave. Is there anything you want to tell me before I meet with Joey?"

Harriet thought back to her conversation that morning with Carrie. Her best friend had tried to explain Craig showed affection by trying to fix things when he saw the need for help. That irritated Harriet, but it also touched her. If she was being honest with herself, her sour mood toward Craig's offer to help Joey had less to do with Craig and more to do with her brother.

Maybe she should accept Craig's offer. After all, she'd been surprised when Carrie said, "Your brother was innocent twenty years ago," which prompted Harriet to point out that her father didn't testify on Joey's behalf. And for the last four hours, Carrie's next words haunted Harriet. "Your father was a complicated man, God rest his soul."

Harriet's twin brother had never been the type to engage in criminal activity. A free spirit like Harriet, for sure, but within the law's bounds. He was a Boy Scout, truly. After receiving his Eagle Scout badge for building handicap ramps for the disabled, he graduated third in his high school class behind their friend Sue Ellen Parker and then Harriet. He went to college on an academic scholarship, worked construction jobs in his summers, and graduated with honors in civil engineering.

It was never clear why Joey got his real estate appraisal license and went into the family business with her father. He'd always talked about building things, like bridges and high-rise buildings. Never once did he mention the desire to appraise real estate. Her father must have talked him into the job. There was no other explanation, and Joey's decision infuriated her. Joey could have gone his own way, done what he loved, and avoided prison.

A whirring motor drew Harriet's attention to the room's center. Nelli cackled while she ran circles around her two opponents, like a chariot circling cowering gladiators in a Roman coliseum. She pumped her mallet in the air. "That was the longest shot in Indie history."

Craig rose to go, but Harriet pulled him back in his seat. "Wait."

She remembered Joey's last words to her before he went to prison twenty years ago. "I don't want you to contact me in prison. Take care of yourself."

She'd tried to visit Joey anyway, but he'd refused her visits, and after that, everyday life and taking care of her husband at the end of his life consumed her. Though she never spoke with Joey again after he went to prison, her thoughts of him—mostly filled with sadness, anger, and frustration, but also, if she was being honest with herself, with love —were never far away.

Was Joey innocent, as Carrie believed? More importantly, why was Chance Landry, the man who ensured Joey's conviction, killed and placed under her house?

"Carrie thinks I might be wrong about Joey's conviction. Given the way he shut me out after he went to prison, I am still upset with him. My brother is so damn stubborn."

Craig smiled at her.

"What?"

"Nothing."

"Anyway, part of me thinks he is guilty. But honestly, I can't be sure he was guilty of anything other than cutting off contact with me when he went to prison. I don't want him to go back to prison for something he didn't do." After a pause, she nodded. "You can defend him."

"I wasn't asking your permission."

Harriet almost said something harsh, but she stopped herself. Craig was more assertive than when she'd met him a year ago. She liked that. "Well, that's up to you."

He nodded.

"Strange times, Harriet. They release your brother from prison, then arrest him again. A collapsed gold mine causes your kitchen to disintegrate, then the police find a dead man with 1830s gold coins under your house. The Indie investment club invests in a gold mine and gold bullion, then the Indie loses ten million dollars, the Standish Company loans it back, and our new Indie board president takes steps to extract the money from the residents."

Yes, these were strange times. "We may have to fight our way to the answers and the solutions." But before Craig could agree, the sounds of a different type of fight filled the air.

The commissioner's whistle shrilled successive blasts, but the whistle did not muffle the curse-a-thon directed at Nelli by her two opponents, or Nelli's creative invective in return.

One woman used her mallet to swing at Nelli like a baseball player trying to hit a knuckleball, but Nelli gunned her electric motor and avoided the blow. When the woman missed, her momentum spun her around like she was engaged in the Olympic hammer throw event.

The other woman brought her mallet over her head, ready to hammer Nelli into the carpet, but Yeager snatched the weapon from her hands and pulled her to the side.

The fracas brought the true whites—normally quiet observers—to their feet, and servers and cooks poured in to witness the smackdown and cheer their favorites. They formed a circle like bettors at a cock-fight, only today, the hens were at it. Nobody called for security. Everyone was having too much fun.

Commissioner Creech darted in and around Nelli and her mallet-swinging opponent like a referee trying to separate two boxers. Nelli's wheelchair spun so fast in a circle it was hard to tell whether the knockout punch she delivered was on purpose or accidental. Either way, Nelli's wheelchair caught the woman on her leg, causing her to trip into the commissioner's arms. She fell on him like a lover in heat returning home from a long business trip.

A collective gasp filled the air. The residents who understood the importance of recorded history raised their phones and snapped photos.

Harriet stood and applauded. She then tapped Craig on the shoulder. "Go if you must."

CHAPTER 9

TWIN BROTHER IN JAIL

Travail walked up a sidewalk bracketed by the North Carolina and American flags to the glass entrance of the county jail. Once through security, an officer pointed him to a door, where he entered and provided his state bar credentials and personal identification. He took a seat and waited.

A framed metal sign hung on a yellow wall. You must wear a shirt and shoes to visit a prisoner, and you must not take guns or sharp objects inside the visiting area. What a surprise. Who would have known without a government sign? Can't be too careful.

A door opened, and a sheriff's deputy stepped out. She looked Travail up and down the way law officers look at lawyers—with mild disgust—and motioned Travail to follow her. They entered a hallway with more yellow walls. This time, they were cinderblock, not sheetrock, and looked as if someone had slapped paint on in a hurry, leaving dried drips here and there.

Travail hadn't been to a jail since he was a summer intern with the public defender's office in college. He didn't like how it felt then any more than he did now. The walls pressed in on him.

The deputy directed Travail to an open cubicle wide enough to hold a folding metal chair. The cubicle was closed off on the left and right by six-foot-tall cinderblock walls that did not reach the ceiling. Travail sat in the chair, placed his notepad on the ledge before him, and picked up the phone attached to the wall. Joey held a phone against his ear on the other side, dressed in an orange jumpsuit.

"I'm Craig Travail. We met early this morning."

Joey didn't answer. He was as indifferent now as he was before.

"Harriet says hello. She is worried about you."

Joey smirked, like he didn't believe it. The introductions were not off to a good start.

Travail glanced at the clock on the wall. He had little time before the video conference hearing that could send Joey back to prison.

"About your hearing—do you want me to represent you?"

As Travail waited for Joey to speak, he wondered how Joey and Harriet felt about each other. This morning, Harriet had said Joey "is who he is" and didn't want to help him, but at the croquet match, her stance softened. She loved her brother, but how did Joey feel about her? He cut her off, after all. And what did Joey want? Did he want help or to be left alone? If he wanted help, he needed to soften up too.

"About the video hearing," Travail repeated.

"They already held the hearing. You missed it."

Before Travail could ask what happened, Joey explained. "They're sending me back to prison for the rest of my term, another four months. Probably safer there anyway."

Safer there anyway? What did that mean? Travail wanted answers, but he needed to cloak them with the attorney-client privilege. "I'd still like to be your lawyer. You may need advice and a reference for a good criminal attorney if you are charged with murder."

"Why do you care about me?"

That was a tricky question. Travail didn't care about Joey. He cared about Harriet.

"Are you sleeping with my sister?" Joey had that smirk on his face again.

"What?"

"You said you are her 'friend.' I figured—"

"You figured wrong."

Joey laughed. "Don't take it personal. It's no skin off my back who sleeps with my twin sister, but they say twins have a sixth sense about each other's lives, and mine says there is something going on between you and my sister."

Joey wasn't wrong. There was something going on between Travail and Harriet. It just wasn't clear what it was.

What was clear was Joey was too direct and too confident for a man in his position. Being direct and confident were traits he shared with his sister.

"I read about you and my sister in the newspaper. Your big court cases together. And how y'all solved an unsolvable mystery. You think you can solve this one?"

Travail didn't answer, partly because he wasn't sure and partly to let Joey make up his own mind about his offer of representation. He wasn't going to beg, because if Joey wanted his help, he'd need Joey to be a willing participant in his defense.

The smirk left Joey's face. "If you want to represent me, have at it. What do you want to know?"

Travail looked at the questions on his legal pad. "Did you violate your post-release supervision terms?"

"Yes."

That explained why Joey was going back to prison, but not why he violated the release terms. "Care to explain?"

"I got a hand-delivered letter saying Harriet was in trouble. I skipped my weekly meeting with the post-release guy and went there instead."

"Went where?"

"The house, the one we met at this morning, the one my dad owned and gave to Harriet."

The deputy hovered over Travail. "You have five minutes."

Travail had more than five minutes of questions left. He had to stay focused. Someone wanted Joey to be in Harriet's house for a reason.

"Who wrote to you?"

"Don't know."

"Did you keep the letter?"

"Nope."

Travail wasn't sure how he was going to help someone who played hide-and-seek with him on every question. "Did the letter say what kind of trouble Harriet was in?"

"No."

"Do you think someone set you up?"

"My, my. You're a quick study."

Joey and Harriet were twins all right. They breathed sarcasm in and out.

"You didn't kill Landry?"

"Nope, but I would have done it if given the chance." He emphasized the word *chance*, and smiled for the first time.

There it was, another resemblance between brother and sister. Similar hair coloring. Similar smile.

"Developers are good liars. Landry was the best. I served twenty years because of him."

Joey's vindictiveness toward Landry would be music to a prosecutor's ears. Travail kept that thought to himself.

"Did you touch the knife?"

"Used it to cut up some fruit. I didn't wear gloves, if that's what you're wondering."

"Time's up," the deputy said.

Travail gave Joey one instruction before hanging up. "Don't talk to anyone about Landry, what happened at the house, or anything related to this matter."

"Even the gold coins?" Another smile accompanied Joey's question.

How did Joey know about the gold coins? And what did he know? Before Travail could find out, the deputy shut down the interview.

Joey placed his phone in its cradle, formed what looked like a "C" with his right thumb and forefinger, and held it up.

Travail had an idea what Joey meant by his hand gesture, but he wanted another look at the coins Yeager found to be sure.

Where did Yeager say he was going to be after the croquet tournament? Something about People's Court in the Indie chapel at happy hour. If he hurried, he could see for himself.

CHAPTER 10

THE PEOPLE'S COURT

Travail made it to the front door of the Indie chapel while something resembling an official proceeding was in progress.

He took a seat in the last row and edged up to see the backside of a man standing at the front row. The man spoke a greeting like an English barrister to another man who sat behind an alter that was bare of religiosity and the sacred vessels that went with it.

"M'Lord, if I may."

The man who spoke wore a black gown and a white powdered wig with a trailing fake ponytail. His body type looked suspiciously like Yeager's.

Behind the alter sat retired judge Roscoe Brady, Chaw to those who knew his tobacco chewing habit, dressed in a blue buttondown shirt with no coat or tie. Chaw stared down the twenty rows to where Travail sat, caught Travail's eye, and nodded.

"M'Lord, we have a case of mistaken identity."

When the barrister turned and motioned to a person to come forward, Yeager's beard gave him away. The residents who filled the pews, holding wine, beer, and mixed drinks, hooted when they recognized the Indie's most infamous mischief-maker.

Someone tapped Travail on the shoulder. He looked up to see

Becky and slid over to make room for her and her boyfriend, Maximiliano Esposito. They carried drinks. Was he the only attendee at happy hour court without an alcoholic beverage?

Becky passed Travail a pamphlet with the words "People's Court Rocket Docket." She pointed to the third case on the list: "The Case of the Unclothed Man." She bit her lip to suppress her smile. "Yeager says you taught him everything he knows about lawyering."

Travail didn't understand. "Is this for real?"

She whispered back. "Another string attached to the Standish Company loan. Residents are required to resolve their disputes with management and defend against rule violation charges in this forum, and the judge decides the result and the penalty. New management thought they'd save money, be more efficient than regular legal proceedings, and win all their cases here. They didn't predict the residents would make it a party, and now they're stuck with the process."

The last time Travail was in this chapel was to serve with Yeager on the "Committee of Heavy Lifting," the label Yeager gave the pallbearer committee. On that day, they struggled with the weight of a dearly departed resident's casket, and Yeager's remark to Travail was loud enough to draw snickers: "Craig Travail, she must have all three boyfriends in here with her."

Knowing Yeager, there'd be laughter in this hearing today too. Not a bad thing, really, after the day he'd had. Travail relaxed and settled in to see what kind of stunts Yeager pulled as a pretend lawyer.

With hands gripped to his lapels, Yeager addressed the witness.

"Now, madam," he said in a tone that suggested he was sorry for the questions he was going to have to ask her, "you stated that my client, Mike Peterson, was naked in your hallway on the night of the fifth, is that right?"

"Yes. It was Mike. That's for sure."

Travail took note of the name. Peterson was the history professor who spoke at the brunch lecture this morning.

Yeager looked down at the paper in his hand. "To use the words in your written statement, madam, you were 'startled by the length and girth' of what you witnessed."

"Length and girth sounds about right."

There were chuckles in the room. Chaw remained impassive. Was that a bulge in his cheek?

"Madam, can you describe specifically what you saw?"

A woman's voice rose from the pew opposite Yeager. "Objection."

It was Bailey Standish, the Indie board chair and wife of Lester Sterling Standish the Third. "Clothing is required at the Indie, and Mike Peterson broke the rules when he walked around the campus naked on the night of the fifth. Can we please move on to the penalty phase?"

"M'Lord, this shouldn't take long. The esteemed prosecutor brought only one witness to prove her alleged rules violation." Yeager said the word *alleged*, with mock sincerity.

Good work, Yeager, to isolate the required proof to one witness, but from what Carrie Roberts had told Travail, tequila made Mike's clothes fall off.

Wasn't the night of the fifth the night each member of the booze club brought a fifth of something special to their meeting for everyone to sample? Word was Mike sampled more than his share of fifths that night, including tequila.

Chaw nodded for Yeager to proceed.

"Back to my earlier question, madam. Can you describe specifically what you saw on the night of the fifth that brought you here today?"

The witness paused, smiled, glanced around at the friendly crowd, and said, "A penis." She paused again, then added, "With great length and girth."

The audience broke into laughter. Chaw, unlike how he behaved in a real courtroom, let it slide.

"One last question, madam. Did you get a good look at Mike's face that night?"

The woman's face reddened. She shifted in her seat. "Can't say that I did."

"Because?"

Yeager handed the witness a wine glass with red liquid. She sipped her courage.

"Why didn't you see his face?"

"Because I wasn't looking at his face."

The audience howled. Someone shouted, "You go, girl."

Yeager faced Judge Chaw. "M'Lord, since the witness cannot identify the naked man's face, we move for dismissal of the charge."

"Granted," Chaw said, with a barely perceptible smile on his face.

The audience responded with raucous applause while Yeager's grateful client gave Yeager a hug.

Becky slid closer to Travail. "That was a fascinating lecture Mike gave this morning. He's so knowledgeable about the Charlotte Gold Rush."

Travail smiled. Good work, Yeager. An expert who can help us and who owes you one.

Bailey waved her arms to shush the crowd. "Quiet. We are here to do serious business."

She addressed the judge. "I charge the witness, Audrey Blunt, with perjury in the first degree." She looked at Blunt. "Stay put. We try your case now."

"M'Lord," Yeager offered. "I am happy to represent Ms. Blunt. I can clear everything up with just a few questions."

Over Bailey's objection, Chaw gave Yeager the green light.

"Madam, your last words were that you did not look at my client's face on the night of the fifth. Is that true?"

"That's right." The witness did not seem nervous.

"And because you did not make a positive ID of my client's face, you are now charged with making the whole thing up?"

"I suppose I am, but I didn't make it up."

Curiosity caused the room to quiet. Yeager nodded for her to continue.

"I didn't need to see his face. I used to date Mike."

"So you were familiar with—"

"The length and girth of his you-know-what. Yes I was."

The audience laughed.

"But you said you were startled."

"We hadn't dated in a few years. He caught me off guard."

"So you're innocent?"

"I wouldn't call myself innocent, but I know what Mike looks like from the waist down."

Judge Chaw tapped his knuckles on the table. "Not guilty."

Bailey was furious. "They can't both be not guilty."

Becky leaned over and whispered to Travail. "Audrey is a specialist in mining and metallurgy."

Sure she is.

Travail exited his row and moved up the center aisle against traffic to catch the barrister and his two clients before they left. "Congratulations, Counselor. Excellent work."

"Craig Travail, you made it to my first trial."

"And your second. Would you like to introduce me to your clients?"

"Sure thing."

Yeager did the honors, and Mike Peterson and Audrey Blunt were glad to make Travail's acquaintance. They talked while they walked from the chapel to the main building.

Mike hadn't changed from his Jimmy Buffet outfit. Audrey, a beautiful woman with piercing blue eyes and short cropped hair, wore a long, flowy Bohemian dress and brown suede booties that made her look relaxed and confident. They seemed to fit well together.

Their personal lives aside, their specialties were interesting and relevant to what had happened at Harriet's house. But before Travail could dig beyond the surface, Mike said, "We know about the collapsed mine shaft, the gold coins, and South End Mining Company. We're happy to help any way we can."

"We?"

Mike took Audrey's hand. "Audrey and I got back together on the night of the fifth. We promised Yeager that if he could get us out of this pickle, we'd return the favor."

Audrey smiled at Travail. "Glad to be of service."

Travail thanked her. "What does a metallurgist do, exactly?"

"They extract precious metals from mined ore, and they process and shape the metal."

"Where did you learn about mining?"

"Before I retired, I worked in several mines, including the Haile Gold Mine in South Carolina where they've done open pit and underground mining."

"Do you know anything about gold mining in Charlotte's South End in the 1830s and whether mining is possible on the same land today?"

"I have a good understanding about the process."

"What about the history?"

"That's Mike's department. Let us know when you want to talk." She squeezed Mike's hand, and they walked hand in hand into the main building.

"Well, Craig Travail, looks like we've got some excellent experts. Love birds, too, at least until Mike wanders around the Indie naked again and another former girlfriend recognizes him."

Travail remembered why he'd come to the chapel. "Do you have the coins you found at Harriet's house on you?"

Yeager fished in his pocket and handed them over. Travail turned them in his hand, and on every coin, the mark was there, imprinted on the coin, confirming what he'd remembered when he saw them this morning. Just like the "C" Joey had made with his thumb and forefinger.

If they were lucky, perhaps the "C" represented Joey's new life in Charlotte when freed from jail. But if they weren't lucky, the "C" might stand for Joey's conviction for a crime he didn't commit.

It was time for Travail to pick up the pizza. Harriet and Yeager would be at his place at six thirty, and they had a lot to talk about.

CHAPTER 11

HOSPICE DINNER AND A DRINK

After the "Croquet Fight of the Century," as Yeager labeled it, Harriet got a text from Carrie asking her to come to her room at the Collins Center at five thirty to meet her hospice nurse and sign a hospice form, adding: "I need an emergency contact for hospice who is not dead, dying, or insane, and the pickings at the Indie are slim."

Harriet entered the healthcare center to see nurses hustling to fill medication orders and checking charts on their computer screens. She turned left at their station and collided with a laundry cart being pushed by an aide. The sour smell gave the soiled cargo away, causing Harriet to hold her breath until the aide passed.

Harriet exhaled as she took stock of Carrie's hallway. This was death row, and today, hospice was here with the admittance paperwork to help Carrie execute her sentence with as much dignity and as little pain as possible. There was nothing Harriet—a natural-born fixer her entire adult life—could do to change the trajectory of Carrie's journey. Harriet wiped her eyes and put on her cheerful face. She flung Carrie's door open. "Is this gossip headquarters?"

Carrie sat upright in a recliner, her wheelchair and hospital bed beside her. A woman in scrubs—early fifties, perhaps—sat across from her with a clipboard and a pen in her hands. They both turned their heads at Harriet's interruption, and Carrie burst out laughing.

"That," Carrie said, pointing at Harriet, "is what an emergency contact looks and sounds like when she's late. Harriet, meet Nanette, my hospice nurse. Nanette, meet Harriet."

Carrie pointed at her wheelchair. "You can practice sitting in that thing for when your legs give out in twenty years."

Harriet maneuvered herself into the wheelchair. She knew she wouldn't have anywhere close to Carrie's gumption if she lived to be ninety. When she sat, the chair rolled backwards, and she fumbled for the brake.

"On the right." Carrie pointed at the wheelchair, then turned to Nanette and got back to business. "Where were we?"

Nanette cleared her throat and looked at the clipboard. "This is the non-resuscitation form."

"Meaning if I croak, you won't try to un-croak me. Give me the pen."

As Carrie signed, she asked Harriet if she was on a tight schedule, "because we got a few things to cover after Nanette leaves."

"Just dinner with Craig and Yeager."

Carrie handed the form and pen back to the nurse. "You cooking?"

"Craig is picking up pizza, and we're eating at his cottage."

The door opened, and a young man came in with a dinner tray. Carrie held up her hand to him and said, "Not tonight, Jimmy. I'm having dinner with my friends. Let Julia next door have mine. She hates your mush as much as me."

Carrie leaned over to Harriet and said, "Text Yeager and your boyfriend and tell them to bring the pizza to my room. None of that veggie stuff. Ground beef and onions."

Harriet was about to protest, but Carrie's eyes said she would not have it. Harriet typed the text while Carrie signed the emergency contact form and made Harriet's role official. She now rode shotgun on a trip she didn't want to take.

Nanette explained how things would work. The Collins Center staff would look after Carrie day-to-day, and Nannette would visit her once a week to see how she was doing, adjust her medication, and offer help. And "when the time comes," she would visit Carrie as often as needed. Nanette lowered her voice when she said "when the time comes," but elevated her voice when she said, "You no longer have to contact your doctors for medication. Hospice will handle everything."

"That's a relief. Isn't that a relief, Harriet? You don't have to fetch my prescriptions anymore."

Harriet didn't respond. She knew she couldn't fetch the narcotics Carrie was going to need. The room felt cramped.

"Now," Nanette said to Carrie, "are there questions you have for me?"

Carrie fixated on the large photograph of a three-story wooden oceanfront hotel she'd had Yeager haul from her cottage and hang where she could see it. In her sentimental moments, Carrie talked about spending her summers at this hotel when she was in high school. The hotel had been owned and run by her grandmother, "one of the finest hotels on the East Coast," Carrie had told Harriet. "Guests ate and slept on the American plan, what my grandmother described as 'three hots and a flop.'"

Carrie pulled herself away from the picture and the memories it evoked and focused on Nanette. "How much time do I have?"

"I wish I could say, but every case is different."

Carrie jeered. "You sound like Harriet's boyfriend lawyer."

Harriet watched Nanette to see how she responded to Carrie. She did so with a smile. "I like you, Ms. Carrie. You've got spunk."

"Ever know of spunk to beat cancer?"

"Spunk can do surprising things."

Carrie adjusted the woven throw that covered her legs. "Nanette, I am a gossip, but I despise dishonesty by my doctors and nurses."

"I will always be honest with you. If I don't have the answer, I will try to get it, and if there is no answer, I will let you know."

"Like when I ask you questions about God? Is she real? That kind of thing?"

Harriet jerked her head, but Nanette seemed nonplused. She teased

Carrie. "I might have to play lawyer with you. Maybe turn the questions back to you."

Carrie thanked Nanette, got the all clear from her to "do as I please as long as these steroids keep me going," and said goodbye.

"I'll walk you out," Harriet said to Nanette.

Once out the door and out of Carrie's earshot, even though they could hear Carrie yell "don't talk about me behind my back," Harriet asked the question that had bothered her during the entire interview. "Really. How long does she have?"

Nanette placed her hand on Harriet's arm. "I told the truth. Every patient's journey is unique." Nanette looked at Carrie's door. "But I have a feeling your friend will not go until she's ready, until she has done whatever it is she feels she still needs to do on this earth. Ninety days at the most, but again, you never know."

Harriet welcomed Craig and Yeager and helped them with their pizza boxes, lemonade, breadsticks, and dipping sauce. Carrie extended her arms. "About time y'all got here. Harriet and I were about to gnaw off each other's ankles."

Yeager gave Carrie a bear hug that lifted her from her recliner. He placed her back down with a laugh. "No heavier than a bag of peanuts. This deep-dish pizza should fatten you up."

Carrie snorted. "What they feed me here keeps me thin and crispy."

Harriet addressed Craig, who was still in his coat and tie. "How'd it go with Joey?"

Carrie interrupted them. "Save your lawyer report for after dinner."

For the next fifteen minutes, everyone ate while Carrie told stories about the Indie residents. It was hard to know how much Carrie told was true or false, but Harriet felt lighter with her friend in her element. Their laughter lit up the dreary setting at the end of a no-way-back hallway.

"Now," Carrie said, pushing aside her plate, "let's get to the business at hand."

"Business?"

"Harriet, if you think I am going to sit on the sidelines while you, Sherlock, and Watson here try to solve another mystery—" Her banter turned into a wince, and she grabbed her back.

As if on cue, a staff nurse stepped through the door. "Time to take your medicine." And next, "let's get you into bed and get you comfortable. You've had a busy day."

With that behind them, Carrie addressed the trio who sat around her hospital bed. "I know y'all think I'm about to walk the plank, but I need to be focused on something other than death. I need to be a part of your team on this one."

Craig and Yeager deferred to Harriet, but she didn't want to upset her friend. What they were about to face wasn't suitable for a ninety-year-old with only a few months to live. She paused, trying to choose the right words to decline Carrie's offer.

Carrie must have seen the answer coming in Harriet's eyes. "Oh come now, Harriet. What's it going to do? Kill me?"

Yeager laughed. "If Harriet won't have you, you can be my investigative assistant. You know what everybody's up to before they do."

"Your assistant? Ha. You can be my assistant. And another thing, everybody. I know all about Joey's wrongful conviction. I attended every day of that trial. Travesty of justice."

Carrie's comment hit Harriet hard. It was the second time today she'd heard Carrie say Joey was innocent. Had she been wrong about Joey all those years he'd been in prison? It was a dark thought, one she'd have to address.

The light in the room had gotten too dim for Harriet's taste. She turned on several lamps, including a small light on the corner desk. When she finished, Carrie told her, "Grab my iPad, in the top drawer, so I can take notes about Craig's visit with Joey today."

When Carrie was ready, Craig explained Joey would have to go back to prison to serve the four-month balance of his sentence for violating his parole. "But there is a chance he might never get out. The police found his fingerprints on the knife in Landry's back, and Joey admitted to me they were his."

This news caught Harriet's attention. "Why didn't you tell me about the fingerprints?"

"I wanted to confirm them with Joey first."

Harriet looked away at the thought of Joey's fingerprints on the murder weapon. She didn't know or understand what he'd endured. Had he been pushed to do the unthinkable? She didn't want to believe it.

Craig didn't either. "The fingerprints are a complication, but someone set Joey up. They sent him an anonymous letter saying Harriet was in trouble, which put him at Harriet's house when the police showed up. And before anyone asks, Joey didn't keep the letter and has no idea who wrote it."

Carrie looked at Yeager. "How about you? Anything to report on Joey's situation? I know you haven't been sitting on your hands with those gold coins in your pocket."

"I am picking up Brian Tartly in the morning. He's taking me to his coin shop to take a closer look at the coins."

"What for?" Harriet asked. "Doesn't he know what they are?"

"The coins looked funny to him."

"Funny how?"

"Like they might not be real."

Another surprise, if it was true. "Surely, my father didn't have fake coins."

Craig looked down at his hands, and Harriet called him on it. "What aren't you telling us, Craig?"

"Joey knew about the gold coins at your house."

Harriet inhaled. How would her brother know about the coins if he didn't know about Landry's body under the house? "Did he say what he knew?"

"No. We ran out of time, but I'm not sure he would have told me. He wasn't very forthcoming with his answers."

Carrie got Harriet's attention. "It's time we talked about your father's obsessions."

Harriet felt pressure in her chest, a sensation that came over her when she had to talk about her father. The digital clock with the time and day for people who can't tell the difference between weekdays and weekends stared at Harriet from Carrie's nightstand, a reminder the clock on their investigation was ticking.

Harriet cleared her throat. "My dad, as Carrie said, had his obsessions. One was work."

"Workaholic," Carrie added.

Harriet nodded in agreement.

"What did he do?" Craig asked.

"A little bit of everything."

"Mostly real estate," Carrie added.

Harriet huffed. "Who is telling this story, Carrie, you or me?"

"You, but not very fast. Remember, I have cancer."

Yeager laughed, and Harriet picked up her pace. "Dad was a real estate appraiser. He started his business when he graduated from college and built it into a successful operation. He first appraised residential properties but moved to commercial. He developed a coveted list of banking, business, and developer clients, and his business grew.

"He hired my brother when he graduated college, and after Joey worked for him and learned the business for twenty-five years, Dad moved the company's offices to South End. One reason for the move was to be closer to home—the house uptown you saw this morning—and the second reason was to get on the ground floor in South End. He always felt it would be developed as Charlotte grew. He was right. For the next five years, they appraised every tract in South End. No one knew the buildings or the terrain better than Dad and Joey."

Harriet could feel Carrie's eyes on her.

"Tell them the third reason."

How should she put it? That her father was crazy? Delusional? Focused on something that didn't exist? A dream. A legend. All of the above. She settled for the facts.

"My dad believed he could mine gold in uptown Charlotte. And when that didn't pan out—no pun intended—he got the idea there were gold coin hoards to be found in Charlotte."

Harriet paused long enough for Craig to ask her how her father died. Carrie supplied the answer for Harriet. "Suicide, but I call it gold fever. A fatal disease."

"Enough about my father." Harriet needed to breathe.

Carrie set her iPad aside. "They should hear the rest."

"Fine. You tell it then."

Carrie looked at Craig, then Yeager. "Her father's given name was Rick Penman, but from a young age, Rick loved to collect pennies. His primary school friends nicknamed him Penny, and it stuck to him like glue his entire life."

Carrie shifted her position in her bed and continued. "Penny's passions became his obsessions. His childhood coin collecting hobby became a lifelong commitment that ruined his marriage and affected his relationship with his children. His collecting became focused on gold coins, and he developed a keen interest in Charlotte's gold mining history. Because of that, he connected with Lester Standish—everyone called him Junior—and the two attended coin trade shows and worked together on business deals, until their most consequential deal sent Joey to prison. They were partners in a venture to develop South End."

Craig was curious about facts that didn't appear to matter to the conversation. "How do you know so much about Harriet's father?"

"We knew each other as children, and we became high school sweethearts. If things had gone differently, I might have been Harriet's mother." Carrie laughed. "Good thing for her she didn't get my genes."

Harriet couldn't help herself. "If I had your genes, Carrie, I'd be watching reality TV, reading romance books, and telling sordid tales until my nineties." Her tone was part playful and part *let's get on with it.*

Carrie dipped her chin at Harriet and smiled a thin smile. "It's not a bad way to go through life, Harriet."

"The end of the story, please."

"Fine. Fine. Harriet knows Penny and I stayed friends over the years, even when things weren't going well for him at home. What she doesn't know is he, like me, loved a good story, and he was a pretty good writer too. Said he was going to write a book someday about treasure hunting. We both had dreams."

Carrie looked out the one window in her room, and a far-away look came into her eyes, which prompted Harriet to steer the conversation back to center, back to Joey being set up for Landry's murder. "We can talk about my dad and his obsessions later. Joey is the one in jail."

Carrie said, "Fair enough, but they need to know what Joey got wrapped up in twenty years ago, especially since your boyfriend is going to represent him, Harriet." She emphasized the word *boyfriend*, and Carrie and Yeager laughed.

Harriet huffed. "Are y'all demented? Enough with the boyfriend thing."

Carrie smiled, as if to say, *you take over, Harriet.*

"Here's the short version of the story. Dad and Junior set out to buy the below-ground property rights in South End's Gold District. They thought they could use the property to mine gold and build a gold mining museum at the site of the old Rudisill Mine. Junior got the property owners to agree to sell if their property appraised for less than a certain value. Dad got Joey to do the appraisals. The sales went through. One seller claimed fraud. Joey ended up in jail."

Harriet could tell Carrie was tired. "That's enough for tonight." She stood and the men did too, before they heard movement near the half-opened hallway door.

"Yoohoo, anybody home?" An elderly woman with platinum hair in a flattering bob walked in with a vase filled with flowers. "Sorry to interrupt, Carrie. I wanted to bring you something to lighten up your room."

"Come right in, Celia, and have a seat."

"No. You've got visitors. I'll come by another time." Celia placed the flowers on the nightstand next to Carrie's bed.

"Please do. And thank you. The flowers are beautiful."

"They're from my grandson Sterling and his wife Bailey." Celia winked at Carrie, said hello to Craig, and introduced herself to Harriet and Yeager, who returned the courtesy. She then slipped out as quietly as she came in.

Harriet wondered how long Celia had stood outside the door. Then to Carrie: "Why are Sterling and Bailey Standish sending you flowers?"

"Probably because Celia told them they needed to be good neighbors."

Yeager expressed his doubt. "Seems suspicious."

"Everything seems suspicious to you, Yeager. Look at it this way: Celia has influence with her grandson and granddaughter-in-law, and I have a new ninety-year-old friend who I can ply for information."

"Time to let Carrie rest." Harriet said it more firmly this time.

Carrie raised both hands over her head. "Hold on. I found out some news from Jenny after Bailey fired her. You will not like what I have to say."

A nurse entered the room and asked Carrie if she needed anything. Carrie shooed her away and adjusted her blanket on her legs.

"Jenny—High Brow to Yeager—stuck her beak into a place she shouldn't, and they fired her to try to silence her, but she called me. They might as well have published the story on the evening news.

"Anyway, she learned who drafted the documents for the Standish Company's ten-million-dollar loan to the Indie. It's someone who despises us, and who hates Mr. Lawyer here in particular. She believes the man is helping the Standish Company do what it is planning to do and has been in the middle of what has already happened."

Harriet and Craig exchanged glances. Yeager said the name. "Robert Elkin, that scumbag lawyer. It's him, isn't it?"

"One and the same. Although 'scum bag' is typically slang for 'lawyer.'" She laughed. "Except for Mr. Lawyer here, of course."

Harriet was sure they'd shed themselves of Elkin after the state bar took his law license. Unfortunately, he'd avoided prison, but Harriet assumed that without his license, he would wilt away, never to bother them again. She chastised herself for being so naïve. Elkin was exactly the person who would hold a grudge, and they had given him every reason to do so. They'd beaten him at his own game. Worse, they'd embarrassed him, caused him to lose his managing partner position, and exposed his secret society. What did he have to lose? He'd hit rock bottom. If he was involved with the Standish Company, it couldn't be good for them.

Craig interrupted Harriet's thoughts with more news. "Late last night, I received a disturbing unsigned email from a *vengeanceissweet* email address that said my retiree friends are about to suffer financial ruin, untold heartbreak, and trials and tribulations. I suspected Elkin. What Jenny learned confirms it."

So that was that. Elkin was back. So be it. They had work to do. Come morning, it would be time to get started.

Travail decided it was time to come clean with Harriet. Maybe not entirely, but he had to begin somewhere. "Buy you a drink?"

"It's been a long day. I'm exhausted."

"Indie bar, on the way to your cottage. Just the one."

She consented, and they walked in silence from the health center to the main building. The bar was empty, which suited Travail. "What's your poison?"

"White wine."

"I'll have the same," he said to the bartender.

They sat at a corner table overlooking Lost Cove Lake and tapped glasses. "To finding the truth," Travail said.

Harriet nodded and took a sip. She put her glass down and set her hands in her lap. "What's on your mind?"

He couldn't just come out and say how he'd ruminated about his feelings for her and his feelings for his late wife, and how those twisted feelings tied him in knots in recent weeks and kept him up late the night before, so he stumbled. "You look nice."

She laughed. "I've only slept one hour in the last eighteen hours. I look anything but nice."

That was the thing though. Harriet's appearance was more than coiffed hair and designer jeans, not that she did either. It was wild red curls and a real-life persona. He loved that about her, but could he tell her that?

Travail sipped his wine to steady his nerves. Damn. This was worse than the first time he asked a girl on a date in high school, not that he was about to ask her on a date, or was he?

"I know this is not the best time, and the show is only two days away, but I have tickets to the Blumenthal on Thursday night for *Hamilton*. Have you seen *Hamilton*?"

"I have."

"Oh."

Harriet paused. "I'd see it again though."

"You would?"

"I would." She touched her wine glass to her lips.

Had she said she'd go to *Hamilton* with him? No. She'd only said she would see *Hamilton* again. But then, he hadn't actually asked her to go, and she, being Harriet, knew it.

Harriet was going to make him ask, and if Rachael was looking down on him now, she'd be in stitches.

Season tickets to the Blumenthal had been Rachael's idea, and he'd never cancelled them after she died. But he had never gone to a show again either.

One night when they left *Jersey Boys*, Rachael put her arm in his and said theater was good for the soul. "When I'm gone, take a date in my place. When the world has you down, theater is your uplift."

Travail laughed at the suggestion he would outlive Rachael. "You're the one who eats well, does yoga, and drinks five gallons of water a day. You will outlive me by twenty years."

"That may be true, dear, but if something happens to me, I want you to go to the theater and take someone with you that you care about."

That exchange led to a debate Travail lost. Rachael said if he died first, she would not date again—it had less to do with her pining for lost love and more to do with the freedom not to have to put up with a man in the house again—but if she died first, he'd be helpless without a woman in his life. He argued otherwise, but her questions about where to look for what at the grocery store, how to run the appliances in the house, and how to pay the electric bill left him cornered.

In the three years since Rachael died, he had done his best to survive, figuring out the day-to-day household bits sufficiently to get by. What he hadn't figured out was the remedy to Rachael's last point: loneliness.

When they came home from the show, Rachael told him to sit, and she got serious. "I hope it never comes to this, Craig. I hope we live to be ninety and die in each other's arms, but that is not how life works. If I go first, I want you to promise me something."

"What?"

"Promise me that if you find someone you care about, you will not let my memory stand in your way."

"You want me to marry someone else?"

Her response was fresh in his mind, like he heard it yesterday. "Who said anything about marriage? I want you to be happy."

She'd offered him a loving gift, one he'd refused to open. Would that change now?

Harriet interrupted his thoughts. "Are you okay, Craig? You're awfully quiet."

"I'm okay."

But really, he wasn't. The ride early this morning with Yeager brought home how little he knew about Harriet and how much he wanted to know. If she had a twin brother in prison, she should be able to tell him. If she had issues with her late father, she should be able to confide in him. And he should be able to tell her how uncomfortable he felt, and about how he felt for her.

Harriet displayed patience by her silence. It was his move.

"Would you like to go to *Hamilton* with me this Thursday?"

"I'd love to."

PART II

DAYS TWO AND THREE - DIGGING FOR EVIDENCE

CHAPTER 12

THE DEVELOPER'S LAIR

Lester Sterling Standish the Third was an early riser. No one beat him to the punch. It's what his grandmother Celia taught him when she schooled him on her success. "The best way to out-hustle the competition, Sterling, is to out-hustle the competition. You can't buy real estate if you're not there to make an offer at the right time. You can't develop real estate without the right connections, engineers, lawyers, and builders. And you can't do any of that well without good planning and hard work before the sun is up, while the sun is up, and after the sun goes down."

The sun was not up when Sterling entered the elevator cab to whisk him to the twenty-third floor of the most recently constructed South End office tower. The top floor had the best view of the territory he intended to conquer. With years of planning, he'd finally harvest what mattered in South End, the wealth below ground. His father, Junior, would be proud.

After he got off the elevator, he faced the main entrance to his company's office, a solid oak double door with a metal sign trimmed in gold that read Standish Company. He put two fingers to his lips and placed them on the sign before turning left and walking to the end of the hall to a forgettable door with a forgettable sign that read "Utility

Closet." He smiled at his joke. The dictionary defined the word *utility* to mean "useful, profitable, or beneficial," which is what he intended the space to be, but most people would see the door and think mops and brooms.

Sterling placed his thumb onto a digital lock in the door and the dead bolt retracted. His footfall engaged the interior lights, and when he'd walked five paces, the door's dead bolt clicked back in place, sealing him off from prying eyes and ears.

Only one other person knew what went on in this space, and he'd be arriving just about now. The lock whirred again, and the man stepped inside.

For thirty years, the man had provided legal services to the Standish Company, but recent events in the man's life turned his professional career upside down and he needed a job. Now disbarred but without prison time for his sins, the once-well-connected managing partner of an Am Law 100 law firm had come on bended knee. The man could not practice law any longer, but he knew enough law to save the Standish Company outrageous sums they'd otherwise pay since the billable hour—now more than $1,700 an hour at some Charlotte firms —was out of sight of reality. More importantly, the man had experience crossing legal lines.

Sterling welcomed him. "Morning, Robert."

Elkin grunted in return, his way of saying good morning. His days managing a big law firm were over, but he often wore silk shirts and designer suits, as if he believed he was still the captain of the ship.

While Elkin got settled, Sterling thought back to three months earlier when he'd hired Elkin in his quasi-legal role and how malleable the man had been. He'd asked Elkin, "Why do you want to work for me?"

"I know your business. And I know what you're planning."

Sterling hadn't been certain it was a good idea to hire Robert Elkin. The newspapers sold a lot of copy based on his misdeeds. "Not sure you'd be a good fit."

"No more a crook than you." Elkin was blunt. And probably, if

Sterling was being honest with himself, he was correct. The glaring difference being they never caught Sterling doing anything illegal.

But being a crook wasn't enough. Sterling knew how to find crooks. He'd pressed Elkin to find out if he could offer more than criminal mischief. "I need money to reach my goals. Can you help?"

This was when the interview got interesting, when Elkin, as down and out as he was, revealed how he could add value to Sterling's plans. "When you want money, you need to go to people who have it. And when you want it quick, you go to people you can manipulate, whether by fear, greed, or a good story." Elkin had dropped a brochure on Sterling's desk. "Go to people who have saved money from their lifetime's work and who love to invest in a 'sure thing.' Isn't that what you call your project, a sure thing?"

Sterling had known nothing about the Independence Retirement Community until Elkin showed him the flashy brochure. "Of all the retirement communities in Charlotte, why there?"

"I have my reasons."

"No secrets, Robert."

Elkin's face reddened as he told how the Indie changed his life for the worse. "I plan to destroy the Indie. I have special plans for three residents who screwed up my life."

"So this is about revenge?

"Revenge with an upside for you, but I also want my law license back. I miss practicing law more than I thought I would, and I am good at it."

"I doubt you can get your license back after the crimes you committed."

"Leave that to me. What matters now is putting Indie money in your pocket."

"Who are the three Indie residents?"

When Elkin mentioned their names, Harriet's rang a bell. "Was her father Penny Penman?"

"Yes. She's the daughter of your father's killer."

Sterling had lost many nights of sleep thinking about Penny Penman. Twenty years ago, shortly after Joey Penman's appraisal fraud trial, Chance Landry told Sterling and his grandmother Celia that Penny killed Junior. Celia decided the family would not go public with the information to avoid publicity and more heartache. Junior's death was heartache enough, she said. Sterling went along, but his desire to avenge his father's death never abated.

Now Sterling couldn't believe his luck. The daughter of the man who killed his father was Elkin's target. He relished the idea of Elkin inflicting pain on Penny Penman's family.

Sterling asked one last question in Elkin's job interview. "Will your fixation on hurting your enemies interfere with getting me the money I need?"

"My fixation dovetails perfectly with your plans."

Elkin explained how.

Sterling remembered the good feeling he'd had when hearing of the scheme's ingenuity, and when Elkin asked for a meager salary, Sterling's answer was quick. "You're hired."

That was three months ago. Today, Elkin was at work early, like he'd been every day since he started work for the Standish Company.

A bulletin board hung above Elkin's desk. He tinkered with it daily, adding photos, diagrams, maps, and notes. The board looked like the kind the FBI used when they tried to solve a crime with many suspects. Elkin's bulletin board did not focus on suspects. It focused on prey.

His first items on the board were pictures of Craig Travail, Yeager Alexander, and Harriet Keaton. Each photo had a to-do list beside it. Next, Elkin pinned an aerial photo of the Independence Retirement Community to the board, identifying the buildings, lakes, and cottages. Thin yellow yarn stretched from each person's photo to the place on the map where they lived. Sometimes, Elkin spent hours in front of the board, never losing his focus.

What would he do with his board this morning?

Elkin laid a newspaper on his desk, took his scissors, and carefully cut out an article. After smoothing the article flat on his desk with his hands, he tacked the article to the board.

Taking a length of red yarn, Elkin measured the distance from

Harriet's picture to the news article, cut the yarn to match the distance, and tacked one end to Harriet's picture and the other end to the article.

Sterling stepped closer to Elkin. "What's the article about?"

"A murder."

Sterling leaned in to read the headline. "Local real estate developer found dead near the Rudisill Gold Mine." A picture revealed Chance Landry to be the deceased real estate developer.

"How did he end up there?" Sterling emphasized the word *there*.

"Interesting word choice, Sterling. Wouldn't the innocent question be, Who would want to kill Chance? or, How did it happen? You jumped to, How did he end up there?"

Sterling snapped back. "I haven't seen Chance since I fired him two days ago for demanding that ridiculous sum of money."

"Is that right?"

"Yes, that's right."

Sterling took the offensive. "Who do you think killed Chance?"

"Many people had a motive to kill Chance. Maybe it was Dan Barnard. He wasn't on board with Chance's blackmail threat. Most likely, it was Joey Penman, but the police may believe it was you or Bailey, considering what you had to lose if Chance talked. Maybe your plan was a two-for-one. Kill Chance, and set Joey up for the murder. You hated the Penman family after Penny killed your father."

Sterling didn't like the conversation's direction. "Don't forget, Robert, you work for me."

Elkin grinned. "I do. But we're deep in the weeds together. You need me as much as I need you. We don't want to cut off our noses to spite our faces, do we?"

Sterling fought to regain control. "You said you'd bring the agreements with you today."

"I have them right here." Elkin dug into his briefcase, took out the documents, and handed them to Sterling.

"Brief me."

"You're holding ten subscription agreements, each for five hundred thousand dollars. That's ten Indie residents who invested their retirement funds in the South End Mining Company. Also included in the stack are the loan documents for the ten-million-dollar loan to the Indie. I recorded them yesterday at the register of deeds. You're welcome."

Sterling smiled as he flipped through the subscription agreements. Elkin had been true to his word. He'd trained a sales group to promote investing in the South End Mining Company, and they made the sales.

"And the bullion coins?"

"Fifty residents bought the coins for $100,000 each. You made a tidy profit. The coins were worth twenty cents on the dollar."

"And the money for the stock and bullion?"

"Deposited in the bank yesterday."

Excellent. The operation's first phase was now funded. That meant more money to move dirt and more capital for lender financing.

The only documents in the stack that bothered Sterling related to the ten-million-dollar loan. He didn't enjoy tying up Standish Company capital in a retirement community, but his grandmother had asked him—more like, told him—to make the loan. She didn't want to move into an insolvent retirement community. Elkin said it would work out for the best. "They won't be able to pay the loan off in time, and you can foreclose and sell the property for more than the loan's value. Four months from now, you'll make good money on the loan."

Everything was falling into place. And yet? "Are you sure your Indie friends won't cause problems? They beat you last time."

Elkin slowed his speech. "They will not beat us, Sterling. We will stay one step ahead to the very end. Yesterday, we placed listening devices in Carrie Roberts' room and in Harriet's cottage. We will know what they know when they know it, and we will know what they are planning."

Elkin reached into his briefcase for a document he handed to Sterling. "This is the icing on your cake. The South End Mining Company's engineering report is complete. You've got a green light."

This was fantastic. Sterling took his time reviewing the report's three sections, starting with the first section about the mine's history. In 1826, a Charlotte gunsmith, while hunting deer on Rudisill Hill, discovered gold in the surface rocks. Count Rivafinoli, the German-educated Italian associated with the London Mining Company, heard the news and brought significant capital and laborers to mine the Rudisill Gold Mine in 1830 as a commercial enterprise. Over the next one hundred years, the mine changed hands many times, but since the late 1930s, no one had worked the largest and most productive gold mine in Charlotte. That would soon change.

Section 2 focused on Charlotte's failed effort to turn the Rudisill Mine into a tourist attraction. In 1965, the director of the Mint Museum of Art suggested reopening the Rudisill Gold Mine as a tourist attraction after reinforcing it for safety and equipping it with shuttle cars. In 1976, city planners recommended the city consider the idea, but lack of funding and other city and state priorities got in the way. If the city wouldn't do it, Sterling would.

Section 3 addressed the issues and solutions. The primary roadblock to reopening the mine and developing an underground museum were the unknown conditions of the mine—the integrity, openness, and precise locations of the tunnels and shafts—and the fact much of the mine was below the water table, an impediment that could require continual pumping of water, making the project difficult to manage and potentially cost prohibitive. However, the engineers concluded, after much study, South End Mining Company could bring the Rudisill Mine back to life, mine gold for profit, and create a premier tourist attraction that would increase property values and celebrate Charlotte's gold history. Everything was coming together.

"You verified this report?"

Elkin nodded. "I worked closely with the staff, pushed them to be thorough, and made sure the report was perfect. You can use the report with your lenders and shareholders."

Sterling reflected on his father's legacy in the Standish Company. Junior—even Sterling called him that—often seemed too conservative with the business. Only after his father died and Sterling learned his father's true plans for South End did he realize he'd been wrong about Junior, who had the courage and foresight to buy the land below the surface. Now, with modern technology and proper permitting to address noise, rock removal, and water dispersion, mining was possible again. Sterling would make amends and honor his father by completing Junior's work. The fact he would become rich doing it was a delightful bonus.

Sterling retreated to his twenty-foot maple desk with a panoramic view of the South End Gold District. From twenty-three floors up, he could see the excavators' progress. The treasure hole—a rectangular pit along the Rudisill gold vein on Mint Street—and the dump trucks hauling ore and dirt, made Sterling forget about the nitty gritty and focus on the prize.

The engineering report vindicated his gamble to get a head start on the project under the guise of building something else. He could worry about bribing officials and obtaining gold mine permits later. For now, he'd enjoy the view.

"Dig," he whispered. "Dig, you beautiful, lovable, earth-moving machines. Dig."

CHAPTER 13

COIN SHOP EXCURSION

Yeager high-stepped it from his cottage to the main building's breakfast buffet, where Brian Tartly, their coin expert, waited on him.

Brian waved at him from a two-top. Yeager waved back, filled his plate to overflowing with French toast and syrup, and navigated his way to Brian through the tables filled with the early risers, mostly men who had difficulty sleeping and no problem being first in line for breakfast. Two women occupied the last table he had to pass to get to Brian. He tried to cut around them without being seen, but he didn't escape.

"Good morning, Yeager." Celia Standish dabbed her mouth with a napkin and smiled. "I hope it's okay if I call you by your first name."

"That's fine. Good morning to you." He didn't like small talk with the Standish family, but if he was going to speak with any one of them, Celia seemed to be okay.

"How is Carrie doing?"

"If you ask her, she's got the hiccups. We're just glad she has good care."

"Me too. The Collins Center is a wonderful healthcare center. One reason I chose the Indie." Celia pointed across the table. "Do you know my granddaughter-in-law Bailey?"

"He knows me," Bailey chirped. "Tried to play me for a fool in the People's Court yesterday." Bailey raised her knife and pointed it at Yeager. "Don't underestimate my power."

"Now, Bailey, be polite." Celia lowered her voice. "Bailey has taken on a big job to keep the Indie financially sound. I'm sure the pressure will subside, and we will all get along nicely."

"I hope so." Yeager also hoped their conversation would end soon. He could smell the sweet syrup on his fluffy French toast.

But Celia continued. "You and your friends seemed to be under some pressure in your serious meeting when I visited Carrie yesterday. I hope everything is okay. Are y'all worried about anything?"

Yeager remembered the witness-prep guidance Craig had given him before he testified in the Meck Dec case last year. Answer only the question asked. Don't volunteer. This is not a cocktail party where conversation is lob, talk, lob, talk. Celia had made several statements and asked only one question.

At a cocktail party—assuming they served beer—Yeager might have responded to her statement about them being under pressure by saying, "You're damn right we're under pressure, and yes, that was a serious meeting, because all hell is about to break loose and we are working to prevent it."

As to her statement that she hoped everything was okay, he might have said he also hoped everything would be okay "because things are not okay at the Indie by a long shot, what with Landry dead in Harriet's basement, her brother in jail, gold coins without a home, questionable investments for the residents, the Standish family's Indie takeover, and Robert Elkin's illicit work behind the scenes." But Yeager didn't say those things.

As to her one and only question about whether he was worried about anything, the answer was easy. Sober as he was, he wasn't worried about the worst, not with Craig, Harriet, Carrie, Becky, and others on his team, but that's not what he said.

"I am worried, Celia. I'm worried my food is getting cold." Yeager laughed, said "good day," slid by the Standish women, and sat beside Brian Tartly, who'd ordered pancakes.

"What was that about? Looked like you were being cross-examined."

Yeager said they'd talk about it later and dug into his breakfast. Between bites, they discussed fishing, Brian's love life, and upcoming events at the Indie.

When they finished breakfast, Yeager said they needed to stop by the business office. The business secretary, who was Yeager's friend, was not at her desk, having agreed to his request that she take a break at this specific time. He took out the key Jenny Montgomery had kept when Bailey fired her and slipped to him the day before, looked around to be sure they were alone, and used the key to enter the office.

Brian followed. "Why are we here?"

"The safe. Watch the door and make sure Bailey doesn't get here before we leave."

Yeager took a scrap from his wallet with the combination Jenny had given him and worked the safe's combination lock. When he heard the click, he pulled the lever and opened the safe. In the bottom corner, where Jenny said to look, sat the gold bars the South End Mining Company had put up as security for the investments made by the ten Indie residents.

As Yeager loaded the gold bars into a satchel, Brian whistled. "What you got there?"

"A hunch," Yeager said.

"Looks more like a robbery."

Yeager heard Bailey's voice in the hallway. "We have to hurry." He closed the safe, pushed Brian out the door, and pulled the door shut.

"What are you doing here, and what's in the bag?"

"Came by to say hello to Alice, but it looks like she's on break." Yeager tried not to look strained as he held up the satchel with one arm. "Food from the dining room."

"That is going to stop. We have to get our finances under control. You old people stuff all kinds of restaurant food in your pockets."

"You want the food back?" Yeager lifted the satchel.

"Get out of here." Bailey's bracelets and bangles clanged as she pointed them toward the door.

Yeager grabbed Brian and they hurried to Yeager's truck parked out front, where Yeager put the satchel on the bench seat beside another satchel filled with bullion coins in small plastic bags. "Let's go see what this stuff is worth."

Brian's coin shop was in a strip shopping center off Highway 51. A sign at the door asked customers to ring a bell to be admitted, but Brian tapped on the glass window and waved at someone inside. With a click, the door opened.

Yeager followed Brian into the long, narrow shop. The wall along the right side had built-in bookshelves displaying coin books for purchase. On the left side, a countertop-high glass case displayed coins for sale in many shapes and colors. Behind the glass case, on the wall, were additional glass cabinets filled with more coins. All the glass cabinets had locks on sliding doors. Security cameras stared at Yeager from the top corners of each end of the store.

A man seated near a cash register placed a magazine on the counter and rose to greet them. Brian pointed at the man. "Yeager, meet my son, Burt."

Burt, who shared Brian's thin physique and olive coloring, shook Yeager's hand. "Dad tells me you want me to assay some gold coins and gold bars for you."

Yeager placed the small plastic baggie with the coins he found near Landry's body on the counter, followed by the residents' gold bullion coins and the gold bars. "You got a safe?"

Burt pointed to the door behind him. "Back there. Don't worry. I will lock everything up nice and secure."

Yeager looked at the glass cabinet below Burt, where two coins on display caught his attention. Burt pulled a key off his belt, unlocked the case, and removed the two coins.

"You've got a good eye, Yeager. We keep a few Charlotte Mint coins on display because of their local origin." He handed them to Yeager to inspect. "One is the quarter eagle. The other is the half eagle. I have more in the safe."

"The quarter eagle looks like the ones I found. Where did you get these?"

Brian answered for Burt. "Not off dead bodies, that's for sure."

Yeager regretted telling Brian where he'd found the coins, but since Burt was doing the work, he confided in Burt too. Come to think of it, Harriet was right. He had a hard time keeping a secret.

"How will you know if the coins I found are real?"

Burt pointed to a small machine near him behind the counter. "We test the metal. Much easier than it used to be. In the early days of gold mining, people spit on coins and rubbed them against an abrasive surface to see if the gold would rub off and show another metal underneath, or they bit the coin because lead is softer than gold."

Yeager never knew why people in old Westerns bit their coins. Now he knew. "How are these coins different from bullion coins?"

"They are what we call a numismatic coin. They get their value from more than just their metal content. How rare they are, their present condition, and whatever role they played in history have a lot to do with how much someone will pay. Bullion coin value is determined solely by the precious metal the coin contains."

"That's why you can charge thousands for a rare coin the size of a dime?"

"Correct."

Yeager thought about the sales pitch for the bullion coins. "The people who sold us the bullion coins told us they would offer a hedge against investment losses in the stock market."

"That's possible, as long as you paid fair value for them."

Yeager pulled a flyer from his pocket with the price list and handed it to Burt, who said he would check the current prices for precious metals of this grade and size and compare those prices to what the residents paid. "Keep in mind, gold bullion prices, while predictable in the long term, can fluctuate."

"Brian says my numa-whatever—my rare—coins looked funny."

Burt examined the rare coins in Yeager's bag. "Dad's eyesight is not what it used to be, but I have a colleague who is an expert who will know for sure." He touched a few coins and held them up to the light. "Truth be told, even the most experienced collectors could be fooled if they are forgeries."

Yeager rubbed his beard. If someone forged the coins, who? And why were the coins in Harriet's house? And, for that matter, what was their connection to Landry's murder?

Burt put all the coins in the safe and returned to collect the gold bars. When he lifted the bars off the counter, he paused.

"What's the problem?"

Burt moved his hands up and down. "Just a thought, Yeager. Nothing to worry about."

CHAPTER 14

TRIAL TRANSCRIPT TEASERS

Travail skipped breakfast and headed to the gym to jump-start a habit he'd neglected in the last few months. He'd need to get in better shape to keep up with Harriet.

On the path around Freedom Lake, he ran into Becky. "Quite a board meeting yesterday."

She nodded her agreement as she sat and fiddled with one shoe on the very bench Travail spent time on the day he'd first arrived at the Indie a year ago.

This was the place where his life changed, where he met Yeager and Harriet on this very spot. Yeager went for a buck-naked frigid swim, and Harriet scolded Yeager for shooting fish in the lake. A lot of time had passed since then. He focused on the present.

"Did you know our new board members would be at the meeting?"

"I got a call from Jenny before the meeting. She told me Bailey had fired her. She was upset and didn't give details."

"Yeager and I plan to speak with Jenny today at my place at eleven. Can you join us?"

"I'll be there."

At the gym, Travail ran into Nelli. She was doing curls with free weights while she sat in her wheelchair. "Morning, Counselor."

"Good morning, Nelli. How are you feeling after your skirmish yesterday?"

"Never better. Pumping iron to be ready for regionals." Her laugh was contagious, causing Travail to laugh, too, until she asked about Harriet. "How's your girlfriend today?"

How many times did they have to tell people he and Harriet were not boyfriend and girlfriend for anyone to believe them?

"Don't get your tighty-whities in a bunch, Craig. You and Harriet are a perfect match."

Travail inhaled. He didn't say he'd asked Harriet on a date. Too much information.

"By the way, I have some news for your investigation."

Travail froze. At this rate, it wouldn't take long before everyone at the Indie, including Bailey Standish, knew about their investigation.

"Here's the scoop. Dan Barnard was Landry's business associate. They both worked for the Standish Company for many years."

"How do you know?"

Nelli worked the weights with one arm, then the other. "Dan's daughter had an accident last year. He thought she would die, but she survived and ended up in a wheelchair. Dan was a mess and leaned on me for advice. He loves that girl more than anything. A bit of a strange bird, but his heart is in the right place, at least where his daughter is concerned.

"Dan has some baggage, but here's what interests me: he's feeling guilty about things he's done in his past for the Standish Company. Said so himself this morning, but he had to leave before I could get him to say what those things are. They must be serious, though. He kept looking at his hands as he talked and had a pained expression on his face."

"He could feel guilty about things that have nothing to do with us."

"Yeah. Nah. He went on a rant about Landry. Said he was glad the man was dead. He also said he didn't like Elkin. Said he was glad we whipped him last year."

Interesting. Dan might be an excellent source. "Thanks, Nelli. That's helpful."

"Does that mean I'm on the investigative team?" She didn't wait for an answer, but pointed instead at the machine for one's abs. "I'd start there if I were you, Craig."

Travail didn't start there, but he got his heart rate up on the elliptical, did some free weight work, and performed some yoga-like stretches.

While he stretched, he thought about Dan Barnard, the man who testified against Joey, who Yeager didn't trust, and whose heart might be in the right place. Then his mind turned to Chance Landry, the thread that held the mystery together. It was time to tug on that thread.

Travail found a cardboard banker box filled with papers on his porch with a note from Harriet taped to the box. "Joey's court files. Help yourself."

He put the box on the kitchen table, made coffee, and fed Blue. As he doled the canned food into Blue's bowl, he spoke to his companion. "What do you think we're going to find in these twenty-year-old court files, old boy?" Blue nudged the bowl and tried to lick the spoon, indifferent to any evidence other than the food in front of him.

Travail emptied the files on the desk in his spare bedroom, his modern-day law office. He first made two stacks, one with the trial docket and charging documents and another with the daily trial transcripts. His third and fourth stacks were the prosecution and defense exhibits. He did not locate any appeal documents.

What was he looking for exactly?

If Joey was charged with murder, Travail needed to know the facts in the case that sent Joey to prison for twenty years, including what Chance Landry said at the trial. His gut told him Landry's death had its origins in the trial, and while revenge by Joey was one explanation for Landry's death, Harriet didn't believe it and neither did he. He didn't want to let her down.

He also needed to know more about the Standish Company. Maybe their involvement in South End that led to Joey's conviction would explain their present plans.

He sipped his coffee, grabbed the docket sheet, and settled in his chair. His first surprise was the defense attorney's name. "I'll be damned. Roscoe Brady."

Blue, who had settled at Travail's feet, looked up at Travail, as if he too were surprised Roscoe had defended Joey.

Travail hadn't known what legal work Judge Brady had done before he served on the bench, but it made sense he had been a criminal lawyer. He'd have to pay Chaw a visit to get his take on the trial. But first, he had some reading to do.

After scanning the testimony of the prosecution's witnesses, Travail determined the evidence favored the prosecution and incriminated Joey.

The prosecution first called Chance Landry, who introduced himself to the jury as a man who always wanted to go into real estate development but who got his start, instead, working for South End Environmental.

"Tell us about South End Environmental's work and your role."

"The company's mission was to protect the environmental conditions of South End property. The plan was to buy up underground property to clean up pollutants in the soil caused by mining and industrial work. My job was to negotiate the purchase contracts with South End property owners."

Yea. Right. The story was too altruistic for Travail's instincts, because in his experience, companies bought up underground property rights to exploit minerals for their own gain.

Still, given the outcome of the trial, Landry must have come across well to the jury, a thought that troubled Travail when he realized he knew nothing about Landry. He placed a quick call to Carrie who was happy to share what she remembered from the trial.

"Six feet tall. Confident. Casually but smartly dressed in dark slacks and a camel-hair blazer"—she remembered the blazer even after twenty years. He was "a good looking man," she said, whatever that meant. And he was "full of the gift of gab." In other words, a practiced liar. The perfect con man.

"Who performed the appraisals to determine what South End Environmental paid the property owners?" the prosecutor asked.

"Joey Penman, with the Penman Appraisal Company."

"Did you ever suspect the appraisals were fraudulent?"

"I did not. These were commercial properties with environmental issues that limited their value. When the appraised values on the properties came in low, it didn't seem unusual."

"If that's true, why are we here with a fraud case against Mr. Penman?"

Travail could imagine the prosecutor holding the nail so Landry could hammer it into Joey's coffin. "Joey used fake sales contracts with false sale prices as his comparable sales data to generate the appraisals on the properties."

"How did you learn these sale contracts were fake?"

"A real estate agent named Dan Barnard figured it out and brought it to my attention. Joey deceived Dan's client with an artificially low appraisal, causing his client to sell for less than the property was worth. Dan and I reported Joey's fraud to the North Carolina appraisal board, and they revoked Joey's appraiser license."

The prosecutor marked several contracts as prosecution exhibits, and Landry identified them. "Those are the fake contracts Joey used to generate the appraisals."

The prosecutor had no more questions for Landry, the court ordered a short break, and when court resumed, Roscoe Brady cross-examined Landry.

"Mr. Landry, I represent Joey Penman. I have a few questions about your experience before taking the job at South End Environmental. You didn't have any environmental degrees or experience before you took the job, did you?"

"No, sir."

"A new thing for you?"

"I suppose."

"A new thing for South End Environmental, too, wasn't it?"

"I am not sure what you mean."

There was no break in the transcript, but Travail sensed Roscoe paused before he asked his next question to let the jury wonder where he was going.

"South End Environmental was formed the same day they hired you, correct?"

"That's right."

"Who founded the company?"

"Don't know."

"Who hired you?"

"Can't say."

"You mean you can't say or you won't say?"

"Can't say. The hiring documents were full-blown legalese. I signed a confidentiality clause. Thought nothing of it."

"Did you know Junior Standish when you took the job?"

"I did not."

Travail stopped reading. He couldn't discern Landry's facial expression from the typed transcript, but his instinct told him Landry was lying.

If Junior and Landry knew each other when Landry took the job at South End Environmental, maybe South End Environmental was a front for the Standish Company to buy the land rights. Maybe that relationship unraveled, leading to Landry's murder years later.

Roscoe's next two questions resulted in several adamant denials.

No, Landry did not receive compensation from the Standish Company.

No, South End Environmental didn't intend to sell the land it purchased to the Standish Company.

"That came later," Landry said.

"How convenient."

The prosecutor objected, and the judge told the jury to ignore Roscoe's comment as to how convenient it was that the sales to the Standish Company came later. Travail smiled at the lawyer's trick. The limiting instruction was often worse than the improper comment itself. The comment was now underlined for the jury.

Landry explained his company sold the land rights to the Standish Company only because "we wanted nothing more to do with the land after Joey's appraisal fraud."

"What did the Standish Company pay for the land?"

"We sold it for the price we paid, plus our expenses."

"Did they pay you an additional fee?"

"No, sir."

"You're sure?"

"Objection."

"Sustained," the judge said. "Mr. Brady, if you have evidence the Standish Company paid Mr. Landry an additional fee, you can show him the evidence; otherwise, move on."

Roscoe moved on. If he had a hunch Landry was in Junior Standish's pocket, he must have lacked the evidence to back it up.

"Mr. Landry, did you prepare the fake contracts and give them to Joey for him to do his appraisal work?"

"Absolutely not."

"Which, the preparation of the fake contracts or giving them to Joey?"

"Neither. I don't know why you would say that."

Neither did Travail, because there were no more questions by Roscoe. He must have known Landry was a crook who set Joey up, but if he did, he either didn't have a trump card or, for some reason, he had it but didn't play it.

Travail skimmed Dan Barnard's testimony and learned Dan put the finger squarely on Joey. Another witness against Joey. Not good for Joey's defense.

Worse, the prosecutor introduced email communications showing Joey forwarded the fake contracts to others, including Landry.

Roscoe objected. "These emails are undated and unauthenticated. It's impossible to determine who created them."

The judge overruled Roscoe's objection, but this was before lawyers knew as much as they do now about metadata—the stamps that reveal creation dates and other data—and when courts were quick to treat email with the same respect as a signed letter.

Junior Standish's testimony was neutral. He denied Landry was his front man, but he didn't accuse Joey of fraud, only said Joey did the appraisals. Even so, the emails' smoking-gun persuasiveness, combined with the testimony of Landry and Barnard, must have swayed the jury, especially when Joey didn't testify.

The fake contracts—regardless of who created them—led to Joey's conviction. Did they lead to Junior's death too? And to Landry's murder twenty years later?

Travail pushed away from his desk. There were too many unanswered questions. He stood and stretched. Blue did the same. They walked down to Lost Cove Lake so Blue could chase the ducks and Travail could think.

Two things from the transcript surprised Travail. Number one, Judge Chaw could speak without tobacco in his cheek.

Number two, nobody testified on Joey's behalf. Not his father. Not Harriet. Not his business associates. He'd have to ask Roscoe why, assuming Roscoe could remember the case.

But first, he needed to get ready for his brunch-time guests so he could discover the truth about what happened to the Indie's ten million dollars and learn about the present-day possibility of mining gold in uptown Charlotte.

CHAPTER 15

WHERE DID THE MONEY GO?

Travail set out water, lemonade, and a grocery-store deli tray with crustless egg salad sandwich squares, along with cheese bites, fruit, veggies, and olives, while Jenny Montgomery, Mamie Snyder, Becky Trainer, and Yeager settled into chairs in his den.

Questions needed answers. Like, what happened to the ten million dollars in the Indie's reserve and operating accounts? Why did Bailey fire Jenny Montgomery as bookkeeper and excommunicate Mamie Snyder from the board? And were Jenny or Mamie complicit or at fault with respect to the missing money?

Travail thanked everyone for coming. To Jenny and Mamie, he said, "You don't have to answer our questions, but if you do, we will be grateful."

Becky seconded Travail. "We want to get to the bottom of the missing money, and we can't do that without your help."

Yeager added levity. "Math is not my strong suit. I'm here to support you, and for the food, of course." He picked three olives and two sandwiches off the deli tray, popped the olives in his mouth, and circulated the tray to his left.

Jenny responded for her and Mamie. "We're glad to help if we can. We know you're the good guys." To Travail, she said, "I am sorry I took my anger out on you yesterday. I'd just been fired, but that's no excuse. You've been kind to me and very professional in board meetings."

"Think nothing of it. We've all been dealing with unfortunate surprises." Travail opened his palms. "How would you like to begin?"

Jenny, who was all business now—like she was whenever Travail had seen her do her job—placed her paperwork on the coffee table, revealing her gold wedding band and diamond engagement ring, but nothing else on her hands. She wore a notched one-button sky-blue blazer with matching slacks.

Mamie, who had to be thirty years older than Jenny and in her early eighties, sat to Jenny's left, wearing a lightweight cream turtleneck sweater with matching wide-legged ankle-length slacks. She clutched a square handbag with a multicolored scarf tied to the handle. Her shoes were gold-toned ballet flats with a bow.

Jenny cleared her throat. "As everyone knows, about two months ago, I took family and medical leave for eight weeks to care for my husband, who had back surgery, and during that time, Mamie was kind enough in her position as board treasurer to look after the day-to-day accounting and financial books."

Everyone turned their eyes on Mamie. She looked paler now than when she arrived. Surely she hadn't stolen the money.

Mamie reached out and touched Jenny on the shoulder. "You don't have to cover for me. I did a bad thing."

Mamie was not the type of person to do a bad thing. Residents and staff liked her, and she didn't fit the embezzler profile. According to the Gossip Queen, "she's a socialite with a cash pile to her name. Her money will certainly outlive her."

Mamie continued. "I was an English major, not a math major, but I like to be helpful." Mamie looked at Yeager, who was neither a math nor English major. He smiled in return.

"A few days after Jenny took her family leave, I got a call from an FBI agent who told me hackers had accessed our accounts and were about to steal our money. That was the bad news. The good news was he led an FBI task force sting operation, and if I cooperated with the task force, I could protect the Indie's money and help prevent other retirement communities from losing their money. It seemed like the right thing to do. To cooperate."

Mamie reached in her handbag, took out a tissue, and dabbed her eyes with it. "Jenny has been through my notes. I have a hard time talking about this because it's all my fault. I'd like her to tell it."

Jenny placed a hand on Mamie's arm before she picked up her folder and looked at her notes. "It was a scam. Over the two months I was on leave, the FBI pretender checked in weekly with Mamie. He earned her trust. He explained he needed the account numbers and wiring information for the operating and reserve accounts because they were going to need to move money from them, over time, into safe bitcoin lockers to protect it from the criminals. Mamie provided the information. He emphasized this was a confidential investigation and she couldn't tell anyone about it. To do so would jeopardize the Indie's funds and the investigation."

Jenny shook her head, as if in disbelief. "In hindsight, the scheme's direction was obvious, but who could imagine people so callous as to steal from a retirement community?"

Travail felt his muscles tighten. He wanted to shake the people who would do such a thing. But there was no one to grab onto. At least not yet. He made his feelings known to everyone present. "Those kind of people are evil, devoid of empathy."

Yeager reached for another sandwich. "I'd go as far as to say there is a special room in hell for their kind."

Mamie whispered "thank you," and Jenny smiled, sipped her water, and continued. "Whenever the FBI agent needed to make a transfer to supposedly protect Indie funds, he sent Mamie an automated request for approval. She had the authority to approve the transactions, which she did."

Becky interrupted Jenny to ask Mamie a question. "How many times did you approve transfers?"

"At least ten times over eight weeks."

"And you didn't notice the account balances had dropped?"

Mamie lowered her head. "I was gullible. He told me not to check the accounts, because if I did, the hackers who monitored the accounts would see I was paying attention and would move the money before the FBI could protect it by their methodical approach."

Becky tried to offer solace. "I worked as a forensic bank examiner, and from my experience, your case is not unique. These criminals play on people's fears. You feared your friends and neighbors would lose their money. Your heart was in the right place."

Travail followed Becky's lead. "I agree with Becky. You tried to do the right thing. When did you realize it was a scam?"

Mamie looked at Jenny to respond.

"When I came back from leave last week, I met with Mamie to review the accounts. She handed me the mail she'd collected for me in my absence. I was about to open the monthly bank statement when we got a knock on the door. That was a big day."

Mamie agreed. "That's when we met Celia and Bailey. They waltzed in like they owned the place."

"And two days later, they did," Jenny added.

Blue nudged his way between Jenny and Mamie, where he eyed the food tray. Yeager picked the tray up, took several cheeses from the top, and motioned for Blue to come to him. He kept Blue fed while Jenny finished her story.

"When they walked into the business office, they said they were there to introduce themselves and set up a new resident account for Celia. She planned to move in the next day. This was normal for the move-in process. What happened next was not."

Yeager fed egg salad squares and a few olives to Blue and himself as Jenny continued. "Bailey made an unusual request. She asked to see the most recent bank statement."

"Did she say why?" Becky addressed Jenny, but Mamie responded.

"Bailey said she wanted to be sure her grandmother-in-law didn't move into a community with insufficient capital. I remember this because I felt good about my work to protect the Indie's money."

"Was that about the time all hell broke loose?" Yeager talked while he dropped a carrot in Blue's mouth. Blue chewed it and spit it out.

"Something like that," Jenny acknowledged. "While they were

there, I opened the latest bank statement. I wanted to put Bailey in her place by showing off our healthy numbers, but when I looked at the statement, I saw nothing but zeros. The accounts were empty. I was so stunned, I didn't know what to say. I handed them to Mamie. She was speechless."

Travail's phone buzzed. Caller ID said it was Harriet. "Let's take a quick break. Help yourself to something to eat before Yeager finishes it off."

When he answered, Harriet got right to the point. "Dan Barnard will be at my place at one today. He was reluctant to come, but when I dropped Nelli's name like you suggested, he agreed. Bring Yeager with you."

"We will be there."

"Also, Carrie wants you, Yeager, and me to come to her room at four thirty today to review where we stand and meet with Roscoe Brady. Does that work?"

"Why didn't you tell me Roscoe represented Joey?"

"It didn't seem important at the time. It is now. Can you be there?"

"At your service."

"And finally, Peaches wants us to go dancing tonight."

Travail couldn't read Harriet's expression through the phone. Tonight was the salsa dance extravaganza in the community room Peaches had pestered Travail to attend, and he'd declined, more than once. Now Peaches was trying to twist Harriet's arm. Was Harriet interested in going?

"Come on, Craig, salsa dancing? See you at one at my place."

When Travail's call with Harriet ended, Jenny took everyone through the hectic two days when Bailey blew her top about the zero balances. "What started with Bailey's threats to sue the Indie ended with the Standish Company, via Bailey, taking over 'for the good of the Indie.' Mamie and I wanted to call the police."

Mamie nodded. "I hoped the police could help us get the money back."

Yeager gobbled the last two egg salad squares. "Let me guess. Bailey didn't want that?"

"She said it would stain her grandmother-in-law's good name for picking a retirement home that could lose ten million dollars in sixty days. If we reported it to the police, she said she would make sure—with the help of their 'damn good lawyer'—that we went to prison."

Travail had gotten a similar reaction from Bailey at the board meeting. Why didn't she want the police involved, really? Something was off.

Travail took his time to word his next question. "Do you think Celia and Bailey knew about the missing money before they saw the bank statement?"

Jenny scrunched her brow. "Not Celia. She seemed surprised, but didn't blame us. Bailey, on the other hand, laid into us with a speech that felt prepared, and it was Bailey more than Celia who didn't want the police nosing around. That was suspicious."

Mamie agreed. "Bailey told us what was going to happen and called her lawyer to tell him to put things in motion, as if they'd already talked about their plan."

Jenny explained how Bailey forced the ten-million-dollar loan on the Indie. "The following day, Bailey handed us what she called the non-negotiable loan documents and a phone number to call to discuss them while she stood there. Guess who answered the phone?"

The answer was easy for Travail. "Robert Elkin."

"You're a talented lawyer, Craig Travail." Somehow, Yeager had found a pretzel bag after the deli tray was empty. He bit into a pretzel and tossed the other half to Blue.

Travail ignored Yeager and motioned to Jenny to continue.

"Until then, I had never had the displeasure of speaking with Elkin. He was abrupt. Rude. Told us where to sign or else. We felt like we had no choice and thought the loan might buy us some time to sort things out. Mamie signed as treasurer, and I witnessed her signature. Then Bailey fired me and told Mamie she was off the board."

Travail had a far-fetched theory. Was it possible the Standish Company stole the Indie's money and loaned it back? Perhaps Elkin arranged it. And if he did, maybe he facilitated the gold bullion and mining stock sales to Indie residents. Like the email said: *financial ruin*.

A vehicle crunched gravel in the driveway. Travail thanked Jenny and Mamie, saw them to the door, and welcomed Audrey Blunt, their gold mine expert, into his cottage.

Travail offered Audrey water or lemonade, because Yeager had demolished the deli tray. She chose lemonade, and they got down to business.

Audrey had done her research on the Rudisill Mine and South End Mining Company, and she'd looked at the marketing materials for the mining company investment.

"The mining company stock is a high-risk investment."

Travail didn't disagree with her assessment, but he needed to hear her explanation. "Why?"

"It's difficult to profitably mine gold through traditional underground methods in old shafts deep below the surface in a developed area. To mine these shafts and put miners underground to chip away at the rock, you'd have to refurbish the shaft infrastructure and shore the tunnels up first. The biggest challenge would be to pump the groundwater out so the miners could do their work. That's hard to do as developed as the area is today. And then there are the permitting and environmental issues."

Travail had done some research on modern-day gold mines, including the Haile Gold Mine in South Carolina where Audrey had worked. "Is open pit mining possible in South End?"

"Not without government approval. Even then, it's a long shot."

"A long shot?"

"North Carolina regulates open-pit mining. A permit is required, and there is a public-hearing process to get it, where the mining company must present a reclamation plan and what they plan to do to remove the gold. The public can object, which seems likely given the number of townhouses, condominiums, and apartments in South End, and the fact the Rudisill vein begins at the edge of the Wilmore single-family residential neighborhood. I doubt the neighbors will be excited about the idea. Mining can be loud and disruptive."

"How long does the permitting process take?"

"Funny you should ask. South End Mining Company has a public hearing scheduled. The Department of Environmental Quality will decide the permit's fate no later than thirty days after the hearing."

"When is the hearing?"

"Ninety days from now."

"And if they cannot get the permit?"

Audrey was sorry to tell them that "anyone who invested in that gold mine is likely to lose their money."

Yeager piped up. "What if they already started mining for gold?"

"That would be against the law."

Becky and Yeager stole glances at each other. Travail caught them. "What are you two not telling us?"

Yeager caved. "The dig has started. We couldn't say anything. They made us sign non-disclosure agreements."

Now the non-disclosure agreements in the subscription packages made sense to Travail. "You agreed not to reveal their plan to dig for gold while they work on the underground mixed-use development, didn't you?"

"They said we'd forfeit our investment if we revealed the plan. It seemed like nothing more than a timing thing, a way to keep a lid on the big dig to avoid claim jumpers. Nothing illegal."

"Surprised you kept it a secret, Yeager."

"I had five hundred thousand reasons to keep my mouth shut, Craig Travail."

"Y'all should have told me this. I can't help you if I don't have all the facts. Not that it matters now, but non-disclosure agreements to hide illegal activity are unenforceable. And now, you could be charged as accomplices." His words had a bite.

Audrey shook her head. "If the government catches the mining company digging for gold without a permit, it will come down hard on them, and the mining company will fold."

Becky stated the problem. "And when they do, we'll lose our $500,000 investments."

Audrey added the most sobering comment. "It seems you will lose either way. Either the government shuts them down or they find it impossible to make a profit."

Becky turned to Travail. "Was the fine print any help? Can you get us out of this investment and get our money back?"

"Less than a 1-percent chance based on the contract language. A lawyer, or should I say, a former lawyer, with a goal to make them stick, wrote the subscription agreements."

And yet, Travail thought, there is the exception they teach in law school. "If we can prove they fraudulently induced you to invest— meaning they deceived you—you can void the contract and win a judgment for damages, but this requires legal action, and if you win, you need to hope the company is not bankrupt. If it is, the judgment will be worthless."

Yeager remained optimistic. "We still have the gold bars as security for the investments."

"Have you received any news about their value?"

"Stay positive, Craig Travail. I know the lawyer in you can't help it, but stay positive."

Looking at his watch, Travail was positive of one thing. It was time to go to Harriet's house to find the dirt on Dirt Man Dan.

CHAPTER 16

THE DIRT ON DIRT MAN DAN

Dan Barnard felt the squeeze with Travail, Harriet, and Yeager staring at him, waiting for him to answer Travail's question.

Dan's mouth was dry, but he'd refused Harriet's sweet tea offer. He needed to focus. He avoided Yeager's stare. The man was an irritant, too loyal to Harriet and her brother to see Dan's side and too quick to blame Dan for Joey's situation.

Travail sat in a club chair across from Dan, close enough to make Dan sit as far back into the sofa as he could. He liked Travail, but lawyers made him nervous. They were like mosquitos with their questions, as they tried to sink their needle-like mouthparts under your skin and suck your blood while injecting their saliva. He swatted Travail away with his response.

"Repeat the question, please."

"When did you first meet Junior Standish, Sterling's father?"

Dan looked at the coffee table, where he, following Elkin's instructions, had hidden a listening device. Because Sterling, Bailey, and Elkin would hear everything he said, he had to be mindful of his words. He touched the small leatherbound Moleskine notebook in his pocket for reassurance.

"Do you need me to repeat the question one more time?" Travail said *one more time* like his voice was in slow motion.

Dan disliked sarcastic lawyers even more than regular lawyers, although he couldn't remember when he'd met a lawyer who wasn't sarcastic.

Travail persisted. "Let me be more specific. Did you first meet Junior before or after Joey's conviction?"

"After, I think, but it's been twenty years, so don't hold me to it."

"Who introduced you?"

This was the hot seat, and Dan needed to wiggle loose. "Are you going to ask all the questions? Not give them a chance?" Dan pointed to Harriet, then Yeager.

"It's a simple question, Dan." Harriet's voice had an edge. "Who introduced you to Junior?"

"Chance Landry. Satisfied?"

Dan turned to Yeager. "How about you? You got a question."

"Sure do, Dirt Man. Why did you testify against Joey and then carry the water for the Standish clan for twenty years? What did you get for it?"

Dan didn't like Yeager's nickname for him or the second part of his two-part question. He answered the first. "The district attorney subpoenaed me to testify in Joey's trial because he used fake contracts to prepare the appraisal on my client's property."

Travail took charge again. "Do you know who funded South End Environmental?"

"How would I know that?"

"Maybe Landry told you."

"He didn't." Dan was not a good liar, but he tried to look irritated as he thought about the truth that rested in the notebook in his pocket.

"Was the plan for South End Environmental to buy the underground property rights and transfer them to the Standish Company later?"

"I don't know what Chance planned or didn't plan about those property rights." Another lie. He patted the notebook in his pocket. Stick to the plan.

"Did Landry have a falling out with Junior?

"I don't know." What Dan didn't say was the falling out happened the night Junior died, also recorded in his notebook.

"Did the Standish Company promise you a job if you testified against Joey?

"That is an insult." Dan's entry in his notebook showed why.

Harriet's tone displayed her displeasure with him. "You also testified against Joey in civil cases where property owners sued him and got judgements against him totaling several million dollars, which he could not pay."

"I had no choice. They subpoenaed me."

Harriet's next question tried to shame him. "Why didn't you do more to find the truth about the fake contracts Joey used for his appraisals?"

Dan had done more, and he'd discovered the truth, but he couldn't say that in this room. He put on an act for his bosses, who listened.

"Harriet, how do you know Joey didn't create them?" He hoped he sounded defiant enough to please the eavesdroppers.

She didn't answer.

Travail changed the topic. "You went to work for the Standish Company after Joey's trial, correct?"

"Nothing wrong with that."

"The Standish family has been good to you, haven't they?"

Dan had liked Junior. He was a kind man, unlike his son, Sterling. Celia treated him with respect too. When Sterling took over from Celia, Dan retired, but he agreed to help the company from time to time, but only because Celia asked him to help her grandson and because he needed the money to help support his disabled daughter.

"I enjoyed working for the family."

Travail's next question came from left field. "Do you know who killed Junior?"

It was a question Dan had known the answer to for the past twenty years. He glanced at where he'd placed the listening device.

"Did you hear my question?"

Of course he heard it. Celia Standish had asked him the same question, and later, Sterling and Bailey, and he'd had no choice but to protect Chance and go along with Chance's version of what happened until Chance died. If he hadn't played along, Chance would have killed him like he killed Junior. Now, if he changed the story to tell the truth, his association with Chance could make him an accomplice. Best to stick to the story for the benefit of the listening device.

"Penny killed Junior."

"My father was not a killer. Who told you that?"

"Chance said it happened after Joey's conviction. I'm sorry if that brings you pain, Harriet, but I am being as honest as I can be." Which meant he wasn't being honest at all. Dan looked at where he had placed the listening device.

Travail focused on Landry's death next. "Do you know who wanted to kill Landry?"

"You mean other than the many men and women he mistreated? The list is long."

Harriet took her turn again. "Do you think my brother killed Landry?"

This was a question that deserved an honest answer, but Dan couldn't give it because the people who listened wanted Joey to take the blame. He knew Joey didn't kill Chance because he knew who did. If he went off script, he would be the next victim.

"I don't know what to think, Harriet. From what I've heard, it doesn't look good for Joey. I'm sorry."

Travail again. "What about Robert Elkin?

"What about him?

"Nelli told me you don't get along with Elkin. Do you think he killed Landry?"

Dan knew he wouldn't get in trouble for confiding his dislike of Elkin. The man rubbed people the wrong way, and he'd given Dan too many unpleasant tasks. If it weren't for his loyalty to Celia and his need for the money to support his daughter, Dan would have refused Elkin's demands weeks ago. "That doesn't mean I think he's a murderer. Come to think of it, Elkin got along with Chance better than anyone."

It was Harriet's turn again. "What's your alibi, Dan?"

Dan didn't have an alibi. He was at the Rivafinoli Passage when Chance died, but he couldn't say that. He also couldn't tell them what led up to the murder, how Chance came to him and told him he wanted to retire and planned to blackmail Sterling. "I am going to demand five million dollars. If Sterling doesn't pay, I will tell the world how Junior swindled his way into South End and how Joey was innocent." Dan had protested because if Chance did this, he would expose himself and Dan for their role in Joey's conviction, but Chance ignored him. He made his demand, Sterling refused, and a few days later, Chance was dead.

Dan said what he had to say. "I'm not on trial, Harriet. I don't need an alibi."

Yeager wanted to know why Dan had pushed the Indie residents to invest in South End Mining Company, but Dan was tired. He worried he might mess up his answers. "I have to check on my daughter. She suffered an accident, and we almost lost her. Her husband is good to her, but he needs help, and I like to do what I can."

Harriet walked Dan to the door.

"One last question, Dan." Travail spoke from across the room.

"What do you know about the gold coins found on Landry's body?"

Dan knew exactly why Chance Landry had gold coins on him. "No idea."

Harriet and Dan stepped out on her front porch. He reached behind her and eased the door shut. "Piece of advice, Harriet. Check under your coffee table."

He placed his Moleskine notebook in Harriet's hand. "This is for you. It explains what really happened, up to a point. If you call me as a witness, I will say you coerced me to write these words. My daughter comes first. I wish you, your brother, and everyone here at the Indie the best."

Harriet gripped the notebook, what might be their first break in Joey's case. She didn't know what to say.

She looked past her previous anger that clouded her eyes and took stock of Dan for the first time. He wore fitting, dark wash jeans, a crewneck short-sleeve cream t-shirt, and gray lace-up casual shoes. A meticulous man. Was he a meticulous recordkeeper?

Dan walked a few steps, stopped, and turned. He looked at Harriet with sincerity written on his face. "I wish Robert Elkin, Sterling Standish, and Bailey Standish the absolute worst."

CHAPTER 17

GARDEN VARIETY SURPRISE

Around the time Dan Barnard left Harriet's cottage, a caller reached Detective Sizemore's voicemail and left an anonymous tip using voice disguise software.

"The gun that killed Chance Landry is buried in Harriet Keaton's garden at the Independence Retirement Community. Pay particular attention to the bed of goldenrods."

To secure his warrant, Detective Sizemore gave the judge a recording of the anonymous tip and an affidavit explaining they found Landry's body in Harriet's uptown house. The judge issued the warrant to search Harriet's garden at 3:30 pm.

The detective and his crew would be at the Indie by four.

Anytime Harriet needed to relax, meditate, blow off steam, or escape the real world, nothing did it like tending to her plants. She needed to think after she'd read Dan's notebook, and her garden was the perfect place to do it.

She adjusted her red-brown overalls, pulled her long-sleeve t-shirt down to cover her arms from the sun, adjusted her wide-brim hat, and knelt in the dirt.

She'd been at it for about an hour—her watch said it was three thirty—and was bent over using her hand shovel when she heard heavy breathing in her ear and smelled wet dog.

"Blue. You've come for a visit." She nuzzled her nose to his. He wagged his tail.

"Don't forget about me." Craig approached from ten feet away.

Harriet stood, kicked dirt from her green muck boots, and pulled her leather-palmed garden gloves from her hands. "You want me to nuzzle your nose, Craig?"

Craig blushed, and Harriet laughed. "Are you here to help me with my garden?"

Craig said "sure" in the tone of a person who preferred to use a yard service to care for their property. But he was a good sport. He fetched her wheelbarrow, loaded it with pine bark, and rolled it in her direction. She pointed to the spot and at a rake. Craig did as he was told.

They worked side by side for the next ten minutes with their hands in the dirt, which, in Harriet's opinion, was where relationships formed. When you plant seeds and nurture them, life happens.

Last night's invitation to see *Hamilton* offered a hint Craig cared about her as more than a friend. And for reasons unknown to her— reasons she needed to understand if they were going to become closer —the moment was hard for him.

Now it was time for her to be more transparent about her feelings and her past. She went inside and returned with two glasses of iced tea, handed one to Travail and tapped his glass. They sat beside each other on the back steps for a break.

"I am sorry I haven't been open with you about my family history."

"That's okay."

"No, it's not. I care about you, Craig, and I want to be open with you. Open about my family from now on, and open about how I feel."

Craig nodded and dipped his head. "How do you feel?"

"I feel we aren't telling each other how we feel."

"I feel the same way."

They laughed. The loop trapped them, but at least they were talking.

Craig gazed across the lake, not looking at anything in particular. "My wife. Her name was Rachael. She would have liked you, Harriet."

She placed her hand on his. "I'm sorry we never got to meet."

He laughed. "It was her idea we go to the play tomorrow night."

"Excuse me."

"I mean—she said, if I found someone I cared about I shouldn't let my memory of her stand in my way, but that's the problem, see. I don't want to forget her. I'm not cancelling our date. It's just that—"

"We're dating now?"

Craig gulped.

"I'm teasing, Craig." She grabbed his hand and pushed it to his heart. "You shouldn't forget about Rachael. My husband never said what Rachael said, but not because he wasn't a good person. We just never talked about it. He died at fifty. Too young. My heart died with him."

"I'm sorry."

Harriet stood and brushed herself off. "And then I watched *Shawshank Redemption*, and a line in that movie made a difference. 'Get busy living or get busy dying.' I chose living."

She reached her hand out and pulled Craig up from the back step. "How about I give you a tour of my garden?"

She offered him room to say 'I'd rather not,' and sensed he struggled with whether to do it for her sake or whether to pass up the offer for his own sake. She knew his likes better than he thought she did. He couldn't care less about landscape architecture. To him, plants were plants.

He said, "of course," but she knew he only said it because he was worried about or cared about her, which was sweet.

"Can you tell the difference in Yeager's yard, the one he inherited from his mother and never properly took care of, and my yard?"

Craig looked around Harriet's yard, then across the lake to Yeager's yard. "He has bigger trees?" He said it like it was a question.

"Noooo," she said. "It's not about size, you dolt. Look closer."

Craig compared the two yards again. "You have more plants."

"You're getting warmer, Craig, but only because you've gone from twenty below to freezing."

"How about you tell me?"

"How about I do."

Harriet explained Yeager's yard—the standard for Indie cottage owners—is not what she wants to see when she steps out of her house. "I am not a fan of boxwoods, azaleas, and knockout roses, especially when they are in lines and pruned to grow into balls. It's a lazy attempt at gardening and does nothing for the environment."

"So you don't like my yard either?"

"At least the plants in your yard are alive. Yeager shoos the landscaping staff away from his dead plants. Thinks he can manage his yard from his riding mower."

Craig looked around again at Harriet's yard.

"See any more differences?" she asked.

"You have more color."

"Of course, Craig. It's because I like variety." She couldn't help herself when she said, "Peaches says variety is the spice of life. Do you agree, Craig?"

Craig blushed and mumbled something inaudible. Harriet grabbed his elbow. "Follow me." Blue came along too.

As she showed Craig around her yard, she explained layering. "We don't need to block the house with plants, flowers, and grasses in rows. We need a natural look. Gaps in the plants are good. Different size plants and grasses are good." Craig nodded, but didn't comment.

"You also have to consider what to plant where. The front yard gets more sun. Let's start there with the trees. What tree is that?" Harriet pointed with her trowel.

"It's purple. Or, maybe pink. Purplish-pink."

She swatted his shoulder with her free hand. "They don't name trees the purple tree or the pink tree. It's an Eastern Redbud, known as the harbinger of spring because of its early blooms. It supplies nectar for butterflies. Bobwhites and chickadees, my favorite birds, eat the seeds."

"I know you like birds, Harriet. You have ten bird feeders."

Harriet took a moment to admire the redbud. It was lovely, the one thing in her life that brought back fond memories of her father. It was her father's favorite tree.

But it was the Eastern Redbud tree, not her family, that had stood the test of time.

"Dad helped me plant this tree when I moved here twenty years ago, just before Joey was arrested and put on trial."

Harriet pressed her lips together as she felt the pain of loss. "Less than a year later, Joey was in jail and my father was dead."

Harriet gathered her emotions and continued her garden-tour lessons. For the next five minutes, they walked her property, and Craig pretended to care as Harriet went on about her trees, shrubs, and flowers. She was so engrossed in the shapes, characteristics, and scents of her garden that she almost failed to hear Yeager scream at them.

From the gravel path fifty yards away, and while in a full sprint, he yelled to "look at your phones," the tail of his flannel shirt trailing behind. Harriet's phone was ten yards away, next to the wheelbarrow. Craig pulled his phone, found Yeager's text, and showed it to Harriet: *Detective coming to search Harriet's garden.*

When they looked up, Yeager was by their side, huffing and puffing. He got his wind back and explained.

"Front gate let me know the cops have a warrant. A perk of my helping out with security. They made sure to give them a wrong turn to take, but it won't stall them for long."

Across the lake, an official-looking vehicle and a police car sat in front of a cottage whose address was close but not the same as Harriet's.

Yeager was frantic. "Harriet, did you see any disturbed ground in your garden today?"

She walked to her bed of goldenrods, a basal rosette of leaves close to the ground that looked nothing like what they'd be in their late summer glory, and pointed at them. "There. Behind the goldenrods. I thought it was rain or a critter that disturbed the ground."

Yeager grabbed a shovel from the ground, elbowed his way past Harriet, and jabbed the shovel in the ground. Harriet gave Craig an assignment. "Go dig holes over there and over there. Turn the dirt over." He did as he was told.

The cops' vehicles were on the move and would be here in less than three minutes.

Yeager's shovel hit something metallic.

He bent down, pulled a plastic bag from the ground, and removed a small handgun from the bag.

Harriet put her hand over her mouth. The vehicles were less than a football field away. "Take it with you. Escape through the woods."

She placed her hand on Yeager's shoulder. "Wait."

As the vehicles approached a stand of trees, she counted down. "Three, two, one. Go."

Yeager took off for the woods. The vehicles were out of their site line for five more seconds.

Harriet motioned to Craig to come to her, and they walked around the side of the house to meet Detective Sizemore and two police officers. Blue ambled up to their side and barked at the uninvited guests.

"Good afternoon, Detective. Welcome to my home. How can I help you?"

"We have a warrant to search your garden." He gave her the paper and walked around them, pointing to areas here and there for his officers to search.

Harriet and Craig sat on Harriet's back deck while the police executed their search warrant. Detective Sizemore leaned on the wooden rail with his back to them, where he watched his officers' work and puffed his cigar. "There are a lot of holes in your garden, Ms. Keaton."

Harriet didn't answer. The detective turned around. "Do you have an explanation?" He waved his cigar, and the smoke created a circle that framed his head.

Harriet didn't like being searched. Besides the damage to her garden, it violated her privacy. "Turning dirt is a good way to nurture plants."

The detective grunted. "If you read the warrant I gave you, you'd know what we're searching for."

"Didn't bother to read it. I just assumed by your officers' focus, you are searching for the secret to growing healthy goldenrods."

The detective turned on Craig. "Are you helping your client commit a crime? You were digging in her garden."

"Didn't know it was a crime to help your neighbor in her garden."

Detective Sizemore yelled to his officers. "Find it?"

"No," said one officer, then another.

Harriet walked to the detective's side and looked over the wooden porch rail at the work the officers were doing to destroy her goldenrods. "I gave Craig my garden tour earlier, but you arrived before I could tell him about the goldenrods. Would you like to know why I like them?"

The detective was silent, his gaze on the officers with their shovels.

"I love goldenrods for their traits. Drought tolerant, they attract pollinators and have healing properties, an excellent anti-inflammatory and a nice boost to the immune system. Goldenrods navigate change and uncertainty with confidence and independence. Ironically, people often mistake goldenrod for ragweed. Throws them off. Is that what happened here? Did my goldenrods throw you off? Did they turn out to be a pest instead of your golden delight?"

"I'm not sure what game you're playing, but it won't serve you well in the end."

Harriet raised her voice to the man who held the power. "I can assure you, Detective, I don't think this is a game. You're being played. My guess is you received an anonymous tip that you hoped would let you take a shortcut to close your case. Easy-peasy. Let's blame Landry's death on Joey and his twin sister. After all your experience, does that sound suspicious to you, that things would fall into place for you so easily?"

Detective Sizemore scratched his head like one of his preambles to a gotcha question, but he had no response. "Stop your work," he yelled to his officers. He crushed his cigar on the rail and threw it in the holes where the goldenrod used to live. "I will be in touch, Ms. Keaton."

When they were alone, Craig asked Harriet what she was thinking.

"I think I need a subscription to *Garden & Gun*."

"What?"

"If I am correct, Craig, we found the gun that killed Chance Landry. In my garden."

Craig looked over the rail where Yeager dug his hole in the goldenrod. "Maybe we should tell the detective Elkin tried to frame you and your brother."

"And how do we do that without implicating me? We have nothing on the creep but our past conflict with him, an unsigned email he may have sent to you, and his employment with the Standish Company. That's not proof."

"Then we need to get proof."

"I agree."

Harriet called Yeager on her phone. "You okay?"

"Never better."

"I owe you one."

"Just glad I got there in time."

Harriet looked at where Yeager vanished with the gun. "Where's the—"

"Do you scuba dive, Harriet?"

"Once. Why?"

"I bet your trench-coat detective friend doesn't scuba dive. Even if he did, we have enough lakes at the Indie, and I still have a good arm from my days as a high school pitcher."

Harriet teared up at Yeager's bravery on her behalf. They could have seen him, chased him down, and caught him with the evidence, but he didn't flinch to shield her from trouble.

Craig showed quick support, too, shoveling in all the wrong places. She glanced at him while she talked. He appeared to be ruminating on what happened and what was next to do. She could tell he wanted to help her and her brother in the worst way.

How's Craig Travail?"

"He's trying to think like a lawyer, again."

"As he should, Harriet. As he should."

CHAPTER 18

BETWEEN THE LEGAL LINES

Travail knocked before he entered.

"Come," Carrie Roberts yelled.

He walked in with the flowers he'd brought for Carrie to find Judge Roscoe Brady in conversation with her, she in her recliner, and he occupying her wheelchair with a bulge in his cheek and a Styrofoam cup in his hand.

Roscoe wore dark-wash jeans, a long-sleeved buttondown in a subtle check with the collar open and the sleeves rolled up, and a wide belt. And, of course, the cowboy boots he was known for in legal circles almost as much as his tobacco habit.

Off to the side, Harriet sat in a wooden chair near Carrie's only window, where the afternoon sun cast a beam across half her body, leaving her other half in shadow. The image was a perfect metaphor for Harriet's personality these days, the bright, energetic doer determined to help others juxtaposed against the dark, melancholy worrier about her brother and friends.

Travail set the flowers on Carrie's bedside table, and Carrie said, "Thank you, dear boy, for your kindness. What are they?"

From the corner by the window: "He doesn't know."

Travail leaned into Harriet's quip. "They're yellow, Carrie, to brighten the room."

He took a seat in a wooden chair between the judge and Harriet, but not before shaking the judge's hand.

Yeager burst into the room with a candy box. "Nothing but the best chocolate for my favorite patient."

Delighted, Carrie instructed Yeager to hide the candy from the medical staff under her clothes in the hutch.

With that accomplished, Carrie pointed to Roscoe, the reason they'd been invited to this meeting. "Roscoe and I were friends long before he began that nasty, disgusting habit. He knew Harriet's father."

Travail went first. "How did you know Penny?"

"Penny and my dad had a common interest in coin collecting. He was often at my dad's house when I stopped by to visit. It's how I came to represent Joey in his trial years ago. Penny asked me to represent him." Roscoe addressed Harriet. "Sorry about the outcome."

Harriet slid her chair closer to the group. "You did the best you could. Thanks for helping Joey and for meeting with us now."

Carrie clapped her hands. "I call this Indie Murder Club meeting to order."

Travail frowned at Yeager, who leaned back and raised his arms. "It was Carrie's idea, Craig Travail."

"Oh, wait, before we begin, I have something to show everyone." Carrie held up a flat metallic item with a small wire and dropped it in her water glass. "Found that thing under the flower vase delivered courtesy of Sterling and Bailey Standish, our new Indie king and queen."

Carrie brushed her hands against one another as if to be done with the petty crime and pointed to Harriet. "Let's start with a review of the information Dan Barnard provided."

Harriet opened Dan's notebook. "Junior Standish set up and funded South End Environmental and put Landry in charge as his front man. South End Environmental never intended to clean up any pollutants in the soil. They bought the properties for their mineral value at discount pricing based on fraudulent appraisals, intending to transfer the property to the Standish Company at their cost. Landry convinced Dan Barnard that Joey committed appraisal fraud."

Harriet looked up from Dan's notes. "According to Dan, Joey was innocent." She read aloud what Dan had written. *When I figured out the appraisal of my client's property was based on the use of fake contracts for the comparable sale data, I told Chance, and he pinned the fraud on Joey. I assumed Chance was telling the truth and that Joey was guilty. But after Joey's trial, I discovered Chance had created the fake contracts himself and then misled Joey.*

Carrie chirped. "I knew Joey was innocent. Anything in his notes about Junior's killer?"

Harriet nodded and read aloud again. *Chance Landry killed Junior Standish. I was in the room when it happened. Although I know Joey didn't kill Chance, I can't, and won't, say who did. I have to protect myself and my family.*

"Interesting." Carrie continued as their leader. "Roscoe, your thoughts?"

"I never believed Penny killed Junior, and while Joey had twenty years to think about what Landry did to him, Joey never struck me as a killer either."

Travail followed up with a question for Roscoe. "I read Joey's trial transcript. Why did you suspect Landry was the front man for the Standish Company?"

"Junior put an incentive in the deal for Landry. The lower the land prices, the higher Landry's commission. The arrangement was not illegal, but Landry had much to gain from low appraisals that generated low purchase prices. Landry created the fake contracts so he could make more money for himself."

Travail glanced at Harriet. Had she relaxed a little, knowing her brother was not a fraudster? Or did she realize, like him, Joey's motive for killing Landry was stronger now than ever? Sure, a guilty person might hold a grudge against their snitch, but it was quite another kind of emotion—more powerful than a mere grudge—that an innocent person might hold against their accuser for a crime they didn't commit.

If Dan didn't identify Landry's killer, the prosecutor would pick Joey for the crime.

Travail had another question for Roscoe, but he didn't know how to ask it without appearing to challenge Roscoe's competency in how he defended Joey.

Roscoe saved him the trouble. "You're wondering why I didn't use the information to Joey's advantage, aren't you Craig?"

Travail nodded. "I am sure there was a good reason."

"Not a good one. But there was a reason."

Before the judge could explain, the hospice nurse dropped in.

"Nanette, so good to see you." Carrie introduced Nanette around the room. Nanette said she could come back, but Carrie said "nonsense" and asked the team to take a ten-minute break.

When everyone returned, Harriet asked Carrie for a medical update.

"Still dying, but today is not the day. Where were we?"

Roscoe shifted the chaw inside his right cheek. "Joey didn't want anyone to think Penny was involved in the scheme."

"I don't understand," Harriet said. "Why would they think that?"

"Your father asked Joey to do the appraisals, and Landry took advantage. He gave your father the fake contracts and asked him to pass them along to Joey. Penny did not know the contracts were fake when he delivered them to Joey, and Joey trusted his father that the contracts were legitimate. Those contracts became the basis for what a willing buyer and willing seller would pay, and they caused Joey to appraise the properties for lower than their actual value."

"Then why didn't you call my father as a witness? He could have pinned the crime where it belonged: on Chance Landry." Harriet was anything but relaxed.

"If Penny testified Landry gave him the fake contracts to give to Joey, Penny's story would look self-serving and could cause the jury to blame both father and son—and cause the state to charge Penny as an accomplice. If Joey testified, he'd have to lie about Penny's role in order to shield him. Joey didn't want to implicate his father, and he wouldn't lie, so he took the hit, so his father wouldn't take the fall."

"My father should have stepped up for Joey." Harriet's voice was raised with what sounded like a mix of anger and frustration.

"It was not Penny's fault," Carrie said.

Harriet extended her palm to Carrie. "I know you mean well, but don't tell me not to blame my father. His obsession with gold coins and gold history in his later years reached such a level it drove my mother away, turned him into an aloof father, and due to the distraction, caused Joey to spend twenty years in prison for a crime he didn't commit."

"All I meant was it was Landry's fault."

Travail wanted to reach to Harriet, to offer comfort, but her stiff posture held him off. He turned to Roscoe instead.

"Why did the judge give Joey twenty years? That seems excessive for that kind of non-violent felony."

"It was, and I told Joey so. I wanted to file an appeal, but he said no. He gave up."

The judge turned his head away and spit in his cup before sharing another surprising fact. "Penny insisted on paying for Joey's defense, but his payment method was unusual." The judge reached in his pocket and placed ten gold coins on Carrie's tray table. "I never bothered to get them appraised, but maybe now, I should."

Yeager looked them over. "They look like the ones I found under Harriet's house."

Carrie picked one coin up off her tray table and examined it. "I'd put these somewhere safe, Roscoe. They look like coins Penny showed me a few years before he died, part of a coin collection he'd built. Thieves stole thirty coins from him after someone—he suspected it was Chance Landry—leaked he was a gold coin collector. He said Landry must have overheard him discuss his collection with Junior. These might be valuable."

Travail looked at the coins and then at Harriet. "Do you think the coins the police found under your house are the coins your father collected, the ones he mentioned to Carrie?"

"Dad was a small-time collector. I don't know what he'd collected, but I assume the coins that fell out of the kitchen floorboards were his, probably the collection he told Carrie about. Makes sense, because he was always hiding things for fun."

A kitchen staff member came in with Carrie's dinner. Roscoe scooped up the coins before the staffer placed the food on Carrie's tray table. When the orderly left, Yeager's Jitterbug phone buzzed. He glanced at the phone. "It's the coin shop."

Yeager put his phone on speaker. He asked Burt Tartly to share what he'd found with the group.

"Bad news, Yeager. The gold bars are mostly pyrite on the inside. It's a metal often mistaken for gold with the nickname 'fool's gold.'"

"What are they worth?"

"Next to nothing, except in converting the metal to chemical compounds for manufacturing paper or rechargeable batteries."

"That ain't good. Any idea how that happened?"

"Someone drilled into them. They siphoned the gold and replaced it with pyrite. They went to a lot of trouble to deceive you. The bars are real. They even have official serial numbers.

"How did you figure it out?"

"Pyrite is not as heavy as gold. I felt the difference in weight when you were in the shop, and I remembered a case I read about years ago where a buyer in New York bought gold bars and discovered something similar. The bars had tungsten cores rather than gold. That made me test the core on your gold bars. Wish I had better news."

"Not your problem, Burt. What about the rare coins we found under Harriet's house? Better news, I hope."

"Afraid not. The metal is gold, but they are forgeries."

"Not worth thousands."

"Nope."

That was a twist. Why did Penny collect forged coins?

Yeager stroked his beard, probably wondering the same thing. "Hey, Burt, three time's the charm, buddy. Give us the good news about the gold bullion coins the residents purchased."

"They should hire a good lawyer. It's precious metal, but they paid five times their value."

Yeager ended the call, and the group fell silent until Carrie poked them. "Thoughts, anyone?"

Travail's mind was on the future, focused on the residents' legal options to sue for their losses and the uncertainty of collecting, even if they won.

Harriet's mind was stuck twenty years in the past, on her father. "I can't believe my father trafficked in forged rare coins. I am sorry he deceived you, Roscoe."

Yeager's mind was in the present. "Damnation, Craig Travail. Gold bars are a bust. Time to shine up your courtroom shoes." And to Harriet: "There's probably a good explanation for the forged coins that were under your house, and I bet the coins Penny gave Roscoe are the real deal. We'll figure it out."

Carrie laughed. "That's what I love about you, Yeager. You have enough optimism to make a sloth think work is exciting."

"What's a sloth?" Yeager's tone was playful as he eyed Carrie and tugged on his beard.

"An animal that is so slow and sluggish it takes up to a month to digest its food. Neither you nor your stomach are stuck in low gear."

Harriet stood. "On that note, let's get dinner. I'm starved."

She gave Carrie a hug and Carrie hugged Harriet back. "Two things, dear. Leave Dan's notebook with me for my bedtime reading. And say hello to Peaches for me tonight."

CHAPTER 19

SAUCY DINNER DANCE

Harriet was low on energy and needed food after their long day. Craig and Yeager were game to go to dinner with her, but Roscoe declined—he didn't say why—and left them before they reached the dining room.

When they arrived, the staff had diverted dinner traffic to the hallway on the left.

The handmade sign at the roped-off entrance said: *Salsa on Your Plate and On the Dance Floor*. An arrow pointed to the hallway, where the line had formed.

Harriet considered other options, her hunger having caused her to forget about the dinner dance extravaganza she'd had no intention of attending. She was about to bail for home and eat leftovers when Peaches appeared out of nowhere.

"Oh, yes, yes," Peaches squealed. "You came." Wearing a black velvet, stretchy mesh dance dress with a deep V-neck and tassels below her breasts and along her skirt bottom, she swished her way past them and pulled the rope aside. "Shortcut."

Yeager pushed Harriet to follow Peaches. "Might as well eat, Harriet."

Peaches winked at Harriet. She purred at Craig.

Seeing how cute Craig looked in his discomfort, Harriet took a deep breath, grabbed Craig's hand, and led the way. "Of course we'll eat. Might even dance. We wouldn't miss this event for all the gold in the Carolinas."

Peaches led them across the empty dining room from the back to the front of the buffet line. Along the way, she pointed out the colorful Latin American foods, "to match the evening's mood."

Her pronunciation was awful as she mentioned the desserts: tres leches cake, arroz con leche, alfajores, dulce de leche, flan, "and those dough-like things that mimic penises are called—"

"Churros." Yeager grabbed two, dipped them in chocolate sauce, and stuffed both in this mouth.

Peaches leaned into Craig with her chest's full weight and said, "Avoid those, Craig. They're called Mexican Wedding Cookies." She slipped her arm through his and pulled him away from Harriet.

When they passed the main dishes, Harriet's mouth watered. There was a chicken dish covered in a Mexican sauce with dried chiles. A beef stew with shredded flank steak, tomato sauce, peppers, and onions. A round patty made of plantains, pork cracklings, and garlic. A flatbread stuffed with cheese and refried beans. A seafood dish. And hot dog tacos that drew Yeager's attention.

Craig's color returned. "The chef outdid herself. And you did too, Peaches."

Yeager stuffed a hot dog taco in his mouth and smiled in agreement.

Peaches motioned to them to stand still, and with a flourish, she opened a door and let the line of hungry residents fill in behind them. Then to everyone: "You're in for a big night, and if you like this food, don't miss our special dinner event next month, our *Taste of Sex* night where you can taste six sexy foods guaranteed to get you in the mood, and that's according to science."

Peaches giggled. "Avocado. Ginger. Asparagus. Oysters. Arti-chokes. And dark chocolate, my favorite. What's your favorite, Craig?"

Harriet couldn't help herself. "Yes, Craig, what's your favorite?"

He swallowed his answer.

A Latin American beat burst from the built-in speakers in the ceiling, where normally, they'd play 1940s acoustic big band music. Peaches snapped her fingers, twirled her skirt, and shouted to the crowd, "Eat up, everyone. Then we party."

Harriet, Yeager, and Craig were the most underdressed residents. Harriet wore brown slacks, a white sweater, and beige print scarf. Craig sported his khaki pants and long-sleeve blue dress shirt. Yeager donned blue jeans, his brown flannel shirt, and his faded tan ball cap. They looked like safari guides to the multi-colored animals who followed them down the buffet line.

After they filled their plates—Yeager filled two—Yeager connected with Nelli and her rowdy friends at the bull table. Harriet and Craig settled into a two-top overlooking Freedom Lake, over which the sun balanced on the horizon.

Peaches came by and lit the candle on their table as the ceiling music softened and the house lights came down. While she worked her mood magic, a server delivered two signature cocktails to the table. Peaches pointed to the drinks and hummed the song about the lime and the coconut before she described the mix. "Besides the lime and the coconut—and the rum, of course—your Brazilian Batida cocktail has passion fruit syrup. Those garnishes are pineapple leaf and grated nutmeg. So, so yummy."

Peaches flitted away, and Harriet relaxed for the first time today, glad Peaches was gone. She lifted her glass. "Here's to helping friends and family."

Craig clinked his glass to hers. "Amen to that."

The candlelight flickered between them as Craig cut into his chicken empanadas and took a bite. Harriet remembered how she used to watch her husband when he ate. It was a pleasant memory. A comfortable feeling to have a meal with someone you cared about.

Craig looked up. "You aren't hungry?"

"Just thinking."

"Lots to think about."

Craig was right. There was a lot to think about. The Indie's future was at stake. Her friends' retirement assets were at risk. Her brother might go to jail again.

Harriet took a bite of her fried plantain. "I wish Carrie could be here. She'd love it, and she'd compile enough gossip to last her months."

Craig agreed. "She's one of a kind."

"There are a lot of one-of-a-kinds at the Indie, Craig, who don't get enough credit for who they are and the differences they've made in the world. Young people think retirees are all the same. Just old people who don't matter."

They ate in silence before Harriet added, "You are one-of-a-kind, Craig. What you've done in your career and what you've done for the Indie since you got here matters."

Travail looked down, away from the praise. "I should thank you for pushing me."

Harriet laughed. "No thanks necessary. Pushing you out of your comfort zone has been an enjoyable new hobby, Craig."

Harriet took another bite and thought about the people here tonight. Particularly the ones she didn't know very well. "We should get to know each other better. I mean, really get to know each other before it's too late."

Craig coughed, grabbed his cocktail, and took a sip.

"I meant our neighbors, Craig. Look around."

"Oh."

"What did you think I meant?"

"I don't know. Yes. Everybody should get to know everybody." Craig shoveled another spoonful of his entrée into his mouth.

Harriet laughed. "You are one-of-a-kind in more than one way, Craig, but you don't seem to think so. And that's why I like you."

Peaches glided by to see "how you love birds are doing" and to remind Craig that "you owe me a dance tonight."

"You will have it," Harriet said to Peaches, and then tilted her head and winked, causing Peaches to shake her tassels and cackle with joy as she left their table.

"Why did you do that?"

"She's just flirting, Craig. Do you remember what that is?"

"Not really."

"You don't say."

They finished their meal in silence, Craig in his thoughts and she in hers. Outside forces wanted to destroy her brother and friends, and she'd felt lonely the last few days.

If she were being honest with herself, she never grieved her husband's death twenty years ago the way she should have. She tried to be the strong woman everyone said she was. And now, her best friend had only a few months to live, and she didn't want to say—didn't know how to say—goodbye to her.

Glancing at Craig, she realized she'd thought about him a lot in the last few days. Of course, she was glad he'd made the first move—the invitation to *Hamilton* tomorrow night was nice—but then again, at their ages, who made the first move was less important than it had been when she was a young woman. She'd be the one to ask him to dance.

"Let's have some fun tonight, Craig. Forget about our problems. Tomorrow will be another day."

Craig looked like somebody had run over his dog. "You mean dance?"

Harriet laughed. "I bet you slayed the girls in the day."

Peaches tapped on a microphone and said, "Listen up, everyone. Time to make your way to the community room. Our dance instructors await."

Harriet stood, extended her hand across the table. "I assume you can dance."

"Not salsa." The confused look on his face was priceless.

"Dancing is wonderful exercise, Craig. It won't kill you."

Harriet dragged Craig along with her to the community room. Might she find her footing again?

The staff had cleared the room's tables, chairs, and croquet wickets. It was wide open for doing the rumba, cha-cha, samba, or whatever salsa dance their instructors had in mind.

She and Travail joined the crowd of residents standing against one wall, waiting for what to happen next she wasn't sure.

"You just never know, do you?" Harriet poked Travail in the ribs.

"What?

She pointed. "Roscoe."

"I'll be."

The retired judge, with his broad shoulders, was resplendent in a black shirt and black pants that Harriet thought could have been Spandex. He wore a wide belt with a gold buckle and had his arm around a woman Harriet recognized as a new resident. No tobacco in sight.

She looked around at the crowd. Their laughter made her happier than she'd been in a while, and their colorful clothes masked, if for just one evening, their mortality. The shoes alone made the stay worthwhile. Men's footwear comprised mostly black lace-ups—leather, mesh, or leatherette—with one exception of white jazz shoes, while women wore the most stylish ones their feet could take—flats and varying heel heights and styles, mostly sparkly. Not a white sneaker with Velcro straps in sight. The thrift store must be empty.

Peaches moved into the center of the room, wiggled her hips, and clapped her hands together. A vigorous looking man and an alluring woman stood beside her.

The man, whose arms, chest, and legs were well-toned, wore a black tank top and tight matching pants. His light brown skin shone and his dark hair was short on the sides and combed straight back on top. His five o'clock shadow and the thin gold chain around his neck added provocative interest. Oh, if only Harriet were in her twenties again, she and her friends would have a good time swooning at the possibilities.

The woman was no less intriguing than the man, with her jet black hair that flowed down her back. She wore form-fitting black dance shorts that clung to her hips and upper thighs, a white cropped top that lifted her breasts, and silver bedazzled high heels that accentuated her shapely legs. Harriet elbowed Craig when she noticed his focus on her.

Peaches introduced their instructors. "Meet Dominic and Valentina." She snapped her fingers, and the ceiling speakers boomed.

The instructors entertained the crowd with a dance that was beauty in motion, if not sex on the dance floor. Harriet put her hand to her mouth at their in and out movements, at their seductive eyes and graceful hips, and at their twists and turns and dips and spins that made it look way too easy.

When the music stopped, Valentina folded herself into Dominic's chest and leaned her head back. He pressed one hand into her low back and leaned over her. His other hand grazed her breast. He buried his face in her neck. The residents applauded with gusto.

Harriet nudged Craig. "That shouldn't take us too long to learn."

He gulped.

The instructors invited everyone to the dance floor. "We're going to work on basic steps first," Dominic said. "The leaders start with their left foot and the followers with the right foot. Leaders forward. Followers back. In a rocking motion."

"Watch us," Valentina said. She stepped back with her right foot as Dominic stepped forward with his left. They stepped back to their original position. They did the same with their other feet. "Left foot forward and together. Right foot back and together. Quicks and slows are the easiest. Quick, quick, slow. Quick, quick, slow. Now, you try."

For the next ten minutes, the residents stumbled into and onto one another, but they had a grand time, if the laughter was any sign. Harriet picked up the tempo and movements faster than Craig, but eventually they had the basics down.

Next, Dominic and Valentina taught a quick turn that involved holding hands with a partner. Harriet raised her right to Craig's left, and they touched. Craig looked unsure. If she didn't loosen him up, she'd be dancing with an anchor, so she twirled like the instructor said, and Craig held his position without falling.

Valentina came to their side and repositioned their hands for a different turn. "Move your hips and feet. Quick, quick, slow. Quick, quick, slow."

As they danced, Valentina pulled on Craig's hand and encouraged Harriet to turn under his arm. They finished with a flourish, bumping into Yeager in the process.

"Atta boy, Craig Travail. A lawyer who can dance. Don't see that every day."

Harriet guided Travail to Peaches and joined their hands. "Show him what you got, Peaches."

Travail mumbled, "I'll get you for this," as Peaches carried him away.

Harriet stepped back and admired the expressions on the dancers' faces, especially the discomforted look on Craig's face as Peaches tried to mimic Valentina's sex on the dance floor moves.

Yeager and Nelli were a misfit team if she ever saw one. But they were having a blast, with her in her wheelchair and him on two legs that seemed as coordinated as a wobbly moose.

Becky, their friend and forensic banking expert, and her beau, Maximiliano Esposito, were smoother than most. Had they done this before?

Mike Peterson and Audrey Blunt, the murder club's newfound gold history and mining experts, clutched each other tight in the slow dance of the year, as if the position was familiar. At least Mike had his clothes on.

And Roscoe put two and two together with his date, who seemed to know her way around a dance floor.

The evening went by fast. One dance after another. Until—as Harriet detected in Craig's eyes—enough was enough.

"Walk me home, Craig?"

On the way to Harriet's cottage, they listened to the low bullfrog baritone chorus. Harriet pointed to where the sounds emerged. "Those are mating calls."

Craig looked toward the lake but said nothing.

She didn't know why she liked to tease Craig. She'd done it to her husband, and before she married, she'd done it to her boyfriends, not that she had that many. Maybe it was her way to relax, to calm herself around men when they got close.

They stopped on the gravel path when they reached the turnoff to Harriet's cottage. Harriet didn't want the night to end with Craig because when it did, she'd have to face their many problems. Her brother's fate. The Indie's fate. Their friends' fate.

Craig looked across the lake at his place and then beyond Harriet's shoulder to her cottage. She could sense his indecision.

Truth be told, she wasn't sure, either, but this moment of intimacy between them had been building over the last year. What was about to happen—if it happened—was inevitable, even though she had concerns about where it might lead for them. Would it bring them closer together? Or push them apart and damage their friendship?

No doubt, she cared for Craig. Very much. They'd been through troubled times together, and they'd been there for each other. That wouldn't change.

Harriet put caution to the side and made a decision. After all, they were adults, and with some men—the good ones, anyway—it was necessary for the women to make the first move in these situations.

She reached forward, took his hand in hers, interlocked her fingers in his, and led the way up the path to her cottage and into a new chapter in their lives.

She lit a candle in her bedroom. "How about one more dance?"

Craig clasped his left hand in her right hand and put his right hand in the small of her back. She took a step forward, where their bodies touched.

Leaning closer, she whispered in his ear. "Remember, Craig. It's quick, quick, slow. Quick, quick, slow. Don't get in a hurry."

CHAPTER 20

GOLD DISTRICT POWER PLAY

The next morning, Travail stumbled around Harriet's kitchen in his t-shirt and boxers, made coffee and toast, filled two cups with steaming java, and loaded two small plates with buttered toast, jam, and a few pieces of cheese he found in the refrigerator. He returned with them on a tray to the bedroom, where Harriet sat up in bed in a loose-fitting silk gown, scrolling through her phone.

"Craig. Such a gentleman. But you'd better not open the shades. The neighbors will talk."

He set the tray between them on the bed and looked at the window coverings. Should they talk about what the neighbors will talk about? He wasn't sure he was ready, so he pointed to her phone instead. "What's the news of the day?"

"No reports on a murder charge in the Landry murder, but I found somewhere for us to eat for lunch today."

She handed the phone to Travail for him to see.

The luncheon event was billed as: *The Golden Future of South End: A Free Lunch and Learn Sponsored by the Standish Company.*

Travail followed Harriet and Yeager into a popular South End brewery for the Standish Company event. The smell of hops filled his nostrils and beer flowed. Chatter filled the room.

He was dressed about right for the luncheon in his dark slacks, a print buttondown shirt with the collar open, and matching casual shoes and belt. Yeager was in his khaki pants with a wide belt, a clean flannel shirt, and brown dress boots. Harriet wore a green floral fit-and-flare dress with short sleeves, along with taupe kitten-heel pumps. Travail only knew they were a "fit-and-flare" dress and "kitten heel" shoes because Harriet told him so when he complimented her appearance. It was like listening to Harriet give her garden tour.

"How about a pint, Craig Travail?"

Travail shook his head. It still hurt from the specialty cocktails and his late night out. Beer wasn't the antidote.

"I'll get you one anyway cause you need to blend in, Craig Travail. Like the spies do." Yeager winked at Harriet and headed to the bar.

Travail tiptoed around Harriet. She behaved like nothing had happened between them last night. Would their night together change things? Affect their friendship? Or would the night fade into the background of their shared experience?

Harriet darted toward an information table and Travail followed. An attractive middle-aged woman whose name tag said "Caren" welcomed them. "What brought you here today?"

Harriet led off. "We're interested in the Gold District's history."

"And what is planned for the Gold District," Travail added.

Their comments ignited Caren's passion. "There is so much gold mine history in South End and so many opportunities. I love volunteering my time in the Gold District. Do you know the Standish family?"

They both nodded.

"Sterling and Bailey are so generous. They have big plans for South End."

Harriet continued her sleuth-like approach, as Yeager had suggested. "That is exciting."

Caren pointed to different areas in the room. "Over there we have South End maps and pictures, and over there on the wall is a life-size gold history timeline." She reached under the counter and pulled out a thick document. "Here is the latest South End Vision Plan." She handed it to Harriet. "I hope you will consider being a supporter."

They thanked her and headed to the maps first. One map showed the South End area designated as the Gold District, with zoning, area demographics, and building locations. Another map included red stars designating the gold mine locations, including the Rudisill Gold Mine.

"Looks like real estate is the actual gold," Harriet muttered, her dissatisfaction evident.

Next, they strolled along easels that depicted South End "Property Success Stories," where "small businesses prosper." Coffee shops. Restaurants. Apartments. Arcades. Boutique retail stores. And more.

Harriet left Travail and walked on until she reached the wall-sized timeline. Travail caught up to her. "What are you looking for?"

"Something that might help me understand my father's gold history obsession." She pointed to the entries for the dates 1837 and 1845.

1837 – John Penman acquires the Rudisill Mine.

1845 – Penman sells Rudisill Mine, gives up mining ventures.

Travail and Harriet walked closer to read the footnote for the 1845 entry, which said newspapers reported that John Penman, sometimes referred to as Captain Penman, was a Methodist preacher before he arrived in America and may have returned to preaching after he gave up mining. Harriet laughed. "Maybe if Dad had become a Methodist minister instead of a prospector for gold coins, we would have dodged Sterling and Bailey Standish and Joey would be a preacher instead of a prisoner."

A shadow appeared on the lower portion of the timeline, and Travail felt a presence behind him. Either the crowd had grown, or someone looked over their shoulder.

"Well. Well. Well. If it isn't Craig Travail and Harriet Keaton." The voice and its pretentious cadence—what Travail hadn't missed hearing for a year—carried above the conversational hum in the room.

Travail and Harriet turned to face the man who'd tried to ruin their lives once before and who was back for sweet vengeance.

The irritating voice poked at them again. "Is your retirement community bus out front? Are you on a senior-citizen field trip?"

Travail challenged him. "I got your email."

Robert Elkin held his ground. "I don't know what you're talking about, Craig."

Their adversary was dressed in a well-tailored, dark blue suit, a pale blue spread-collar shirt, and a yellow print tie. He wore black wingtip shoes and a black belt with an engraved buckle bearing the Jefferson coat of arms.

Harriet stepped forward, crowding Elkin. "We know what you've done and what you're up to."

"Do you? Are you sure?"

Elkin fixed his eyes on the Gold District timeline. He reached around Harriet and put his finger on the date 1849, which said, *Gold discovered in California. Many Carolina miners go to California.* He sneered at Harriet as he kept his finger on the date. "Here's the moral to the story. Good times don't last forever. There's boom and there's bust. To be more specific, the golden age of retirement living at the Indie is about to bust. The good times are about to end."

Yeager walked up with amber ale pints in each hand and handed one to Travail. He raised his glass and said, "To Robert Elkin's imprisonment, a terrible lawyer and all-around-mean-person who has only gotten worse with age."

Elkin narrowed his eyes at Yeager, much the way he did a year ago when he first met Yeager outside the Indie chapel. "I'd be careful if I were you, Yeager."

"Or what?" Yeager stepped forward.

If Yeager released his frustration on Elkin—turned him into a newt as Yeager liked to joke about from time to time—Travail would have to open a full-blown criminal law practice. He put his hand on Yeager's shoulder.

"Robert, is everything okay?"

The man who spoke wore a modern slim-cut suit, medium blue, with straight-leg ankle-length pants, and a pink spread-collar shirt, with a pink and blue paisley tie and pocket square. His socks were blue and pink and his belt and dress shoes, brown.

Harriet was quick to peg the intruder. "You must be Sterling Standish, the boy wonder who rode his grandmother Celia's coattails and who is intent on destroying the Indie to make a buck."

Sterling curled his lip and narrowed his eyes. "If that's Southern manners for 'thank you for saving my retirement community,' the South has truly fallen."

Harriet didn't back down. She kept her focus on Sterling and pressed him. "Does your grandmother know your plans to make a profit at the expense of the Indie?"

"I don't answer to my grandmother. I support her now, although why she wanted to live at the Indie is beyond me. She could have lived in an uptown penthouse with full concierge services or a seven-thousand-square-foot home on the Quail Hollow golf course with servants. Instead, she chose condo life with two trout ponds and an embezzler for a bookkeeper."

Yeager downed his pint and tagged his way in for a go at Sterling. "How do you think it will play in the news that your mining company lied to us, and provided worthless gold bars as security to entice us to invest in your mining stock?"

Sterling glanced at Elkin and Travail tried to read his expression. Was that surprise on Sterling's face? Or realization they'd been caught?

Either way, Elkin had an answer. "Yeager, you seem to forget you signed a non-disclosure agreement and your risky investment—fully disclosed as such—came with an arbitration clause. Whatever beef you have with the Standish Company and its subsidiaries, you must pursue in a private forum, and if you leak anything to the public, you will pay handsomely for that mistake." Elkin smiled his devilish smile. "Please make that mistake. It will please me to see you make your financial demise permanent."

Elkin was correct about arbitration. Travail had studied the venue clause this morning when he reviewed the subscription agreements again and learned the investors could not bring legal action in court. They had to file a private arbitration, presided over by a retired federal judge. Any party could hire a representative to defend them, even someone who is not a licensed attorney. Very convenient for Elkin.

A voice from the podium came over the speaker system. It was the woman named Caren with a welcome message.

"That's my cue," Elkin said. "I have the honor to give the blessing."

As the scrum separated, Yeager had choice words about Elkin doing a blessing, something about it being like a horned goat offering communion.

From their table in the back of the room, Travail, Harriet, and Yeager watched the festive lunch unfold. Following Elkin's blessing, a slick video described South End's history, starting with Count Chevalier de Rivafinoli's work at the Rudisill Mine in 1830. While the video played, servers brought steak and potatoes and beer pairings, putting the guests in a good mood.

Donation cards were on the table to support the work of the Gold District, along with sheets listing properties for sale.

When the ten-minute video finished, Caren rose, told the guests to keep eating—dessert was on the way—and introduced the keynote speaker, Lester Sterling Standish the Third, "whose company has a big surprise for South End."

When the applause died, Sterling cozied up to the crowd with a story about his father.

"Junior Standish saw a vision for South End to be the premier multi-use community for work and play in the Southeast, both above and below ground."

Sterling paused, perhaps for effect. "My father also wished to bring attention to and celebrate Charlotte's gold mining history. He couldn't do it in his lifetime, but I am here with an announcement that would make my father proud."

Sterling used a remote device to flash an image on the screen.

"This is a press release my company sent out to all major news outlets this morning. It may be hard to read on the screen, but it announces a major financial contribution by the Standish Company to reshape South End's Gold District and bring Charlotte's gold history to life for all to enjoy. Copies are being handed out."

Sterling changed the slide to show an architectural mock-up of a museum.

"To celebrate the bicentennial of Count Chevalier Vincent de Rivafinoli's arrival in Charlotte, the Gold District 2030 Vision Plan includes developing several surface parks, including one above the Rudisill Gold Mine, like the one in this image."

The image on the screen looked like the location next to Harriet's house, where all their troubles began two days ago.

But it was the next two slides that caused the audience to stir. In the first slide, visitors boarded mining cars wearing hard hats with headlamps. In the second slide, the cars traveled horizontally below the surface and then descended vertically to explore underground mining shafts. It looked like a ride from Disney's Magic Kingdom.

Sterling continued. "Through creative design and engineering, visitors will experience an underground mine as it was in Count Rivafinoli's time—being able to go where it happened—bringing to life the most prolific and longest-running gold mine in Charlotte's history."

Elkin stood and whispered to Sterling while Yeager whispered in Travail's ear. "I have to say, Craig Travail, that looks like a pretty cool ride to me."

Travail whispered back. "But not a cool investment."

Sterling's next words to the audience didn't agree with Travail's assessment. "I've just had word the city is fast-tracking their decision for what will become a South End centerpiece, driving tourism and excitement to the area and helping improve and expand development." At his exuberance, the crowd broke into applause.

Harriet whispered to Travail and Yeager, "He said nothing about mining gold, or about where he got the money to do it."

Travail's cell phone buzzed.

He pointed at the phone and said to his friends, "County jail."

He put the phone to his ear. "Hello."

"This is Joey. Guess I need a lawyer. They just charged me with murder."

Travail pressed his phone to his chest and whispered the news to Harriet and Yeager.

Harriet grabbed the phone from Travail and spoke to her brother. "Joey, I'll be there in thirty minutes."

CHAPTER 21

TWINS AGAIN

Harriet picked up the phone on the wall and stared through the glass at the brother she hadn't spoken with in twenty years. The yellow-stained cubicle and metal chair with no pads on the seat or back set the perfect mood for the visit.

"How ya doing, Sis?"

Joey wore an orange jumpsuit, which made him look old and tired. He leaned forward, with one elbow on the six-inch shelf and one hand holding the phone.

Harriet leaned in too. "You could have called, written, something."

"Wouldn't have mattered."

To her, it would. It would have mattered a lot. Joey had always been the fun one, and even though they were the same age—her mother actually delivered Harriet first so she was the big sister by a few minutes—she'd loved being with the brother she idolized as a child.

They'd shared a room until they were twelve. Joey always called the top bunk. They'd played with the same toys. Didn't matter if it was dolls or footballs. They'd competed but had fun doing it. Their parents left them alone to take care of each other, and they did.

Through high school, Harriet was the brains and Joey the brawn, although he was smart too. They leaned on each other, shared their joys and heartaches, and when they went to college, they visited back and forth.

Joey would always show up on Harriet's spring break, even if it was not his spring break, and they'd take a trip together, mostly by car. National parks were their escape. Wide open spaces, nothing like where he sat at the moment. Joey didn't deserve to be in a cage.

Until now, Harriet had never asked Joey about his career choice. "Why did you reject the offer to work in construction in New York? It's what you wanted to do. If you'd left, none of this would have happened."

"Dad needed me."

That was like Joey. Putting others first.

"You didn't ask my opinion."

"You would have tried to talk me out of it."

"Would that have been so bad? Would it have been so terrible not to get caught up in Dad's mess and end up in prison all these years?" Harriet clenched the phone.

Joey changed the subject. "Why are you here and not your boyfriend?"

Harriet's normal response would be to snap back at the boyfriend comment, but the question made her think. When did you call someone a *boyfriend* at this stage of life? When you slept with them once? Or was there another term for that?

Carrie might use a slang term to describe what had happened between her and Craig. She'd say they "hooked up." It sounded clinical to Harriet, more like two co-joined dogs in an open field after they'd done the deed, rather than two consenting adults who'd made love.

Her face turned pink.

Joey grinned. "I see I'm on the right track with you and my lawyer."

"Joey, look around. Does it feel you're on the right track?"

A sheriff's deputy handed Joey a one-page document that Harriet had given her. "From your lawyer."

Joey looked at Harriet for an explanation.

Into the phone, Harriet explained. "I can't help it if she mistook me for a lawyer."

Harriet pointed at the paper. "Your real lawyer prepared that for you to sign. It's an arraignment waiver. Sign it, unless you plan to plead guilty."

Joey held the pen the deputy had given him above the line where he needed to sign and paused. "You think I'm guilty, don't you?"

"Yes, for shutting me out for the last twenty years. Of murder, no."

Joey laughed. "Same ole Harriet." He signed the document and handed the pen and paper back to the deputy who had waited beside him until he signed, probably to make sure Joey didn't stab himself with the pen.

Harriet hesitated, but she needed to know why her brother cut her off. "Every letter I mailed to you came back. You wouldn't let me visit you in prison. Why did you do that to me?"

Joey's eyes glistened. For a millisecond, his face belonged to eight-year-old Joey, the boy who'd had dreams of being a firefighter, police officer, or astronaut, and later, a builder. "My life was over when I went to prison. I wanted you to forget me and live your life."

"We could have leaned on each other, Joey, like we did when we were young."

Joey didn't look convinced.

Then she played the twins card. "There were times these past twenty years when I hated you for turning away from me." Harriet teared up. "I never forgot you though. You are my twin brother, and that means something."

Joey put his hand on the glass. "I'm sorry."

Harriet put her hand up to Joey's. "Me too."

The deputy delivered the signed paper to Harriet and leaned over her. "You have ten minutes," causing Harriet to change the subject. "Carrie says hello."

"How's she doing?"

Harriet told him about her cancer. "She's handling it better than I am."

"Sorry to hear she is sick. I always liked her. Dad did too."

Joey looked over his shoulder, as if to see whether anyone was within earshot. "The last time Dad visited me in prison, he said he gave Carrie something important to give to you and me when they released me from prison."

"She hasn't said a word about it."

Joey fiddled with the telephone cord. "It had to do with Dad's obsession with nineteenth-century Charlotte gold coins."

"Oh, that. We know about the forged coins. Dad was the criminal, not you."

"I don't think—"

"Joey, stop defending him. He let you take the fall for him, and he trafficked in forged gold coins."

Joey tilted his head forward as if in prayer, and then looked up. "Harriet, I am going to ask you to trust me. Our father was not a criminal."

"The coins he buried in the floorboards, which we've confirmed are fake, say different. Doesn't that bother you?"

"Dad was always hiding things, Harriet. Think about it. At every birthday party until the sixth grade, he ran a scavenger hunt for us and our friends, complete with his handwritten maps and clues, and prizes at the end of the search.

"And whenever he gave us a gift, it came with a catch. Don't you remember the time he gave us flashlights, then hid the batteries with a clue where to find them? And when we found them, we found another clue about what to search for at night with our new flashlights? I am not surprised Dad hid coins in the floorboards."

Harriet nodded. "He did love puzzles. But none of that explains the forged coins."

"You're right, but Dad was not a criminal."

Joey's chin dipped, and he tugged at the collar of his jumpsuit. "There's something else. But you can't be mad."

Harriet focused her full attention on Joey's face, pushed the hand-held phone tight against her ear, and leaned toward the glass partition. "No promises."

"Dad told me something else the last time he visited me in prison that I should have told you. An oncologist diagnosed him with cancer. He had less than six months to live. He said—"

Harriet cut him off. "Dad had cancer? Why didn't you tell me? Why didn't he?" She was more hurt than angry.

Joey hung his head. "He insisted I not say a word. Your husband was dying, and Dad didn't want to add his healthcare needs to your plate. He said he didn't want to—"

"I would have taken care of him. Despite what he did to you, he was still our father."

"I know. I encouraged him to tell you about his illness, but he refused. A few months later, he committed suicide. After that, it didn't matter."

Harriet felt a heaviness come over her body. "Why tell me now?"

"He told me about his cancer when he told me he gave Carrie something important to give to us. He seemed happy, despite the diagnosis, like he'd put things right with whatever he gave to Carrie."

Harriet's voice was flat, emotionless. "We may never have to know what Dad gave Carrie if we can't get you out of jail before she dies and she takes her promise with her."

The deputy told Harriet she had two minutes left.

Harriet did a rapid data dump on Joey about what was going on at the Indie and their suspicion that he was the victim of Elkin's revenge plot with the Standish family's help. "You didn't kill Landry, did you?"

Joey sat back. "On television, the lawyer never asks their client if they did it. They might not like what they hear."

"Stop joking."

Joey's face was blank, but Harriet knew her brother. She knew he held information back, as surely as the instinct one twin has about how the other twin feels or thinks.

"Joey, do you know who killed Chance Landry?"

Joey looked down and fiddled with his hands again.

"Simple question, Joey."

Joey looked Harriet in the eyes. "I do."

"Who was it?"

"I can't tell you, and I can't tell the court. If I do, the jury will never believe me."

"Why?"

Joey looked around. "Because I was there when Landry died."

The deputy sheriff tapped Harriet on the shoulder. "Time's up."

CHAPTER 22

TIME FOR MORE PRESSURE

A few miles away, five people gathered at a coffee shop in South End near the Rivafinoli Passage, where one person among them murdered Chance Landry.

They were close enough to hear the heavy machinery's rumble from the construction work near the Rudisill Mine. Somewhere in that hole—which got deeper by the day—South End Mining Company was hard at work digging ore from the earth.

Four of the five people set up camp at a corner table where Sterling Standish, the meeting organizer, chastised Bailey. "Why did you bring Celia with you?"

Sterling's grandmother waved at him from the coffee bar.

"She wanted to come see your work in South End. After the luncheon, I offered to take her back to the Indie, explaining we had this meeting, but she said she'd be happy to wait for me while we met." Bailey lowered her voice. "Honestly, she's been nosy."

"About what?" Elkin asked.

"Who killed Chance and the company's plans for South End."

Sterling waved back at Celia and called, "We won't be long." He whispered to Bailey, "This is our company now."

To Elkin, their consigliere, Sterling aimed his first question. "Will the murder charge against Joey stick?"

Elkin nodded. "The evidence strongly incriminates Joey. Unfortunate for him, but good for us."

"Keep me updated." Then to Dan: "I've listened to the conversation at Harriet's house where the lawyer ambushed you with pointed questions. What do you think they know?"

"Not much. They don't accept Penny killed Junior, but they don't have any evidence otherwise, and they don't know the truth about Joey's appraisal-fraud conviction. I'm sure they don't know who killed Chance or who put his body under Harriet's house."

Sterling looked around the table. "Any news from Carrie Roberts's room?"

Bailey said no. "Something went wrong with the listening device."

Sterling eyed Elkin. "What about the gold coins found under Harriet's house?"

"Impounded in the murder investigation, but not to worry. I have a plan to get them."

"And the real gold coins? The ones that belonged to Penny?"

Elkin didn't bother to look at Sterling when he responded "They're just a rumor in the numismatic world, Sterling. He probably sold them before he died to fund Joey's defense twenty years ago. They're long gone."

"Gone but not forgotten, Robert. I don't believe Penny sold his coins before his death. I believe he hid them somewhere, like he hid my dad's coins in his kitchen floorboards, and we are no closer to finding those coins today than when we first started looking twenty years ago.

Sterling's frustration showed in his raised voice. "Pay attention, everyone. I want Penny Penman's coins. You need to do better." His emphasis on the words *do better* was loud enough to cause Celia to look in their direction.

The bracelets on Bailey's wrists sounded like wind chimes when she shook them down her arms, placed both hands on the table, and addressed Sterling. "We're on it."

"Agreed," Dan and Elkin both said, before Elkin leaned toward Bailey. "When residents fail to pay their assessments in four months, you need to foreclose on their units. Increase the pressure."

Sterling agreed. "Full speed ahead. The family responsible for my father's death must pay dearly. And their friends too."

Elkin grinned. "I couldn't agree more, Sterling. I couldn't agree more."

PART III

FOUR MONTHS LATER - TRIALS AND TRIBULATIONS

CHAPTER 23

A MURDER TRIAL BEGINS

It was nearly noon on their second consecutive day in court, a steaming hot Tuesday in early August. The courthouse air conditioning worked overtime to keep up.

Travail was sure Judge Cheryl Williamson had broken the county record for selecting a jury in a murder trial. His co-counsel on the Joey Penman defense team, retired judge Roscoe Brady, agreed, being the first to praise her for it when the lead lawyers and their teams gathered in her chambers before opening statements.

"Save the sarcasm, Roscoe. You were the slowest judge in your day because it gave you more time to chew your tobacco, but as you can see, I don't chew." She pulled on her cheek to show nothing inside her mouth but her teeth. "And by the way, no chewing in my courtroom."

Travail had never had a trial with Judge Williamson, but her reputation for moving trials faster than a speeding bullet was legendary.

He glanced at prosecutor Liza Fortuna, a rising legal star who a local media outlet had named in their annual list of *40 under 40 professionals on the move*. She was the only lawyer on this year's list, and she had something to prove. With her plan to run for lead district attorney in the coming election, and by the media frenzy she'd stirred up about this trial, she would use Joey's case to prove her mettle to voters. Her campaign manager was none other than Robert Elkin, and her campaign war chest was flush with more cash than any other candidate.

The judge picked up the ballpoint pen she was famous for and clicked it twice. "Any last matters we need to address before we knock out your opening statements to the jury?"

Fortuna was first. "We're ready to proceed." Her associate, a young man who looked like he'd just graduated from law school, remained silent.

Roscoe deferred to Travail, who said, "We're ready." But he didn't feel it.

The last four months had proved a letdown to the team's hopes. They'd interviewed many witnesses with nothing positive to show for it, double- and triple-checked the accuracy of the prosecution's fact disclosures—there were no gaping holes in the prosecution's case—and spent hours at the police station grilling Detective Jimmy Sizemore on his investigation and what he planned to say in court. He was a broken record in the prosecution's favor. "Your man did it."

Nelli took a run at Dirt Man Dan—after all, he'd come to rely on her advice in caring for his disabled daughter—but he clammed up, worried someone might overhear them, even though they were alone.

Yeager tried to butter up Celia and Bailey Standish for information, but the butter didn't stick to Bailey, who said, "Stuff it, Yeager."

Celia was kinder, hosted Yeager for dinner twice, and wanted to know who murdered Landry if it wasn't Joey, but she said she didn't know what Landry had been up to for the Standish Company or who might want to kill him, adding, "I am out of the business loop, a downside of retirement."

Travail could relate. He'd been out of the legal loop after Elkin pushed him out of their law firm a year ago and he ended up at the Indie.

The only person who should have been forthcoming was Joey, but Joey refused to tell his defense team who'd murdered Landry. Worse, he admitted he was at the scene when Landry died. He said he didn't kill Landry, but he wouldn't say who was there or why they were there when it happened. It would help to know more, but Joey held back.

The more they pressed Joey, the more he deflected. "The killer had their reasons." It was as if Joey agreed with the murder.

Harriet had pleaded with her brother, to no avail. "You can't take the fall again, Joey." But he was stubborn, something Travail had learned was a Penman family trait.

Judge Williamson stood, which meant the conference was over. "One last thing." She aimed her eyes and pen at Liza Fortuna. "I will not be happy if anyone tries to turn this trial into a media circus. We will try this case in my courtroom. Not in the media. I don't care who wants to get elected to what."

Travail liked Judge Williamson's directive, but it wouldn't keep the media away. This morning, Amanda Rogers, Channel 24 News, greeted him at the courthouse door, just as she'd done at the Meck Dec trial last year. "Glad to see me, Mr. Travail?"

Amanda Rogers had held her microphone toward Travail. "Care to comment on the trial? The prosecutor says she's got an ironclad case against your client."

"They don't make *60 over 60* lists of professionals on the move, so, no, no comment."

Travail was polite to the reporter, but he wasn't happy to be near her. The media boiled an entire day in court down to one sound bite or headline, which never told the full story and often strayed from the case's nuanced facts. One slip of his tongue and he'd be the next sound bite to go viral, and not in a good way for his client. Better not to comment.

Rogers dropped her microphone to her side and laughed. "I like you, Mr. Travail. You're relatable. The jury will like you too."

Travail didn't know what it meant to be relatable. Did it mean he was old and sweet? A retiree with a kind face? Or, maybe it was his new outfit.

He blamed Harriet for having to get rid of what she called his "baggy and outdated suits" for Joey's murder trial. The salesperson had recommended a charcoal-gray suit, with a spread-collar shirt. Though he preferred the buttondown, she said the spread collar was more styl-ish. She tried to sell him the purple shirt, but he had to draw the line somewhere. He chose the light blue he liked and bought the suit to go with it. Maybe he'd made the right choice. Maybe traditional light blue was what was relatable.

Or maybe the reporter thought he was relatable because he was an over-the-hill lawyer defending a murder case. Looking out for the underdog. How cute was that? And how interesting they let him leave the complex to play defense attorney. Like a field trip for retirees.

Harriet nudged Travail as they walked from Judge Williamson's chambers toward the courtroom. "What are you thinking?"

He sighed. "I am thinking retirement is exhausting."

"Are you really that tired from our salsa spend-the-night party?" she teased.

Travail's body tensed, and he blushed at her little joke.

The salsa dinner dance that led he and Harriet to her bedroom seemed like ages ago. But the four-month rocky road that followed was fresh in his mind.

Since that night, they had dated off and on, but not in a public way. That was his doing, and he could tell his modesty irked Harriet. But then again, she wasn't that keen on having a boyfriend anyway—though he wasn't sure the boyfriend label fit yet—so they suffered stops and starts. One thing he'd learned: dating after sixty-five wasn't much different than teenager dating.

Harriet poked him in the side. "Relax, Craig. You have a murder case to win."

That was true. He had a case to win with the facts against him, and while ordinarily that would create enormous pressure, it didn't feel as scary as when he asked Harriet for their first date. Little did he know they would salsa dance and sleep together the night before that date, not how he'd imagined a mid-sixties courtship—with the cart before the horse and all that—but Yeager put things in perspective when he found out the next morning where Travail had spent the night. "I'm glad you ain't no lollygagger, Craig Travail. Clocks tick fast in retire-ment. You can't afford to be no lollygagger."

With his inimitable wisdom, Yeager made Travail laugh, and his date with Harriet to the musical that night was relaxed. They left *Hamilton* with Harriet singing Broadway tunes down Tryon Street, comforting him about their previous night's sleepover by telling him not to worry because nobody except them—like the song's lyrics in the musical said—was in the room when it happened, the room when it happened.

Their back-to-back spend-the-night party and musical-date-night led to more dates where, bit by bit, they opened up about feelings they'd been reluctant to share. But with Travail being overprotective and Harriet being who she was—a force for change and a strong woman who didn't need a man to protect her—they often clashed. Like every time he thought back to his wife's accident and encouraged Harriet to be careful and she reacted. "I am a woman, Craig, not a child. There is a difference. I can take care of myself."

Before Travail could apologize and make recompense for his over-protectiveness, Harriet would say she needed to breathe. That was code for *we need to take a break*. She took a week to breathe after their first spat and two weeks to breathe after their second.

Travail soon realized he needed to be careful not to tell Harriet to be careful, and if he did that, she might give him the opportunity to be more careful.

This morning, he reminded himself not to tell Harriet to be careful in court, and she was loose, even playful, despite Joey's weak case. He was afraid she had more confidence in him than he did in himself.

Travail couldn't predict Joey's fate with the court any more than he could predict his fate with Harriet. Maybe Joey would get off, and maybe he and Harriet had a chance to make things work, because even as they learned each other's flaws, they kept finding reasons to be together.

Who knows? Maybe their relationship could blossom, flaws and all, where they did the best they could with each other and with the things they cared about and did together. Like Joey's defense and their work to help their Indie friends.

As they stepped into the arena, with its beige walls and taupe wood furniture, now was not the time for relationship worries.

Every courtroom table was inlaid with black leather to match the black juror chairs and courtroom computer screens, a reminder serious business would soon occur.

Travail placed his briefcase on the defense table and looked around to get his bearings. An octagonal feature on the ceiling with interior white lights looked like a rocket engine's underside. A reminder they were about to blast off and he needed to buckle up.

During Liza Fortuna's headline-grabbing opening statement, she railed against the parolee who killed the man who sent him to prison, her voice rising and falling in all the right places for her election-year performance. The act was "premeditated" and "vengeful" and worse, took the life of a man who'd only done his civic duty to "speak in court against a man who committed fraud." To hear her tell it, Landry was the law-abiding saint to Joey's lawless sinner.

"When the evidence is in, you will have more than enough facts to convict Joey Penman of murder beyond a reasonable doubt." She sat in triumph, shiny sweat on her cheeks.

Travail said nothing in response, except to preserve his right, should he choose to do so, to make his opening statement later, before he presented his witnesses.

The judge looked at the clock. It was 12:45 p.m. She turned to the jury. "We will be in recess until two thirty. Don't discuss the case among yourselves or with anyone else."

Prosecutor Fortuna called Detective Sizemore as her first witness. He walked to the witness chair without his usual cigar. Still, his rumpled brown suit gave him that familiar look of experience, the feel of a hard-working detective, and not somebody who sat in an office all day and wore the latest fashion. Travail was sure the jury would like him. He was the relatable one.

After Fortuna established Sizemore's credentials—he'd started as a beat cop after the police academy and worked his way up to detective, where he'd solved more murders than anyone in the department—Detective Sizemore set the scene the night they found Landry's body.

"A neighbor called the fire department early in the morning to report an explosion at Harriet Keaton's house."

"Explosion?"

"That's what they said it sounded like. The fire department arrived and found the kitchen floor had collapsed, and upon further investigation, they discovered Landry tangled in the debris over the collapsed mine shaft. We showed up to find the defendant in the living room, waiting for us to arrive."

Roscoe nudged Travail, but Travail didn't object to the speculation. Detective Sizemore couldn't know what Joey was thinking, but why draw attention to the comment? He could use it later against the detective.

The prosecutor turned to the cause of death. "Was there an autopsy?"

"There was."

"Can you share the results with the jury?"

Fortuna glanced at Travail, but he didn't object. He and Roscoe had discussed their strategy. If the prosecutor tried to get all the cause-of-death evidence in through one witness, they'd let her do it to cut down on the number of prosecution experts presented to the jury.

"A single bullet to the head killed him."

"Time of death?"

"Between 1:00 and 3:00 a.m."

Fortuna approached the witness with an evidence bag containing a knife. She showed it to the detective.

"Was this knife on the scene when you found the victim?"

"Yes. It was sticking in Landry's back. We confirmed the knife belongs to Ms. Harriet Keaton. It came from her kitchen. It had the defendant's fingerprints on it."

"Interesting." Fortuna let her comment about Harriet's knife and Joey's fingerprints on it hang in the air before she turned her attention to the cyber evidence.

"Detective Sizemore, did your team discover relevant evidence on the defendant's mobile phone?"

"We did. Someone had deleted information from the phone, but our cyber forensic team recovered text messages between Landry and the defendant."

The prosecutor asked permission to approach the witness and to use a demonstrative aid to show the text stream to the jury.

Travail didn't object. He'd confirmed with Joey the text messages, though damaging to Joey's defense, were authentic. Any objection would only give the messages more weight.

Fortuna's assistant attorney set up an easel and placed on it a poster board that displayed sentences inside text-like bubbles, with names beside them.

"Can you use this demonstrative exhibit to relate to the jury what the victim and the defendant said to each other in their texts?"

"I'd be glad to. Landry—"

Fortuna interrupted. "Excuse me, Detective. Can you tell the jury the date of a text when you read the text to the jury?"

"Certainly. Landry sent his first text to the defendant one month before he died. It said, *Now that you're out of prison, we need to meet.* Defendant responded the same day with, *Why would I want to meet with someone like you?*"

Detective Sizemore edged closer to look at the poster. "Landry sent his next text one week before he died. It said, *I have unfinished business with your father. You know what I want and how to provide it.* Defendant responded, *You can rot in hell for all I care.*"

Prosecutor Fortuna used her pointer to tap on the next set of texts on the poster. "And these texts?"

"Sent around five the evening before the defendant killed Landry."

"Objection. The detective is not the jury, Your Honor." Travail said it with a combination of disdain for the detective and respect for the rule of law.

Judge Williamson agreed. "Detective Sizemore, the jury will judge the facts, not you." To the jury, she said, "Ignore that last comment."

Liza Fortuna used the moment to stretch things out. "Detective Sizemore, please identify the last texts. Take your time."

The detective enunciated his every word. "At 5:00 p.m. on March 31, Landry sent a text message to the defendant that said, *Meet me at the Rivafinoli Passage in South End. 1:30 in the morning. I will make it worth your time.*

"Defendant responded a few minutes later with, *How will it be worth my time?*

"One minute later, Landry said, *Your father didn't kill Junior. I know who did.*

"Defendant didn't respond to that text before Landry sent another text an hour later that said, *Do you want to clear your father's name?*

"A few minutes later, defendant responded with, *What do you want in return?*

"Landry responded immediately with, *The coins.*

"At 11:30 p.m., Landry followed up with, *Are you coming?* Defendant sent the last text just before midnight, saying, *I'll be there.*"

The prosecutor returned to her table. "Can you tell the jury how far it is from the Rivafinoli Passage in South End to Harriet Keaton's house, where you found Landry?"

"Only a few blocks. Her house is in the Wilmore neighborhood, next to South End and the old Rudisill Mine."

The detective explained he'd walked the distance himself. "Her house was a convenient place to hide the victim until the killer could move the body."

Travail thought about objecting to the implication Joey used the house as a temporary spot to hide the body, but the jurors were probably already there, so he held off.

"A few more questions, Detective Sizemore."

The prosecutor reached into a box beside her and pulled out a clear plastic bag about the size of a bowling ball filled with shiny coins. She struggled with the bag's weight as she held it up with one arm for the witness and jury to see.

"Did you find these coins where you found Landry?"

"We did."

The audience murmured.

"Could you describe the scene?"

"Coins were everywhere, but mostly on the body."

Detective Sizemore made eye contact with Travail, as if he were thinking about whether he should say something else, and then he did. "It looked like the defendant left Landry with the coins he wanted."

Travail rose to object, but it wasn't necessary. Judge Williamson addressed the detective's misstep without his request. "Members of the jury, ignore the detective's speculation."

She then pointed her ballpoint pen at the detective, clicked it, and said through gritted teeth loud enough for the jury to hear, "If you do anything like that again in my courtroom, you will be sorry."

Fortuna begged the court's forgiveness, and with the court's permission, approached her witness with the coins. "Do you know what kind of coins these are?"

He took one coin from the bag and examined it. "These are copies of gold coins made at the US Mint in the 1830s."

Travail doubted the detective was qualified to testify about the authenticity of 1830s gold coins, but an objection would only make it appear the coins were important.

"You said 'copies.' Do you mean they are counterfeit?"

"Actually, the correct term is 'forged.' Counterfeit coins are those intended to be used as currency in place of the real thing. These are knockoffs of rare coins, not for spending as currency, and of no value to collectors. Professor Fortenberry, who I believe you plan to call as a witness later, explained the difference to me."

Travail could picture the headline on the evening news: *Murdered man covered in forged gold coins*.

"You mentioned a hole in the ground, Detective. Can you explain?"

"We brought in experts from UNC-Charlotte who concluded the hole under the kitchen floor of Ms. Keaton's house opens to a shaft in the old Rudisill Mine that began operations in around 1830."

Fortuna slowed down and feigned a puzzled expression. "That's all very interesting, detective, but what do gold mines and gold coins have to do with this murder?"

"Nothing, until we found the handwritten note in Harriet Keaton's house."

"The note?"

"Yes. The one in the defendant's handwriting."

The detective waited. This wasn't his first time as a prosecution witness. He let the suspense build.

The prosecutor played along. She tilted her head. "What did the note say?"

Travail didn't object because Joey admitted to him he'd written the note. Joey didn't explain why, but the note was authentic.

Detective Sizemore turned and faced the jury. "The note said, *Meeting. 1:30 a.m. Chance wants the coins. He can die trying.*"

Several jurors wrote on their pads. Others nodded, as if they'd just solved a riddle.

Fortuna took her time marking the handwritten note as a prosecution exhibit, walking it up to the detective, and having him identify it. "Yep. That's the note."

Fortuna thanked Detective Sizemore, handed the devastating exhibit to the clerk, and returned to the prosecution table. She took her time on the way, smiled at the jury when she got there, and turned to face the judge. "No more questions, Your Honor."

With that painful evidence inflicted on the defense's case, the judge announced a brief recess. They were back in session in ten minutes. "Your witness, Mr. Travail."

"Thank you, Your Honor." Travail knew he had to treat the detective with respect. This wasn't a rogue cop with a penchant to lie, but he wasn't perfect, either. Every witness makes mistakes.

"Detective Sizemore, you said when you arrived at the scene that morning, it appeared as if Joey had been waiting for you. Did I get that right?"

"You did."

"He wasn't packing a bag?"

"No."

"He wasn't trying to exit the back door?"

"No."

"He was just there, waiting for the police to show up?" Travail emphasized the word *waiting*.

"That's right."

"Detective, do you recall telling me when I interviewed you about this case that the firefighter who came on the scene said the same thing?"

"I don't recall what I told you, but what you describe is accurate."

"That Joey was just waiting for the fire department to arrive?"

The detective nodded. "Yes."

"Don't you find it odd that a man you say committed a murder and hid his victim's corpse under the house hung around for a chat with the firefighters and police?"

"Criminals do stupid things."

Several jurors nodded, as if they were familiar with stupid criminal behavior.

Travail didn't flinch. "One stupid thing he never did was confess to murder, correct?"

"He probably would have if you hadn't showed up and told him to keep his mouth shut."

The same jurors who knew about stupid criminal behavior, plus a few others, laughed, as did some gallery members. Travail looked at Judge Williamson. "Your Honor?"

The judge pointed her ballpoint pen at the detective. "You know better than that."

She then turned to the jury and was true to her word; she wouldn't tolerate the detective's shenanigans in her court again. "Detective Sizemore is not a comedian. You must ignore his claim defendant would have confessed if the detective were allowed to talk with him. Detective Sizemore is not that good."

The detective shifted in his seat and didn't look at the jury.

The evidence bag with the knife sat on the clerk's desk in front of the witness. Travail approached the clerk, collected the evidence, and placed it on the witness box ledge. He pointed to the knife.

"Detective, what did the autopsy report conclude about that knife's role in the cause of Landry's death?"

Detective Sizemore shifted in his seat again. "It had no role."

"Excuse me?" It was Travail's turn to feign surprise.

"The knife did not kill Landry. The bullet did."

Travail scratched his head, mimicking the motion Detective Sizemore had used on him and Harriet the night they arrested Joey. "Are you saying the knife went into Landry's back after he was already dead?"

"That's what the autopsy said."

"Just to be clear, you're saying someone stuck a knife with my client's fingerprints on it in the back of a dead man?"

The courtroom quieted as if everyone was curious to hear the answer. Detective Sizemore hesitated, then looked at the prosecutor.

Judge Williamson clicked her ballpoint pen. "Eyes on Mr. Travail, Detective. You don't get to call a friend for help. Answer the question."

"It looks that way."

"You mean it looks like someone stuck this knife with my client's fingerprints on it in the back of Chance Landry after he was dead?"

"Uh-huh. I mean, yes."

It was Travail's turn to use the word the prosecutor had used. "Interesting."

He paused before he turned to the gun. "Did you find the murder weapon?"

"We did not."

Travail leaned forward, still upset over the effort by someone to plant evidence on Harriet.

"Who told you, Detective, that you would find the gun that killed Landry buried in Harriet Keaton's garden at the Independence Retirement Community?"

"It was an anonymous tip."

"You tore her garden to muddy shreds. Did you find the gun in her garden?"

"You know I didn't." The detective's tone suggested he had lost patience but so had the judge. "Just answer the question, Detective."

"I did not find the murder weapon in her garden."

Detective Sizemore locked eyes again with Travail as if he were thinking about adding a postscript to improve his answer to benefit the prosecution, but he remained silent. Maybe his decision had to do with the clicking ballpoint pen ten feet from where he sat.

Travail took a calculated risk when he wrapped up his cross-examination.

"Detective, your work in solving murders has earned you honors and commendations. Have you ever had a case where all evidence pointed at a particular suspect, only to find out later, someone had framed the suspect?"

"I have."

"How many times?"

"Only once in thirty-five years."

"So it's not unheard of?"

The detective conceded. "It's rare, but not unheard of."

Roscoe placed his hand on Travail's back, a signal between the two that this was the best time to stop, when the evidence gave off a scent of reasonable doubt. And given the time on the clock, it was a nice way to end court for the day.

CHAPTER 24

SETTLE OR ELSE

Travail led his legal team on foot from the Mecklenburg County Courthouse toward the Charles R. Jonas Federal Building. Harriet said their walk uphill to the square and the three blocks beyond after their day sitting in court "will do you and Roscoe good."

A few months earlier, Travail had filed a mini class action by every Indie resident who bought gold bullion or invested in South End Mining Company against the Standish Company and its subsidiaries. Late last week, the arbitration association had appointed a retired federal judge, Thomas Dooley, as the arbitrator. He set their status conference for six-thirty today to allow them to finish their day at the county courthouse.

This was going to be a long day, to be sure, and as Travail walked uphill, he felt the weariness a sixty-six-year-old lawyer should feel when they try to tackle a murder trial and a multi-million-dollar financial fraud case in the same week.

Dooley was more eager beaver than Judge Cheryl Williamson. It was said by those who had appeared before him that Dooley pushed hard, took no flack, cracked the occasional joke, and in the end, did the right, fair thing. Travail was glad Dooley was on their case.

On the way to the federal courthouse, they passed the square at

Trade and Tryon where twenty-foot-high bronze sculptures guarded the four corners. Roscoe, who surprised Travail with his art knowledge, provided commentary.

"The four figures represent how we got here as a city and where we're going."

Roscoe spit tobacco juice in his Styrofoam cup. Harriet groaned.

"What's that statue represent?" Travail pointed to what looked like a strong African American man holding a sledgehammer before his thick chest.

"Transportation," Roscoe said. "After the gold rush, railroads made Charlotte into what it is, and men like that built the railroads. The mill-worker represents industry. The woman with the child represents the future."

The light changed, and they walked across Tryon Street.

It felt like the last figure looked away from Travail, as if he didn't care to acknowledge his presence. He wore a floppy hat, with the lid raised in front to reveal a full nose, chiseled face, and thick goatee. He held a gold mining pan. Roscoe pointed at him and said, "Commerce."

Minutes later, they stood on federal building grounds, once home to the first branch of the US Mint. A sidewalk led to the entrance of a two-story sandstone structure, where six columns supported a triangular portico offering minimal cover.

Behind the two-story section were five or six additional stories. White clouds floating in the blue sky above the higher stories looked like puffs of smoke, giving off the impression the building spit out steam billows.

They cleared security and took the elevator to the designated floor, where Judge Dooley met them and ushered them to his office.

"Now that I am retired from the federal bench, I don't have any law clerks, but they let me use my office for private arbitrations, and I get to dress more casual now."

Judge Dooley's navy-blue sport coat, a bit baggy, and his khaki pants, a bit tight, showed their age, but he didn't seem to care. He wore a blue traditional oxford buttondown. No tie. His shoes were well worn and could use a polish.

But Travail was not fooled by the judge's appearance. Even in his relaxed clothes, he was not a jurist to underestimate. One best be prepared in Dooley's presence.

They entered a spacious room with a fantastic view, especially if you liked Triple A baseball. The judge's desk was a billiard-sized mahogany beast that took up one end of the room, while spacious upholstered seating took up the room's center.

At the other end was a conference table big enough for sixteen people. Robert Elkin and Sterling Standish faced them from their seats on the table's other side. Neither rose to greet them.

Dooley shrugged. "So that's how it's going to be." He invited Travail's team to sit. They took chairs across from their opposition.

"Before we get started, let me tell you about creatures that die when they mate."

Travail and Harriet exchanged glances. Roscoe grinned at Dooley's panache.

"There is the mayfly, of course. Very short lifespan after they mate. And there is a marsupial mouselike creature in Australia that goes at sex like gang-busters and then poof, its immune system collapses. Dead as a doornail.

"Salmon swim so hard to spawn upstream, they wear themselves out. Many die before they make it back to the ocean. But those aren't the most interesting examples."

Elkin looked at his watch, and Dooley noticed. "Mr. Elkin, do you have a date?"

"Your Honor, my client is very busy with his South End development project and this frivolous arbitration is—"

The judge waved his hand. "We'll get to that. You need to listen."

Dooley jotted some notes, stopped, and jotted some more, before he read off the names on his list. "Praying mantis, octopi, redback spiders, wasp spiders, green anacondas. There are probably more. Do you know what they have in common, Mr. Elkin?"

"I do not." Elkin said it as if it mattered not who knew the answer to the question.

Dooley ignored Elkin's indifference. "These creatures eat their male mates after sex. It's the worst one-night stand you could ever have." Dooley laughed, and Roscoe joined him.

Travail remained quiet. He didn't know what this National Geographic lesson had to do with the arbitration process, but he was sure the retired judge, with his many years on the bench, would tell them if they waited. Dooley didn't disappoint.

"The process you've chosen mates you together in a legal fight. Arbitration, like court, will have a winner and a loser. The fight will get heated, maybe not as heated as sex and not nearly as exciting, but you will break a sweat. You will either kill each other in the process—financially, that is—or, more likely, one side will win, and after they do, they will eat the loser."

Travail hadn't heard this speech given in his continuing education courses, but he liked it. Much more interesting than the standard spiel.

Dooley walked to the door. "I am giving you thirty minutes to work this out." He closed the door and locked it. From the outside.

Sterling raised his voice at Elkin. "Is it legal for him to lock us in here? With them?"

Harriet crossed her arms. "Don't think for a second we want to share oxygen with you."

Elkin ignored Harriet and focused on Travail. "Control your girl-friend, Craig. She's a paralegal. Needs to learn her place."

Oh, boy. That was the wrong thing to say. Travail glanced at Harriet, knowing a reaction was coming. She stood, grabbed the six-foot coat rack behind her, shook the coats loose, flipped the rack forward, and thrust it across the table at Elkin like a medieval jouster.

The rack's prongs stopped short of body contact, but the threat startled Elkin. When he pushed back to avoid the blow that never came, his chair flipped over backward, and his head slammed against the floor. Travail froze to his seat.

Elkin, flat on his back, moaned, and Roscoe added the exclamation mark. "Looks like she showed you the proper place for a smart-mouthed disbarred lawyer, Robert."

Judge Dooley stuck his head in the door. "Everything okay?" He glanced at Elkin on the floor. "What happened to you?"

Elkin rolled to his knees and pointed at Harriet. "She assaulted me."

The incident took Travail back a year earlier to when Elkin taunted Travail by demeaning his wife's death, prompting Travail to react in a blind rage and tackle him to the ground. Harriet's reaction made him think. Maybe he and Harriet were compatible.

"I didn't touch him, Your Honor. I just wanted to see how he would react. He seems a little jumpy."

Sterling seethed. "Call your security, Judge." He spoke like he gave directions to a lowly subordinate.

Dooley ignored Sterling and kept his eyes on Elkin. "Looks to me like you tried to mate with a praying mantis." He closed the door, but not before adding, "You have twenty minutes to resolve your case, or when the time comes, I will resolve it for you."

Elkin turned his chair upright, retook his seat, and aimed his wrath at Travail. "Your arbitration claims are bogus. When you lose—and you will lose—your clients will pay our attorney fees."

Harriet sniffed. "Not much of a threat, Robert. Isn't minimum wage the going rate for a disbarred lawyer?"

Sterling ignored Harriet and addressed Travail. "This is a waste of my time. I have a business to run. Cut to the chase. What do you want?"

"Refund the money the residents invested with interest."

Sterling laughed. "That's ridiculous. Not happening."

Harriet leaned toward Sterling. "You misled my friends." She emphasized the word *misled*.

Sterling leaned back and scoffed and Elkin bristled. "That is for the judge to decide."

Roscoe caught Sterling's attention. "Your disbarred lawyer pulled a fast one on you, didn't he?"

"What are you talking about?"

"I bet he told you the state will approve your permit to dig for gold."

Sterling jerked his head toward Elkin. "How does he know about the permit process?"

Elkin waved him off. "Easy to figure that out. The state hearing is a matter of record."

Roscoe continued to annoy Sterling. "The permit decision is due this Friday, isn't it?"

"What if it is?" Sterling looked unsure.

"How are you going to dig for gold when the state denies your permit?"

Sterling turned on Elkin. "You said the permit was a no-brainer."

Harriet had the last word in their negotiation. "The only thing that is a no-brainer in this room is what's between your disbarred lawyer's ears."

Judge Dooley unlocked the door and entered. "Do we have a settlement?"

Hearing nothing, he said, "Okay. We will hold the arbitration this Saturday after your murder trial and see who survives this coupling."

CHAPTER 25

NOT THE PEOPLE'S COURT

While Travail, Harriet, and Roscoe were in court dealing with the testimony of Detective Sizemore, Bailey Standish tacked a sign on the Indie boardroom door that said *Night Court.* Underneath the sign, she tacked a decree signed by herself as board president.

The decree made clear this was no longer the People's Court. There were new rules. New processes. And a new location, the boardroom in the main building. Not one judge but two, and Roscoe did not make the cut. Bailey made sure the rules, location, and judges favored her goals.

She'd decided the best course of action was to deal with the slew of residents in default on their assessments with brutal efficiency. Their four months was up.

Bailey's decree prohibited alcoholic drinks and spectators. Only the accused and their representatives could be in the room, and the court would hear cases one at a time.

She'd found the word *sequestered* on the internet and dropped it into the decree. Until your case was called, the court sequestered you to the library, where she'd tacked another sign that read, *Night Court Waiting Room.*

The decree also prohibited *laughter, frivolity, and stupid English barrister costumes.* Above Bailey's signature were the words, *This is serious business.*

Bailey made herself and Celia the new judges. The court would serve as prosecutor and jury. No need to waste time. Bailey would present the facts, let the residents plead their cases, and then she and Celia would rule against them.

Bailey knew what she was doing. She'd had practice running her sorority honor court in college. When a girl broke the rules, Bailey held a hearing and doled out the punishment. How could this be any different? Celia would do as she was told.

Bailey had posted a third document to the Night Court door. This eight-by-sixteen-inch docket provided the schedule for the evening. There were forty-eight resident names with times beside their names. All were delinquent in paying their assessment. Each had five minutes to state their case. If they kept to the schedule, Bailey's court would finish its work in four hours. Twelve residents per hour.

Everyone with a case before the court had to be in the waiting room when the court began or they'd forfeit the chance to defend themselves.

Although the sun was still shining, Night Court began at five o'clock. Two reasons for the start time. One, it disrupted the dinner schedule. Hungry residents, some of whom would have to wait hours in the library until their case was called, would be too famished and out of sorts to put up an effective fight. Two, they could begin while Travail, Harriet, and Roscoe were still at the courthouse dealing with Joey's murder trial and finish before they returned from their conference with Judge Thomas Dooley. Yeager would be no match for what Bailey had planned.

Bailey assigned Dan as bailiff. His role was to shuffle the deadbeats to and from the court and keep the court train running on time.

Five minutes before Night Court began, Yeager pushed Nelli into the boardroom. They both wore white wigs and black robes.

Bailey was furious. "Did you not read my decree? No stupid costumes. And why is she here?" Bailey pointed at Nelli.

"Nelli Nimble is my second chair. We represent the people you want to railroad."

"NASCAR to you," Nelli added. "Still the fastest chair at the Indie. Second to none, except for today when I am second to Yeager in your kangaroo courtroom."

"Whatever, but ditch the robes."

Yeager lowered his voice. "You sure about that?"

"Absolutely, and hurry up. Court starts in two minutes."

Yeager lifted his gown over his head to reveal he wore nothing underneath but his red, white, and blue American flag boxers and cowboy boots. "I like to travel light." He rubbed his right hand across his hairy belly while Nelli struggled to pull her gown over her head.

"Stop. Stop." Bailey was apoplectic. "I don't want to see your knickers, Nelli."

Celia laughed and put her hand over her mouth. Bailey gave Celia the evil eye. To Yeager, Bailey shouted, "Put that back on."

Yeager shrugged and did as he was told. "This doesn't seem too efficient, if you ask me. You rule one way. Then you reverse yourself."

"Nobody asked you."

Bailey's heart raced and she took a deep breath to calm herself. She was in charge, not Yeager. "I can assure you, Mr. Alexander, I will be very efficient tonight."

Dan stuck his head in the room as the clock on the wall turned to five o'clock. "Are you ready, Bailey?"

"Yes, bring in—"

Yeager interrupted. "Madam Judge, if I may."

"No you may not."

Nelli picked up her phone and dialed a number.

Bailey protested the distraction. "What are you doing?"

"Calling Amanda Rogers at Channel 24 News. She can have a media truck here in twenty minutes for a special interest story about the new railroad you've opened here."

Bailey didn't want the media here. "Put the phone down, Nelli. Your first chair, or whatever the hell you call each other, can speak."

Yeager bowed. "Grateful to you for that, Madam Judge."

"Stop calling me that." Bailey felt her heart rate speed up again. Celia put a hand on Bailey's forearm and patted it.

"As you wish, Bailey." Yeager tucked his thumbs under his armpits, puffed out his chest, and said, "We request the court combine all cases as one case. There is a *common nucleus of operative facts* at play here." Yeager laughed. "Craig Travail taught me those words."

"Denied." Bailey had her plan, and this wasn't it.

Yeager maintained his composure. "If you intend to proceed in this manner, each accused will call up to five witnesses for their individual cases, as the bylaws allow. It will take weeks."

Nelli waved her phone at Celia. "And Channel 24 News will provide daily coverage."

"Unbelievable," Bailey shouted.

Yeager raised his hand. "However, there is a middle ground, a shorter way than your four-hour charade and our multi-week marathon, without cameras."

Celia leaned over and whispered to Bailey. Bailey nodded and said, "We're listening."

Yeager picked up a document and looked it over. "These cases are all the same. You imposed assessments that are unaffordable. People can't pay. You want to kick everyone out. We can address the rights of all the parties in one fell swoop with one witness. The hearing shouldn't take more than fifteen minutes."

Bailey was suspicious, but she liked the idea of one fell swoop. "Any other conditions?"

"Just one. The outcome will be the outcome for all, and the resident we call before you can speak for everyone."

"Done. Call your one resident. Let's get this over with."

Dan's head poked through the crack in the door like a turtle poking its head out of its shell. "Who do you want me to bring in?"

Nelli smiled at Dan. "Tell everyone they can go to dinner."

Bailey didn't understand until Yeager spoke. "We call Celia as our one witness."

"Wait. What's going on?" Bailey looked at Celia. "Did you know about this?"

"I did not, but I don't mind answering their questions. I'd like to go to dinner too."

This felt like a lawyer trick, but Yeager wasn't a lawyer. He just played one. What were they up to? Bailey looked at the clock on the wall. "Fine."

Celia came around and sat in a chair at the table next to Yeager and Nelli.

Nelli spoke first. "No need to swear the witness. I trust her, except when we play cards together." Nelli and Celia grinned at each other.

Yeager agreed that no swearing was necessary. "Evening, Celia."

"Hello, Yeager."

"Do you enjoy living here?"

"Very much so."

"How are your cats?"

Bailey interrupted. "Celia's cats have nothing to do with this case. The clock is ticking on your fifteen minutes."

Nelli put a sticker on a document and handed it to Yeager. He handed it to Celia. "This document is Exhibit 1. Do you recognize it?"

"These are the Indie bylaws."

"Very good."

Yeager turned and received another document from Nelli and handed it to Celia. "This document is Exhibit 2. Do you recognize it?"

"This is the declaration establishing the Indie Owner Association."

"You've read them?"

Celia nodded. "I was a businesswoman. Can't help myself."

Bailey had not read them, but she didn't need to read them. She was board president. She was in charge. What she said went.

Yeager grinned. "Do you know whether these bylaws and this declaration are binding on the residents?"

"Yes. When you buy property here, your rights as a property owner are subject to the rules in these documents."

"I see. What about the board? Is it bound to these rules?"

"Of course."

Bailey sensed a trap. "Yeager, these cases are about forty-eight residents not paying their assessments."

"Which are stupidly high," Nelli added.

"Shut up, Nelli." Bailey turned on Yeager. "Whether the assessment is high or low, don't you agree residents have to pay their debts?"

Yeager smiled at Bailey and didn't answer. Turning back to Celia, he continued. "Do you know the difference between a common assessment and a special assessment?"

Celia asked to look at the bylaws to refresh her memory. She flipped through them until she found the page she sought.

She put her finger on the page and moved it from left to right. "A common assessment is an assessment made as part of the regular budget cycle. The board creates a budget, and as part of that budget, they set the residents' dues for the coming year to meet the expense obligations in the budget."

"And a special assessment?" Yeager asked.

"That happens outside the regular budget cycle, usually for a lump-sum amount to address an unexpected expense."

Yeager addressed Bailey. "Will you *stipulate*—that's another word Craig Travail taught me—the assessments the board made four months ago were special assessments?"

Bailey hadn't focused on the difference. "What do you think, Celia?"

"Yes. We should stipulate. The board was in the middle of the budget year when it made these assessments. These were special assessments."

"Fine." Bailey pointed at Yeager. "You have five minutes to finish your case."

"Celia, did you read these documents before the board issued the assessments four months ago?"

"I did not. I'd just moved in and was new to the Indie and the board." She paused. Then: "Now that I know what the documents say, I should have looked at them before I voted yes on the assessments."

Remembering how lawyers looked surprised when they knew what was coming, Yeager drew back, offering his best imitation of shock. "Why is that?"

"Indie bylaws require a 67-percent resident vote to approve a special assessment."

"That vote didn't occur, did it?"

Bailey realized what was about to happen. "Stop right there, Yeager. You are out of order. Celia, don't say another word. The issue today is simple: did the accused residents pay their assessments? That's it. Nothing more."

Bailey ordered Celia to rejoin her and take the seat to her side. With Celia settled, Bailey asked Yeager for her own stipulation. "Do you agree the forty-eight residents have not paid the board's assessments?"

"Yes, but the assessments violated the Indie bylaws."

Bailey called the question. "All in favor of filing liens and foreclosing on the units owned by the forty-eight residents who failed to pay their assessments, raise your hand."

Bailey's hand shot up, but Celia's arms remained by her side.

"Celia, raise your hand."

"They don't owe the money. We didn't follow the bylaws."

Nelli chimed in. "We knew you'd be honest, Celia."

"Tie goes to the runner," Yeager said. "We win. You lose."

Bailey shoved her chair back, stood, and stomped to the door. "You will hear from our lawyer."

Yeager opened the door for her. "Please tell Robert Elkin we said hello. And tell him how well we performed today. Harriet is right. It's not that hard being a lawyer."

CHAPTER 26

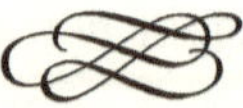

THE PROSECUTION PILES ON

The next morning, Travail dodged Channel 24 News star Amanda Rogers and her cameraman and ducked into the Mecklenburg County Courthouse for the third day of Joey's murder trial. It was only Wednesday, and he was already tired for what was shaping up to be a long week with the back-to-back murder and arbitration cases before him.

As he made his sprint into the nine-story justice building with its white concrete walls and glass windows, Travail passed under the Mecklenburg County seal above the courthouse's covered patio. He and Harriet had admired the images on the seal last year before the Meck Dec trial, particularly the colonial-era quill and parchment honoring the first American Declaration of Independence. There was no gold nugget on the seal, but there were two images that represented time periods before and after the gold rush era.

On one side of the seal was a farm and silo, representing the county's rural roots, with its good dirt, green landscape, and abundant trees. On the other side were skyscrapers, reflecting the city's growth in the twentieth century to become the New South city of commerce.

The gold rush in between gave Charlotte an economic boost to the financial engine it became. It was an essential and unique part of Charlotte's history, but most Charlotte residents knew nothing about the period, something Penny Penman had tried to rectify. Travail reflected as he passed through security on how Penny's zeal led them to this day.

Harriet and Roscoe waited for him in the foyer near the elevator, where they greeted him and Roscoe punched the elevator button.

On the ride up, Harriet handed Travail briefs from their pre-trial investigation on the prosecution's next three witnesses, the one from Central Prison, the one from the Wilmore neighborhood, and the one from Queens University.

They entered the courtroom to a larger crowd than the day before. It probably had to do with the television coverage last night about the dead man found in a mine shaft covered in forged gold coins.

Joey was in his seat at defense counsel table looking rested and at ease. "Morning, Counselor. How did you and my sister sleep last night? I know she snores."

Travail marveled at Joey's ability to remain calm while on trial for murder. His joke—which normally would unnerve Travail—helped him relax. For a few seconds, Travail thought about saying, "Joey, I have to tell you, it's hard to get much sleep when I'm in bed with your sister." But instead, Travail smiled, happy Joey was confident, even if Travail wasn't.

On the opposite side of the courtroom, Liza Fortuna spoke with a man in the gallery's first row who wore an ill-fitting suit he must have borrowed for his testimony today. Beside the man was a woman in a dark blue suit wearing an alert, serious expression. Travail pegged her for a plainclothes officer. The man she watched was most likely the witness from Central Prison.

In the next gallery row on the prosecution side, Sterling and Bailey whispered to each other. It wouldn't surprise Travail if they had delivered all three of today's prosecution witnesses to the prosecutor, wrapped in a bow. Or it could have been the man who just joined them.

Roscoe chuckled. "Elkin is moving slow this morning, Harriet. Your lesson sank in."

Harriet sniffed. "Wasted effort. Every time we put him under a rock, he crawls back out, slimier than before."

The bailiff yelled, "All rise," and bellowed his oyez routine while Judge Williamson quick-stepped it to her perch.

Once the jurors were in their seats, the judge barked at the prosecutor to "call your next witness."

The man with the ill-fitting suit stepped forward and took the oath. He was stocky—around five feet five and maybe a hundred and eighty pounds—had a crew cut, and a scar on the right side of his square face.

Fortuna sat upright. "State your name for the jury, please."

"Terrence Lamb. But everyone calls me T."

"Do you know the defendant?"

"Sure, I know Joey. Shared a room with him. Told you that yesterday, didn't I?"

"Do you mean you shared a prison cell with the defendant?" Fortuna kept her voice steady. "And please, just answer the questions asked."

"Fine. We shared a prison cell for a few years at Central."

"Why were you in prison?"

"Got caught."

"Doing what exactly?"

Travail could see by Fortuna's stiff posture, T tested her patience. Maybe that was a good sign. Maybe the witness was malleable.

"I stole a few vehicles."

Fortuna took a breath. "When you say 'a few,' are you referring to fifteen to twenty high-end vehicles stolen in a car theft operation, for which you were the mastermind?"

"If I was a mastermind, I wouldn't have got caught, now would I?"

Judge Williamson aimed her ballpoint pen at Fortuna. "Before you bury this witness and leave Mr. Travail no work to do, maybe you could ask him a relevant question."

"Of course, Your Honor. I didn't want the jury to think I was withholding anything about the witness's character."

Judge Williamson was quick as ever. "They know what kind of character Mr. T is."

"It's just T, judge." T smiled, as if he were enjoying his day off.

The judge ignored the witness. "Anytime, Ms. Fortuna."

The prosecutor flipped through her notes. "Mr. Lamb, did the defendant ever confide in you while you shared a prison cell?"

"Said he wanted to kill that bastard Chance Landry."

"How did that come up?"

"About a year ago, he talked about his upcoming release. We got to jawing about our crimes and what we wanted to do when we got out. Me, I wanted to—"

Fortuna interrupted. "Mr. Lamb, could you stay focused on what the defendant said to you about what he wanted to do when they released him from prison?"

"Like I said, he wanted to kill that bastard Chance Landry. His very words."

"You're not making this up?" Fortuna asked.

"Why would I?"

"Has anyone in the government promised you anything for your testimony?"

It was subtle, but the witness paused for a split second. "Nah. Government didn't promise me nothing. It's my civic duty."

Fortuna passed the witness, and Travail pounced.

"Mr. T, is stealing expensive cars your civic duty?"

"I said my name is T, not Mr. T." The witness gritted his teeth. "Mr. T was a Black TV character. I ain't Black, as you can see."

Travail bored in on T.

"Why do you want to make it clear to everyone in this courtroom that you are not a Black man? Why do you need to point that out?"

"I ain't one. That's all."

"And that's important, how?" Travail stressed the word *how*.

Fortuna was on her feet. "Your Honor. Mr. Lamb's race is immaterial."

"Apparently not to T, Your Honor, since he is a white nationalist who hates Black people."

Judge Williamson clicked her ballpoint pen three times in rapid succession before she lashed out. "That's not evidence, Mr. Travail. You know better."

"Sorry, Your Honor. I got ahead of myself. Please allow me to lay the foundation."

Judge Williamson said "proceed" and Travail mentally prepared to set the trap while he wondered whether it would work. What would the jury think when they learned what Joey had told Travail about T's prejudice? Would they refuse to care, or would his behavior disgust them? Either way, he hoped T was too smug to detect the snare Travail had crafted.

"Were you a member of any clubs in prison?"

"One social club."

"For white people only?"

'Sure. The Blacks had their own club."

"But you were never a white nationalist? Never a part of any organization that demeaned Black people?"

The witness looked at the jury. "Nah, like I said, we had our club, and they had theirs."

"You're sure about that?"

"Yep."

"That's the truth?"

"It is."

"Like it's the truth my client told you he planned to kill that bastard Chance Landry?"

"Yep. That's what he said."

Travail whispered to Harriet, who handed him a one-page document. He placed his finger on the page.

"Were you quoted in a flyer—one published by and for your white-people-only social club—saying, 'It is a scientific fact whites are superior to Blacks. Slavery was a good thing for this country, and we need to bring it back.'"

"That's private property." The snitch spit out his words.

Travail looked at the paper. "Oh. You're right. The flyer says you have to be Aryan, swear allegiance to Hitler, and believe in white supremacy to be a member."

T looked away from the jury and shuffled in his seat.

"You lied to the jury, T. You are a white nationalist who hates Black people."

T didn't respond.

Travail pushed harder. "Is lying one of your civic duties? Is that why you're here today, to do what you do so well, to lie?"

T's face tensed, and he balled his fists. "Screw you."

Judge Williamson motioned to the bailiff and the plainclothes officer to come to the bench. She whispered to them, and they flanked the witness box.

She aimed her ballpoint pen at T and made sure he and everyone else in the courtroom heard what she had to say. "If you curse again, I will hold you in contempt."

Travail glanced at the paper he held, crumpled it, and tossed it in the bin below the table. It was a prop. He didn't have the real thing, only Joey's recollection of what he'd seen in prison.

Harriet smiled at him. She'd prepared the prop, and when he'd seen it a few minutes ago for the first time, he'd almost stumbled on his words. It was a list of sexy salsa dances and how to perfect the moves. A list of plants would have been better.

"Any further questions for this witness, Mr. Travail?"

"Your Honor, I am sure the jury has a good grasp of T's character by now. Therefore, I only have a few questions related to his motive for being here today."

Travail steadied his voice. "Mr. T, since you're such a truthful man, is it true your appearance here today is not the first time or even the second time you've testified about something someone in prison allegedly said to you?" He stretched out the word *allegedly*.

"You know that's true, or you wouldn't have asked the question."

"Quite right," Travail said. "I enjoy being truthful, which is why we did some research to learn the truth about the prizes you win for your civic duty here today.

"Turns out, each time you testify for the prosecution, your prison conditions improve. Better food. Better accommodations. Favors from the warden. And one time, the state reduced your sentence by three years. These weren't handwritten deals—because you'd have to admit to that in court—but they weren't coincidences."

The witness still seethed for being shown up. "So?"

"Do you remember telling Joey that you had a good thing going, that all you had to do was tell the police and prosecutor what they wanted to hear and you'd get a day out, get to stay in a nice hotel, eat a good meal, and bank some perks?"

"I don't remember that."

Travail shrugged. "I didn't expect you would, T."

To the judge, Travail said, "That's all we have."

The judge ordered a fifteen-minute recess and told the plainclothes officer in a voice loud enough for the jurors to hear to "remove Mr. T from the courtroom and return him to Central Prison, where he belongs."

The prosecution's next witness would not be as easy to discredit as the prison snitch, and his testimony would be deadly to Joey's defense.

When Travail quizzed Joey about the truth of what the witness was going to say, he was unhelpful. All he said was, "It's not what it looks like."

Chad Breeden stepped into the witness box, took the oath, and answered questions about his background, experience, education, and character.

On the morning in question, he walked home from a bar in South End to the house he rented in the Wilmore neighborhood. He identified an image of Harriet's house as the one he passed by on his way home that morning.

"What time was it when you passed Ms. Keaton's house?" the prosecutor asked.

"It was around two in the morning."

"What did you see?"

"A person crawled out a basement door on the side of the house, brushed himself off, and walked toward me."

"Could you see the man's face?"

"Not at first. But I was curious. So I waited. When he came into the front yard, the streetlight gave me a clear view. He waved. I waved back."

"Did you know him?"

"No."

"But you got a good look at his face?"

"I did."

Liza Fortuna paused for dramatic effect. "Is the man you saw that morning in this courtroom? Take your time. I want you to be sure."

Breeden looked at the defense table and pointed his finger. "That's him."

"Your Honor, will you ask Mr. Penman to stand so we can be sure he is the man Mr. Breeden has identified?"

The judge clicked her ballpoint pen. "Stand up, Mr. Penman."

Joey stood and looked at the witness.

Fortuna continued. "Is the man standing at defense counsel's table the man you saw emerge from Harriet Keaton's basement at around two in the morning on April 1?"

"Yes. That's him."

"You're sure?"

"Absolutely."

Fortuna looked pleased as she turned the witness over to Travail.

Joey had been no help to the defense team in how to deal with Breeden's testimony. He neither admitted nor denied he was under the house. Nor did he explain why he stayed at the house after the kitchen collapsed when he had to know—if Chad Breeden was telling the truth —that a dead man was in the basement, and worse, that the dead man was Landry, the man whose testimony sent him to prison.

Travail and Roscoe had role-played what might work on cross-examination. Three things came to mind. One, Breeden had been drinking. Two, it was late. Three, it was dark outside.

But the distance from the sidewalk to the house's corner was only twenty feet and the streetlight was bright, not to mention the moon was visible that night, which gave off even more light. The witness's friends confirmed Breeden was not a heavy drinker, and he was sober when he left them to walk home. He was out late only because he had the next morning off.

Breeden was a recent Wake Forest business school graduate, with honors, having won the book award in his business ethics class with a perfect score. He worked for a reputable Charlotte consulting company, where he came in early and left late. He had excellent credit, no criminal record, and a reputation for being an honest guy.

And on top of all that, he'd recently taken an eye test to be a private pilot—to fly small planes to honor his father who died in the air force—and his eyes tested perfect, near and far.

"No questions, Your Honor."

Travail watched Professor Jeffrey Fortenberry, a supposed expert in rare gold coins and criminology and the last witness before the lunch break, take the witness stand.

The prosecutor had the professor share his credentials with the jury —which included several fancy degrees and practical experience in criminal law enforcement—and then asked him to examine the coins found on the victim. He pulled on gloves and examined several gold coins with a magnifying glass. It was a good show.

"These are replicas of coins manufactured at the Charlotte Mint in the 1830s."

"Are you saying they're forged to look authentic?"

"Yes, and whoever made them did excellent work."

"Does that concern you, sir?"

"It does." Professor Fortenberry scrunched his brow. "These coins could fool skilled collectors. Someone could sell these coins for twenty times their actual value to unsuspecting purchasers."

"So, they're valuable?"

"Yes, but only to a criminal."

Travail kept his powder dry and did not object.

"Professor Fortenberry, you've had experience assessing crime scenes, correct?"

"I have."

"You've consulted with police on the significance of items found at crime scenes, as they related to the crime, correct?"

"That's true."

"Were you in the courtroom when Detective Sizemore testified?"

"I was."

"Did you hear his testimony that the forged gold coins you just testified about were found under the defendant's sister's house, on the victim?"

"I did."

"Have you investigated the scene where the body and coins were found and familiarized yourself with the investigative files and exhibits in this case?"

"I have."

"Do you have an opinion based on your education and extensive experience and the evidence in this case about the significance of the coins and how they relate to the murder?"

"I do."

Travail stood. "We object, Your Honor. Speculation."

The judge addressed Ms. Fortuna. "Do you have evidence the forged coins belonged to defendant or to the victim, or that either of them possessed the coins on the night in question?"

"No, Your Honor, but Professor Fortenberry has an opinion, based on his experience, and his understanding of the facts and the type of people who possess such coins that—"

Judge Williamson held up her hand and turned to Travail. "What do you have to say?"

The jurors were paying close attention, and Travail took advantage.

"Your Honor, the professor is no more an expert on the facts in this case than the jury. And it matters not the kind of people who might possess those coins, because there is nothing unlawful about possessing them. They're not meant as currency. They're nothing more than souvenirs. The professor will only be guessing as to how the coins ended up under the house, and if he wants to say they have something to do with the murder, that's a guess too."

Fortuna snapped back. "Your Honor, the professor's opinion will fit the evidence in the case. Particularly, the statement in defendant's handwritten note found at the house." She looked at a copy of the exhibit. "The note specifically says, *Meeting. 1:30 a.m. Chance wants the coins. He can die trying.*'"

Travail, with an eye to swaying the jury back to his side, said to the judge, "That's fine, but where is the prosecution's evidence that the coins under the house are the coins referred to in the note? And for that matter, how did they get under the house? Who knows? Maybe the person who stuck the knife in Landry's back put them under the house in an attempt to frame my client."

The audience murmured, and the jurors sat up.

Fortuna's face turned red. "I object to Mr. Travail testifying, Your Honor."

The judge held up both hands. "Stop, everyone." She had the bailiff remove the jurors from the courtroom, explaining to them, "We have to take up this evidence issue."

When they were out of the room, Judge Williamson addressed Fortuna. "Do you know how the coins got under the house?"

"Not with certainty, Your Honor, but—"

Judge Williamson held up the palm of her hand. "Evidence, Ms. Fortuna, the beyond-a-reasonable-doubt kind."

Fortuna hesitated, then shook her head.

"Do you know who owned the coins?"

"No, Your Honor."

Roscoe whispered to Travail, and Travail looked at Sterling Standish in the first row behind the prosecutor and then at the judge. "Your Honor, perhaps the prosecution would like to call Sterling Standish, Junior's son, to testify about the coins, and then I can cross-examine him about his interest in this case. He's sitting right there." Travail pointed.

The judge clicked her ballpoint pen. "Ms. Fortuna?"

The prosecutor spoke with Sterling, but he shook his head.

"We won't be calling Sterling Standish to address this issue."

Judge Williamson looked frustrated. "So, Ms. Fortuna, you have nobody to testify about facts relating to the coins, only a professor to offer his opinion?"

"That's true, Your Honor, but—"

The judge held up her palm and stopped Fortuna from saying more while Travail and Roscoe whispered to one another.

"Mr. Travail, do you or your co-counsel have something to add?"

Travail stood. "Your Honor, I believe it would help us resolve this evidentiary issue if I am allowed to *voir dire* the witness outside the presence of the jury."

"Proceed."

Professor Fortenberry, who still sat in the witness chair, waited for Travail to ask his questions.

"Professor, you said the forged coins were valuable, but only to a criminal."

"Yes."

"And, of course, you're aware of the note saying Chance Landry wanted the coins?"

"I am."

"Are you prepared to back up your earlier statement by confirming to the jury that since Chance Landry wanted these coins, he was the criminal?"

"Ummm. That wasn't exactly what the prosecution asked me to do."

"I can see why. Am I correct that you were going to suggest that my client possessed criminal intent with respect to the coins, maybe even killed Landry over the coins?"

"Well, they were in his sister's house, and they caught him there."

"Aren't you getting a little beyond your area of expertise, Professor? The fact is, you have no idea how the coins got under the house, do you?"

"No."

"And you don't know who they belonged to or what the person who owned them was going to do with them?"

"No."

"Enough." Judge Williamson got the bailiff's attention. "Bring in the jury."

When they were back in their seats, the judge ruled.

"Members of the jury, the court will not allow this witness to speculate about how the coins in question got under the house, or who owned them, because he doesn't know, and you are not to infer any criminal conduct because of the coins."

When the judge finished, Travail asked for one more thing. "Your Honor, we move to strike Professor Fortenberry's entire testimony."

"Grounds?"

"Relevance. The coins make for good headlines, but Chance Landry did not choke on forged gold coins. His entire testimony was a sideshow, or to be more precise, *hogwash*."

Fortuna objected to Travail's use of the word *hogwash*. That suited him fine. The more the word was mentioned in front of the jury the better.

Judge Williamson touched her chin with her ballpoint pen and smiled. "I don't recall studying the hogwash motion to strike in law school, Mr. Travail."

Travail smiled back. He didn't tell her it was a motion he learned from esteemed English barrister Chuck Yeager Alexander.

Judge Williamson turned to the jury. "Members of the jury, I will not tell you to disregard the professor's testimony as *hogwash*, because *hogwash* is not a legal term. But I will tell you to disregard it, because none of it is competent evidence in this murder case. Defendant's motion to strike the entire testimony is allowed."

Hogwash was a simple word, really. Easy for the jurors to remember.

Perhaps when the jurors thought of Professor Fortenberry's testimony on their lunch break, they would think *hogwash* and wash their hands of him and the gold coins.

CHAPTER 27

DIRT MAN WITNESS

Dan Barnard returned to the courtroom after the lunch break and took his seat in the gallery knowing he was the next witness the prosecution planned to call. There was no need to rush to the front. This experience would not be pleasant.

Judge Williamson fixed her eyes on the prosecutor. "Call your next witness."

Fortuna looked at the audience. "Dan Barnard. Come forward."

Dan took the oath and answered the preliminary questions about his name, background, credentials, and employment history for the jury. Next, the prosecutor took him back to a time he would have liked to forget.

"When did you first meet Chance Landry?"

"I represented a client in South End who sold their underground land rights to South End Environmental. Landry was the environmental company's representative."

"This was around twenty years ago?"

"Thereabouts."

Fortuna guided Dan through several questions about the client he represented, the property they sold in South End, and Joey's involvement in the appraisal. She did not ask him about Junior Standish, and

Dan did not volunteer Junior's name or role because Sterling had made it clear to him that Dan must not tarnish the family name. "Stick to the story, or else."

Dan caught Harriet's stare. No doubt she hoped he would share what he knew to save Joey. Unfortunately, he would disappoint her.

Travail was occupied with his notes and didn't look up at Dan. Roscoe studied Dan, but Joey's expression toward Dan was blank, probably because Joey knew what Dan knew and understood if Dan shared what happened to Chance, his words would only make Joey look more guilty. Dan felt sorry for Joey, but Dan couldn't help him. He had his daughter to think about.

"Did you report the defendant to the appraisal board?"

"Landry and I did, yes."

"Why?"

He followed the script. "The appraisal Joey prepared on my client's property was fraudulent."

"Did the appraisal board suspend his appraisal license?"

"They did."

"How did that make you feel?"

"Objection." Travail was on his feet. "The witness's feelings are irrelevant."

Dan didn't agree. He'd felt guilty for the last twenty years about how Chance deceived him and how Chance took advantage of Joey. And now, both he and Joey were paying the price again for their association with Landry, but in different ways. Most likely, Joey would go back to prison for a crime he didn't commit. And Dan's conscience would never let him rest.

Judge Williamson sustained the objection, and Dan kept his mouth shut.

"Did you and Landry cooperate with the authorities?"

"We did."

"You testified at Joey's fraud trial?"

"Yes."

In Dan's witness preparation, the prosecutor had used the word *corroboration*. Dan looked the word up. Now seemed like a good time to use it. "Landry testified about the fake contracts and how Joey used them to create the fraudulent appraisals. I simply corroborated Landry's testimony as it related to the actual value of my client's property."

"Did the jury convict the defendant?"

"Yes."

"And the court sentenced him to twenty years in prison?"

"Yes."

"That's all we have, Your Honor. Mr. Barnard's testimony establishes defendant's motive for Chance Landry's murder."

Travail had hoped Dan would help Joey, but he didn't. He turned his head to observe Elkin, Sterling, and Bailey, their actual opponents. They occupied first row spectator seats behind Fortuna. His gut told him that Dan was worried about what they might do to him if he testified to what really happened, what he'd written in his notebook gift to Harriet.

If Travail tried to cross-examine Dan about what was in his notebook, Dan might push back and solidify the case against Joey. He had to use another tactic, one that didn't impugn Dan's credibility, in case he ever decided to help Joey.

"Mr. Barnard, if Chance Landry's prior testimony against Joey is the motive for his murder, why are you here?"

"I don't follow."

"Both Chance Landry and you testified against Joey, correct?" Travail emphasized the words *and you.*

"Uh huh."

The court reporter spoke to Dan. "Please say yes or no."

"Yes."

Travail paused. He wanted to be sure the jury got the point. "Since you and Landry both testified against Joey, is it fair to say Joey would have the same motive to murder you as he did Landry?"

"If you put it that way, I suppose that's true."

"And yet, here you are, alive and well." Travail's sing-song cadence punctuated the words *here you are, alive and well*.

Liza Fortuna was on her feet. "I object, Your Honor. Just because the defendant didn't kill Dan Barnard doesn't mean he didn't kill Chance Landry."

Travail's response was quick and clever, an effort to create reasonable doubt. "Your Honor, what Ms. Fortuna says is her prosecutorial bias. A more logical conclusion is that if Joey sought revenge on those who testified against him, he would have targeted Dan Barnard first, the person who initially accused him of fraud. And yet, here Mr. Barnard is, very much alive."

Judge Williamson ordered the lawyers to the bench and put her hand over the microphone, but her voice carried. Likely, the jury heard her admonish the lawyers to "save your jury arguments for later." During her tirade, the clerk handed the judge a note. She read it and shooed the lawyers away. "Back to your seats."

"Members of the jury, we're going to break early today. I have an emergency matter in another case that requires my attention. We will pick up with Mr. Barnard's testimony in the morning. In the meantime, don't discuss the case with anyone, and don't read or watch any news about the trial."

Harriet decided it was time she had a one-on-one with Dan.

He'd left the courtroom in a hurry and was not in the hallway. She took the steps at a brisk pace. When she walked out the courthouse's front entrance, she caught sight of the back side of Dan's gray-and-blue-plaid sport coat and navy slacks. He stood at the intersection on the courthouse corner, waiting for the pedestrian walk symbol to flash. She stepped beside him.

"We need to chat, Dan."

Dan kept his head down as they crossed the street. Elkin, Sterling, and Bailey looked at them from the opposite corner.

They followed the sidewalk to the next light, turned left, and found a bench on the old courthouse's front lawn. Harriet dispensed with pleasantries.

"Why did you lie about Joey committing appraisal fraud?"

"I didn't lie. The prosecutor asked me what I testified to in the past."

"Why didn't you say you knew Landry set Joey up with the fake contracts?"

"How would that have helped? If I did that, the jury would conclude Joey had a perfectly logical reason to kill Landry."

They sat with their thoughts for a few minutes and watched vehicles carry people to and from shiny uptown office towers. Dan spoke first.

"I wanted out from the Standish Company when Sterling took over, but I needed money to support my daughter's medical rehabilitation expenses, so I continued to do odd jobs for the company. Things I am not proud of." His voice was low and his tone was apologetic.

Harriet put her hand on Dan's back. "You can make this right."

"You don't know who we're dealing with."

"I think I do."

Harriet kept her hand on Dan's back, realizing his daughter's future, not his own safety, was the key to whether he would help Joey.

She kept her voice soft, but reassuring. "If the worst happens to you for saving my brother's life—and I pray nothing bad will happen to you—I will be sure to help with your daughter's expenses."

Dan blinked. "You promise?"

Harriet nodded. "Yes. I do. I give you my word."

Dan sat for a few minutes without speaking, before sitting up straight, like he was ready to take on a laborious task.

"Where do you want me to start?"

"At the beginning."

Dan talked without interruption.

He confirmed Roscoe's suspicions at Joey's trial twenty years ago and added flesh to the factual bones in the notebook he'd given to Harriet.

"Landry was greedy. He insisted that a clause in his agreement with

Junior provide the more he saved Junior on the land prices, the more commission Junior paid him.

"Landry admitted to me, when he was drunk one night, that he fabricated the fake contracts. It was Landry's way to create low appraisals that led to low sales prices and higher commissions, and he set Joey up to take the fall if something went wrong. He said it was bad luck I came along with my client's complaint about Joey's appraisal."

Dan turned next to what happened the night Junior died.

"After Joey's conviction, Junior called a meeting at his house with Landry and me to discuss the next steps in South End's development. It was one of two nights I will never forget."

Dan closed his eyes, as if he were watching the twenty-year-old events in his head. He took a deep breath, opened his eyes, and described what happened that night.

The problems started when Penny pushed through Junior's front door and yelled for Junior, who pushed Landry and Dan into the next room so Penny wouldn't see them. Still, Landry and Dan were able to hear every word of the argument between Penny and Junior.

Penny shouted at Junior. "You betrayed me. Joey was innocent."

Junior kept his voice steady. "Calm down, Penny. The prosecutor made me testify. Served me with a subpoena. I didn't want Joey to go to prison."

"You are my partner. We had plans. Now, you've ruined everything."

"We still have plans, Penny. We can still develop South End like we dreamed. And we can use the gold coins we've collected to promote the gold mining museum."

Penny wailed at Junior. "Fire Chance. He's why Joey is going to prison."

Landry opened the door and stepped into the study, holding a knife. Dan followed, but kept his distance from Landry.

"You want Junior to fire me, Penny? Make your case. And I'll make mine for why it will never happen."

Penny stepped toward Landry and didn't flinch at his knife. "You knew Joey was innocent. And you lied to the court about it." Penny's eyes were wide.

"Is that true?" Junior asked Landry.

"Yes, but you won't fire me."

"And why is that?"

"Your rare coin collection. Get the coins, and I will explain."

Junior went to his safe in the next room and returned with a canvas tote bag that jingled when he carried it. He pushed aside a row of books on a coffee table held up by two brick-like bookends and placed the bag in their place, causing one bookend to fall to the floor.

Landry pointed at the tote bag with his knife. "Let Penny look inside. He's the expert."

Penny pulled two coins from the bag and examined them. His mouth fell open. "Are they all like this?"

Landry sneered. "Every single one."

Penny tossed the two coins to Junior. "They're forged."

Junior caught one coin. The other coin hit the floor. His face was flushed and his voice raised when he addressed Landry. "You were supposed to buy legitimate rare gold coins. What happened to the millions of dollars I gave you to build my collection?

"I used some of the money to pay a forger to create those coins, and I spent the rest. It's why I'm here tonight. I need more money. I plan to use those coins to get it."

Junior addressed Dan and his voice was sharp. "Did you know about this, Dan?"

Landry laughed. "Dan wasn't smart enough to know about the forged coins." Landry pointed at the tote bag. "You can hand those over, Junior."

Junior handed the tote bag to Penny instead. "Take these." Then to Landry: "I'm curious. Why do you think these coins will prevent me from firing you?"

Landry had an ugly look on his face. "If you fire me, Junior, I will tell the district attorney about your plan to sell forged rare coins to unsuspecting collectors."

Junior's body tensed up. "I never had such a plan."

Landry pointed at the canvas tote bag Penny held. "That's Exhibit A."

Penny dropped the coin bag. With his face contorted and spittle flying from his mouth, he launched himself at Landry. The knife fell free as Penny and Landry tumbled to the floor.

Dan picked up the knife and stepped back as Landry rolled Penny over, grabbed his head, and banged it on the floor again and again. It looked like the end for Penny, until Junior made a flying tackle and knocked Landry off him.

Junior struggled with Chance, but Landry was stronger. He picked up the heavy bookend that had fallen to the floor and smashed Junior in the head until Junior stopped moving.

Dan paused in telling the story. His body shook and Harriet put her hand on his shoulder again to calm him. "Take your time, Dan."

He turned to Harriet. "I was shaking then like I am now. I didn't know if Chance would go for me or Penny next? I picked up Junior's coin bag, put it in Penny's hands, and pushed Penny to the door. I told him to get out, that I'd deal with Landry.

"I still held the knife, but Chance held the cards. 'You're tied to me now,' he said. 'If I go down, I will make sure you go down too.'"

Dan hung his head. "I'm not proud of it, Harriet, but I capitulated. Within five minutes, we had our story straight: Penny killed Junior in a rage and stole Junior's coins. Your father must have hidden them in his kitchen floor. Chance came back for them twenty years later after Joey got out of prison. Junior's coins killed Chance. They could be why Joey goes back to prison."

Dan looked drained from the effort it took him to relive that night. Harriet almost felt sorry for him—almost. Knowing for sure her father didn't kill Junior and knowing the truth of it had been concealed was too much to absorb. And at the moment, too much to forgive.

A horn honked, and a truck pulled to a stop. It was Yeager. "Y'all need a ride?"

Harriet waved him on. "I'll catch a ride with Dan." She felt oddly tied to him now. And she felt that Dan might now be amenable to helping Joey. Turning to him, she said, "Let me buy you an early dinner."

After a short walk, they entered double doors under the "Eats" sign at Mert's Heart and Soul, a family-owned restaurant that served delicious Low Country dishes. A hostess led them across a tile floor with a variety of colored checkerboard squares to a table with a red tablecloth. Terracotta orange walls served as the backdrop for framed Broadway show posters, local celebrity photos, and sketches of African American singers like Ray Charles and James Brown. A stainless-steel counter and kitchen were open to view from the dining area.

Harriet perused the menu. "I recommend the soul rolls, the fried green tomatoes, and the smoky BBQ beef ribs. If you're a chicken wing man, I suggest the jumbo chicken wings served with two sides and cornbread. The gumbos are tasty. If fish is your favorite, they have catfish and whiting, both fried, of course. Actually, I can't think of a menu item I wouldn't order, but I am going to start with the okra soup."

After they placed their orders, Harriet returned to the past. "You said the night Junior died was one of two nights you will never forget. What was the other night?"

"The night Landry died."

"Tell me what happened."

Dan lowered his head. "There is a reason I can't do that."

Harriet tried another approach. "I am going to say a name. Say 'hot' if they had a motive to kill Landry and 'cold' if they didn't. Let's start with Sterling Standish."

"Hot."

"Bailey Standish?"

"Hot."

"Robert Elkin?"

"Hot."

"You?"

"Hot. I hated the guy. Chance threatened to lie about my work with him for the Standish Company if I ever turned him in."

"But you didn't kill him?"

"Didn't have to."

"What about Joey? Hot or cold?"

"Hot. The jury thinks so too. But he didn't do it. I told you that already."

The server placed Harriet's homemade Low Country okra soup before her, along with a chopped BBQ sandwich. Before Dan, she placed the chicken wing dinner with sides of red beans, okra, and tomatoes. She put the hot, moist cornbread on the table between them.

As they ate, Harriet tried to narrow the suspects. She asked about Sterling's, Bailey's, and Elkin's motives. Dan complied with answers between bites. She made mental notes so she could brief Craig and Roscoe.

On their walk back to Dan's car, Dan asked Harriet to forgive him. "Tomorrow in court, I will do my best to clear Joey, short of identifying the killer."

You're a good person, Dan. Thank you."

Dan dropped Harriet at her cottage and said he'd see her in court in the morning.

Harriet never saw him again.

CHAPTER 28

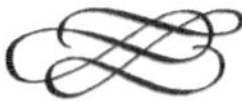

DIRT MAN DOWN

Travail's Thursday morning preparation in the courtroom felt hopeful, thanks to what Dan told Harriet last night and his willingness to cooperate today.

Sitting at defense counsel table, Travail reviewed his list of questions one last time and made notes in Dan's notebook as he waited on court to begin. He didn't want to make a mistake with the factual gift Dan had given them. Dan's testimony might free Joey.

Joey was his usual positive self, and there was light in Harriet's eyes. Roscoe's cowboy boots had a swagger in their steps.

On the prosecution side of the courtroom, the vibe was urgent. Fortuna and her associate were deep in conversation, but her voice carried. "Barnard should have been here this morning for our prep meeting. Where is he?" Travail's antennae twitched. Something was up.

The bailiff swung his head as if it were on a swivel to catch sight of Judge Williamson coming in behind him and up to the bench. He called the court to order with flare.

The gallery quieted, but before the judge called for the bailiff to bring in the jury, the prosecutor stood. "May I address the court?"

"Do we have a problem, Ms. Fortuna?" Judge Williamson leaned forward.

Fortuna looked at the audience and back at the judge. "Dan Barnard, our final witness, is not here yet, Your Honor."

Judge Williamson had shown her proclivity for moving the trial forward, and she didn't pause now. "You better have him here in the next ten minutes, or we will move on. I am sure the defense won't mind, given what he said yesterday."

Travail stood, knowing what was at stake. "The defense will mind very much, Your Honor. We have no objection to a short recess for the prosecution to find their witness."

The judge did a double take at Travail's comment. "You planning some Perry Mason theater for us, Mr. Travail?"

Travail's heart beat fast, but he remained composed. "Your Honor, we just want our client to be able to exercise his constitutional right to cross-examine his accuser."

The judge sniffed. "So, no Perry Mason moment. Pity. You're just trying to set yourself up for an appeal if you can't cross-examine the witness."

She didn't give Travail a chance to respond before she got the bailiff's attention. "Inform the jury we have a thirty-minute delay." She pointed at both benches with her pen and said, "If he is not here by then, we will discuss striking his testimony from the record."

Detective Sizemore leaned over the rail separating the audience from the lawyers to hear what the prosecutor had to say to him. He nodded and left the courtroom, presumably to search for Dan Barnard.

The courtroom was at ease for thirty minutes. Travail's team fidgeted at the possibility Dan might not show up. Had he gotten cold feet? Surely he wouldn't skip town, given his daughter's needs. Traffic might have delayed him. Perhaps he experienced car trouble.

Judge Williamson returned in thirty minutes on the dot, ready to proceed. Detective Sizemore opened the courtroom door ten seconds later and walked with long, quick strides toward the prosecutor. Fortuna listened to what he had to say and drew back. "What?"

Judge Williamson must have heard her. "You have news, Ms. Fortuna?"

The prosecutor, who'd been nothing but forceful with her words to this point, stumbled. "We, uh, Your Honor, just now, Detective Sizemore, well, it seems, they found Mr. Barnard. But. He's dead."

Harriet gasped. Joey and Roscoe sat up straight. Travail couldn't believe it. Dan. Dead.

The only people in the room who didn't have a surprised look on their faces sat behind Fortuna. Neither Sterling nor Bailey looked like they regretted or mourned their lost employee. Their faces were tight, like someone puckering their sphincter muscles to deceive a polygraph test. Elkin thumbed items on his phone, seemingly indifferent to the breaking news.

Travail's hope for Joey evaporated from his body, leaving behind despair as the solid accumulation in his heart. They'd had a reasonable chance to set Joey free with Dan's testimony, and now he was dead.

The bad breaks in Joey's case kept getting worse, and now, Travail had lost access to the steering mechanism for Joey's defense.

Dan, a man who'd made mistakes but who had reformed and agreed to help Joey, had lost his life and left his daughter behind to deal with her serious disabilities without his help. The whole thing was a tragedy. There was too much death, and it needed to stop.

Travail sensed Harriet was about to unravel. Her head was down. He put his hand on her hand, but she didn't look up.

The judge kept her composure. "I am very sorry to hear that news. Did he die of a natural cause?"

Fortuna deferred to the detective, who spoke with confidence. "Dan Barnard did not die of a natural cause."

"How are you so confident, Detective?"

"Because of the bullet hole between his eyes, Your Honor."

The gallery exploded in excited conversation, and Judge Williamson banged her gavel to restore order. "Enough." When the room quieted, she aimed her gavel at the detective. "Was it suicide?"

"It was not suicide, Your Honor. The gun that killed Dan Barnard was nowhere to be found."

The judge looked at the defense team and said, "What do you want to do? And don't you dare use the word 'mistrial.'"

Roscoe, who'd handled many criminal trials, stood and took over for Travail, and Travail was glad to let him take the lead while he sat back and held Harriet's hand beneath the table.

"Judge Williamson, I don't see any way around a mistrial. Dan Barnard's testimony supplied the prosecution's evidence of motive, and the defendant cannot cross-examine the witness. A limiting instruction will not cause the jury to forget what the witness said."

The judge grumbled as she pointed her pen at Roscoe and clicked it.

"You served a long time on the bench, Roscoe, and you taught at judge's conferences. You know a mistrial is unnecessary if I give a limiting instruction to the jury and the prosecution offers another witness to provide their evidence for motive." She looked at the prosecutor. "Can you do that, Ms. Fortuna?"

Fortuna looked at the defense table before addressing the judge. "We can, Your Honor. We call Harriet Keaton as our next witness."

Travail sat forward while Roscoe pushed back. "She's not on their witness list."

Fortuna was quick. "We didn't know we'd need her. We withheld nothing."

Judge Williamson agreed. "Defense counsel will have thirty minutes to prep her."

Travail let go of Harriet's hand and stood. "But Ms. Keaton is our paralegal."

"Shouldn't take long to prep her, then. A witness is a witness, Mr. Travail."

Not this witness. Unlimited time would not be enough time to train Harriet on how to be a witness, even after she pulled herself together. She would be too intent on defending her brother. In fact, she'd probably lose her temper, or become too aggressive, like her sarcastic wordplay with Detective Sizemore the night they found Landry.

Harriet must have read his mind. When he sat, she straightened her spine, patted her hair, and whispered in his ear. "I can handle this, Craig."

Roscoe reasserted himself with the judge. "Your Honor, calling another witness does not remove Dan Barnard's testimony from the jurors' minds. You're only allowing the prosecution to corroborate his testimony with another witness, while denying the defense its constitutional right to cross-examine."

"Barnard is dead. What part of 'I have ruled' do you not understand, Roscoe?"

With Dan's death, they'd lost their best chance to turn the tables on the prosecution, and now, they risked a fiery Harriet on the stand. Travail wasn't sure how the jury would take to her. Something else bothered him more. Who killed Dan?

What Travail was about to say to the judge would draw a harsh response, but he felt in his bones, it had to be said.

"Your Honor, Dan Barnard's death is a tragic loss for his friends and loved ones, but it is also a loss for my client. Someone murdered him to prevent his testimony today."

The judge's eyes peered deep into Travail's. "Based on what facts?"

She picked up her pen and clicked it twice. "Facts are important in a courtroom, Mr. Travail. Maybe not in Congress or the executive branch where narcissistic political beings who lean far right or left want to bend the rules to accomplish their goal to make everyone into their image, but in this room, where we take our time to understand exactly what the facts are before we act, facts matter."

Travail tried to make his case. "After court yesterday, we learned Dan Barnard would testify that—"

Judge Williamson held up her hand. "Stop. What you were about to say is not evidence. Do you have any credible evidence someone murdered Barnard to prevent his testimony today?"

"Someone used the same execution method on both victims, right between the eyes. The person who killed Landry also killed Dan, and it wasn't Joey. He was in the county jail."

Fortuna responded in kind. "That is rank speculation, Your Honor.

It's just as likely the defendant hired an assassin who killed Barnard and made it appear like a copycat murder. As you recall, Barnard's testimony yesterday was devastating to the defendant."

Travail knew Joey didn't hire anyone to kill Dan because he had no reason to kill their best witness. Dan's testimony today would have created reasonable doubt, but based on the judge's directive, Travail couldn't share with the court what Dan would have said to the jury.

What Dan knew had gone to the grave with him. Now, with Dan's direct testimony lurking in the jurors' minds and the prosecutor ready to skewer Harriet, their job was more difficult than ever.

The judge denied the motion for mistrial. "However." Judge Williamson directed her attention to the detective. "How much do you know about Barnard's death?"

"Very little. Autopsy will be this week."

"Speed it up. Find out the bullet's caliber and whether it is the same caliber that killed Landry, along with anything else that connects the two murders."

Detective Sizemore left in a hurry.

Judge Williamson shuffled the papers on her desk, clicked her pen, and made a note on her pad. "Mr. Travail, in my experience, murder investigations take time. I do not plan to wait for the police to complete their investigation before we complete this trial."

Judge Williamson addressed the jurors when they were in their seats.

"I apologize for the delay this morning. We learned that Dan Barnard, the prosecution witness you heard from yesterday, is no longer available to testify. And now, the prosecution has decided to call Harriet Keaton, Mr. Travail's paralegal and the defendant's brother, as a witness. You are not to consider anything Mr. Barnard said in his testimony yesterday because he is not here today for the defense to ask him questions."

Part of Travail looked forward to seeing what Harriet did as a witness. He suspected she would be volatile, but he didn't think it would take less than ten seconds for Harriet to mouth off.

"You are the defendant's twin sister?"

"Yes."

"For how long?"

"Ever since we were born."

"I meant, how old are you?"

"You have a funny way of getting to the point."

Travail heard chuckles from a few jurors and gritted his teeth. *Be respectful, Harriet.*

Judge Williamson clicked her pen twice, lifted it in Harriet's direction, but addressed the prosecutor instead. "Ms. Fortuna, their age is not relevant." *Score one for Harriet.*

"Ms. Keaton, are you aware your brother performed appraisals on property in South End twenty years ago?"

"Yes."

"What do you know?"

"I know he worked for my father's appraisal company, and my dad gave him the assignment."

Fortuna pressed Harriet. "Anything else?"

Harriet puffed. "Yes. Someone other than my brother committed the crime of appraisal fraud, and the Standish family, who is feeding you information on this case, hopes to keep that fact a secret. They're sitting behind you. In the first row. But you know that."

Time stopped in the courtroom while everyone looked to where Harriet pointed. Only three people sat in the first row. Sterling and Bailey, whose mouths were open, and Elkin, who offered a respectful sneer.

Fortuna caught up with the moment. "Wait. Your Honor. Objection. Motion to strike."

"To what?" the judge asked.

"Speculation. Hearsay. Unfounded accusations."

Travail didn't move or say a word. Things were trending on a proper course without his need to step in.

Judge Williamson clicked her ballpoint pen. "Tell you what, Ms.

Fortuna. I will give you a wide latitude. You can ask this witness all the questions you want about how she knows the Standish family wants to keep it a secret who killed Landry."

Fortuna stumbled. "But?"

Travail suppressed a smile. If he were in Fortuna's shoes, deciding what to do would be difficult. She did not know what Harriet would say next, but if she didn't attack Harriet's credibility, the comments about the Standish family would hang over the prosecution's case like a not-guilty cloud. Harriet was correct she didn't need to go to law school to master the art of the trial. Nor did she need Travail to prepare her to testify.

Fortuna fumbled with her notes.

"Ms. Fortuna?" The judge tapped her pen on her bench.

Before Fortuna could answer the judge, two first-row subjects of Harriet's scorn—Sterling and Bailey—stood and peppered Fortuna with inaudible words, no doubt concerned about the Standish family's reputation.

Judge Williamson pounced on the disturbance. "Make your helpers behave, Ms. Fortuna. Get them in line or I will."

The prosecutor told Sterling and Bailey to sit. She turned to Harriet, and with her lips pursed, she went on the attack. "Ms. Keaton, you didn't see who did what with the appraisals, did you?"

"Ms. Fortuna, you didn't see who did what either. You were probably in middle school."

Fortuna looked rattled. "Just answer the question. Yes or no. You didn't see who did what with the appraisals twenty years ago, did you?"

"You don't want me to explain how Joey did not create the fake contracts, and how someone set him up, just like he is being set up for Landry's murder? If you don't want to ask me, ask the Standish family. They know what happened."

Fortuna yelled "objection" and "motion to strike" while Sterling yelled "bullshit" and Bailey yelled "bitch."

The gallery went from murmur to full-on uproar. Jurors leaned forward, gaped at the maelstrom, and spoke among themselves.

Judge Williamson banged her gavel six times to restore order. "Clear the courtroom, bailiff, except for the parties, their legal teams, and those three." She pointed her pen to the first row behind Liza Fortuna.

After the bailiff had cleared the courtroom, the judge walked from behind the bench and stood before and between the two counsel tables. "I don't know who to hold in contempt first. Should I start with you, Ms. Fortuna, for asking the stupid question that led to this riot? Or maybe I should start with Ms. Keaton, who lit the match, tossed it on the fire, and added gasoline. Perhaps those two—" She pointed at Sterling and Bailey. "—for interrupting court and using profanity." Nobody responded to the rhetorical lecture.

Judge Williamson paced back and forth, and her clicking ballpoint pen matched her steps. "Ms. Fortuna, I do not know what you hoped to gain by calling Ms. Keaton as a witness. Perhaps you thought you could embarrass her and cast a shadow on the defense. Whatever your reason, you clearly underestimated your witness."

Travail glanced at Harriet, who didn't seem bothered by the Pandora's box she'd opened. She had taken a tremendous risk, which could have backfired and sunk the case. If Fortuna had asked Harriet to identify the person responsible for the appraisal fraud and she had identified Landry, Joey's motive for killing Landry—the criminal who set him up—was a lock.

But Harriet was clever. She knew Fortuna would be hesitant to ask that question. And she layered in a hint about the Standish family's role in what happened to Joey twenty years ago, and what was happening to him right now. Those were not admissible facts, but the scene would be hard for the jury to forget.

"Here's my ruling. Flagrant fouls on all sides. Off-setting penalties. Replay the down." Judge Williamson walked to within Liza Fortuna's discomfort zone. "You need to decide if you are going to continue to examine Ms. Keaton or whether you will introduce evidence of defendant's motive some other way."

With the jury back in place and the courtroom duly chastised by the judge to remain quiet, Fortuna made her next move. "We excuse Ms. Keaton as a witness."

"As you wish," the judge said.

Harriet, who had returned to the witness chair before the jury came back, came down and looked at the jury. More than a few smiled at her.

The prosecutor asked the court to take judicial notice of an exhibit, a certified copy of Landry's trial testimony at Joey's fraud trial, along with another exhibit, the jury's guilty verdict and the court's twenty-year sentence for appraisal fraud. The judge accepted the evidence into the record and the prosecution rested.

Travail liked the timing for when the prosecution finished its case, with Harriet having the last word. What started this morning as hope had shifted 180 degrees to despair, and now, the needle had moved back toward hope. Not all the way back, but in the right direction.

Now what?

It was the defense team's turn to present evidence. And they'd lost their best witness to a bullet in his forehead.

CHAPTER 29

THE VERDICT

Travail had to decide whether to call Joey as a witness in his own defense. He imagined how Joey's cross-examination would unfold if he did.

"You say you were there when Landry died?"

"Yes."

"But you didn't kill him?

"No."

"Someone else did."

"That's right."

"Their name?"

"I can't tell you."

"How convenient."

Added to that was the problem of the eyewitness who saw Joey crawl out from under Harriet's basement. Joey said the witness got it wrong. "It's not what it looks like," he'd said, although he didn't deny the witness saw him. Travail could foresee how Joey would make that evidence worse when the prosecution questioned him.

"Do you remember Chad Breeden's testimony?"

"I do."

"He said he saw you crawl out of the basement, where they found the victim."

"It's not what it looks like."

"Did you put Landry under your sister's house?"

"No."

"Because, actually, that's what it looks like."

"I know."

"If you didn't put him there, who did?

"I can't tell you."

"Was it the same person who killed him?"

"No."

"But you won't tell us who it was."

"You wouldn't believe me if I did."

Travail could envision the prosecutor's closing argument: "Ladies and gentlemen of the jury, the defendant expects you to believe—expects you to be so gullible to accept that—he did not kill Landry because someone else did, even though he won't tell you the killer's name."

The prosecutor might build her momentum like this: "The defendant also expects you to believe that him crawling out from under the house where they found Landry's corpse is not what it looks like, even though that is exactly what it looks like. He claims he didn't put Landry there, that someone else did, and he says we wouldn't believe him if he told us who did. The fact is, if the defendant admitted to the truth, we would believe him, because he was at the murder scene, where he killed Landry, and he was under the house, where he hid Landry."

The prosecutor might stick her landing like this: "When a defendant tells you something is not what it looks like despite the simplest explanation—like the evidence right before your eyes—the simplest explanation is always the correct one. He is guilty."

Travail couldn't risk that kind of closing argument or the cross-examination of Joey to make it possible. There were too many unanswered questions. Why was Joey at the murder scene? What was Joey doing under the house? Who was Joey protecting? And why?

When Travail and Roscoe asked Joey these questions, Joey resisted, forcing Travail and Roscoe to accept the fact Joey's testimony would sink him. What to do instead?

Travail and Roscoe were ready to move on to other options, but Harriet was not. The anteroom where they met with Joey to discuss strategy was a tight fit. Both the space and their choices boxed them in.

Harriet expressed her ire toward Joey in her rigid posture and in her words. "Joey, we're busting our butts to help you, and you won't help yourself. Why?"

"It's complicated."

Travail felt compassion for Joey, but also for Harriet. This case hadn't helped repair their twenty-year rift. It only made it deeper by the day. The more Joey refused to assist in his defense, the more agitated Harriet became.

"You owe me an explanation, Joey. I am your twin sister. You need to open up." She inched close to his face. "Tell me why you won't save yourself."

Joey looked sympathetic but resolute. Finally, he explained why. "To protect you."

"I don't understand."

"They said they'd kill you if I talked."

Harriet's eyes widened.

Joey dipped his head and wiped his eyes. Harriet hugged him tight, while Travail and Roscoe waited.

When Joey lifted his head, Harriet kept a firm grip on his shoulders. "You don't have to protect me, Joey. We are a team."

Joey looked to Travail, as if for guidance.

Travail's guidance came in the form of a question. "Who threatened to kill Harriet?"

"I didn't recognize his voice. It was muffled, like the phone's speaker was covered with something."

"When did he call?"

"Between the time Landry died and the time the police showed up that morning. He said if I revealed who killed Landry, he would kill Harriet."

Harriet seemed to like what she'd heard. "We can use this, Craig. Get the phone records, use them as evidence, and have Joey explain the phone call."

"Phone records will show only that a call took place, probably from a burner phone. Anyone could have made the call. I don't think it will help Joey's defense."

"But?"

Roscoe agreed with Travail. "If Joey can't identify the mystery caller, the story will sound so made-up that Joey becomes not just a liar, but a terrible liar. From there, it's easy for the jury to find their way to a guilty verdict."

Joey had regained his composure. "Doesn't matter who called. I won't risk your safety, Harriet."

Harriet turned her feelings on the lawyers. "This is absurd. Joey went to prison for a crime he didn't commit to protect my father. And now he could go to jail for life to protect me. You need to do something, Craig." She toppled her chair and slammed the door on her way out.

The stakes had risen. Besides Joey's freedom, Harriet might never forgive Travail if he botched Joey's case, and for all the gold in town, he wasn't sure what to do.

Joey looked at Travail. "What are our options?"

"We need to decide if we are going to call witnesses. If we don't, we get the last argument to the jury. If we do, we need to be sure our witnesses will help your case."

"Do you have any witnesses in mind?"

"We have a suspect list based on what Dan told Harriet."

"Who?"

"No surprises here. We have Sterling, Bailey, and Elkin."

"Their motives?"

Travail turned to his notes and started first with Sterling. "According to Dan, Landry blackmailed Sterling a few days before he died. Five million dollars was his price to keep quiet about the Standish Company's role in securing the underground property rights. If he talked, he could endanger the success of the Standish Company's projects in South End and ruin the company's and Junior Standish's reputations. This was an excellent motive for Sterling to murder Landry, because, as the saying goes, a dead man tells no tales.

"Something else about Sterling," Travail said to Joey. "You knew the truth about the fraudulent appraisals, and you were out of prison. That was a threat to Sterling. It might explain why Landry's body ended up under Harriet's house when you were there. Sterling could frame you for the crime. Two birds. One motive."

Travail explained how Bailey had a similar motive to murder Landry.

"The day before Landry died, Bailey confronted Dan about a conversation she overheard between Landry and Dan, where Landry told Dan about his blackmail conversation with Sterling. Dan confirmed the blackmail scheme to Bailey but swore to her he was not involved. Although she loved her husband, she loved his money more. If Landry was dead, he could not pressure Sterling to part with the company's money."

Looking at his notes, Travail explained how Elkin's motive was twofold.

"Elkin was Sterling's fixer. If Sterling wanted something done, Elkin did it. Number one, Sterling told Elkin he wanted the blackmail problem with Landry to go away, and he didn't care to know the details. Number two, Elkin wanted revenge against the Indie and told Sterling how fortuitous it was they had just released Harriet's brother from prison. It was Elkin's idea to dump Landry's body under Harriet's house."

Travail set his notes on the table. "Dan told Harriet he was 100-percent sure about the accuracy of these facts."

Joey took a deep breath after listening to Travail's report. "Can I borrow your phone, Craig?" Joey reached out his hand. "I need to call her, get things settled."

Travail handed over his phone, and he and Roscoe went into the hallway. A sheriff's deputy stood guard outside the door.

A few minutes later, Joey opened the door and waved Travail and

Roscoe back into the room. Travail hoped Joey had reached Harriet and helped her calm down. "All good?"

"Time will tell."

The bailiff knocked and stuck his head in the door. "Court will resume in five minutes. The judge says to be ready to call your first witness."

It was decision time. They had Sterling, Bailey, and Elkin under subpoena, and Travail had his questions ready, but everything Travail had against them was based on a dead witness.

Sterling, Bailey, and Elkin could deny any pointed allegations, and when the prosecutor demanded the defense put up or shut up regarding Travail's "scandalous and speculative allegations" against the witnesses, the levy might crack and Dan would not be coming back from the grave to plug the hole. Still, Travail had to do something, make some effort to defend Joey, even if it was just a Hail Mary pass. "Let me take a run at them. Someone might break."

Joey turned to Roscoe for a second opinion.

"How many gotchas have you seen in all your years as a judge, Roscoe, where the witness confessed to the crime during a blistering cross-examination by the defendant's lawyer? Tom Cruise got Jack Nicholson to 'handle the truth' in the movies, but that was fiction. What's the chance Travail can get Sterling, Bailey, or Elkin to cop to the crime?"

Roscoe took out his chewing tobacco pouch and laid it on the table. "No offense to Craig—he's a talented lawyer—but he has about as much chance of doing that as I have of getting Judge Williamson to let me chew this in court."

Joey placed his hands on the table. "It's settled then. We don't call any witnesses. We take the last argument to the jury, and you create reasonable doubt. That's my verdict."

They returned to the courtroom to find Harriet in her seat. Travail leaned in and gave her a half hug. "How are you doing?"

She shrugged.

"I am glad Joey spoke with you after you left us."

Harriet jerked her head. "What are you talking about?"

Before Travail could explain, the bailiff put the court back in session while Judge Williamson strode to the bench. Travail looked at the outgoing calls on his phone. He didn't recognize the number Joey had called.

"Mr. Travail," the judge said, "are you making a phone call?"

"Just silencing my phone, Your Honor." He clicked the phone to the off position and set it in his briefcase.

Roscoe stood. "Your Honor, defense moves for acquittal at the close of the prosecution's case."

The judge clicked her ballpoint pen. "How many motions like that did you ever grant as a judge, Roscoe? Never mind, doesn't matter. Motion denied."

Roscoe sat.

"Mr. Travail, you may call your first witness."

"Your Honor, the defense does not intend to call any witnesses."

There was a murmur in the courtroom, but Judge Williamson stifled it with her gavel. The judge looked at the clock.

Roscoe popped up again. "Now that the evidence is in, we renew our motion for acquittal."

"And I renew my denial. We will excuse the jury until tomorrow. The charge conference to review jury instructions will be this afternoon at three in my chambers. Arguments start at nine in the morning. One hour for each side. Then the jury will decide."

The schedule worried Travail. No juror wanted to ruin their weekend with unfinished business. They might have a verdict before the end of the day on Friday.

Harriet left the courtroom without another word with Travail.

Yeager walked up and asked if Travail needed anything.

"Yes. Check on Harriet. She's mad at me for not defending her brother the way she thinks I should."

CHAPTER 30

THE REAL VERDICT

Liza Fortuna began her Friday morning closing argument like a person who wanted more than anything else in her life to be the top dog in the district attorney's office. From the time she was a little girl.

She raised and lowered her voice to make herself heard as she pushed one bad Joey fact after another on the jury, while pulling the jurors closer and closer with every bit of emotion she could pour into her closing argument. A nauseating performance for anyone pulling for Joey.

Fortuna made it sound like failing to render a guilty verdict would be the worst miscarriage of justice since they crucified Jesus Christ. Joey was the worst recidivist—ten times worse than any criminal ever to sully the halls of the Mecklenburg County Courthouse.

Fortuna paced back and forth before the jury. Pointing at Joey, she hammered home his precise whereabouts on the night in question—the text messages that put him with Landry, and the witness testimony that put him under the house where they found Landry—what she called evidence of the defendant's opportunity to kill Landry and dispose of him.

She picked up what she called her best exhibit—Joey's handwritten note found in Harriet's house—held it up for the jury to see again, and read the words aloud: *Meeting. 1:30 a.m. Chance wants the coins. He can die trying.*

The handwritten note, she said, was solid evidence of Joey's premeditation to meet with Landry and do what needed to be done when Landry demanded the coins—kill him.

"After the deed was done—after Joey killed Landry—he hid the victim under his sister's house until he could move him somewhere else."

Fortuna spewed disdain for the defense's weak effort to refute her rock-solid case, and she pushed the motive for the crime down the jurors' throats.

"Think about it. Landry is the reason Joey Penman spent twenty years in prison. Is there any better motive for murder than revenge?"

Fortuna paused.

"Joey Penman breathed betrayal for twenty long years. And when, at long last, he had his chance, he exhaled revenge."

The one thing Liza Fortuna didn't mention was the jailhouse snitch. There was no need. Her argument lined up perfectly without him. To a T.

Travail intended to use a more deliberate approach to his closing argument. Reason over passion, which was what he would need to try with Harriet to get in her good graces again.

Since he'd told Harriet about the team's decision not to call witnesses, she placed the blame for that decision on Travail as lead counsel and made him *persona non grata*.

Whatever emotional connection Travail and Harriet had made in the last four months came to a halt. She ghosted him when he tried to text her. This morning, she didn't say hello. Instead, she punched down.

"How could you back down from a fight, Craig? It's not like you to give up. You could have destroyed Sterling, Bailey, and Elkin." She was thinking with her heart and not her head, and at the moment, her heart was with Joey, not him.

As he readied himself to speak for Joey, Travail was in second-guess mode. Maybe he was wrong not to call Sterling, Bailey, and Elkin as adverse witnesses. Joey didn't think so, but he was a client, not a lawyer. Roscoe didn't think so, but Roscoe had been a judge for too long.

A trial lawyer had to take chances in court to win tough cases. He hadn't taken a chance, and it pained him to think he might have been wrong, that Harriet might lose her brother again, and that he might lose Harriet.

Reasonable doubt was the goal. That was his focus.

Travail reminded himself to be himself. Not to get too high. Or too low. Not to be someone he wasn't. He walked to the middle of the courtroom and faced the jury.

"Members of the jury, thank you for your attention this week. Joey Penman's life is on the line. He is seventy years old. If you convict him of murder, he will die in prison. That's why you need to be sure of your verdict—sure of the truth of what really happened—beyond a reasonable doubt."

Travail explained the burden of proof was on the state, not the defendant, to prove guilt beyond a reasonable doubt.

"The Constitution says my client does not have to present evidence. He does not have to prove his innocence. And he does not have to risk his freedom by taking on a skilled cross-examiner who will twist his words and make him look guilty when he's not."

Travail paused.

"Think of the bullseye on the dartboard as the spot the prosecutor aims for when she presents her case. She must land her dart very close to the bullseye to prove her case beyond a reasonable doubt. My client doesn't have to play darts with the prosecutor. He prevails when the prosecutor misses."

Travail paused again.

"There is an undebatable fact you know to be true. The government does not bat 100-percent in law enforcement. They are known to get things wrong from time to time."

Several jurors nodded.

Travail glanced at Fortuna. "Sometimes, the government can become like a dog with a bone, frothing at the mouth to gobble a win. And while there is nothing wrong with passion for your case, it's not up to the defendant to snatch the government's bone out of their mouth and explain why the bone is not real and why, instead, the bone is a cheap, plastic knockoff."

Travail paused again. "But that's what I plan to do."

Travail glanced at Harriet. Her sour expression hadn't changed from the one she had on her face when she'd chastised him this morning.

Yeager, who sat in the gallery's first row, gave Travail several head nods, letting him know he had a cheerleader.

Roscoe was attentive to the speech, but probably bored with the lead-up. He'd heard many defense counsel arguments about the burden of proof resting with the prosecution.

Joey looked on, but it was hard to tell where he was focused, almost like he didn't believe Travail's argument was the key to his freedom. Like it didn't matter.

Travail asked Roscoe to bring forward a demonstrative aid. He placed a poster on the easel that once displayed text messages between Landry and Joey. Bold letters at the poster's top said: *How the Prosecution Missed.*

Travail pointed to the first item on the list: *The Missing Gun.*

"The gun is quite important. It's what killed Landry. Not the knife. The knife found its way—conveniently, I might add—into Landry's back with Joey's fingerprints on it after Landry was dead." Travail emphasized the word *after* and then asked a question. "Why would Joey stab a man he'd already killed? That sounds more like a move somebody else would make if they wanted you to believe Joey killed Landry."

Travail pointed to the second item on the list: *The Missing Eyewitnesses.*

"If this is such an ironclad case, beyond a reasonable doubt, where are the eyewitnesses? Who saw what happened? Who heard the shot?

Travail pointed to the third item on the list: *The Missing Investigation.*

"The authorities did not investigate the murder as they should have because they were sure—they jumped to the conclusion—they had their killer the night they found Joey in the same house with Landry's body.

"Unfortunately, this kind of rush to judgement is a common problem in law enforcement overburdened by many cases. They catch what they think is a break—a parolee in the house with the corpse of the man who sent him to prison—and they pre-judge the case."

Travail looked at Detective Sizemore, who sat in the second row behind the prosecutor's table. "Members of the jury, if I were the investigator on this case, I would want to know who thrust the knife with Joey's fingerprints on it into Landry's back and why they worked so hard to frame Joey for Landry's murder."

Travail looked behind him and locked eyes with Elkin, then Sterling, then Bailey, who sat together in the first row behind the prosecutor. He hadn't called them as witnesses as Harriet wanted, but he was sure the jury hadn't forgotten about them, thanks to Harriet. He pointed at them for the jury's benefit. "I would also want to know why those three people have such an interest in being sure Joey takes the fall for Landry's murder."

Fortuna objected. "That is an improper argument, Your Honor, not based on the evidence."

"Sustained. Members of the jury, ignore the reference to the three people seated in the first row behind the prosecutor."

Roscoe grinned. Harriet didn't smile, but she didn't look as angry. And the jury kept their focus on the three people in the first row behind the prosecutor.

Travail pointed to the fourth and final item on his demonstrative aide: *Missing Common Sense.*

"Common sense screams for attention in this case."

Travail took a marker and circled the word "common sense." He stepped back and admired his work.

"Ask yourself these two questions. If you killed someone, would you put them under your sister's house? You would not. More importantly, would you wait at the house for the police after the kitchen collapsed? Again, you would not. Only an innocent person with nothing to hide would wait for the police. Not someone who'd just committed murder."

Travail thanked the jury, said he knew they would take their duty seriously, asked for a verdict of not guilty, and returned to his seat. On the way, he spotted Celia Standish in the gallery. She dipped her head in his direction, as if she approved of his argument.

Judge Williamson sped through her instructions to the jury. Just before noon, she sent the jury out to select their foreperson and begin their deliberations. She ordered lunch to be taken to the jurors so they wouldn't lose time in reaching their verdict. The courtroom was "at ease" until the jury returned.

Prosecutor Fortuna had the good graces to shake Travail's hand. "Just doing my job."

Travail felt no ill will toward her. He'd once been a young lawyer trying to win his first big case, and there was nothing wrong with showing passion and zeal. It was too bad Elkin and the Standish family deceived her about the facts.

Detective Sizemore approached, no more friendly than when they'd first met. "Didn't much care for your speech. I've always done things the right way."

Now it was Travail's turn to explain. "Just doing my job, Detective. Any update on Dan's murder investigation?"

"I just received a text from forensics. The bullet that killed Barnard was the same caliber as the bullet that killed Landry. If you will excuse me, I have to find Barnard's killer."

Travail hoped the detective had listened closely to his jury argument and that while he looked for Dan's killer, he would think more about why Robert Elkin, Sterling Standish, and Bailey Standish have such an interest in being sure Joey takes the fall for Landry's murder.

Travail, Roscoe, Harriet, and Joey went to their anteroom to wait on the verdict with the deputy sheriff standing guard outside the door.

Joey cleared his throat. "I am grateful for all the hard work everyone has done for me. Thank you, Craig and Roscoe, for being my lawyers. Thank you, Harriet, for being by my side. Everyone did the best they could."

"Knock it off, Joey. You act like it's over. Even if you lose this round, I will figure out a way to prove your innocence." Harriet spoke as if Travail and Roscoe were not in the room.

"I am going to ask you to do me a favor, Harriet."

"What favor?" Harriet's eyes narrowed.

"If I lose this case, don't hold it against Craig, Roscoe, or me. Can you do that for me?"

"You shouldn't ask me that."

"I know, but this is important. Will you promise?"

Harriet slumped back in her chair. She continued to avoid Travail's eyes when she mumbled her response. "For you, Joey, yes, I promise."

Harriet paid close attention to the jurors as they filed into the courtroom. They weren't looking toward the defense team. They kept their eyes on the judge.

They'd only been out for two hours. It was a very short period to deliberate a first-degree murder case.

The foreperson rose and faced the judge, who put the process in motion of delivering the verdict in open court. "Hand your verdict sheet to the bailiff to bring to me."

Judge Williamson looked at the verdict sheet, remained impassive, and handed the verdict sheet to the clerk. "Take the verdict, madam clerk."

The clerk rose and faced the foreperson: "Has the jury reached a unanimous verdict?"

"We have."

What is the jury's unanimous verdict on the question: *Is Joey Penman guilty of murdering Chance Landry in the first degree?*

"Guilty."

Harriet took a deep breath as the verdict sucked the air from the room. Not again. Poor Joey. This was a terrible miscarriage of justice.

Travail dropped his head. Roscoe patted him on the back.

Joey was stoic. Harriet could not see through his mask, even though he was her twin brother, linked to her by biology and shared experience. They were a pair. And the pair was about to be separated for the second time, this time, forever. Surely, he felt as she did, that there was no justice in the world.

Yeager leaned forward from the first row. "Don't worry, Harriet. This ain't over."

But when the clerk polled the jury, and one by one, they agreed with the guilty verdict, it felt over. Twelve people who didn't know Joey the way she did had stamped him a murderer.

The judge excused the jury, and they filed out while anger and sadness battled each other for space inside Harriet. Her heart ached. She felt lost. What next?

Judge Williamson addressed the date and time for their next hearing. "Sentencing will occur on Monday at 10:00 a.m. in this courtroom." She asked Travail if there was anything further he wanted to address today."

"Just one other matter, Your Honor. Ms. Fortuna received a request today from retired federal judge Thomas Dooley to release the forged coins in the court's possession—the ones identified in this case—to his custody for a private dispute as to their ownership under his jurisdiction. She is agreeable, as is Ms. Keaton, who owns the house where the coins were found. With your permission, the prosecutor will release them to the federal marshal who is here to pick them up for Judge Dooley."

"Permission granted."

Judge Williamson picked up a collection of ballpoint pens and banged her gavel to end the jury portion of the first murder case Travail ever tried and lost. If Harriet could have her way, he'd never take another one.

The clock said it was 4:00 p.m., and Harriet was not in a good frame of mind. Joey was about to return to jail, and he had something to say to her.

She spoke first. "I love you, Joey."

"I love you too, Sis, but I need a second favor from you."

She tried to lighten her mood. "You're getting greedy, aren't you?"

Joey smiled. "My second favor is for you to trust me when I tell you I have a plan."

Harriet perked up. "A plan?"

"Of course, Harriet. I'm your twin. Why would I roll over?"

"I hoped you wouldn't."

"You need to get one thing for me."

"Anything."

"I need the forged gold coins the police found under the house. Do everything you can to get that federal judge to release them to you."

Before she could ask why, the deputy sheriff grabbed Joey by the arm and escorted him to a side door in the courtroom.

When the deputy sheriff took Joey away, Harriet teared up. She accepted Yeager's bear hug and squeezed him tight for at least a minute. He'd been her good friend for twenty years and always looked after her. She trusted him and felt safe in his arms.

Harriet wasn't sure how she felt about Craig at the moment. Sure, she trusted him and she felt safe with him, but she'd wanted him to call witnesses to defend Joey and he didn't. Could he have done more? Should he have done what she asked? Maybe. But as much as she liked to kid him about how easy it was to be a lawyer, she knew that wasn't true. Maybe she was being too judgmental. Maybe she was blaming Craig for circumstances beyond his control.

He was a good man and he'd tried his best. She would speak with him.

"There's more bad news." Yeager looked anxious about sharing what he knew.

Harriet braced herself. She wasn't sure she could take any more bad news today. "I'm listening."

"The gold bullion market took a big hit today."

"Oh no." Her shoulders sagged as she thought about her Indie friends who'd invested their assets in gold bullion coins.

"Another thing." Yeager hesitated.

"Yes?"

"Today, the state denied the permit for South End Mining Company to dig for gold in South End."

Harriet placed her hand on Yeager's shoulder. "I am so sorry. What about the gold mine museum?"

Yeager shook his head. "It doesn't look promising."

All of this was terrible news for her friends, but at least they had the arbitration hearing tomorrow. Craig had given the arbitration a fifty-fifty chance. Not the best odds, but better than no odds at all.

Harriet didn't thank God it was Friday. Her brother—even though he said he had a plan—was going back to prison for another crime she was sure he didn't commit. Her Indie friends—even though they would fight for their losses in the arbitration case—had lost much and might not get it back. The Indie—even though it was a community that wouldn't back down—might fall into an unscrupulous developer's hands through foreclosure. And when all that happened, retirement life would never be the same.

Harriet didn't want to move into her house near South End, but she couldn't stay at the Indie if her friends couldn't afford to stay, especially when Sterling and Bailey took ownership and did who-knows-what with the place.

Maybe Judge Dooley would right her friends' financial wrongs tomorrow and maybe they could figure out a way to prevent foreclosure of the Indie's ten million dollar loan. Anyway, one could hope for the best. And she would. Because hope was all she had left.

A sheriff's deputy approached. "Are you Harriet Keaton?"

"Yes."

He handed her an envelope. "You're served."

When she thought her day couldn't get any worse, it did. Inside the envelope was a condemnation notice. In two weeks, the city would demolish her childhood home, now labeled a "safety hazard." If it happened, she couldn't move there if she wanted. The notice had to be Elkin's work. She hated the idea he might win.

When Craig approached, he was so quiet, Harriet didn't know he was beside her until he spoke. "I'm sorry. Will you forgive me?"

"Not your fault, but I do want you to promise me one thing."

"Anything."

"Promise me you will keep fighting."

"You didn't have to ask."

He extended his hand. She took it, and they tightened their grips. Together, they walked away from the field of battle, but not away from the fight.

CHAPTER 31

JUDGE DOOLEY RULES

Travail had difficulty falling asleep. Even after he fell asleep, he awoke several times, wondering what he might have done differently to change Joey's verdict.

When Yeager slipped in and woke him up at the butt crack of dawn, Travail drained two cups of coffee while he did his final arbitration prep work, and he carried a third cup into the federal courthouse where the hearing before Judge Dooley would take place.

Judge Thomas Dooley, like Yeager, was an early riser. That meant the people who appeared before him for his arbitration cases had to get up long before the roosters crowed. To Dooley, early was on time, on time was late, and being late was a travesty of justice.

Dooley had a well-earned reputation in legal circles as a hard worker. Because Dooley worked hard, he expected everyone who appeared before him to do the same. If they weren't so inclined, he figured he did them a favor when he pushed them past their usual pace. That's why he scheduled the arbitration for early on Saturday, after their long week in a murder trial.

Travail didn't mind Dooley's habit of forcing his work ethic on others because Elkin, his opponent today, had never outworked Travail.

At 8:00 a.m. on the dot, at the sixteen-person conference table in

Dooley's office, the judge kicked things off. He was not about pretense. He didn't wear a robe. "This proceeding is less formal than court. The evidence rules don't apply."

Travail sat on one side of the table with Harriet, Yeager, and Roscoe. Elkin sat on the other side with Sterling and Bailey Standish.

"Each side will have one hour to present their evidence on the two financial claims. Then we will address the issue of ownership of the coins. After that, you'll have five minutes apiece to make your arguments. I will take five minutes—assuming I need that long—to deliver my ruling. We will be finished well before lunchtime."

Judge Dooley looked at Travail's witness list. "Mr. Travail, you have ten witnesses on your stock purchase claim. That's too many for the time we have."

"All ten witnesses are residents who have claims. Each invested five hundred thousand dollars in South End Mining Company."

"Are all their claims alike?"

"They are."

"You can do it with one witness, your first one on your list."

The judge asked Elkin, the non-lawyer representative for the Standish Company, whether he agreed. "What say you, Mr. Elkin?"

"A splendid idea, Your Honor. Just splendid."

Yeager was the first name on Travail's list for the stock purchase claim. Not ideal.

Elkin cleared his throat. "Your Honor, perhaps we should do the same on the gold bullion claims."

"How many witnesses do you have on that claim, Mr. Travail?"

"Fifty."

Dooley laughed like he'd heard the most bizarre thing. He asked to see Travail's witness list and put his finger on the first witness on the list. "You can use Nelli Nimble for this group's claims."

How could Travail say no? His strategy had been to call Yeager and Nelli as his first witnesses so he could finish with more sympathetic, less eccentric witnesses. But he had to agree. They were claimants, and they were the first ones on his lists.

Dooley spoke to Elkin. "You can have two witnesses to rebut the claims."

"Mr. and Mrs. Standish will be our two witnesses."

Dooley pointed at the coins on the table. "You can each have one witness to testify about ownership of the coins. Mr. Travail, call your first witness."

Travail asked Yeager to take the seat at the end of the table facing the judge, and Yeager moved there, ready to proceed.

"Mr. Alexander, why did you invest in the South End Mining Company?"

"Dirt Man Dan, I mean, Dan Barnard, laid the groundwork for the scheme. He invited a financial expert to speak on Zoom to the Indie investment club. She was slick, polished, and knew her stuff, or so we thought."

"What do you mean?"

"According to her pitch, we faced an imminent stock market crash, and we could lose our retirement funds unless we invested in gold, which she promised would skyrocket in value when the market crashed. The stock market never collapsed. But the gold bullion market did."

"Who did this person work for?"

"Found out later she and her team had a contract with the Standish Company, who paid them a commission on the sales."

"What gold investment options did the Standish Company's sales team offer?"

"They suggested three options: gold bullion coins, gold futures—which was some kind of stock gambling thing—and stock in an actual gold mine, which sounded pretty cool to me."

Travail told Yeager that Nelli would address the gold bullion claim. "Tell us how you got sucked into the gold mine stock investment."

"The financial expert pitched the South End Mining Company as a solid, risk-free investment. She arranged for other experts to speak with us on the phone and sent us videos. They assured us South End Mining Company would be able to obtain all state and city approvals to dig for gold and build an underground gold mine museum at the old Rudisill Mine."

"Was that true?"

"Nope. Yesterday, the state denied their permit to dig for gold."

Sterling sat up straight. "What?" He turned to Elkin. "Did you know about this?"

Dooley told Sterling to "wait your turn" and waved at Travail to continue.

"Did the Standish Company's sales team misrepresent anything else?

"They promised our stock would increase in value because the mining company's connection to the Standish Company's underground mixed-use development would create an economic boom. But the only thing they've done so far is dig a big hole in the ground."

"Any false promises with the underground museum?"

"Yep. Found out last night the city will only allow a museum on the surface, and even then, only with extensive conditions imposed by the city's planning department. Too dangerous to build one underground, they said."

"That can't be true," Sterling said.

Bailey echoed his disappointment. "I don't believe it."

Dooley tapped the table. "Elkin, if your clients don't keep their mouths shut while the other side testifies, they can wait in the hall."

Elkin leaned over and whispered to Sterling and Bailey in a voice that carried. "Everything is alright. I will explain."

Travail continued with Yeager. "Were you given any collateral for your stock investment if something went wrong?"

"Yes, South End Mining Company put up gold bars as security for the investments, but the gold bars are filled with pyrite—fool's gold."

"Just like your investment?"

"Well said, Craig Travail. Well said."

Elkin took his turn with only a few questions. "Mr. Alexander, did you sign a subscription agreement for your stock investment?"

"Everyone did."

"Did you read it?

Yeager laughed. "It was a hundred pages. Too many words. Legal jargon on steroids. Wouldn't understand it even if I had read it."

"Did your friends—the other investors—read it?"

"I doubt it. I bet you didn't read it either. You probably just hit print on your computer. The boilerplate on that thing must weigh a ton."

Dooley didn't chastise Yeager. He grinned instead.

Elkin continued. "You understand, Mr. Alexander, investing in stock comes with risk—it says so in the subscription agreement?"

"I do, but not the risk your clients would lie to us."

Travail remembered why Elkin was so bad at trial work. Corporate law was his background. One question too many was his lesson to be learned. If he'd been smarter, he would have let the stock subscription language agreed to by the purchasers do the work for him.

Judge Dooley called for Nelli Nimble to testify next. As was her style, Nelli motored in on four wheels, dressed in her pickleball gear this time, with two paddles strapped to her chair. She removed her sweaty headband and her sweatshirt, revealing an athletic tank top. "Morning, everyone. Sorry for the outfit, Judge. Didn't think you'd need me this soon. I had our know-it-all croquet commissioner, Lafontaine Creech, down nine points to one when I got Harriet's text message."

Travail explained to Nelli that Yeager had already covered the evidence on the stock claim. "Please tell Judge Dooley why you and the other Indie residents bought the gold bullion coins."

"They scared us. Made us think the stock market was about to crash. Called us every day. Kept pushing. Called it a hedge against investment losses in the stock market."

"When you say 'they,' who are you talking about?"

"The people the Standish Company hired to sell us the coins. Found out later from Becky Trainer—she's a whiz, by the way, at figuring out what shady companies do—that the Standish Company cut a deal with a group that specializes in buying and selling gold. I looked them up on the internet. Many states have investigated and sued them for selling gold bullion at inflated prices. Turns out, they source their 'gold-like' coins from Chinese factories for huge profits."

"Do you know if you paid fair value for the gold bullion coins you and your friends bought?"

"They said we did, but the write-up we got from a coin expert says we got taken. The coins were worth a lot less than we paid for them, and now, with the downturn in the market, they're not worth much at all."

Travail turned Nelli over to Elkin and almost felt sorry for Elkin when he did.

Elkin talked down to Nelli. "Ms. Nimble, you're not very knowledgeable about the gold bullion market, are you?"

"I thought I was until your clients and their people lied to me."

Elkin tried to recover. "Did you read the paperwork that came with your gold coins?"

"Yeah, I read it. After I got past all the congratulatory sentences about buying gold to protect my future, I had to get out my magnifying glass to read the small print sharks like you put in documents."

"Ahh, so you read about how investing in gold is risky?"

"I did." Nelli shifted forward in her wheelchair and stared directly at Elkin. "It warned against poor market value appreciation compared to stocks and against its volatility—is that the right word?—but what it didn't do was warn against *buying a pig in a poke*. Bet you don't know where that phrase comes from. It originated when people sold piglets in pokes—which were sacks—where the buyer couldn't see what they were really buying. Pig sellers without a conscience sometimes put less valuable animals in the sack. Like cats. Nothing against cats, but that's what your people sold us."

Elkin quit while he was behind.

Judge Dooley ordered a ten-minute break. When everyone returned, Elkin took another step toward being the worst disbarred representative a defendant could hire. "We have decided not to call any witnesses." Sterling and Bailey shot glances at each other and then at Elkin. He whispered to them in a voice that all could hear that "everything is going according to plan."

Travail had a good feeling about their claims. And yet, something was off, because Elkin wasn't flustered. He seemed as indifferent to his sinking case as he was to the permit denials for his client's development project.

Dooley made a note on his legal pad. "Okay then. I have enough evidence to rule on the claims, but before I do, let's talk about who is entitled to the coins."

Elkin responded first. "Thank you, Your Honor. The coins belong to Sterling Standish. He'd like to have them returned."

"Do you have any evidence to support your position?"

Elkin asked Sterling to explain his family's relationship to the coins. "The coins belonged to my father, Junior Standish. Harriet Keaton's father, Penny Penman, killed my dad and stole the coins."

Travail made as much of an objection as he could make in an arbitration. "I realize the rules are more relaxed in this forum, Your Honor, but it doesn't sound like Mr. Standish is speaking from personal knowledge. Was he there when Junior Standish died?"

"It doesn't matter, Your Honor." Elkin handed a sheet of paper to the judge. He slid a copy to Travail. "This affidavit by Dan Barnard says he and Penny Penman were in the room when Junior Standish died. He doesn't say who killed Junior, but he says Penny Penman left that night with Junior's coins. They did not belong to Penny then. They do not belong to his daughter now."

Dooley asked Sterling why he wanted the forged gold coins. "You can't pass them off as the real thing."

"Does it matter what I do with them?" Sterling's voice had an edge. "They are mine."

Elkin placed a hand on Sterling's forearm and addressed Dooley. "What he means, Your Honor, is the coins have sentimental value. They remind him of his father, and he doesn't want them to go to the daughter of his father's killer."

"He could have said that himself."

Dooley pushed the affidavit aside and shifted his attention to Travail. "Who do you represent regarding the coins?"

"Harriet Keaton."

Travail asked Harriet to move to the end seat so the judge could hear her better. He nudged the coin bag in her direction and wasted no time getting to the point.

"Do you own the house where these coins were found?"

"Yes. My father left the house to me in his will."

"Did you have dinner with Dan Barnard the night before he died?"

"I did."

"Did he tell you how Junior died?"

Elkin objected. "This is hearsay."

Dooley shook his head. "It's no different from your affidavit. We will hear what she has to say."

Harriet proceeded. "Dan told me the same thing he said in his affidavit, that he was in the room when Junior died. However, he told me —in fact, he made it very clear to me—my father did not kill Junior. Chance Landry killed Junior."

"What did Dan say about the coins?"

Harriet explained what happened the night Junior died, and in particular, how Junior gave Penny the forged coins before he fired Landry and about the fight that followed. She looked at Sterling. "All those years, you thought my father killed your father. You believed the story Landry told you about my father being the killer until you learned Landry killed your father, and when you did, you killed him."

Sterling smiled like a Cheshire cat. "The jury disagreed. Joey is going to prison, not me."

Ignoring Sterling and addressing the judge again, Harriet explained her theory about how the coins ended up in her basement. "Dan Barnard believed my father hid the coins in the kitchen floorboards at my house, and I agree. When the kitchen collapsed, the coins rained down on Landry's body."

Dooley told everyone he'd heard enough. "What's your argument, Elkin?"

"The coins belonged to Junior Standish, and he never gave up ownership. Harriet Keaton has no claim to them."

"What's your argument, Travail?"

"Junior Standish gave the coins to Penny before Landry killed him.

Penny made Harriet his heir. The coins belong to her. Not to mention what they taught us in first-year law school."

"What's that?"

"Possession is nine-tenths of the law. The coins were on Harriet's property, not Sterling's. He never had possession."

Retired judge Thomas Dooley only needed five minutes to decide.

"Based on the facts presented before me in this case, the Standish Company and its subsidiaries and agents committed fraud in the inducement regarding the sale of South End Mining Company stock and the sale of gold bullion coins. Therefore, I enter this award against them in favor of all Indie residents who purchased stock and coins for the amount of their purchase prices, plus interest." He signed two copies of the award and passed the documents to Travail and Elkin.

"As for the coins,"—Dooley slid the bag in Harriet's direction— "better you have these coins, Ms. Keaton, than someone likely to commit fraud with them."

Travail felt like a lawyer again for the first time since moving his law practice into a retirement community.

When Travail boarded the courthouse elevator with Yeager and Harriet, Yeager gave Travail a slap on the back and an "atta boy" to boot. Harriet seemed extra pleased when she took his hand and squeezed it. She also reached out and took Yeager's hand. They were a good team, odd as it may have seemed at times, who'd just won big for their friends.

Yeager used his free hand to stop the elevator door from closing to allow the rest of the team to join them. Roscoe and Nelli were all smiles when they got on board and in good spirits for the ride to the first floor.

On the sidewalk outside the courthouse, the group made plans to meet for a drink at the Indie bar to celebrate the win. Roscoe went one way. Nelli and Yeager went another. Harriet kissed Travail on the cheek. "Thank you."

Before Travail could respond, he heard Elkin's voice. "Craig, one moment please."

Elkin ambled down the steps and approached Travail. He ignored Harriet, who stood rigid in Elkin's presence.

"Congratulations to you on a case well-handled." Elkin stuck out his hand.

Travail wanted to resist, but he stood before the courthouse with a defeated adversary who extended his hand. And although the glint in Elkin's eye suggested Travail should be wary, Travail shook Elkin's hand.

"Thank you, Robert. I plan to record Judge Dooley's ruling with the state court on Monday. When can my client expect payment?"

"That's the thing, Craig. This was such a perfect outcome. I never liked Sterling or Bailey. My loyalty was to Junior and his mother, Celia, but Junior died, and Celia retired. Sterling and Bailey have treated me like a peasant. They've been so ungrateful, given all the things I have done for their family business. I hoped they would fail—in fact, I orchestrated it—and now they have."

This explained why Elkin was unbothered by his clients' loss, but Elkin's smile suggested there was more coming to explain his amiable attitude.

"I just informed Sterling and Bailey of their overdrawn bank accounts, which shocked them, of course. They're going to hire a bankruptcy lawyer and fight, but bankruptcy will only divide their assets among their secured lenders. I'm afraid unsecured creditors like your clients will receive nothing. Nada. Zilch. All according to plan."

Travail wanted to chastise Elkin for his deceit, but he held back because he blamed himself. He should have dug deeper. He should have seen this coming. After all, Elkin put his plan for revenge in his email. *Your friends are about to suffer financial ruin, untold heartbreak, and trials and tribulations.* He now understood the last line of the email, and it struck him to his core. *You have only yourself to blame.*

Harriet gasped when she realized what this meant.

"And to think, y'all thought I was a terrible lawyer." Elkin made the mistake of smirking at Harriet when he said it.

Harriet reacted with vigor. She slapped Elkin so hard he stumbled backward. She closed the gap. "It was you all along, wasn't it? You wrote the email to Craig. You convinced Sterling to deceive the Indie residents. You made Sterling believe he could dig for gold in South End and build an underground museum. You framed my brother for Landry's death. You, Robert Elkin, are a monster, that's what you are."

Elkin put his hand to his face and rose from his bent position. "Harriet, that one was free because the look on your face is priceless compensation enough. You and your friends ruined my life. It's time for you to suffer for what you did to me."

Elkin walked five paces before he turned around.

"One thing I forgot to mention. Sterling needed to bribe some government officials—that didn't work out for him, by the way—and I gave him the money he needed in exchange for the ten million dollar note on the Indie. Sterling was so desperate I got the note at a 50-percent discount. Yesterday, I filed the foreclosure proceeding on the Indie for their default on the note. One week from next Friday, the court will rule, and the Indie will be mine. I plan to sell it off for parts."

Elkin looked down his nose at Harriet. "Isn't that about the same time the city demolishes your house?"

The sky emptied and raindrops hit the pavement.

How quickly the weather had changed.

CHAPTER 32

CARRIE'S TRIP HOME

Harriet went straight to Carrie's room from the federal courthouse. She found her friend asleep, so she pulled a chair up to her bedside and held Carrie's hand.

This past week, Carrie had slept more and more. When she was awake, she kept the conversation going, but she tired faster and struggled more with the pain. She didn't complain, though, as steadfast as ever in her appreciation to those who cared for her and to those who visited. Harriet wasn't fooled by the short bursts of energy. She could see what was coming. Her larger-than-life friend got weaker by the day. She was nearing the end.

Carrie Roberts had never been an overly religious person, but earlier in the week, they'd talked about what's next, what it was, and what it might be. Carrie had confessed to Harriet she was a believer, optimistic about her future. "I can't wait to meet the woman in charge upstairs."

When she'd said it, a male orderly looked up from his work in surprise, and Carrie had laughed at his reaction until it hurt. "You heard me, Pete. Heaven is a five-star resort. It's got everything you need, a clean, organized place. Ain't no man able to pull that off and run the day-to-day of the universe too."

Harriet had marveled at Carrie's spunk and laughed along with her.

Nanette, the hospice nurse, eased the hall door open and approached. "How's she doing?"

Harriet looked at Nanette. "She's been asleep all afternoon. The staff nurse administered her last morphine dose one hour ago, what Carrie calls her liquid sleeping pill, and it did its job."

Nanette went to Carrie's bedside and touched her on the arm. "Hello, Ms. Carrie. How are you doing today?"

Carrie's eyes fluttered open. "Nanette, you angel you. Good to see you, darling."

Nanette checked Carrie's hands and feet, a routine she followed on every visit now. The bluish tint in Carrie's skin was more noticeable today than yesterday.

"Nanette, I was telling Harriet how good you've been to me." Carrie reached out with both hands and clutched Nanette's hands. "Thank you for everything. I love you."

"I love you too," Nanette said. "You tell the best stories of any patient I've ever treated."

Nanette asked Carrie about her pain and made a note on her electronic pad.

"We're getting close, aren't we, Nanette?" There was no panic in Carrie's voice.

"Everyone's journey is unique."

"Don't bullshit a bullshitter," Carrie teased.

Nanette smiled at her patient. "There are signs, yes. Things have progressed."

Carrie tilted her head in Harriet's direction. "Ain't she a hoot, Harriet? She knows I am running on empty, but she's too polite to tell me."

Carrie had surprised the medical staff with her staying power. She'd pushed her body beyond her predicted ninety days to live, perhaps to get through Joey's trial and see him freed, but Harriet could feel Carrie's time was close.

For the past week, Harriet was by Carrie's side every night until midnight. Carrie told childhood stories. She was quite the dancer, apparently, but her love life, was a disaster, from beginning to end. "That's why I took up romance novels. You should try them, Harriet. The men know how to carry on a conversation, and they are attentive to a woman's emotional and physical needs." Harriet smirked at the suggestion.

Last Monday, they talked about the problems the Indie faced with Sterling, Bailey, and Elkin. Carrie waved her hand like she swatted a fly. "People like that come and go." She said to "pay them no mind, except to give them the ass-kicking they deserve."

Last Tuesday, they talked strategy, how to deliver defeat to their adversaries, and also, about how to deal with failure.

"I've failed a lot in my life, Harriet. There is no better remedy for failure than to get your butt off the ground and keep going."

Carrie told Harriet to remember to be herself. "If things don't work out, you keep going, dear, and you pull all the weak people along with you. You're a leader, Harriet."

Harriet didn't feel like a leader. Not for Joey, and not for the investment club members. She'd bailed on both when they didn't listen to her, and look where they ended up.

Last Wednesday, they discussed Celia Standish. "A remarkable woman," Carrie said. "Quite a force in her day when the men tried to push her around in the boardroom. One time, a director in her company was mansplaining what she should do in front of the all-male board, and she kicked him in the gonads, then fired him." Carrie hooted. "Now that's my kind of girl."

Harriet hadn't seen that side of Celia Standish and was impressed. She was always surprised by people's past, especially those who lived in a retirement community.

"Celia's kind too," Carrie had said. "She visited me to take my mind off Joey's trial. She's worried about what her grandson has done and plans to do. But do you know what she cares about the most?"

"What?" Harriet was polite. She didn't have any empathy for the Standish family.

"Her son Junior. How he was murdered and the possible damage to his reputation as an honest business person."

Harriet didn't respond. Celia would know soon enough Chance Landry killed Junior and that Landry—not Celia's son—was the one with the deserved bad reputation.

It was Carrie who brought up the topic of Craig Travail on Thursday night. "Do you love him, Harriet?"

What a question. Harriet loved many people, but that wasn't what Carrie meant. Did she love Craig?

The answer was complicated, especially when she factored in the tension between them during Joey's trial, but it was a fair question.

"I will tell you a secret, Harriet. There are very few men like Craig available in retirement communities. The good ones are mostly married, or they're about to be dead."

Harriet didn't need that lecture from her friend, and it must have showed on her face.

"I'm not saying you have to marry him, Harriet. Wow. The young people these days."

"I don't need a man in my life, Carrie. I've lived by myself just fine for twenty years since my husband died."

Carrie used what gumption she had left that night to chastise Harriet. "Bright-line rules are for bright-line idiots. When it comes to dating and marriage, rules are more like guidelines."

As they talked, Harriet gave Carrie the benefit of the doubt and wondered if she'd taken the man-free life too far. Were there ways to balance a good man with her independent spirit? But if so, she wasn't sure Craig thought the same.

Carrie continued to press Harriet about Craig. "I know you've slept together. And before you get out of sorts, I haven't put that tidbit on the gossip line. What I want to know is how y'all have handled things after your sleepover."

"My, you're nosy."

But Harriet had no excuse not to confide in Carrie about her and Craig. Carrie wasn't going to be here much longer, and she was her best friend.

"After the salsa night sleepover, we took things slow. I haven't told anyone we're dating, and he's treated my public displays of affection like a cat tolerating a dog's presence. I suppose we're still in the closet with whatever it is we have together."

Harriet illustrated her point with a story. "A few weeks ago, Yeager lectured Craig about his emotional distancing from me in public. 'You worried about catching cooties, Craig Travail? You ought not fight it. That's the germ that keeps on giving.'"

"Good for Yeager," Carrie said. "Did it work?"

"Not really, but it made us laugh. We seem to teeter on an emotional cliff, unsure how to balance spousal memories with what's next in our lives and our feelings for each other."

"How was the sex?" Carrie smiled through her pain.

"You are incorrigible, Carrie Roberts."

"You can't fault me for asking."

"I certainly can."

"Well?"

"What do you want me to say—that it's like riding a bicycle?"

"No, I want you to tell me if the bike was a one-speed or ten-speed, comfortable or rough, fast or slow, that kind of thing. I'm dying, after all."

They laughed that night about dating, relationships, and sex, and Harriet relaxed to the point she admitted that she and Craig made excuses to avoid talking about how they felt about each other. "We keep saying we need to stay focused on our missions to save Joey and the Indie before we talk more about how we feel, but we're failing there too."

Carrie had some advice that rang true. "Craig's love language is his desire to help those he cares about, and he is working overtime to help you, your brother, and your friends. He loves you, Harriet. You better not wait long. Peaches has a sign-up sheet for Craig. She's ready to publish the sheet at the first inkling you and Craig are not joined at the hip."

Last night, Carrie tried to tell funny retirement community stories, but she struggled. Harriet decided not to tell Carrie about the jury verdict. No reason to add to her suffering.

"You need to rest," she'd said to Carrie.

Carrie reached for Harriet and took her hand. "I'm ready," she'd said.

"Ready for what?"

"Ready to go. Ready to get my legs back and walk through the pearly gates. It's time. The good Lord—bless her heart—and modern medicine gave me ninety good years."

Carrie was so brave as she stared death in the face, and Harriet so wasn't. "I'm not ready for you to leave me. I will miss you too much." Tears formed in Harriet's eyes, and Carrie reached up and touched her cheek.

"I appreciate that. I do. But you have a life to live, and you've got a boyfriend now. If that won't keep you occupied and frustrated and happy and tied in a knot, I don't know what will."

Harriet thought about objecting to the term *boyfriend*, but she didn't. She and Craig were something. Harriet didn't know what to call it, even if Carrie did.

"I've lived a good life, Harriet. Made some mistakes, sure. But I wouldn't change a thing. Nope. I wouldn't change a thing."

"Not a thing?" Harriet teased. "You sure about that? What about that time you and Will Miller skinny-dipped in the neighborhood pool and your parents caught you?"

Carrie laughed, then touched her back, the place with the most pain. "I told you about that, did I? That was a highlight, Harriet, part of a life well lived."

Harriet had kissed Carrie good night at eleven thirty last night and had returned home exhausted. After the drama in the arbitration hearing today and Elkin's post-hearing revelation the Standish Company was broke, she had no energy left.

Nanette finished her examination and gathered her things. "Ms. Carrie, do you need anything before I leave?"

"Yes. If you won't tell me how long I have left, tell Harriet. I know she's going to ask you."

In the hallway, Harriet smiled at Nanette. "She's right. I'm curious."

"Could be a few days. Could be less. You never know. I'll be back tomorrow."

Harriet got on her phone and found the text group she'd created with Craig, Yeager, Becky, and Nelli. She tapped out a message. "Hospice says it could be a few days. I don't want to leave her alone. I will spend the night with her tonight and every night. Let's pull three-hour shifts during the day, starting at eight tomorrow morning. Reply with when you can be here."

Her phone pinged, pinged again, and pinged a third and fourth time. Her friends had signed up to cover Sunday from eight in the morning until eight at night. Harriet would come at eight and spend the night, again. How many more nights did Carrie have?

When Harriet returned to the room, Carrie was asleep.

She found an instrumental love-song playlist on her phone and played the songs aloud on shuffle. Carrie would like that. She loved good romance.

On Sunday, Harriet worked in her garden, but kept her phone close. The exercise and fresh air were good for her limbs and her soul after the stressful week and her worries about Carrie.

She texted with her fellow caregivers during the day to check on Carrie. What she learned convinced her the end was near. Carrie slept during most of their shifts.

When Harriet showed up to relieve Craig at eight o'clock, Carrie was asleep. She found Craig by her bed, his hand in hers.

"How's she doing?" Harriet asked.

"They increased her pain medication. She slept the entire time. I did all the talking."

Harriet sat beside Craig and leaned into him. "What did you talk about?"

"Pretty much everything that's been on my mind. She's a good listener."

Harriet touched Craig's nose. "Did you talk about me?"

"The subject came up. It looked like she smiled when I told her we danced all night after our salsa lesson. Quick, quick, slow. Quick, quick, slow."

Harriet gave Craig a light punch on the shoulder. "You didn't."

"Like I said, I talked about pretty much everything on my mind."

"I've got it from here, Craig. Thanks for coming." She walked him to the door and kissed him on the mouth. "About tomorrow?"

"Roscoe and I can handle Joey's sentencing hearing."

"I should be there for Joey." She looked at Carrie in her bed. "And here, for her."

"Text me in the morning, and let me know what you decide. I will pick you up if you want to go." He leaned in and kissed her again.

Harriet returned to Carrie's side and chided her in a soft voice. "I bet you're proud of yourself for badgering me into having a *boyfriend.*"

Did Carrie mumble a response in her sleep, or was the air vent talking to her? Either way, it sounded in Harriet's mind like, "I told you so."

For the next few hours, the nurses came and went, and Carrie continued to sleep. Harriet had missed Nanette's Sunday visit, but Becky had texted to say Nanette felt the time was near.

At around midnight, Harriet dozed in the recliner when she heard Carrie's voice, softer than she'd ever heard it. "Harriet?"

Harriet raised the recliner, shifted to a straight-back chair, and pulled up to Carrie's bedside. She gripped Carrie's hand.

"I'm here, Carrie. How's my Gossip Queen doing?"

Carrie smiled a serene smile. Her head rested on the pillow. "I have to tell you something important."

"What's important is for you to be comfortable. Are you comfortable?"

"It's about your father."

Harriet didn't feel like talking about her father on what might be her best friend's last night, but Carrie was insistent. "Please."

Harriet fluffed Carrie's pillow, positioned her head, and stroked her hair. "Tell me whatever you want to tell me."

"Your father left you and Joey a package. He trusted me to keep it safe." Carrie's voice was tired. "He instructed me to give it to both of you when they released Joey from prison. He wanted you to open it together. Now that he's out—"

Carrie winced. Harriet pressed the call button and told Carrie to relax. The staff nurse came in with the morphine and administered it under Carrie's tongue. When they were alone again, Carrie told Harriet how to find the package. "Look in my bedroom closet. There is a safe. The combination is SAFE#SEX."

Harriet wanted to laugh, but she teared up instead.

"My will, the instructions for my funeral, and my lawyer's name and contact information are in the safe. My lawyer is holding the package for you and Joey.

"Your father said the package is very important. Something about his life's work. For you and Joey. Something you could work on together now that he is out of prison." Carrie must have dreamed Joey was free.

Harriet whispered to Carrie. "Time for you to sleep. I love you so much." She didn't tell Carrie that she and Joey would never open their father's package because Joey was going back to prison for life.

Instead, Harriet poured all her energy and focus into the room for Carrie, wasting none worrying about what might happen to her brother, her friends, or the Indie. She was present. She was here for her best friend.

A breeze rustled the curtain in the open window. Carrie startled, then reached both arms up toward the ceiling and moved them together as if she were trying to embrace something or someone. She did it twice more. Her eyes were glassy but open wide. She had a hard-to-describe look on her face. The closest thing that came to Harriet's mind was joy.

Carrie relaxed, dropped her arms to her side, and closed her eyes.

Harriet slid into the hospital bed next to Carrie. She remembered the good days with her friend. Their happy visits. The teasing. The laughter. The way Carrie brightened her days when Harriet was down. And also the days they sat together in grief and held hands after they had lost loved ones. She'd never known anyone like Carrie and she couldn't imagine life without her. She laid her head beside Carrie's.

A teardrop fell from Harriet's face and onto the bed. More followed.

As tears streamed across her face, Harriet hummed the song *You are My Sunshine* into the ear of the woman who'd brought so much light into her life.

Harriet tried to be strong despite the growing hole in her heart. She told herself she was ready for Carrie's trip to begin, if only to end Carrie's pain. She said a silent prayer for her friend's safe passage, took a deep breath, and in a soft voice, almost in a whisper, Harriet sang the song *Somewhere Over the Rainbow*.

She sang about a place way up high. About a land she'd heard about in a lullaby. She sang until her voice caught and she could sing no more.

She kissed her friend on the head one last time and gave her a blessing. A wish upon a star. "You need to fly, Carrie, just like the bluebirds fly."

Choking back sobs for the next ten minutes, Harriet did the only thing she knew how to do. She held her friend close until the Lord called her home.

PART IV

BALANCING THE BOOKS
– THE NEW NORMAL

CHAPTER 33

DIRT MAN REPRISE

Harriet, Craig, and Roscoe arrived thirty minutes early at the courthouse to meet with Joey before his sentencing hearing. They dodged the cameras and news star Amanda Rogers, whose Sunday night feature about the *Gold Mine Murder* had received high marks in the ratings.

Harriet walked hand in hand with Craig. He hadn't hesitated to take her hand, even in public, attentive to her fragile state. She'd told him she was fine, and she tried to be strong for Joey's sake, but he must have sensed how she really felt. Inside, she was a wreck with Carrie's death and what was about to happen to her brother.

Joey was not as forlorn as Harriet expected he would be when they entered the anteroom guarded by the sheriff's deputy. Unlike the coat and tie he wore during the trial, today he wore orange prison scrubs, as if the state didn't expect he'd need to change for the rest of his life.

Harriet wrapped her arms around Joey. "I'm so sorry."

"Not your fault, Sis. Everything will be fine."

Was Joey delusional about his prospects? Or did he really have a plan? And if he did have a plan, what was it, and did the plan have a chance?

Harriet pressed her brother to tell her how everything was going to be fine. "Did you bribe the judge? Buy her a lifetime supply of ball-point pens?"

Joey laughed. Nothing like that. His confidence felt misplaced, but Roscoe and Craig ran with it. In an upbeat tone, Roscoe talked about how the hearing would work. And Craig sounded positive as he explained the points they would make and the statements they would present to the court on Joey's behalf.

"No offense, Craig and Roscoe, but shaving a few years off a life sentence won't help."

Joey's comment was like a cold shower, but Joey was right. They needed more than a good sentencing hearing presentation. They needed a miracle.

A knock on the door was a nice interruption.

While Roscoe went to the door, Joey addressed Harriet. "Did you get the coins?"

"I did. But why do you need them?"

Before Joey could answer, Roscoe opened the door and revealed Celia Standish on the other side.

"Excuse me," Celia said. "May I speak with Joey?"

Roscoe stepped aside so Celia and Joey could see each other from where Celia stood. "Good morning, Joey. The plan is in motion. I hope it's not too late."

"Thanks, Celia. I'm grateful. We have the coins."

She nodded and left.

When Roscoe closed the door, everyone peppered Joey with questions.

Harriet was first and was emotional. "What in the name of why-are-you-talking-to-Celia-Standish is going on, Joey?"

Craig was next, putting two and two together about the phone call Joey had made with his phone during the trial. He held up his phone for Joey to see. "You called Celia with my phone last week, didn't you?"

Roscoe asked what needed to be asked. "What plan is in motion?"

But before Joey could answer any of their questions, there was another knock on the door. This time, the bailiff appeared. Court was about to begin, and while Harriet wanted Joey to explain, the explanation would have to wait.

Harriet's mind was a jumble as they walked in the courtroom. She was confused as to why Celia Standish was being helpful and why she wanted the forged coins.

The courtroom audience was sparse compared to the jury trial, except for the media, whose numbers had grown. They'd want to update their sensational stories about the murder victim in the gold mine with a report on how much time the judge gave the gold mine killer. Murder and justice played well on the local news.

Judge Williamson wasted little time. "The formal evidence rules do not apply in this proceeding. We will start with the prosecution."

Liza Fortuna handed the judge a copy of the sentencing statute and asked her to impose the maximum sentence. As she put it, the maximum was appropriate "for Joey Penman's heinous and unpardonable crime of first-degree murder."

To Travail, the judge said, "Does your client wish to make a statement of remorse about the murder?"

Joey stood and faced the judge. "I will not apologize for a murder I didn't commit."

The sour expression on Judge Williamson's face was not a good start for the defense.

"Fine. Does counsel for defendant have any written statements?"

Roscoe handed the judge several signed statements from people who knew Joey and vouched for his character. The courtroom was quiet while she read them. "Anything else?"

Craig stood. "Your Honor, I'd like to remind the court of the underwhelming evidence in this case that—"

The judge cut him off. "We're not here to try the case again. You can make that argument on appeal."

Craig sat and conferred with Roscoe.

"Anything else from the defense?"

Harriet wasn't a lawyer, but from her practical experience and observation of lawyers doing their work in court over the last year, she knew nothing miraculous was coming. All was quiet while the defense team huddled. Until it wasn't.

The courtroom door slammed open, and Yeager ran toward the defense table. The bailiff stepped in Yeager's path, perhaps thinking he was going to wreak havoc.

"It's okay," Craig advised the bailiff. "He's with us."

Out of breath, Yeager whispered to Craig and handed him an item from his pocket. Travail appeared to ask Yeager a question and Yeager appeared to respond.

"Gentlemen, is there something you'd like to share?" The judge clicked her ballpoint pen.

"Uh, yes, Your Honor." Craig patted Yeager on his shoulder. "With the court's permission, we'd like to use the court's video system to play a short video on behalf of our client."

Prosecutor Fortuna stood. "We object, Your Honor. The defense team has not shared—"

The judge held up her hand to Fortuna and looked at Craig. "Mr. Travail, will this video complete your presentation?"

"It will, Your Honor."

The judge allowed Craig to proceed, and Craig handed the flash drive to the clerk, who inserted it into her computer and punched a button. The bailiff dimmed the lights and lowered a retractable screen from the courtroom ceiling.

The courtroom quieted as the video began to play.

A four-door sedan stopped beside a curb well known to Harriet. The curb was in front of the house she and Joey grew up in, the same house her father gave her, where the police found Chance Landry's body.

The driver, wearing a hooded sweatshirt, walked to the vehicle's rear, opened the trunk, and struggled with something inside. Leaning into the trunk, the driver pulled a package over the trunk's lip.

The camera revealed two legs from the waist down in dark slacks and loafers.

Harriet inhaled.

Reporters whispered.

The judge shouted. "Pause the video."

With a crime in progress frozen on the screen, the judge glared at Craig. "What is this, Mr. Travail?"

Craig paused, and Liza Fortuna filled the gap. "That is not mitigation evidence, Your Honor, nor is it character evidence." Fortuna pointed at the screen. "That is a person removing a body from a car trunk."

Craig pleaded with the court. "Please, Your Honor. From what I understand, this won't take long. The rest of my client's life is on the line."

Judge Williamson motioned to the lawyers to sit, and for the next thirty seconds, she tapped her ballpoint pen on the bench at the pace water might drip from an old faucet. Finally, she made up her mind and pointed at the clerk with her pen. "Play it."

Media members moved to seats closer to the video screen and set up with their pads and pens to record what happened next.

Reaching into the trunk, the driver pulled the body forward, bending the figure's legs under the bumper and folding the body's midsection across the driver's right shoulder. One shoe fell off the body's foot as the driver stumbled, appearing to struggle with the body's weight.

As the driver walked toward the camera with the body slung over a shoulder, their face was hidden from view by the forward tilt of their head. They were on the side of Harriet's house, with the junkyard on the screen's left.

The camera moved and jumped, as if it was not in a fixed position, meaning someone held the camera. Harriet had an idea who it was. She looked at Joey, but he remained focused on the screen.

By now, everyone must have assumed the body being carried by the driver was that of Chance Landry. But who was the driver? The hood concealed the driver's face.

The courtroom had an eerie silence about it, except for the sounds of media members scribbling on their pads and the sounds of the driver and camera person crunching ground in the video. A dog barked in the distance.

The driver lowered Landry's body to the ground next to Harriet's basement entrance, then turned away from the camera and disappeared around the house's front, where it sounded like the front door opened and closed.

The camera shifted its focus to the right and locked on the lighted kitchen window on the back of Harriet's house, revealing a person's silhouette in the window.

A minute later, the light inside the kitchen went out.

Easing the camera's view back to the house's side, the camera showed the driver return and crouch over Landry with a knife in their hand. It had to be the knife from Harriet's kitchen.

Rolling Landry over onto his chest, the driver used one quick motion to stab Landry in the back with the knife. A collective gasp filled the courtroom.

Before crawling into the three-by-three-foot basement door, the driver turned Landry's feet toward the basement entrance. Then, with considerable effort, the driver grabbed Landry by his legs, and pulled his body out of sight.

A few minutes later, the driver reemerged. When an owl screeched, the driver turned to face the camera. The lights from the junkyard and the moonlit sky left no doubt.

The driver was Dirt Man Dan. No question about it.

What the hell? Harriet guessed the driver would be someone with the Standish Company, but not Dan.

Harriet had trusted Dan. She had believed everything he told her. And she had believed him to be a good person, despite his history with the Standish Company and notwithstanding his testimony against Joey many years ago.

But this video? This was a gut-punch, knocking the wind out of her faith in Dan's narrative and his credibility. The jury believed Joey moved the body. Had they known Dan did it, Joey would be free. Harriet's body shook, fed up with the never-ending deception.

Seconds later, the courtroom filled with the sound of a muffled implosion on the video, causing Dan Barnard to look through the crawl space door and then run off, climb in his vehicle, and speed away. Static lines appeared on the screen.

The clerk stopped the video, and when the bailiff turned on the overhead light, Amanda Rogers of Channel 24 News hustled to the exit, waving to her cameraman to follow her. Judge Williamson didn't move, except to chew on a ballpoint pen.

The video froze Fortuna and her associate to their seats.

Media members chattered.

Craig and Roscoe whispered to each other.

Serene was the best way to describe Joey's reaction, and Yeager appeared undone by the surprise.

Harriet leaned over the rail, grabbed Yeager's arm, and pulled him close. "Where did you get the video?"

"Celia Standish."

It was now obvious to everyone in the courtroom familiar with the trial that what Chad Breeden testified to in court was not what it looked like after all.

The prosecutor—and the jury—believed Joey put Landry's fresh corpse under the house. But Joey didn't do it. Dan Barnard did.

Craig looked Harriet in the eyes. Then he smiled.

Harriet held her breath as Prosecutor Fortuna scrambled to save her case. "Your Honor, this video proves nothing about who killed Landry."

The judge waved at Fortuna to sit. "Hold that thought. I want to hear Mr. Travail's reasons for his motion to overturn the verdict."

"It's very simple, Your Honor." Craig picked up his notepad and looked at his notes. "During closing argument, the prosecutor said this: 'After the deed was done—after Joey killed Landry—he hid the victim under his sister's house until he could move him somewhere else.' Her conclusion, and the circumstantial evidence the prosecutor claimed was so powerful for the jury to rely upon to reach that conclusion, was factually wrong. This video proves—without a doubt—Joey Penman did not put Landry under Ms. Keaton's house."

Warmth radiated through Harriet's body at their stroke of good fortune. Dan was the prosecution's witness. They used him to make their case.

Craig continued. "We weren't able to cross-examine Dan Barnard, a key prosecution witness. That's a denial of due process, but worse, the prosecution charged Joey Penman for doing what Dan Barnard did."

The judge turned to the prosecutor. "What do you have to say?"

"Someone could have doctored the video—it is probably a deep fake—and even if it is accurate, defendant and Barnard could have worked together."

"She's got a point, Mr. Travail. The video doesn't exonerate the defendant of murder."

Roscoe stood. "If that is how you intend to rule on the motion to dismiss all charges, Your Honor, we renew our motion for a new trial. This evidence—especially when it involves a prosecution witness—could lead the jury to reasonable doubt. This is not for the court to decide, but for the jury."

Judge Williamson tapped her pen on her pad as she considered her ruling.

The second hand on the big wall clock ticked off at least sixty seconds while everyone held their breath.

Finally, the judge put down her pen, clasped both hands together, and leaned forward. "The court grants the motion for a new trial. Any other motions?"

Craig was quick. "We move the court to release the defendant pending retrial. There is no forensic evidence tying Joey to the murder except his prints on the knife, but Dan Barnard stabbed Landry in the back, not Joey. There is no gun. There is no witness who saw Joey murder Landry. If the prosecution retries Joey, it will be on a wisp of insufficient evidence. Joey should not have to sit in jail waiting for the prosecutor to figure out how to save face."

Harriet felt dizzy from the legal back and forth. Was there a chance they would release Joey from prison? It seemed too good to be true.

The prosecutor rose to speak, but Judge Williamson stopped her with a question. "Considering this recent evidence, Ms. Fortuna, do you plan to pursue the murder charge against the defendant?"

"We need more time, Your Honor, before we can make that decision."

"Second question. What is your position on the bail amount for defendant's release? Notice I did not ask you whether you think I should set bail."

"This is a first-degree murder case, Your Honor. Courts rarely set bail."

Judge Williamson clicked her pen twice and pointed it at the prosecutor. "It isn't typical for a prosecution witness to hide the murder victim's body either. How much?"

"Ten million."

"Too much. I set bail at two million dollars. Anything else from the parties?"

Celia, who appeared from nowhere, spoke up. "Your Honor, my name is Celia Standish. I employed Dan Barnard for many years and feel terrible about this miscarriage of justice. I would like to post Mr. Penman's bail. May I do that?"

"Money is money, Ms. Standish. See the clerk about the details."

Harriet didn't understand Celia's motives, but without her intervention, Joey would be serving a life sentence.

Celia's generosity was so unlike a Standish. A mystery, to be sure, and one she'd normally like to solve. But not now.

Today, she didn't care about Celia's motives. They were about to release Joey.

One hour later, with the bail paperwork completed and Joey wearing oversized jeans and a summer flannel shirt Yeager had run out to secure for him, the defense team gathered with Joey on the sidewalk outside the courthouse. Harriet put her arm around her brother and told him to look up and take a deep breath. "It's called freedom, and you deserve every bit."

Detective Sizemore approached the group, cigar in hand, and asked if he could have a word with Harriet and Joey. Harriet stepped in front of Joey. "What do you want, Detective?"

"We have re-opened our investigation into Landry's death. We will work Landry's and Dan's cases together. Would you and Joey be willing to assist our investigation?"

"That depends."

"On what?"

"What does your gut tell you?"

Sizemore scratched the back of his head like he'd done the morning they first met in a house above a collapsed mine shaft, and with the hand holding his cigar, he patted his stomach. "I don't believe Joey killed Landry, and I think the two murders are connected."

Harriet responded for she and her twin brother. "Drop by anytime, Detective. You know where I live, and Joey will be staying with me."

CHAPTER 34

A BOMBSHELL MEMOIR

After they returned from court that afternoon, Harriet called the funeral director and answered her questions based on Carrie's specific wishes. "Cremation. No relatives. I will write the obituary. Small service. At the Indie. Flowers."

The will in Carrie's safe appointed Harriet to be her estate's executor. A note clipped to the will identified Vance Dagenhart as Carrie's attorney for her estate. Another note, addressed specifically to Harriet, said: *Vance Dagenhart has custody of Penny's package for you and Joey because Dagenhart can keep a secret.*

Twenty years was a long time to keep a secret, but Harriet knew Dagenhart was a person who could do that. He had helped her, Travail, and Yeager solve the mystery of the Mecklenburg Declaration of Independence one year earlier.

Harriet called Dagenhart, and he answered his own line.

"It's good to hear your voice, Harriet, but I'm sorry it is under these circumstances. Carrie Roberts was a wonderful person, a genuine character, and a creative storyteller with a sense of humor. How can I help?"

"Carrie's instructions said you would do the legal work for her estate. As her executor, I'd appreciate your help."

"I would be honored."

Harriet felt relief. She knew Dagenhart would do good work and make the experience easier on her. She thanked him, then hesitated.

How could she ask Dagenhart about the package her father left for her and Joey without appearing self-centered at a time like this? But she had to ask. It had been important to Carrie.

"Carrie told me that you had something for my brother and me, something that—" She hesitated again.

"It's okay, Harriet. I know what you're asking about."

"What am I asking about? I have no idea what it is."

"Your father's memoir, of course."

"Oh."

Harriet was underwhelmed. She didn't know what to expect of the mystery package, but she didn't expect a memoir. She didn't even know her dad had written one.

"'Oh' is right." Dagenhart said. "How would you like to go on a treasure hunt?"

"Excuse me."

"I will explain everything, but Penny's instructions were clear. I am only supposed to release the memoir to you and your brother together. Can you arrange that?

"Fortunately, my brother's schedule is wide open. How about ten tomorrow morning at your office? I can bring Carrie's will."

"Splendid. I look forward to seeing you."

Harriet drove and Joey rode shotgun to Vance Dagenhart's office. "I don't mind driving, but we need to get you a driver's license. Your first step to an independent life."

"I don't have a car."

"We'll add that to the list."

Joey laughed. "I promise to get out of your hair. I don't want to be a burden."

"A burden? Ha. I plan to put you to work on our mystery-solving team. Free room and board until our happy ending."

"Whatever you say, Sis." His tone was playful.

After they entered the South End district off Morehead and drove up Mint Street, Joey pointed ahead to a construction site on Harriet's side of the road about a block in the distance. "Looks like the gold mine project."

Harriet turned left in front of the site and looked out Joey's window. The hole was about twenty yards wide and fifty yards long, bordered by a ten-foot-tall chain-link fence. A work stoppage order hung on the locked entrance. "That's about the right location."

Joey was reflective. "Dad would have loved to see that project succeed. It's why he went into business with Junior."

Harriet groaned and gripped the steering wheel tighter. "Look where that led. Death for Dad. Jail for you. Bankruptcy for Sterling."

"Things are not always as they seem."

She glanced his way. "You've been saying that a lot, Joey."

Harriet turned into the below-ground parking deck under Dagenhart's office building.

Like other Charlotte law firms, Dagenhart's firm had made the move to a new high-rise office building in the Gold District. They boarded the elevator to the tenth floor.

Harriet hadn't visited the Gold District since they arrested Joey four months ago. Their childhood home, soon to be destroyed, was only four blocks away. She put her hand on Joey's shoulder. "After the meeting, we should swing by the house and check on it."

"Suits me."

Dagenhart greeted them wearing a classic-fit navy suit, white shirt, and red tie, more conservative than contemporary business casual attire. Harriet liked that. Classy. He showed them to the conference room.

He took the chair at the head of the table where two spiral-bound documents, each of them two inches thick, waited. Joey and Harriet took seats to his left and right. He offered them water or coffee, but they declined.

Harriet handed Carrie's original last will and testament to Dagenhart. He thanked her and pushed one of the bound documents toward Harriet, the other toward Joey. "Those are for you."

The cover on the documents read: *Penny Penman: A Treasured Life*.

Harriet read the title and snapped her head in Dagenhart's direction. "Is this a joke?"

Dagenhart's message on the phone suggested the memoir would lead to a treasure hunt, whatever that meant, but she didn't think it meant this. She put her finger on the memoir's title. "A Treasured Life? Seriously? That's our treasure hunt—reading about what our father thought was his treasured life?"

She was still mad at her father for what happened to Joey. Thrusting her chair back from the table, she jumped up and turned for the door. "Come on Joey. We're leaving."

"Please," Dagenhart said. "Let me explain. I've kept this secret for twenty years. All I need is ten minutes of your time."

Harriet eyed Joey, who hadn't moved from his seat. He shrugged. "We came down here, Sis. Might as well hear what he has to say. Besides, you can't judge a book by its cover."

Dagenhart cleared his throat. "It might help to start with the backstory."

Harriet plopped in her chair. She didn't understand why her father had written a memoir and why it required such secrecy and special delivery conditions. And there was the suggestion he'd lived a treasured life. That irked her, too, with the way he'd abandoned his family.

"Your father was a successful man."

"We know." Harriet's tone was dismissive. "He built a successful appraisal business." She didn't say he destroyed it too.

"I am not talking about his real estate work. I mean his success as a coin collector."

Harriet and Joey looked at each other, and Joey corrected Dagenhart. "That was just a very busy hobby. Dad liked coins. He tried to get Harriet and me interested, but we had better things to do than collect old coins."

Dagenhart smiled. "Y'all really don't know, do you?"

"Know what?" Harriet asked.

Dagenhart leaned back. "Did you ever wonder why you never moved into a bigger house, why you never took expensive vacations, why Penny rarely bought a new suit, and why he made just enough money to support his family and pay his employees a living wage?"

The answer was obvious to Harriet. "He was tight as a tick with his money."

Joey laughed. "I'll say. His nickname—Penny—had double meaning. Dad pinched his pennies his entire life."

"Except in one area." Dagenhart sounded confident when he said it.

But Harriet was tired of the game. "Not to be rude, but we have several pressing issues, like finding out who killed the man they say Joey killed." Harriet touched the bound document before her for an explanation.

"Right, right. I'll get to the point. When your father achieved his ultimate success, the universe gave him a vision to write a memoir."

"About being an appraiser?" Joey's tone said he was as puzzled as Harriet.

"No. Forgive me. Your father became the most respected numismatic coin collector in the South. Nobody knew rare coins like your father, especially the gold coins the government minted at the Charlotte Mint during the nineteenth century."

Harriet slumped back. "Doesn't sound like a very exciting book."

Dagenhart grinned. "It would be if you were the person curious to know how a man could collect twelve million dollars' worth of rare gold coins, with no one knowing he'd done it."

Harriet sat up. "Twelve million? What are you talking about?"

Joey straightened his posture, too, apparently as interested as Harriet in Dagenhart's answer.

"Penny did not die penniless. He died a very rich man."

Harriet shook her head. "No, he didn't. I handled his estate, and all he had left was the house near South End and enough money to settle his debts. He'd already sold his business for practically nothing after it ruined Joey's life. There was nothing in Dad's will about gold coins worth twelve million dollars."

"He didn't have the coins in his possession when he died." Dagenhart turned to Joey. "He gave you a hint the last time you saw him."

"The last time Dad visited me in prison, he said nothing about a memoir, only that Carrie had something to give to Harriet and me when they released me from prison. It had something to do with his obsession with coin collecting. He always wanted to get us interested in his hobby."

Joey looked at the cover of the memoir. "Now that I think about it, he also said Harriet and I would be financially secure with a little creative thinking on our part. It didn't make any sense then, and it doesn't make any sense now."

Dagenhart pointed at the bound documents in front of them. "He was talking about his memoir."

Harriet's throat was dry. She reached for the water pitcher, filled a glass, and downed it. She tapped the memoir. "How is this going to set Joey and me up for life?"

"Your father wanted to make amends for not being there for you, and for what happened to Joey. And he wanted to give you an adventure, something to bring you back together, the way you were as children."

Harriet leaned back in her chair and twisted her head from side to side, trying to loosen her neck, stiff from the stress this conversation had caused. "We're seventy, not seven. I'm sorry, but I don't understand why he went to all this trouble. Why didn't he just put the coins in a lock box and give you the key?"

"We're almost there, Harriet. Patience, please."

Joey laughed. "Harriet is not known for that personality trait."

She glared at Joey, and Dagenhart continued. "Before things went wrong for Joey, the world was right for Penny and his children. You didn't need his support. You didn't need his coin collection. He decided to write a memoir about his life, with particular focus on the history of the Charlotte Gold Rush, how he collected his coins, and how a reader could find his treasure."

"To clear his conscience?" Harriet asked.

"Partly, but also—"

Joey interrupted. "To offer a scavenger hunt to the world."

Harriet scoffed. "Who does that?"

Dagenhart continued. "Penny got the idea from a book he read. It was billed as the ultimate treasure map, with clues to find treasure a millionaire collected and hid around the United States, everything from rare paintings, to antiquities, to sports memorabilia, to precious metals and rare gems. Penny thought if he hid his rare gold coins in Charlotte and wrote about Charlotte's gold rush, people would learn about the history he loved. He asked me to do the legal work to publish the memoir."

Harriet was confused as to Dagenhart's role. "I'm sorry. I thought my father gave the memoir to Carrie to keep for us."

Dagenhart nodded. "He did. When he decided not to publish, he made changes just for you. He gave one copy to Carrie and one copy to me. He hoped one of us would survive long enough for Joey to get out of prison. When Carrie got sick, she gave me her copy to keep it safe."

Joey picked up the memoir and took a closer look at the title. "Why didn't he publish it?"

"You and Harriet. With you in prison, his cancer diagnosis, and his decision to commit suicide—which I tried to talk him out of—he wanted the two of you to have his treasure. And his story. And a chance to bond with each other again."

Harriet looked at the two documents on the table. She thought about the financial crisis at the Indie and she thought about what twelve million dollars could do to alleviate that crisis. But then she thought about Penny's folly, gritted her teeth, and pushed the memoir aside.

Dagenhart raised his eyebrows. "You're angry?"

"Yes. I am. Because nobody who loves their children cuts them out of a twelve-million-dollar inheritance to create a treasure hunt for the world and then changes their mind, only to hide the inheritance and make his children solve clues to find it. And nobody in their right mind does that knowing someone else could find the coins or they could be lost or destroyed during the twenty-year period before his children learn about the treasure."

Joey stayed calm. "You're talking about our father, Harriet, the man who loved to leave us clues to find our allowance."

Dagenhart pushed the document back to Harriet. "He wasn't in his right mind. He wasn't thinking about the passage of time or what might happen to the coins before you found them. Giving the clues to you instead of the world was his way of being sure you'd find the coins. If nothing else, he had faith in your abilities."

Harriet looked at the document, then at Dagenhart. "You're telling me this memoir will lead us to a treasure worth twelve million dollars?"

"Only if you solve the clues it contains."

Joey asked a question on Harriet's mind. "Does anyone else know about the memoir?"

"Nobody else has a copy. But—"

There was always a "but" involved, especially with a lawyer.

"But what?"

"Your father told his business colleague, Junior Standish, about his coin collection, but not where he hid the coins. I don't know if Junior told anyone what Penny told him, but Penny made an effort to cover his tracks. He destroyed all paper and electronic copies of the memoir except the two bound documents in front of you. My copy has been in my safe for twenty years. Carrie's copy has been there for the last three months."

Harriet picked up the memoir and held it up to Dagenhart. "Have you read it?"

"No."

"You weren't curious?"

"I didn't say that."

"Why then?"

"I made a promise to your father. Now I've fulfilled it. What you do with the information is up to you."

∽

Harriet texted Craig. "Round up the troops. Dinner at my place at six. Steaks on the grill. Joey and I have big news about a way to save the Indie. Tell Becky to bring her boyfriend."

They stopped first at a print shop and paid to make extra copies of Penny's memoir. Their next stop was the house they'd grown up in.

When they pulled up to the curb, they sat and took in the view. Joey said what Harriet was thinking. "It's seems so much smaller now than when we were kids."

Harriet nodded. "This is what happens when you return to your childhood home. You find your castle reduced to the size of a dollhouse."

There was a condemnation notice tacked to the front door. Joey went one way while Harriet went for the notice. She ripped it off, balled it up, and threw it on the porch. She then caught up with Joey on the side of the house where Dan had pulled Landry into the basement. Joey pushed aside barricade tape and opened the crawl space door to reveal the mess of kitchen joists and floorboards over the open mine shaft.

Joey pointed. "That's where Chance's body was. Otherwise, looks about the same as it did that night."

Harriet tugged at her brother's arm and led him into a stand of trees on the property that separated it from the dirt lot with the Rudisill Mine pump shaft.

She put her hands on Joey's shoulders and turned him around, so they both faced the street, tucked within the tree cover. "Is this where you hid when you made the video?"

"Nothing gets by you, Harriet."

"More, please. How did you know Dan would bring the body here?"

"Elkin called Dan that morning, right after Landry was killed, and told him to put the body under your house."

"Why?"

"Vengeance. Elkin saw an opportunity to cause you heartbreak and get me out of the way while he implemented the rest of his plan for the Indie.

"Dan didn't know it was your house and I didn't tell him. I got back to the house before he did and filmed what happened."

"You're still not going to tell me who killed Landry?"

"Nope. If I expose the killer, your life is in danger. Look what happened to Dan."

"Joey, did it occur to you that the threat to kill me has nothing to do with protecting the killer's identity and everything to do with making sure you go back to prison for a crime you didn't commit? Which, I have to tell you, will be worse than killing me."

"Yep."

"So?

"So we need to pick up the steaks."

Harriet pulled the baked potatoes out of the oven to cool and then fixed a green salad with Granny Smith apples, chopped walnuts, red onions, and a lemon vinaigrette dressing. At the other end of Harriet's kitchen counter, Joey readied the steaks with salt, pepper, garlic sauce, and Harriet's special marinade of red wine, oil, and a pinch of saffron.

"What's that?" Joey pointed at the small electronic-looking object on the counter.

"A listening device I dismantled." Harriet set the object on a cookbook, grabbed the meat mallet Joey had used to pound the steaks, and smashed the object. "Just to be safe."

Yeager arrived first and licked his lips while Joey prepped the steaks.

"Surprised you're early, Yeager." Harriet waved the mallet at him and laughed.

"I never miss a free meal."

Craig showed up next. Harriet rewarded him with a peck on the cheek and a stack of dishes to set the table. "Thank you, dear," she whispered. Then she grinned at him.

When Nelli arrived, Harriet handed her two beers. "One for you and one for Yeager. Make yourself at home."

Roscoe showed up only to be frisked by Harriet, who took his tobacco pouch. "Not tonight, Roscoe. Wine is in the fridge."

Becky and Max, a handsome couple if Harriet ever saw one, arrived last. She hugged them and pointed to the bar. "Help yourself to vodka, bourbon, or scotch. If you prefer, there's beer and wine too. Dinner will be ready in twenty minutes."

With everyone seated at the table and their plates overflowing with food, Harriet asked them to hold hands. She said a short blessing.

"Dear Lord, we give thanks for close friends and family, here and wherever they may be, living or departed. We ask you to watch over us and them in the days to come. Give us courage to do what needs to be done, and…" Harriet opened her eyes to see if Joey looked at her. It was something they did as children during the blessing. A silent form of rebellion. Their secret. He looked at her and smiled. All other eyes around the table were closed. "…and Lord, give us the strength and ability to solve life's riddles to help those we care about."

"Amen, let's eat." Yeager lathered steak sauce over his medium-rare grass-fed beef, cut a juicy piece, and stuffed it in his mouth. "Mmmmm, that's good."

Nelli took a bite of buttered baked potato with sour cream and chives. "Delicious."

Becky especially liked the salad. "The apples and walnuts are light and tasty."

Everyone else weighed in about how much they enjoyed the meal. The food and Harriet's and Joey's moods put them in good spirits. For the first time in months, everyone relaxed.

Harriet wondered whose curiosity would get the best of them. Who would ask the first question about her big news? Her bet was on Craig because lawyers couldn't help themselves. To them, questions were like fuel. It kept their motors running. Meaning, it also could be Roscoe.

After ten minutes of eating and conversation, Harriet had her answer. She was wrong about who was most curious. It was Max.

"I hear you have some big news about how to save the Indie. Is it about your father?"

"What do you know about my father?"

"I know about his reputation as a prominent gold coin collector."

"How do you know that? Before today, Joey and I had no idea of his success."

"From the streets." He took a bite of steak.

The Indie rumor was Max had been in the mafia, but nobody in Harriet's circle was sure, and Becky didn't talk about it. Max was an Italian immigrant who'd worked in the construction business in New York until he retired—got out of the game, he'd said—and settled at the Indie, of all places, causing some residents to speculate he was in witness protection.

Harriet and her friends never cared about Max's background. He'd come to their rescue with armed helpers last year when Elkin's father tried to kill them over the Meck Dec, so all things considered, the chances were better than fifty-fifty that Max had some former unsavory business acquaintances in the know about gossip on the street.

"You must understand, Harriet, I keep my ear to the ground. People talk when they think someone has amassed a fortune and hidden it."

"What do you mean by hidden a fortune?" Nelli asked Max.

Max deferred to Harriet, who deferred to Joey, who told everyone what Vance Dagenhart told them about Penny's memoir and the hidden coins.

Nelli whooped. "Twelve million dollars and a treasure hunt to boot. What's the plan?"

Joey gave the answer—"a scavenger hunt"—and while Harriet handed out copies of Penny's memoir, he gave them their homework assignment. "Read the memoir before noon tomorrow. Focus on places Penny may have hidden the coins related to the Charlotte Gold Rush."

"What kind of coins are we looking for?" Becky asked.

Harriet pointed everyone to the photographs in the memoir's appendix. "These pictures show Dad's treasure was mostly quarter eagles, the most difficult coins to collect because of their rarity in circulation. He also acquired two collections of every one-dollar, quarter-eagle, and half-eagle denomination minted at the Charlotte Mint between 1838 and 1861."

Craig, the typical lawyer, was skeptical. "Not to throw cold water on the treasure hunt plan to save the Indie, Harriet, but do you really believe your father collected and hid twelve million dollars in gold coins and we can find it?"

"I know you're doing your job as a lawyer, Craig—seeing the glass half empty—but what do we have to lose?"

Yeager agreed. "Nothing to lose. Everything to gain. Fun time for all."

Craig withdrew his objection and affected a more positive tone. "Did Dagenhart say where Penny may have hidden the coins?"

Joey answered for him and Harriet. "Somewhere in Charlotte."

Everyone groaned at the scope of the challenge. Charlotte was a big city. And to add to the challenge, time was of the essence, as Harriet reminded everyone.

"We have less than two weeks before the foreclosure on the ten-million-dollar loan to the Indie goes through and Elkin shuts down our community. Not to mention, our friends' finances are stretched to their limits by the gold scams that won't be corrected now that the Standish Company is bankrupt. We need to find the coins to make things right, and with so little time to do it, we will need to spread out and cover as much ground as possible."

Harriet didn't say it, but something else was on her mind. She only had two weeks until the city demolished her childhood home. If they found the treasure, she could afford to repair the property, shore up the collapsed mine shaft, and stop the city's bulldozers.

Her final instructions to the group were precise. "Meet Joey here at noon tomorrow to divide up search areas." Then to Yeager: "Take this copy of the memoir to your People's Court client Mike Peterson. If he's naked, dress him, tell him to read the memoir, and tell him to meet me tomorrow at noon in the Indie library, where I can pick his history-professor brain about where Penny may have hidden the coins."

The Godfather had the last word and took his time to make his point. "I have a sixth sense regarding criminal activity. My sense is there are criminals who want the treasure as much as we do, and they are prepared to kill for it. With two people already dead, everyone should be careful."

CHAPTER 35

HOW TO WORK A PUZZLE

The next day at noon, the team gathered at Harriet's cottage, having completed their homework assignment. Even Yeager, although he bemoaned homework that involved reading. "Wish I'd had the audio version."

Joey thanked Yeager for his extra effort and took charge of the team while Harriet left for the Indie library meeting with Mike Peterson.

For the next hour, Joey and the team brainstormed a list of locations to visit based on Penny's memoir and split into three groups: Travail and Roscoe, Yeager and Nelli, and Becky and Max. The teams departed and headed in different directions.

Joey grabbed his copy of the memoir—one of the two originals—intending to join the meeting with Harriet and Mike Peterson. An envelope he hadn't noticed before fell out of the back jacket pocket of the spiral-bound memoir. He picked it up, read it, and decided to hurry. The note was important, and Harriet needed to see it.

Yeager pulled his truck to a stop in front of Harriet's uptown house. He unloaded Nelli's wheelchair and three metal detectors. Once Nelli settled in her chair, he strapped two detectors to the wheelchair's arms so their carbon shafts were at forty-five-degree angles and their detecting coils close to the ground, one on each side of her. This was Nelli's idea. "Faster this way. I can cover more ground."

Yeager and Nelli adjusted her headset and flipped on the machines. She waved to Yeager and took off, moving back and forth across Harriet's yard like a combine planting seeds. Yeager took the third detector and entered the house.

Within an hour, they'd scoured the entire property, including the basement, making it the second time Yeager had crawled on his belly under Harriet's house. Their theory had been that if Penny hid the forged coins on the property, maybe he hid the real coins there too. Unfortunately, the treasure was not there, only a few forged coins the police missed in their search.

Yeager and Nelli repeated the same routine on the empty lot behind the house where the Rudisill Mine pump shaft was located. They failed there, too, but Nelli was practical about their effort. "It was a long shot, Yeager, but it was worth a try."

Next, they loaded their equipment and headed to the two oldest cemeteries in Charlotte.

Yeager figured somebody important to the gold rush period had to be buried at Old Settler's Cemetery, established around 1768, or at Elmwood Cemetery, established later, around 1855, when the town ran out of space in Settler's. "Maybe Penny buried the coins with a corpse that mattered to the discovery of gold."

Nelli drove her metal-detecting wheelchair between graves so as not to tread on the dead, and Yeager swept the tops of the graves themselves. It took most of the afternoon, and like their earlier efforts, they came up empty.

Nelli texted Joey their report.

~

Travail and Roscoe took on the task of visiting local monuments to the gold rush era. They started at the twenty-foot-tall bronze sculpture of the gold prospector at the intersection of Trade and Tryon Streets uptown.

Travail ran his hand along the granite base and looked up at the bronze statue on top. "There is no feasible way to hide clues here for twenty years."

They gave up and walked across the street to observe a twenty-foot-diameter bronze disc that rotated on its axis, one of the first public art installations in Charlotte. "Looks like a big gold coin with a map of the city on it," Travail said.

Again, they saw no way to hide clues on the disc that the public wouldn't discover or that wouldn't disintegrate over time. Roscoe touched the disc and looked back at the gold prospector, his chaw in his mouth. "Even if these sculptures had space inside them for the coins, to put the coins inside them would have destroyed the art."

Travail had an idea. "What if we look for clues at the uptown gold mines, starting with the big three?

"The big three?"

Travail remembered what Penny wrote about them in his memoir. "In around 1825, Samuel McComb opened a mine just a few blocks from here at the site of the Carolina Panthers football stadium after he found a gold vein on his farm. It later became known as the Old Charlotte Mine, and then the Saint Catherine Mine. It was among Charlotte's big three gold mines, along with the Rudisill Mine and the Capps Mine."

Roscoe wasn't on board. "It would be a wild goose chase. Penny said in his memoir this county had around sixty gold mines, more than any other county in North Carolina. Penny would not have made the search that hard on his children."

Travail gazed in the direction of the stadium and, being a lawyer who thought about risk, concurred with Roscoe but for a different reason. "A search of the underground mines would be too unsafe with buildings and parking decks on top of them, and with shafts held up by decayed timbers subject to collapse. I agree. Too dangerous for his children." Travail looked around. "Where then?"

Roscoe suggested one last stop on their way back to the Indie. "Let's check out the gold statue in Myers Park of Hugh McManaway, the confused man who directed traffic at the corner of Providence and Queens Roads even though there were stop lights there. Penny mentioned the statue in his memoir."

The visit proved unproductive. If Hugh McManaway were alive and directing traffic that didn't need direction, he would be less confused than Travail felt. Why mention gold mines, street names, and gold monuments in the memoir, if not to make their job more difficult?

Travail texted Joey to give him the bad news on their search.

Becky and Max strolled hand in hand among the streets of South End, looking for what, they knew not. They followed the streets mentioned in Penny's memoir having to do with the gold rush.

Carson Boulevard honored the family that purchased and ran the Rudisill Mine in the nineteenth and twentieth centuries. Summit Avenue, formerly Gold Street, ran across the Rudisill Mine. The Rudisill gold vein ran along Mint Street, and the city named Catherine Street for the Saint Catherine Mine. And, of course, there was Penman Street, named after Englishman John Penman, who ran the Rudisill Mine and who Penny thought his gold-digging Methodist ancestor.

For several hours, Becky and Max traversed the historically named streets, paying particular attention to the area near Penman Street, what they surmised might be the Penman family's yellow brick road. But nothing stood out to them as a place to bury and preserve a treasure for twenty years. If Penny had hidden his coins along one of these streets, they'd have to dig up the entire Gold District to find them, a search that would take years.

Becky texted Joey they hadn't found any places they thought Penny hid his treasure.

∼

Harriet found a fully clothed Mike Peterson—a good start that he was dressed—standing in front of floor-to-ceiling bookshelves in the Indie library. He had his back to her as he ran his hand along book spines in the fiction section.

"Looking for a good book to read?"

He turned. "Ah, Harriet. Yes. Looking for a good mystery. Maybe a thriller. Got any ideas?"

She plopped her copy of Penny's memoir on the mahogany library table in front of him and pointed at it. "Yes. Right there."

He dropped his copy beside hers. "Already read it."

They took seats across from each other. "Are you a book critic, Mike?"

"I've been known to have my opinions." He smiled.

Harriet tapped Penny's memoir. "Let's start with the themes. Your thoughts?"

"Penny's coming-of-age theme was nice, but not central to the plot. His childhood loneliness and family trauma themes were handled with openness and deftly placed below the surface plot to remind us what he and his family had been through, but again, not the crux of the story. The theme that resonated most with me was how his children were the heroes of his story, not him. You and Joey were his real treasure."

Harriet swallowed. She hadn't expected her jest for Mike to critique her father's memoir to hit her so hard. She felt moisture in her eyes. Because, honestly, she, too, had seen more in the memoir than a treasure map. Her father, like a good memoirist, had been twice as hard on himself as anyone else, and she'd learned things about him she didn't know, things that helped her understand him better.

Her father, in his unique voice, told them about his journey through life, faults and all, and about his passion for Charlotte's gold history that led him away from his children. One line made her cry at the lost opportunities: "I can never repair the emotional harm I've done to my family by my search for my fool's gold. I am deeply sorry for abandoning them the way I did."

Mike's voice softened. "You're not here to talk about book themes, are you, Harriet?"

That was true. She wiped her eyes.

"Vance Dagenhart believes my father hid his rare coin collection in Charlotte at a place of historical significance to the Charlotte Gold Rush."

"Makes perfect sense."

"What do you think about the Rivafinoli Passage, the alley where Landry died, as a hiding place? Dad went on and on about the Chevalier in his memoir, quite impressed he fought for Napoleon in his Italian campaigns, not to mention his influence on gold mining in Charlotte."

"Not a bad guess, but I don't believe the alleyway is the spot. You'd have to knock down brick walls and jackhammer the pavement to find coins."

"Do you have an idea?"

"As a matter of fact, yes."

"And that would be?"

Mike leaned toward her. "The Charlotte branch of the US Mint."

Harriet groaned. She was wasting her time with this man who was supposed to be the expert on Charlotte's gold rush history. "There is no Charlotte Mint anymore, Mike."

Harriet knew this because she had spent Saturday in the federal courthouse, which sat on the exact spot where the U.S. Mint operated until—as Penny mentioned in his memoir—the Confederacy seized it in 1861 and turned it into a military headquarters. It then operated as an assay office until it closed in the early 1900s.

Mike was not dissuaded. "When the Charlotte branch of the U.S. Mint closed for good, the federal government dismantled it, moved the pieces to a new site, and local citizens raised the money and rebuilt it to look like it did before but with a new purpose."

Penny's memoir had mentioned the mint building's history, but Harriet hadn't paid close enough attention. "I'm listening."

"In the 1930s, the Charlotte Woman's Club turned the Charlotte

Mint into the Mint Museum of Art, the first art museum in North Carolina."

"You think my father hid his coins at the Mint Museum of Art?"

"No. I think he hid the last clue there, the clue that will lead to the coins. And I think he hid the coins somewhere very safe to ensure they would be there when you find the answer."

Mike searched on his phone and showed Harriet a picture from the Mint Museum's website. "This photograph shows the current museum's backside, which is exactly what the Charlotte Mint looked like from the front when it made gold coins. It's not used as an entrance now, but the facade is a historic relic, dating back to 1837. Tangible history from the gold rush era. A perfect place for a person in love with Charlotte's gold history to leave a clue."

"You seem pretty sure about this, Mike."

Mike nodded. "So sure, Harriet, that if I am wrong, I will walk naked through the dining hall at dinnertime."

Harriet's mood lifted at Mike's humor. "You win either way, don't you, Mike?"

He shrugged and smiled before the sound of running feet in the hallway caused them both to look at the library door. Seconds later, Joey burst into the room, panting and waving an envelope. "Y'all need to see this. It was tucked in the back of my copy of the memoir."

He forced the envelope into Harriet's hands. It was addressed to *My beloved Joey and Harriet*. It was unmistakably Penny's handwriting.

Harriet fumbled as she pulled a single sheet of paper out and unfolded it.

Dear Joey and Harriet,

I hope my life story will not be too painful for you to read, but it's the truth, and that's the best I can offer you.

Truly, I am sorry for the pain I caused you when I went in search of gold and ignored you. I should have been a better father. A better husband. I should have seen my quest as a fool's errand. My family—you, in particular—were more important than gold, but I was blinded by the quest. I apologize from the bottom of my heart.

Should I apologize for the treasure hunt I'm sending you on? I suspect Harriet is livid about it, but you are both such good problem-solvers. You won all our scavenger hunts as children and you were quick to solve the riddles I gave you. Together, you will have no problem using the memoir to find my coin collection. The coins are yours. I know you will find a good use for them.

Harriet will probably say I should have given my lawyer the key to a lockbox with the coins inside, or at the very least, given you a more direct clue without the bother of having to read my memoir. Below you will find that clue, but I hope you read the memoir too. It is my confession and my apology. And it's the story of your father, warts and all.

A clue: History and art have a lot in common. They are both meant to be celebrated, explored, studied, critiqued, and examined. You cannot go back in time, but you can honor the past by treating it like the artwork that it is. When I am nothing more than a distant memory, you can stand on the ground where I stood and touch the rare coins I gathered if you link the past and the present. Where better to find the coins than where they got their start? Where better to establish your future than by understanding your past?

May you soar like eagles, my dear children.

All my love, Dad.

Harriet and Joey locked eyes. She handed the note to Mike. He read it to himself and smiled. "Did I tell you the story about the gold eagle that hangs on the backside of the Mint Museum of Art?"

Joey's phone buzzed three times. He looked first and showed his phone to Harriet. "Texts from Nelli, Craig, and Becky. They struck out."

Mike had a different spin. "I'd say they did you a favor by ruling out the other locations."

Harriet thought about what the Godfather would say about what she was thinking. "There will be good security, Harriet. After all, it is a museum."

〜

Bailey Standish had stayed as quiet as possible in a small corner of the Indie library reading room, next to the room where Harriet and Mike discussed Penny Penman's gold coin treasure. She'd come to the spot to make notes on the best strategy to recover the money Elkin had lost for them, and she couldn't believe her luck.

Here she was struggling to consider how best to deal with their financial setback when the answer fell in her lap.

For years, Sterling was convinced Penny Penman had collected and hidden a treasure. She hadn't believed him. Until now.

Bailey waited until Harriet, Mike, and Joey left the library and then called Sterling to report the good news. She was giddy when he answered.

Sterling Standish sat alone in his tower in the sky, where he sulked behind the door with the Utility Closet sign. He'd wasted no time changing the door's combination lock to keep Elkin out. The traitor had deceived Sterling, and now Sterling had lost everything.

Who knew it was impossible to dig for gold in South End? Who knew it was a pipe dream to think the state and city would give regulatory approval to the project? And who knew the physical obstacles were too great to mine gold or build an underground museum?

Elkin knew. That's who. And it made Sterling seethe to realize Elkin had scammed Sterling, too, playing on Sterling's weakness, his desire to honor his father's wishes to dig for gold and celebrate Charlotte's gold history.

Sterling—with his eyes wide open now—could kick himself. Why had he been so gullible to believe the engineering report Elkin had doctored was real?

He peered out the floor-to-ceiling window at the sight of the big dig—the hole in the ground into which he had poured so much money —and regretted hiring Elkin and everything that followed, especially what he did to Dan.

During Joey's trial, when they spied Harriet walk off with Dan after he had testified, Elkin said Dan, not Penny, killed Junior, causing Sterling to snap, corner Dan that night at his home, and demand Dan confess to killing his father.

Dan resisted and scoffed at the idea. "I didn't kill Junior."

Angry and unconvinced, Sterling shot Dan in the same place Landry got his—between the eyes. Only now, as Sterling looked down on his South End failure, he knew Dan was innocent. And he knew he'd been set up by Elkin to kill Dan, to remove the only witness who could expose Elkin's role in hiding Landry's body.

The gun Sterling used to kill Dan was from his grandmother Celia's collection, matching pistols that had once belonged to his father. Its duplicate was missing from the folding case when he borrowed the gun from Celia without telling her. He hoped the police wouldn't trace the gun he used to kill Dan to Celia. She'd been kind to him and didn't deserve the mess he'd created.

He looked at the gun on the table and thought about his situation. The gun was an option, although Bailey—even Bailey—might miss him.

If he didn't do what he was thinking about doing, there was only one way for the Standish Company to recover: Penny Penman's treasure.

Over the years, Sterling had heard the rumor and hired people to find it, but they'd run into dead ends. Nobody believed Sterling about the treasure. Not even his wife.

His phone buzzed. It was Bailey.

He answered, listened, and depression gave way to opportunity. By the time the call ended, they had a plan. Surveillance had become their new best friend.

All he and Bailey had to do was follow Harriet and her friends until they found the answer to where Penny had hidden his fortune.

Palming the gun in his hand, the one he'd used to kill Dan, he decided if it became necessary, he'd use the gun again. He had nothing more to lose and everything to gain.

~

On Thursday, Friday, and Saturday, Harriet coordinated visits by Craig, Roscoe, Becky, and herself to the Mint Museum of Art.

Harriet asked Joey and Yeager to stay away from the museum. They complained, of course, but Harriet had her reasons. "When we are reasonably sure we know where Penny hid the answer to the treasure's location, you two will go get it. Your faces need to be unrecognizable."

Harriet now believed Mike's theory. Her father had stashed the answer to where to find the coins at the museum and hidden the coins in a safe place.

Now all they had to do was find out where at the museum Penny hid the answer.

Roscoe, acting very much like the art lover he was but without his tobacco, took tours of the exhibit rooms. Craig, posing as a potential donor, met with fundraising personnel to learn about previous and upcoming capital projects. Becky, who pretended to be a museum history researcher, met with the museum's librarian, where they examined original Mint blueprints and compared the original Mint's design to the existing structure, which had doubled in size twice.

Harriet made friends with the archives director, who gave Harriet a personal tour after Harriet explained she was doing research for a novel set during the Charlotte Gold Rush period. It was a white lie, but a means to an end to help her Indie friends.

The director took Harriet through the upper floors. Now used as art exhibit rooms, they first used the space as the superintendent's residential quarters, the coining room, the assayer's room, and the melting rooms. Harriet glanced at where the entrance was in 1837 and visualized what it was like to welcome miners with their raw gold.

Next, the director took Harriet downstairs to the basement—an area off limits to the public—where the building's basement structure was the same as it was when it was an active mint in uptown Charlotte, with its stone walls, barrel ceilings, and tight quarters. Now the space was used for administrative offices, but at one time, there were boilers, a blacksmith shop, private stores, and an ore-crushing room. Harriet imagined the heat and fumes as they must have been in the 1830s.

On Harriet's last visit, the archives director walked the outside grounds with her. They toured the gardens and stood back to view the original facade and entrance, where an entire economy was born in 1837. Steps rose to a door that helped shape Charlotte's future. Above the door was a gold eagle. The director pointed at the golden symbol of economic independence.

"The original eagle was wooden, with gold leaf, and had a fifteen-foot wingspan, the largest eagle replica in the United States. They repaired the eagle for the 1930s museum opening, but by the early '70s, the wood was too brittle, and they commissioned a replacement. What you see is sixty pounds of polyester resin and fiberglass, gilded with gold leaf, with a ten-foot wingspan. It took a crane to hoist it onto its nest."

The eagle made Harriet think of what Joey told them at the trial, *It's not what it looks like.*

"What's that dark spot under the eagle's breast, between its legs?" Harriet pointed.

"That has been a recurring problem since the museum opened. Fitting, don't you think, that our eagle guards a hornet's nest?"

Harriet remembered her history and nodded. "A hornet's nest of rebellion" is what British general Cornwallis called Charlotte when he was here during the American revolution.

A memory flooded her brain, and she smiled. The answer to the riddle was so like her father, the playful dad she remembered when she was a child. The one with the sense of humor.

In the distance, under a stand of trees hidden from view, Sterling and Bailey Standish watched Harriet and the museum employee carry on their conversation.

They paid close attention when Harriet pointed at the gold eagle above the door.

CHAPTER 36

HOW TO SOLVE TWO MURDERS

Harriet welcomed Detective Sizemore to her Indie cottage and invited him through to her back deck where Craig, Roscoe, and Joey sat at a round picnic table.

It was Monday morning, one week since the court freed Joey on bail, and the detective was here with a few questions for Harriet and Joey. Craig set it up, and he and Roscoe were here as their lawyers. Yeager was absent. He was gathering the clothes and supplies he and Joey would use when they went to the Mint Museum tomorrow.

As he took a seat at the picnic table, Detective Sizemore peered into Harriet's garden.

"I trust you aren't here to do more damage to my plants," Harriet said.

"I'm sorry about the mess we made. Someone led us astray."

Harriet had set out coffee, juice, and biscuits. The detective tamped his smoldering cigar against his palm to snuff it out. He stuffed the cigar's remains in his coat pocket, poured a cup of coffee, and picked up a biscuit.

"You weren't led astray entirely." Harriet said it as if it were an afterthought.

The detective dipped his chin and stared at her over the lip of his coffee cup. "Why do you say that, Ms. Keaton?"

Craig placed his hand on Harriet's forearm and addressed the detective. "Do you consider Harriet or Joey suspects?"

"Not anymore."

Roscoe pushed the detective for the critical addendum. "Can they speak freely without fear of prosecution?"

"Depends on what they tell me."

Roscoe played it safe. "In that case, this meeting is over."

The detective shook his head. "Okay. Okay. Yes. They can speak freely."

Harriet handed him the napkin Craig had used. "Write it on this napkin and then we talk."

When they inked the deal, bordered by a dark coffee stain, the detective asked Harriet his question again. "Why wasn't I led astray—entirely—with the search of your garden?"

"Because someone did bury a gun in my garden. Probably the gun that killed Landry."

Sizemore sat up straight. "Where is the gun now?"

"Not important. What is important is that whoever buried the gun in my garden went to the trouble to frame me." Harriet stared at the detective. "Your turn to share."

Sizemore didn't seem pleased by Harriet's response, but Harriet, Joey, and their lawyers waited him out, and he relented. "A resident saw a woman walk into your backyard carrying a bag the night before we got the tip."

"Was it a plastic bag?"

The detective eyed Harriet. "Yes. The witness was sure of the woman's identity. Said she's caused a lot of trouble at the Indie and made a name for herself."

"Let me guess. Bailey Standish?"

"One and the same."

Harriet folded her arms. "Were you as quick to arrest her as you were to search my garden?"

Detective Sizemore sipped his coffee and took his time to respond, perhaps to give Harriet's sarcasm a chance to settle. "It's not that simple. The witness is eighty-five years old, she didn't have her glasses on, and it was dark. And besides that, Bailey has an alibi from Robert Elkin, who says she was with him at the time."

"Ha. And you believe them?"

"No. I do not. It's why I am here." The detective ate his biscuit and brushed the crumbs from his rumpled suit. "Tell me about Elkin."

Harriet explained their history with Elkin and why Elkin had it out for them. Craig added the piece about the *vengeanceissweet* email he'd received and why Elkin could be a killer, like his father before him.

The detective shook his head. "I hate to break it to you, but Elkin has an ironclad alibi for the time when Chance Landry died. Same for Bailey."

Joey spoke for the first time. "That's accurate."

Detective Sizemore stared at Joey, as he took out his note pad. "Would you like to tell us more?"

Joey glanced at Harriet, who put her hand on his shoulder, as if to indicate it was time to come clean. He nodded.

"Landry and I met at the Rivafinoli Passage. He thought it appropriate, given the gold history. It's a small alleyway. Secluded. Very little activity in the early morning on a weekday."

The detective made a note. "Did Barnard kill Landry?"

"No."

"But he was there?"

"Yes."

The detective waited for Joey to continue.

"There were four of us. Me. Landry. Dan Barnard. And the killer."

Joey raised his hand to ward off another question. "Before you ask me the killer's name, I will tell you what I told everyone else here. Robert Elkin threatened to kill Harriet if I revealed the killer's identity. I'm not going there. At least not yet."

"Interesting." The detective jotted more notes on his pad. "Why did this unnamed person kill Landry?"

"Because Landry admitted he killed Junior."

The detective nodded. "Seems Sterling is our man. He must have killed Landry as pay-back for killing his father."

Joey didn't flinch, his poker face intact.

Craig supported the detective's theory. "Roscoe and I came to the same conclusion, but Joey won't confirm. He's worried about Harriet."

Detective Sizemore didn't push Joey. "For argument's sake, let's say Sterling killed Landry. What did he do next?"

"For argument's sake, Sterling called Elkin for help with the body and left the scene. A few minutes later, Elkin called Dan with instructions to put Landry's body at an address in South End. I asked Dan the address, and he told me. He didn't know that was my childhood home, and I didn't tell him. If I did tell him and he'd put the body somewhere else, Elkin would know that I knew of his involvement. I wanted to hold onto that card."

The detective looked up from his notes. "Why didn't you report the murder?"

"I was a convicted felon who had skipped his parole meeting and was at the scene when Landry died. Reporting the murder didn't seem like a good idea at the time."

Detective Sizemore shrugged. "Go on, then."

"I couldn't tell Dan to take the body somewhere else because it would get back to Elkin and he'd probably set me up as an accomplice. So I hurried to the house and filmed the whole thing. I planned to move the body after Dan left, but the mine shaft caved in and here we are."

The detective made a few more notes and shut his pad.

Harriet watched the detective for any sign that he believed Joey, but his face gave nothing away. "Your thoughts, Detective?"

"Sterling is the prime suspect for Landry's murder." The detective took out another cigar and lit it. "As for Dan Barnard, I think he died because he knew too much. He knew who killed Landry. He knew who told him to put Landry's body under your house. That makes Sterling and Elkin the prime suspects for Dan's murder."

Detective Sizemore thanked Harriet for the coffee and biscuit, apologized again for tearing up her garden, and thanked Joey for the information.

Everyone departed, but not before Harriet informed the detective the Indie was under a financial gun Elkin had pointed at them. "This coming Friday, the court will foreclose on the Indie's ten-million-dollar note. When Elkin owns the Indie, we're done. Please work fast."

CHAPTER 37

TREASURE HUNT SHOWDOWN

Yeager, dressed in button-front cotton coveralls, stepped through the Mint Museum's front door on Tuesday at noon and presented forged paperwork at the front desk. "Shouldn't take but thirty minutes to do the work."

The desk clerk looked Yeager up and down and made a phone call as a precaution. Yeager set the toolbox he hefted on the floor while he waited.

Joey, dressed like Yeager, waited outside, but the desk clerk could see both him and the extension ladder he carried through the building's expansive glass front wall.

The desk clerk hung up the phone. "Our maintenance technician is out to lunch. She won't be back for an hour. Can you wait until she gets back?"

Yeager knew the schedule because Harriet had briefed him. She'd told him if he faced any resistance to act indifferent.

"Unfortunately, we can't wait, and we can't be back for two weeks. It makes no difference to us. We get paid by the hour. But the gold eagle needs to be tightened or it could fall. And those hornets are likely to sting someone at this weekend's event on the back lawn. It's up to you. We'll give the eagle a good cleaning while we're here if you want us to do the job now."

The desk clerk looked at his phone and decided. "Do you know the way?"

Yeager did.

~

Yeager led Joey around the building, past the garden, to the façade with its magnificent eagle perched over the original entrance.

While Joey held the ladder, Yeager climbed with his spray can. Midday was not the best time for what he was about to do, but Yeager popped the can's top, let loose the stream, and doused the nest in white foam. The hornets weren't happy.

Joey laughed as Yeager grabbed both sides of the ladder, threw his legs to the side rails, and slid down the twenty feet like a firefighter on his way to a five-alarm fire. As the hornets chased Yeager, he weaved and dodged and sprayed foam into the air.

Five minutes and a few stings later, Yeager climbed the ladder again, stepped on the porch roof above the Mint's 1837 entrance, and poked the nest. It fell, bounced off the ledge, and tumbled to the ground. Joey bagged the nest, set it aside, and climbed the ladder. They inspected the space below the eagle's breast, previously guarded by angry patriots.

Yeager recalled Harriet's explanation about her solution to Penny's puzzle. Every chapter in Penny's memoir contained an eagle reference. The way Penny told his life story, he had an eagle eye for rare coins at a young age and was an Eagle Scout in high school. At nineteen, he saw his first bald eagle. With his grandfather, he loved watching the Philadelphia Eagles football team. And so on. One chapter covered the Charlotte Mint's half-eagle gold dollars, and another covered the mint's quarter-eagle gold dollars. And then there was the note with the invitation to Harriet and Joey to soar like eagles.

But it was the hornets that sealed it for Harriet. "I know the current nest wasn't there twenty years ago, but Dad would have done his research and known about the recurring hornet problem. He was a detail guy, and he had a sense of humor."

Joey picked the story up from there. "Harriet and I went camping with Dad when we were twelve, and I thought it would be fun to poke a hornet's nest. Dad warned me against it, but I was sure I could outrun them. I was wrong, of course, and got what I deserved. I never heard my father laugh so hard before or since that time, and he never let me live it down. Dad's moral for that story, every time he told it was: 'If you are going to poke a hornet's nest, you better have an excellent reason.' We now have that reason, but when we go, Yeager handles the insecticide."

Yeager was willing to kill some hornets, but to what end? "Harriet, do you really think Penny would hide twelve million dollars' worth of rare coins inside an eagle attached to the Mint Museum's second-story exterior wall?"

"You've been hanging around Craig too long, Yeager. Stay positive. My father wanted Joey and me to learn about his passion. He didn't want us to be arrested. I don't think he hid the coins inside the eagle. I think he hid the answer to where the coins are behind it, protected by the hornets."

Yeager and Joey leaned in close to look below the eagle's breast. There were four Phillips-head screws that held a plate in place on the wall. The plate was in the crevice behind where the hornet's nest had been.

Joey took a screwdriver and removed the four screws and the plate. Inside the cavity was an envelope addressed to Joey and Harriet. In the top left corner, where the return address would normally be, was the name: *Penny Penman*.

With the eagle dusted and cleaned, Yeager walked with a purpose to his truck, the envelope tucked in his pocket, with Joey close behind.

As they made their way, hope for the Indie and their friends was in the air.

Yeager had left his truck at the parking lot's far end, close to Randolph Road. He saw from a distance, it didn't sit level.

When they got to the truck, they knelt beside each other to examine two flat tires on one side. Yeager felt something hard against his head.

"Easy now," the man's voice said. "This gun is no toy."

Joey started to turn his head in the direction of the voice, but the voice commanded him to stop. "Don't move, Joey, or Yeager will have a terrible last day in this world."

"Just shoot them both, and be done with it." The woman's voice was shrill.

The gun pressed tighter against Yeager's head. "All we require is the envelope, and we will be on our way."

"And if I say no?"

The man cocked the gun.

Joey nudged Yeager. "It's not worth dying over."

"You don't know your sister. If I give up the envelope, Harriet will kill me."

"Don't worry. She'll find another way to punish you."

The man tapped the gun against Yeager's head. "Now."

"Okay. Okay. Hold your horses." Yeager took the envelope from his pocket and held it over his shoulder. A hand snatched it away. The pressure against his head disappeared.

They turned to see Sterling and Bailey Standish hop into a waiting vehicle with a driver, who sped off.

Joey borrowed Yeager's phone and made a call. "Harriet, I've got good news and bad news."

Harriet was on her front porch at the Indie when Yeager and Joey pulled up. She waved them inside, where Craig and Nelli waited.

Harriet addressed Yeager. "Tell us about the envelope."

"After we found what we were looking for, I put the envelope in my pocket. We cleaned the eagle—seemed like the right thing to do— and then—"

Harriet turned to Joey. "Can you get to the point? Did you open the envelope?"

Joey's shoulders sagged. "No. We thought we'd do that here. My fault."

A problem, yes, but nobody's fault. "What was on the outside of the envelope?"

Joey appeared to concentrate. "Dad addressed the envelope to you and me and wrote his name in the top left corner. It was definitely his handwriting. The back of the envelope was odd. It featured a drawing of a tree sapling. That's it."

"Describe it."

Joey did the best he could.

Harriet felt an idea form in her head as she walked to the living room window. She looked through the window at the front yard she'd tended for the last twenty years to be sure.

When she turned around, she had a big smile on her face. "It's time we set a trap."

Everyone listened to Harriet's side of a phone call she made to Peaches, the activities director who had been trying in recent weeks to get Harriet to confirm or deny her relationship with Craig.

"Peaches, this is Harriet. We're trying to catch a criminal, and we need your help. Please tell everyone at dinner I will be sleeping with Craig at his cottage tonight."

"Good for you," Peaches squealed, loud enough for everyone in the room to hear.

Harriet ended the call, and Craig stuttered before he hit his mark. "Harriet, I don't understand why you told her to tell people we're sleeping together at my place tonight."

Yeager slapped his buddy on the back. "Craig Travail, there is no sense in you trying to catch up. Just hold on for the ride. Harriet has a plan."

Yeager was correct. Harriet wasn't spending the night with Craig at his cottage. "You are sleeping here," she told him.

"I am?"

"You like excitement, don't you?"

"Um." Craig looked confused. Or was he embarrassed? Harriet laughed.

"In fact, I'd like everyone to sleep over." When she explained why, they understood.

Harriet made a phone call. "Detective Sizemore, please." She waited fifteen seconds for him to answer and explained what she knew and what she needed him to do.

Next, Harriet gave an assignment to Yeager. He left to fulfill her request.

"What now?" Nelli asked.

"We wait."

Harriet walked to the kitchen and opened her pantry. "How about spaghetti and garlic bread for dinner?"

Harriet hosted dinner in her dining room. While they ate, they talked about how to be careful and where to position themselves for the evening.

"Harriet, do you really think they will come tonight?" Yeager asked.

"I do. They're desperate." Harriet walked to the dining room window and raised the shade to reveal her Eastern Redbud. "My father helped me plant that tree. It was the last thing we did together before Joey's trial."

Harriet put her face to the window and peered through it. "Where did you conceal your wildlife cam, Yeager?"

"Midway up the tree. It's got a wide-angle lens with good audio and night vision."

"Perfect."

Harriet offered Key lime pie for dessert and nobody refused. "The after-dinner drink option is coffee. We need to be alert tonight."

They'd already asked the neighbors to keep their lights off tonight.

Harriet noticed the streetlight. At sunset, it would brighten on an automatic timer. She asked Yeager to handle it. "But please, not with your rifle."

"Consider it done."

Early Wednesday morning, around one thirty—the same time of day Joey met Landry in a dark alley in South End four and a half months ago—Harriet snuggled with Craig on her living room couch while Yeager and Joey slept in chairs near them. They had taken turns on lookout, and Nelli was now on duty in the next room.

Harriet was too alert to do more than doze. Her phone buzzed with a text from Nelli. "Bad guys in sight."

Harriet's phone buzzed again. "Three figures. Two men and a woman. One has a shovel."

Harriet nudged her friends awake. "Operation Shallow Dig is underway."

Everyone except Nelli went out the back door and down the back deck steps. Craig and Yeager flared out and took up concealed positions behind opposite corners of the house. Joey and Harriet walked past Travail and stepped into the front yard.

A man on his knees worked the ground at the base of the redbud tree with a short-handled shovel. Sterling stood over him, with Bailey by his side.

"Did you lose something?" Harriet's tone was Good Samaritan helpful, as if she were assisting a stranger in need.

Sterling swiveled and reached into his pocket.

"We're not armed," Joey said. "If that's a gun you're after, I suggest you keep it there. You're liable to wake the neighbors. Harriet tells me retirees are light sleepers."

Harriet added the postscript. "If you wake the neighbors, you won't finish your work." Then she whistled.

Yeager and Craig stepped into view and walked halfway to the street on each side of the yard. The redbud tree was closer to Craig's side.

The garage door lifted and Nelli emerged, motoring her way down the driveway past Yeager and into the street, where she took up her position. "You're surrounded," she yelled.

Sterling pulled a gun from his pocket and held it by his side, causing the man on his knees to stop his work and wait for instructions.

"Keep digging."

Sterling raised the gun and aimed it first at Harriet and Joey, then swept it in an arc that included Travail, Nelli, and Yeager. "This gun has enough bullets for all of you. Don't move. Let us finish our work, and you can live to attend another craft class."

Harriet crossed her arms. "Does that mean you have a few bullets left over after you killed Chance Landry and Dan Barnard?"

"What makes you think I killed Landry?"

"Motive. Opportunity. To name a few."

Bailey interjected with disgust in her tone. "Sterling didn't kill Landry. He only killed Dan, and he did it against my advice."

Sterling raised his voice. "Shut up, Bailey."

Bailey's bracelets clinked as she gestured with her hands. "Doesn't matter. I know you. You will lose your temper and kill them all if you don't get the gold."

Sterling raised the gun and pointed it at Bailey. "If you don't shut up, I will use one of my bullets on you."

The digger's shovel hit something hard. He reached down with his hands and removed loose dirt from the hole. Sterling moved close and looked over the man's shoulder. "Pull it out."

The man retrieved a steel storage box with handles and set it on the ground at Sterling's feet. In the distance, sirens blared.

Harriet looked at the man on his knees. "If I were you, I'd leave now. Things are about to get real for your boss."

Sterling focused on the box as the man backed away. By the time Sterling kneeled and lifted the lid, the man was gone.

Bailey stepped close to Sterling, but as the siren grew louder, she froze. Harriet couldn't help herself. "How do you like being Indie president now, Bailey?"

Careful to keep his gun pointed at Harriet and Joey with one hand,

Sterling used his other hand to shine his phone's flashlight in the open box. The coins' golden hue gleamed.

Flashing lights from two vehicles appeared through the trees on the lake's opposite side. Bailey panicked. "I'll get the car."

She ran toward the street and away from the on-coming vehicles toward a dark blue Tesla. Before she got there, Nelli acted. She rammed Bailey with her wheelchair, fostering a collision that sent them both sprawling to the pavement.

Sterling slammed the lid shut on the coin box and tried to lift the box with one arm, but it was too heavy. He pointed the gun at Harriet as he spoke to Joey. "Put the box in the Tesla. Trunk is unlocked. If you don't, I will shoot your sister."

Two police cars screamed to a halt at the curb. Detective Sizemore was the first one out. He drew his revolver and shouted, "Drop the weapon."

Sterling yelled back. "You drop yours." He circled around Harriet and put the gun to her neck, keeping her body between him and the detective. Joey stood halfway to the curb with the box in his arms.

A second later, Harriet heard a grunt as bodies collided behind her. She turned to see Craig take Sterling to the ground and the gun fly from his hand. Sterling rolled and reached for the gun, but she kicked it away as Craig pressed Sterling to the grass. Shouts and footsteps filled her ears as uniformed reinforcements arrived.

Detective Sizemore put handcuffs on Sterling and read him his rights while an officer appeared to do the same with Bailey in the street. Yeager helped Nelli into her wheelchair, while Harriet picked up Sterling's gun and handed it to the detective. "This may be the gun Sterling used to kill Dan."

"How do you know he killed Dan?"

Yeager reached up into the tree and pulled his wildlife video camera down, ejected the SIM card, and handed it to the detective. "Everything you need to know is on here."

Detective Sizemore thanked Yeager and checked on Craig. "You okay, Counselor? Let me guess. You played linebacker in high school?"

Craig rubbed his shoulder and groaned. "A long time ago."

The detective looked at Joey, who held the box in his arms. To Harriet, he said, "Is there anything I need to know about that box?"

Without turning to look at Joey, Harriet said, "What box?"

Detective Sizemore chuckled. He lit a cigar, took a deep draw, and puffed. He looked at his watch. "I only have a few hours for a nap before I meet with a judge to get a warrant so I can pay an early morning visit to the person who started all this trouble."

Harriet was grateful for his help. "Thank you for coming so fast. Let me know when you find out who killed Landry. Joey won't tell me."

He saluted Harriet. "It's on the list."

Harriet sat on the ground next to Craig. "How ya feeling, sport?"

Craig grunted.

She leaned in and gave him a bear hug. In his ear, she whispered her appreciation. "Thank you for being my hero."

CHAPTER 38

THE GIG IS UP

Yeager, still excited after their early morning adventure in Harriet's front yard, followed Becky and Max into the elevator. Becky punched the button, and the elevator hummed its way to the twenty-fourth floor. It was 8:15 a.m. They were cutting it close.

The detective would be here in the next thirty to forty-five minutes, and they needed to be gone by then. They also needed to succeed.

With less than forty-eight hours before the foreclosure hearing gave Elkin the power to shut down the Indie, Yeager arranged to have Max here to close the deal.

Max Esposito's special friends had done their reconnaissance and now stood guard on the building's perimeter to ensure Elkin didn't escape. Yeager had done his research too.

The Carlington, known as "the pink building" for its desert-rose glass, was a high-end luxury condo association with a swimming pool on the roof. Its units offered a sweeping view of the Charlotte skyline, the development in South End, and the tree-lined neighborhoods that bordered both. Elkin had the best view from a penthouse suite he'd rented around the time he emptied the Indie's bank accounts.

Before the elevator made it to the top floor, Max addressed Yeager. "Does his unit have an outdoor terrace?"

"It does, but why is that important?"

Max patted Yeager on the arm and smiled, leaving Yeager to wonder. He wore what Yeager considered serious attire. Black slacks, a crisp white shirt with a red tie, and a well-fitted blue blazer with a soft check pattern. A fresh white rosebud was pinned to the lapel.

Becky wore a green and white dress covered in flowers. She carried a small tan handbag and a manilla folder.

Yeager wore beat-up jeans and a torn flannel shirt. He wasn't about to wear good jeans and good flannel for Robert Elkin.

When they arrived at their destination, Yeager knocked on Elkin's door, but there was no answer. Max nodded at Yeager, and Yeager knocked again. After a few minutes, Elkin opened the door, but only halfway. He held a mug in his hand. "It's too early for visitors."

When Yeager pushed his way into the suite, Elkin pulled his phone from his pocket and attempted to make a call.

Yeager swatted the phone away and picked it up after it hit the floor.

Elkin chastised Yeager. "I will enjoy watching the police arrest you for assault and trespass."

Max was matter-of-fact when he told Elkin who was in charge. "If you live through our conversation this morning, you can call whoever you want to call."

Yeager liked Max's style. With that bluff, they were off to a good start.

They settled in chairs in the living area, although "settled" was not how Yeager would have described Elkin. He seemed less cocky than usual. Did he know something about Maximiliano Esposito's negotiating skills that Yeager didn't?

"We have a problem, Robert." Max had a deep, confident voice. Being in his eighties did not affect his ability to command a room.

"Your problem is not my concern." Elkin sat with his arms folded. Yeager sat behind him, watching his every move, and guarding against any attempted escape.

Max, who sat across from Elkin, nodded to Becky, who sat beside him. She handed a document to Elkin. "This lists the banking transactions showing where the money from the Indie reserve and operating accounts went after it left the Indie accounts."

Elkin looked at the document and smiled. "I see you are at a dead end. The last account on this list—where the Indie money supposedly went—has no money in it."

"You are correct." Becky handed Elkin more paper. "These documents show how you created a limited liability company to make loans, and how you transferred the Indie's money from the now-empty account to that LLC's account. The money didn't stay in the LLC's account long, but you know this. Your limited liability company loaned ten million dollars to a company in Vietnam who paid back the funds. They did your laundry for you."

Max smiled as he let Elkin know he shouldn't underestimate retired women. "Did you know Becky was a forensic accounting auditor? Your bad luck."

"I don't know what you are talking about." Elkin didn't look as confident as he tried to sound.

Becky pointed to the last page in Elkin's hand. "After your Vietnam cohort cleaned the stolen money, you used five million dollars to buy the note for the Standish Company's loan to the Indie. You have five million dollars of Indie money left in your account."

Max patted Becky on the knee. "Thank you, Becky." He turned to Yeager and asked for the loan-release paperwork.

Yeager reached over Elkin's shoulder and dropped it in Elkin's lap.

"What's this?" Elkin scowled.

Max adjusted the white rose in his lapel. "Something you need to sign."

Elkin read the document. "This says I release the Indie of its obligation to repay the ten-million-dollar Standish Company loan I now own, and I dismiss the foreclosure proceeding."

Elkin threw the paper on the floor and stood. "If you don't leave, you will be sorry. My people will be here soon."

Yeager grabbed Elkin's shoulders from behind and pulled him back into his seat. He came around him, fetched the paper from the floor, and shoved it in Elkin's chest.

Max, whose even tone had not changed during the meeting, stated in a calm voice what would happen next. "You are going to sign that paper releasing the Indie of its loan obligation and dismissing the fore-closure proceeding, and you are going to get on your computer and transfer the remaining five million dollars in your account into this account." He handed Elkin a note with a routing number and account number.

"The hell I will. I am entitled to that money. The Indie ruined my life and stole my law license. That money will help restore my reputa-tion, set the facts straight, and position me with the best state-bar panel to hear my plea."

Max shook his head. "It's over, Robert. Money is not going to restore your law license, especially after what you've done."

"I'm not signing."

Max reminded Elkin of what happened to Elkin's father one year earlier. "He came at us with gunfire and died trying. You are here with nothing but your lies and schemes. How do you think that is going to work out for you?"

Elkin looked at a button on the table next to him.

Max explained it had no value. "We disabled your panic buttons and your bodyguards. We will release them when we're done, but not before letting them know what will happen to them—what my family will do to them—if they don't fire you as their boss. You are alone now, Robert. You betrayed everyone you know, and nobody cares about you anymore."

Elkin drew in, narrowed his eyes, and hissed like a cornered feral cat. "I won't sign the release, and I won't transfer the money."

Max shrugged. "I didn't want it to come to this." He pulled a pistol from his blue blazer and pointed it at their nemesis. He instructed Becky and Yeager to wait for him in the hallway. "But before you go, Yeager, please open the terrace doors. We need fresh air."

Yeager paced in the hallway for ten minutes until Max came out of the penthouse suite and handed a document to Becky. "Notarized it myself."

Then to Yeager: "Tell Harriet a wire transfer just deposited five million dollars into the numbered account she set up."

Yeager grinned. "Well done, Max. Care to explain?"

"We had a pleasant chat on the balcony. Turns out, the man doesn't like heights." Max said not to worry though. "I didn't lay a finger on him."

Yeager couldn't contain his curiosity. "What convinced him?"

The Godfather smiled. "It's a bit of a cliché, but old habits die hard. I made him an offer he couldn't refuse."

Just as the threesome got off the elevator at the ground floor, Detective Sizemore and several police officers came into the lobby. Becky and Max peeled off to the left while Yeager approached the detective.

"Who was that?" The detective looked in Max's direction.

"Who?"

"That man who was with you." Sizemore pointed.

Yeager looked around. "I don't see anyone."

The detective scratched his neck. "He looked like a man on the FBI's most-wanted list."

"Can't help you there. Are you about to arrest Elkin?

The detective patted his pocket. "I have the arrest warrant."

"For Landry's murder?"

"No. We don't have the evidence. This is for felonious concealment of murder and secret disposal of a dead body."

Detective Sizemore looked around the lobby. "You watched the doors like we asked?"

Yeager nodded.

"Is he up there?"

"He's all yours."

The detective shook Yeager's hand. "I'll take it from here."

"What about Joey's case? Do you know who murdered Landry?"

"Not yet, but when Elkin understands the jail time he's facing for his role in hiding a murder, he will cut a deal to identify the killer."

The detective and two police officers boarded the elevator. Yeager dialed Harriet on his Jitterbug. Craig picked up for her.

"Craig Travail. My, my. Harriet has a boyfriend answering service now. Butler will be next, and then—"

Craig cut him off with a question. "How did it go?"

"Timing was perfect. Elkin didn't know we were coming, and the detective never knew we were there."

"What happened?"

"Justice, Craig Travail. That's what happened. Justice. Pure and simple."

EPILOGUE - LABOR DAY WEEKEND

ALL HANDS ON DECK

Travail woke energized. He left his cottage at 5:30 a.m. to swim in the Indie pool and work out at the gym. Having reignited his exercise routine before Joey's trial, he felt whole again, and if he was being honest with himself, had it not been for the change of habit, he might not have become quick, limber, and strong enough to protect Harriet from Sterling. For that, he was grateful.

On his way to the exercise facility, Yeager approached. His neighbor was many things, but in the early morning hours, he was like the man who directed traffic when the stoplights worked just fine. The Indie had a security crew, but Yeager never missed his morning rounds. He tipped his ball cap when he gave Travail the good news. "Nothing suspicious at the Indie this morning, Craig Travail."

"How about a quick workout?"

Yeager coughed.

It was a good sign, letting Travail know the universe was in balance. Had Yeager said yes to a workout, the earth might have slipped off its axis.

Travail quickened his steps toward the main building's lights. Ahead, employees unloaded delivery trucks near the kitchen while a crew assembled a large tent for the day's meals. Beside Freedom Lake, folding chairs dotted the hillside as another crew constructed a stage for the band concert.

They'd held Carrie's and Dan's memorial services on back-to-back days in the Indie chapel to overflowing crowds. They were an emotional two days for the community that caused Peaches and Nelli to come up with the idea for this Labor Day weekend celebration.

The two party planners had behaved like worker ants on a mission to nourish their colony as they planned and executed what needed to happen for the two-day event. The Indie Appreciation Festival, as they'd dubbed it, had replaced all previously scheduled Indie activities for the weekend.

Roscoe funded the event. Turns out, the ten coins Penny gave Roscoe to defend Joey twenty years ago were the real deal. Very rare coins, unaffected by the drop in the gold bullion market. Worth fifty thousand dollars, according to the Tartly coin shop on Highway 51.

The activities today would honor Dan for his better-late-than-never help to Joey and his community service. Day 2 would honor Carrie, because as Peaches explained, there would be food and drink and carousing on Day 1 and everyone needed Day 2 to gossip about it.

Travail knew the ad hoc committee, at the insistence of the soon-to-be-reimbursed scammed residents, planned to honor Harriet and Joey at tomorrow night's steak and lobster dinner. Travail's job was to make sure they attended.

Whoever said retirees didn't have energy like the younger generation hadn't seen today's schedule. First up was the buffet breakfast with Bloody Marys, from eight to ten, followed by lawn games— horseshoes, badminton, cornhole, and more—with fruit plates and mimosas.

Next was a two-hour buffet lunch spread, complimented by wine parings, beginning at 11:30 a.m. And that was just the morning.

When lunch ended, the community would gather in the afternoon to tap their toes to the battle of the old-time bands while they ate home-made ice cream from the churn. And if those weren't enough activities for one day, they'd meet for cocktails on the terrace at five, followed by homemade pizza pie.

The sit-down dinner tomorrow night would be the capstone for the food events and the warm-up for an evening of ballroom dancing. If Travail were lucky, Yeager said, Harriet would teach him the tango, and if she didn't know how, "not to worry, Craig Travail, I will teach you."

Travail definitely wasn't up for a dance with a grizzly bear, and he wasn't sure he was up for the full Indie Appreciation Festival schedule, still trying, as one of the youngest residents, to acclimate himself to the go-go years of a meaningful third act.

He dove into the pool and completed his laps at a relaxed pace.

After he toweled off, he stretched and took a turn on the treadmill, where he reflected on the last few weeks and how they'd tied up loose ends.

"I want Joey to have my father's house," Harriet had said to him.

Travail had prepared a deed for Harriet to give to Joey, but Joey pushed back when she tried to give it to him. "Dad gave the house to you, Harriet."

"Only because you were in prison. You should have it."

They argued like siblings do and reached a compromise. Joey accepted the house but insisted he do the labor for the needed repairs. She argued they had enough money to hire people to do that work, but that was Joey's line in the clay. "I have nothing else to do, Sis."

Harriet relented, but only if Joey got some help. "You're seventy years old. I don't want you to have a construction accident and spend your retirement life dead."

It turned out several Indie residents were good with tools, and two had been general contractors. A few others had grandchildren built like weightlifters. The residents and their kin, working with Joey, shored up the mine shaft sinkhole, repaired the kitchen floor, and removed the debris within a week. Travail filed the paperwork to avoid condemnation.

Meanwhile, the rare coins buried under the redbud tree were a hot topic at the Indie. Everyone wanted to see them. Harriet relented and made them available for the residents to peruse one day after lunch, after which Yeager returned them to Brian Tartly's coin shop, where his son Burt had agreed to keep them secure in the shop's safe until they could be sold. Burt confirmed the coins were authentic and should fetch at least twelve million dollars.

With Max and Becky's help, they'd successfully halted the foreclosure process on the ten-million-dollar loan, and after that was accomplished, Harriet, Becky, and Travail met with Jenny Montgomery—their rehired Indie bookkeeper—to go over the Indie books.

Becky presented Jenny with a file-stamped copy of Elkin's signed release that she'd filed at the courthouse, and Jenny's mouth fell open.

"Why would Elkin do that?" It was the same question Travail had asked Becky, but Becky told him what she told Jenny. "Best not to go there."

Jenny didn't need to go there. The Standish Company loan had replaced their stolen ten million dollars, and now Elkin had forgiven that loan. "The balance sheet looks excellent," she'd said.

With Dan's death and their president Bailey Standish in jail awaiting trial with her husband, Becky called an emergency board meeting to remove Bailey from the board and replace her and Dan with new board members.

Celia spoke first. "I understand why we need to replace Bailey, but I abstain from the vote because she is family. I hope you understand." Travail understood Celia's decision, but he didn't understand how she'd been so unlucky with her relatives and in-laws.

The board voted to replace Bailey with Roscoe. He agreed to the replacement only if they didn't make him president. That was fine because Becky resumed the position.

When no resident volunteered to replace Dan, they voted to put Nelli in his board position. It was either her or Yeager, and they unanimously chose the lesser of two distractions.

"One more thing," Becky had said. "I move to refund all illegal assessments residents have paid and remove any delinquent balances from resident accounts." Celia seconded the motion, and the motion passed

They doled out the five million dollars Elkin wired to Harriet's special account to the ten Indie investors in the South End Mining

Company. They'd spent five million dollars—$500,000 per investor—to gain stock that became worthless. Harriet had one condition for the bailout, which the humbled investors accepted on the spot. They dissolved the Indie investment club.

The fifty residents who'd invested a hundred thousand dollars each in the gold bullion coins were in a different financial dilemma. Their coins might have value someday, but their value depended on the gold bullion market. Harriet and Joey called them together and told them they were going to help them by selling their coins now, at whatever price they brought, along with enough rare coins to make them whole. Everyone in the room clapped when they heard the news. One resident yelled her appreciation. "You're my hero, Harriet. Carrie would be proud."

That left close to seven million dollars from their treasure hoard. To clear Joey's debts, they used two million dollars to pay off the civil judgments still on file against him in favor of the South End property owners defrauded in the appraisal scheme.

Next, Travail filed the paperwork to expunge Joey's conviction. Judge Williamson signed the order. With a ballpoint pen.

Harriet and Joey decided they would keep one complete set of every coin minted at the Charlotte Mint in case Yeager was correct and someone built a gold mine museum one day in uptown Charlotte. They agreed they would donate the coins to such a museum to honor their father if it happened. They also decided, but didn't tell Yeager, they might be the ones to build the museum. Not an underground museum. Something on the surface. They had close to five million dollars left to put toward the project.

Harriet and Joey made a substantial donation to the Gold District in Penny's honor. That was Joey's idea. "Every sign, event, and monument that reminded the public that Charlotte had a golden era is a reminder of my father and others like him who love the history." Like the passage that honors Count Rivafinoli, Yeager said, when he convinced Travail they had to visit it.

They parked near South Tryon and Morehead Streets, because "this is where the count lived in a gigantic house," Yeager said. The house appropriate for a count was gone, and in its place were high-rise build-ings and commercial properties. Yeager brought a walking cane with him. "It doesn't have a gold handle like they say Rivafinoli's did, but it's close enough for government work."

They strolled—Yeager said that's what the count did—from where the count's house stood to the passage he used on the way to the Rudisill Mine. Yeager stayed a few steps ahead—"You can be my assistant, Craig Travail"—because Yeager said that was how Rivafinoli walked with his barber, who dressed and shaved him every day before their daily stroll.

Travail let him have his fun. He was curious to see where all the trouble began, the place where Landry died.

Underwhelmed was the best way to describe how Travail felt upon reaching the Rivafinoli Passage. There was no grand entrance, just a back alley to a few shops and restaurants.

Next to the passage, on the brick wall of a one-story shop—now out of business—someone had painted a mural of a woman wearing a flowing white dress with a high collar that surrounded the back of her neck. Yeager had looked her up, of course. "That's Queen Charlotte, queen of England during and after the Revolutionary War, and she's wearing her coronation dress. They called her the botanist queen. Notice the flowers in her dress, hair, and hand?"

Travail noticed. Harriet and Queen Charlotte had something in common: their love of flowers.

They stood there, waiting for something to happen. But other than almost getting hit by a car because they stood in the secondary street to observe the alley guarded by a queen, that was it. No ah-ha moment. No entrance to a mine filled with gold. Nothing to see. Unless you were Yeager, who saw something Travail didn't. "History is fantastic, ain't it?"

When Travail didn't reply, Yeager slapped him on the back and laughed. "Craig Travail, even lawyers use their imagination from time to time."

Travail took another look. He thought about the history a gleaming city bent on tearing down its past had buried and what it must have been when the Count Chevalier Vincent de Rivafinoli walked through this passage and up to a loud, busy, and productive gold mine in Charlotte's early years. When he closed his eyes, he could see it all. He was grateful for Yeager, a living example of the need to approach history and life with childlike wonder.

In fact, there was a lot to be grateful for, but as Travail tapped the cool-down button on the treadmill, his thoughts turned to the loose ends they hadn't tied up.

They never figured out who bored holes in the gold bars, extracted the gold, and substituted pyrite, and they might never know who did it, but Travail's gut told him Elkin was the thief. It would be just like the man to take that gold and squirrel it away in a rainy-day evil-doer fund so he could use it to take a shot at them after he licked his wounds. Maybe he would go to prison. But even if he did, the man was like a cockroach who thrived in the most extreme environments and who would eventually show up to spoil the picnic.

Regarding who killed Landry, prosecutor Liza Fortuna had become impatient. Facing an upcoming election for district attorney and having lost Elkin as her campaign manager—and his financial support—she needed a public victory after Joey's mistrial.

"I am going to put Landry's killer away," she'd said to Travail on the phone yesterday. "If you or the detective don't give me someone, I'm coming after Joey again."

Travail pushed back. "And you will lose again. Elkin knows who killed Landry. Cut a deal with him."

Fortuna grunted. "That man will not get a deal from me. I was foolish to let him be my campaign manager. He will get the maximum sentence for his crime."

Travail agreed Elkin should get the maximum sentence for what he'd done, but he didn't tell Fortuna that. He prioritized clearing Joey of the murder charge.

"If you don't cut a deal with Elkin, I will call Elkin as a witness in Joey's trial. It will not play well that he assisted you in the first trial, especially when the jury learns he told Barnard where to hide the victim. And if Channel 24 News, for whatever reason, focuses on your decision to hire Elkin as your campaign manager, it could be embarrassing."

"Are you threatening to harm my reputation?" Fortuna shot back.

"No, but Elkin harms the reputation of anyone who does business with him. You'd be better off to focus on getting a murder conviction against the actual murderer."

Fortuna relented, but only slightly. "Detective Sizemore and I have a meeting with Elkin tonight. I will consider making a deal with him, but only if he has solid evidence of the killer's identity."

Travail wondered if she or the detective would have news about a deal today. Harriet was worried about her brother.

Joey didn't seem to be concerned though. That was another loose end they hadn't tied up. Why wasn't Joey worried?

Travail skipped the Indie buffet breakfast and morning activities, knowing Harriet would be there. He had an errand to run and a task to perform at Harriet's house while she was away. He borrowed Yeager's truck, and Blue rode shotgun.

The lawn and garden store had several sizes. As he made his choice, Yeager's advice came to him. "You might as well go big, Craig Travail," as if Yeager knew anything about plants. Still. He chose several three gallon plastic containers of mature plants. Blue welcomed him back to the truck with a howl.

Travail punched in the code to Harriet's garage—they shared more and more with each other these days—and borrowed her wagon, shovel, and trowel. After Blue helped him with the digging, he stood up from his work, brushed himself off, and admired the scene.

The clustered flowers in full bloom on the green stalks were a bright yellow, a remarkable improvement over the shredded plants the detective left behind in this same spot.

What was it Harriet told the detective? "Goldenrod navigates change and uncertainty with confidence and independence."

As for him and Harriet and whatever was brewing between them, it was time to be confident. Time to be like a goldenrod. Harriet, he was sure, would be the one to handle the independent part of their relationship.

Travail stuck an envelope with a note next to the planted flowers that read: *Your subscription to Garden & Gun magazine is on the way. Your boyfriend, Craig.*

When he arrived for lunch, after having dropped both Yeager's truck and Blue off at their cottages and showered and changed, Peaches pointed him to "your reserved table, where your girlfriend awaits you." She winked.

Travail chose black golf pants for the day, because they were nice enough, fit well, and were comfortable, along with a short-sleeve buttondown in a blue, gold, and white plaid. He thought about wearing his tennis shoes and then decided to wear the new casual shoes Harriet suggested he buy—Skechers—as comfortable as his soft fabric golf shoes.

Their entire mystery-solving team was present for lunch and looking good. Yeager, dressed up more than usual for Yeager, told some kind of joke to Nelli, and she laughed. He wore brown cargo shorts, a gold and red western-style short-sleeved shirt—"it is too damn hot for flannel today"—and his best hiking shoes. Nelli wore her signature NASCAR flag earrings, an elbow-length red blouse with ruffles around the collar and down the front, tan cropped pants, and cream and tan tennis shoes.

Becky and Max held hands and sipped wine. Becky wore yellow slim-cropped slacks, a lemon-print top, and white sandals, along with simple jewelry. Her date was dapper as usual. The Godfather sported a white seersucker suit, pushing the dictates of Southern fashion to the edge as Labor Day was upon them.

Joey and Harriet were relaxed in conversation. Joey had been to the store at Harriet's suggestion and bought a new wardrobe. Prison orange was out. Comfortable but well-fitting blue jeans were in, which he wore with a plaid short-sleeve shirt.

Travail took a moment to observe Harriet as she laughed at something Joey said. She wore tan-and-black-striped linen pants, a black linen tank, and cream sandals with a little heel. He supposed she chose, as a nod to their success, several gold necklaces, a gold bangle bracelet, and gold and diamond earrings. She caught him looking at her, smiled, and pointed at her Apple Watch with a black leather band, as if to say, *About time you arrived.*

Roscoe, Travail's co-counsel and recently reinstated People's Court happy-hour judge, stood in his casual slacks, loose-fitting shirt, and cowboy boots—tobacco free at the moment—and shook his hand with an update.

"The district attorney called this morning. They plan to arrest the killer today and drop the charges against Joey. I thought you should be the one to share the good news."

Travail thanked Roscoe but preferred to wait for confirmation.

Yeager had a foot-long bun on his plate covered in onions and relish. "Hope you're hungry, Craig Travail. Big day of good eats at the Indie. Ballpark dogs. Bratwurst. Plenty of toppings."

"There is also the vegetarian burger, Craig." Harriet grinned when she said it.

Travail was confident he wouldn't choose the fake burger. For once, he agreed with Yeager. That would be an affront to his taste buds.

"Saved you a seat." Harriet pulled him in and gave him a kiss on the mouth, without the senior discount. Their friends clapped.

"You enjoy doing this, don't you?"

She laughed.

Nelli went over the afternoon events. "After the band's first set, a motorized wheelchair race will take place around the lake. I expect my cheering squad to be at the finish line. Yeager is my pit boss."

"We'll be there, Nelli," Joey said. "After you ran down Bailey, I doubt anyone can beat you, especially when metal rubs against metal."

"She's a three-time champ," Yeager bragged.

Celia appeared from nowhere to enter the conversation. "I bet she is."

She was dressed in white ankle-length pants, a print top in more vibrant colors than Travail had seen her in before, and a coral-colored cardigan, perhaps in case the weather got cooler later in the day. She wore gold flats and the same jewelry he'd seen her in when he met her at their first Indie board meeting together.

"Hello, Celia," Becky said. "Are you enjoying your day?"

"I am. Very glad I moved here. Sterling and Bailey were against it, but I had a good feeling about the Indie."

Travail had warmed to Celia Standish. "We're glad you're here."

The others echoed the sentiment.

Celia said she had a gift for Harriet. "What's that saying? Lemons into lemonade. In your case, forged gold coin melted into a solid gold ring. A remembrance of what you accomplished."

Yeager whistled. "A wedding ring. How about that, Harriet?"

Harriet told Celia it wasn't necessary, but thanked her for the gesture. "I will wear it on a chain." She glared at Yeager as she said it.

A few awkward seconds went by before Celia addressed Joey. "Thank you, Joey. You didn't have to do what you did."

"You either." Joey got up and gave Celia a hug. "I hope what's coming won't be too hard on you."

"I'll be fine. Look after your sister. And yourself."

Celia paused before she left their table and addressed the group.

"You will hear a lot of bad things about me in the next few days. Please don't think the worst of me. It's not what it looks like."

Celia left and sat with her bridge club friends. Harriet eyed Joey for an explanation. "What's not what it looks like, this time?"

Before Joey said anything, Detective Sizemore and a police officer arrived outside the tent. Travail nudged Harriet and pointed at them. Soon, everyone at their table had their eyes on the detective and the officer.

The detective walked under the tent in their direction. The officer stayed put.

Before Sizemore reached their table, he veered off and stopped at Celia's table, where he leaned down and whispered something in her ear. Celia nodded, spoke to her friends, and left the table with the detective. They arrived at where the police officer stood, had a few words together, and the officer and Celia walked up the hill to the parking area.

The detective turned and headed toward them.

"Joey, what's going on?" Harriet asked.

"It was justified," Joey insisted.

Detective Sizemore greeted everyone, said he was sorry for intruding, but said he had news. "We have made an arrest in Landry's murder." He looked at Joey. "The district attorney will drop the murder charge against you today. On behalf of myself and my department, I am sorry for misjudging you and putting you through the trial."

The table should have celebrated, but like Travail, everyone must have been stunned by what had just happened. "Did you arrest Celia?"

"I did."

Roscoe asked Travail's next question. "What about Elkin?"

"The district attorney cut a deal with him. No prison time. Only community service."

"What community would want that weasel?" Yeager barked.

The detective didn't disagree. "It had to be done. He gave us Celia's name."

"And you trust him?" The skepticism rolled off Harriet's tongue.

"Not a bit. But he recorded his phone conversation with Celia that night. She called him, said she had a body, and needed his help to dispose of it."

Joey offered an addition. "She didn't know Elkin would instruct Dan to put Landry under Harriet's house."

Detective Sizemore exhibited his patented confused look as he addressed Joey. "Anything else you want to share about that night? Anything to explain why Celia killed Landry?"

Harriet supported the detective's query in a tone that said it was time to talk. "This time, Joey, you need to tell us everything."

Joey didn't disappoint.

"Landry was at the Rivafinoli Passage with Dan when I arrived. When Celia showed up a few minutes later, she pressed Landry for information about my fraud conviction and her son Junior's death. Things didn't add up, she said. A source—I later learned it was Dan— had told her Landry had lied to her and the family. Dan wanted to set things straight with Celia."

The detective interrupted to ask a question. "Did you see Celia shoot and kill Landry?"

"Yes, but it's not what it looks like."

Harriet jumped in again. "I wish you would erase that phrase from your vocabulary and tell us what happened."

"When Landry pulled his gun, Celia did the same. Landry wanted Junior's forged coins for either their melt value or to sell them for a profit to unsuspecting buyers. He also wanted Penny's rare coin collection. I told him I didn't know the location of Junior's coins, and I knew nothing about a collection of my father's. He didn't believe me and was in a fidgety mood. I've thought a lot about what happened that night and how I might have prevented it."

Joey set the scene and took everyone through what happened next.

Landry was inside the narrow alley, facing Celia, with Dan a few feet to his left. Celia stood in the entrance to the alley, facing Landry, with Joey a few feet to her right, facing Dan. Landry and Dan were only fifteen feet apart from Celia and Joey.

The gun in Landry's hand pointed at Celia, then Joey, and back to Celia, and as they talked, the gun in Landry's hand continued to move from one target to the other. The whole time, Celia kept her gun aimed at Landry.

Landry taunted Celia. "Put your gun down. Don't make me kill another Standish."

Celia extended her gun hand and kept it pointed at Landry. "Why did you kill my son? He was good to you."

Landry shrugged. "Junior overreacted to my framing Joey, the forged coins paid for with his money, and my embezzlement of the rest."

Dan pleaded with Landry to put the gun down. "You don't want to do this. You came for the coins, not to kill anyone. That's what you said."

Landry turned his gun back on Joey and licked his lips. "Changed my mind. You have three seconds to reveal the location of Junior's and Penny's coins, or you will join your father in the coin collecting paradise in the sky. Three, two, one."

A gun fired.

And Landry fell to the ground.

The detective and everyone at the table were silent, waiting for more.

Joey shook his head, as if to try to shake the memory. "It happened so fast, Landry was dead before he hit the ground. Celia is a woman of many talents. One is how to take dead aim with a gun and hit your target."

Detective Sizemore scratched his head. "You're telling me you will testify Celia shot Landry to save your life?"

Joey nodded.

"That's why you didn't give her up," Harriet said. "You wanted to protect her from prosecution because she protected you."

"She protected me twice. Celia gave the video to Yeager. I sent it to her because I wanted her to know where Dan put Landry's body."

Yeager laid things out in his unique way. "It seems the prosecutor has a sour pickle of a case against Celia."

The detective ignored Yeager. "Joey, why didn't you offer this information sooner?"

"You wouldn't have believed me, especially if Celia didn't cooperate."

The detective scratched his head. "I suppose you're right. Why was she hesitant?"

"She wanted to see if I could beat the charge without her story having to be told. She didn't want to live through her son's death again. It's why she sent Travail the email."

Travail had been considering how to defend Celia when Joey's remark startled him. "Celia Standish sent me the *vengeanceissweet* email?"

"She wanted to motivate you, Craig. Did it work?"

"It did." In fact, the email jolted him, gave him the impetus to take two steps forward, one to improve his personal life, and one to help the community who had adopted him.

Roscoe asked the detective what he thought this meant for Celia.

Removing a fresh cigar from his shirt pocket, Detective Sizemore licked one end, stuck it in his mouth, and rolled it around.

"The way I see things, Fortuna doesn't have any good options. Dan Barnard is dead, and the only witness left is Joey, the man she first charged with murder. She will have to admit Joey didn't do it. Not sure how she will claim Joey is a liar about what really happened. This could cause her to suffer another courtroom defeat, which she doesn't want while she runs for office."

Sizemore removed the cigar from his mouth and pointed it at Joey. "Can you come to the station and give a statement?"

"Happy to do it."

The detective saluted with his unlit cigar and left.

"I have a question," Becky said to Joey. "Why did Celia want the forged coins?"

Yeager answered first. "To make Harriet a wedding ring."

Harriet huffed. "Really, Yeager. I should report you to your middle-school principal."

Joey laughed before he provided the correct answer. "Celia didn't want the forged coins to fall into the wrong hands and bring further shame on her son's reputation. When she learned Harriet set up a trust to care for Dan's daughter, she melted the coins down and, except for the gold she used for Harriet's ring, she sold the raw gold and added the proceeds to the trust. She and Harriet asked Nelli to manage the money."

"I was happy to do it," Nelli said.

Becky and Max excused themselves, and Becky happily took her beau's arm. "We will save everyone seats at the concert."

Travail took a deep breath.

That's it then.

Mysteries solved.

Nelli must have had the same thought. "Hey Yeager, have we solved enough mysteries for you for a while?"

Yeager stroked his beard. "I saw the most interesting thing on the news today about—"

Harriet poked Yeager in the side. "Nope, not having it, Yeager. Not today."

As if to second Harriet's directive, the esteemed Roscoe "Chaw" Brady pulled his tobacco pouch from his pocket, grabbed a plug, and stuffed it in his right cheek. Then, he gave his ruling. "That's enough for now. Case closed."

Travail and Harriet drifted from the tent and stood under a clear blue sky as the band struck up its first tune. The selection was a decent rendition of the Eagles song *Take It Easy*. And while this wasn't Winslow, Arizona, Harriet was a fine sight to see, for sure.

He reached his hand out to her, palm up, and she took it. They squeezed. And together, as one, they walked hand in hand to the sound of music.

Harriet talked the whole way.

"Just because we are boyfriend and girlfriend now, don't think we are getting married. And don't think I am giving up my cottage, because I am not. It is good to maintain boundaries. And another thing. You need to learn to cook and take care of your yard. You're doing better with the exercise and clothing, but your culinary and gardening skills need serious attention."

As Yeager might say, "And so it begins, Craig Travail. And so it begins."

THE END

If you enjoyed reading Deadly Gold Rush, please leave a review online. Reviews are a great way to help authors reach more readers.

AFTERWORD

By growing up in Charlotte and practicing law there my entire legal career, I heard stories about Charlotte's gold rush history. I knew about the Mint Museum of Art because I played Little League baseball two blocks away and went there on school field trips. And I had fun delving into the gold rush history for this novel to discover what I never knew.

If you're interested in more facts about the Carolina Gold Rush, read on.

If not, please skip to the acknowledgments.

And because this afterword is probably longer than it should be—as I said, I enjoyed the history—I've included my sources after the acknowledgments if you want to skip to them.

The Carolina Gold Rush

The first gold rush in the United States sprung from twelve-year-old Conrad Reed's discovery in 1799 of a seventeen-pound gold nugget in Little Meadow Creek in Cabarrus County, North Carolina, not too far from Charlotte. Conrad was playing in the creek that ran through his father's farm when he spied the shiny yellow rock the size of a shoe. He picked it up and found it was heavier than he expected. He showed it to his father, John Reed, who showed it to a Concord silversmith, who told him the rock was worthless.

Unfazed, the Reeds used the rock for three years for what author Bruce Roberts in *The Carolina Gold Rush* called "the world's most expensive door stop." That doorstop turned out to be one of the largest nuggets ever found in the eastern United States. And, yes, the story Yeager told his friends was true. A Fayetteville jeweler swindled ole man Reed by paying him $3.50 for a nugget that was worth several thousand dollars at the time.

When John Reed discovered the jeweler scammed him, he went to the creek and found more gold, and with several partners, they began to search for gold on the surface with slave labor, leading in 1803 to a slave named Peter discovering a twenty-eight-pound nugget just under the surface in Reed's Meadow Creek. It was believed to be the largest nugget discovered at the time in the United States.

When word spread about Reed's good fortune, farmers bought gear to search for gold on their properties, leading to discoveries in Anson, Montgomery, Mecklenburg, and other counties in the state. From around 1804 to 1828, most of the domestic gold coined at the United States Mint in Philadelphia came from North Carolina, and the excitement resulted in thousands of foreigners coming to North Carolina to make their fortunes.

Around 1830, the *Western Carolinian* of Salisbury and the *Miners' and Farmers' Journal* of Charlotte regularly published articles and advertisements to satisfy the public's thirst for information on gold, including where to find it and how to get at it. Other state newspapers fueled the rush with tall tales about nuggets found that were too heavy to lift.

During the early days of the Carolina Gold Rush, miners engaged in what was called branch or placer mining on the surface. Several decades later, miners dug shafts and mined gold underground, by following the vein of gold.

Today, Reed Gold Mine is a State Historic Site where visitors can tour underground mine tunnels, see the restored ore-crushing stamp mill, and pan for gold.

The Charlotte Gold Rush

The April 8, 1929, headline in *The Charlotte Observer* read: "Streets of Charlotte Literally Paved with Gold." In the early 1800s, all those newcomers hoped that was true.

The first recorded attempt to follow a gold vein below the surface in Mecklenburg County was by Samuel McComb on his farm in 1825, and it made him rich. The McComb Mine, which later became known as the Saint Catherine Mine, was near where the Carolina Panthers football team plays today, with shafts to a depth of more than one hundred feet and tunnels in many directions. The Rudisill Mine, discussed in more detail below, dug vertical shafts as deep as three hundred feet, with horizontal tunnels connecting them.

Gold fever led to close to sixty mines popping up across the county, making Mecklenburg the county with the most mines in the state. Many of those mines went by the names of their landowners, but others were more creative, such as the Black Cat, Queen of Sheba, King Soloman, and Yellow Dog.

Working the mines was a tough way to earn a living. Miners often turned their pay into liquor. One northern observer could "hardly conceive of a more immoral community... Drunkenness, gambling, fighting, lewdness, and every other vice exist here to an awful extent."

And yet, even though Charlotte was a lively place—with the taverns and the "Sons of Temperance" making their cases against each other—Charlotte did not devolve to a Wild-West-style saloon town. Businesses thrived by selling to the miners.

With the Charlotte Mint's arrival in 1837 and the numerous mines being worked in the Charlotte area, Charlotte became the mining capital of the United States.

~

Facts are important, but stories are mostly about people and the places they inhabit.

I discovered several interesting people and places from the Charlotte Gold Rush era who inspired the characters and settings in *Deadly Gold Rush*.

The Rivafinoli Passage is a real place in South End. It's not much to look at—a good place for a murder in a novel—but you can find it on Lincoln Street, a small side street in South End off South Church Street. And yes, on a brick wall at the entrance to the alley there is a mural of Queen Charlotte, who was married to insane King George.

Who was this Rivafinoli character, anyway?

Accounts vary, and are likely embellished every time someone writes about him, but he's been described as a flamboyant Italian aristocrat and mining expert who hailed from Milan, Italy, with the titles of count and chevalier.

Rivafinoli (sometimes spelled "Ravafanoli" or "Ravafinoli") came to Charlotte around 1830 at the age of forty-three with significant mining experience in large South American mines. He brought with him more than fifty experienced foreign workers and the financial backing of New York investors and the London Mining Company.

Rivafinoli made improvements in underground mining techniques at Charlotte's largest commercial mines. He dressed in the finest clothes, and lived in a luxurious home at the corner of South Tryon and Morehead Streets, from which he departed daily with his gold-headed cane to inspect his mines accompanied by a manservant.

This bigger-than-life character left a trail that's still celebrated today. John Short, in a piece in *The Charlotte Ledger*, said, "The next time you look at the Corporate Center in the Charlotte skyline, think of the mine shafts below and the cane-walkin', wheelin', dealin', kiss-stealin' son of a gun who captured Charlotte's imagination in the first half of the nineteenth century."

But truth be told, even with his trappings of wealth, his titles, his mining successes, and his storied reputation, the count's time in Charlotte passed quickly. He slipped away in 1832 or 1833, leaving a mountain of debt in his wake.

Into Rivafinoli's void stepped thirty-six-year-old John E. Penman.

John Penman, who is the ancestor of the fictional Penny Penman in *Deadly Gold Rush,* showed up in Charlotte and went straight to the Mecklenburg County Court of Common Pleas, where he, like Rivafinoli had done before him, filed a declaration to become a citizen of the United States, renouncing his citizenship to his home country. The gold tug was that strong.

He was reputed to be a Methodist minister, although it is unclear whether that was before or after his Charlotte gold mining adventures. Either way, the spiritual vocation was nothing like his gold mining lifestyle.

Described as a daring wheeler-dealer and a bit of a rascal, Penman was often in the company of unmarried women, whom he referred to as his sisters. He liked fine wine and parties and was generous with his money, having once placed fifteen hundred dollars in the Methodist Church collection plate after his miners struck a rich vein on Rudisill Hill.

Like Rivafinoli, he was known to enjoy the finer things. He had a manservant named Goodluck, who groomed him every morning, saddled his horse, and rode behind him at a respectful distance. One of his associates, a man named Penworthy, often accompanied Penman to one of several local taverns.

Records show Penman coming and going during the 1830s and 1840s to dodge debts and chase the next big find, but by the end of his days as a gold miner, he had the reputation of one of the most experienced miners to operate in the Charlotte region.

Perhaps John Penman quit because the mining got too hard, or maybe he decided it was time to minister to his Methodist flock.

I picked the Rudisill Mine as the focus for the novel because of its importance to the Charlotte Gold Rush and its staying power. Mining on the Rudisill load lasted one hundred years, from the early days of deep shaft mining to the late 1930s.

Located in what is now the heart of booming South End, the gold vein extends from Summit Avenue (formerly Gold Street) down to Bank of American Stadium where the Carolina Panthers play professional football. The mine is a historical relic hiding in plain sight.

There is a concrete cover over the pump shaft that sits in a gravel parking lot, backing up to the Wilmore neighborhood, just like the novel said. This pump shaft head is the only ground-level reminder of the major producer of gold in Charlotte.

A prospector—some say a hunter stalking deer—found gold on Rudisill Hill in 1826, leading to early efforts to mine the gold with shallow digs, pits, and trenches.

Then along came Rivafinoli, and then Penman, and then the mine changed hands many times over the next one hundred years.

The Carsons were the last to own the operating mine before it shut down in the 1930s—remember, Carson Street? It was one of the streets where the characters searched for Penny's gold coins.

In September 1965, the director of the Mint Museum of Art made a public plea that the Rudisill Mine be reopened as a tourist attraction. He suggested it be equipped with shuttle cars and reinforced for safety, and he tried to shame the city for letting this piece of Charlotte history go ignored. He also complained the city had changed the name of Gold Street to Summit Avenue.

It took a few years, but the city listened enough to solicit studies. The probable condition of the Rudisill Mine, as described in a report to the city in the 1970s was: "Except where thick veins have been mined out, tunnels are likely to be very narrow, allowing only single-file passage of a man and possibly a wheelbarrow.... Commonly, low ceiling height will require a man to walk in a stooped position or even crawl." The report also described tunnels packed with rubble and decaying timbers. Added to that was the problem of the underground water that filled the mines. Not a good report to promote the building of a gold mine museum.

In other words, the Standish family dream was an unrealistic venture from the start.

But a few things did happen to bring attention to the area.

In 2014, a nonprofit known as The Gold District of Charlotte, Inc., was formed to promote the district in Charlotte's South End. So far, they have helped put historical signage in place, helped obtained favorable zoning, generated interest in the history, and created a 2030 Vision Plan—the date 2030 being two hundred years after Rivafinoli arrived in Charlotte.

In addition to street names and markers that honor gold mines and gold miners, a commemorative marker was placed at the site of the Rudisill Mine. While I was doing research for this novel, the marker was there, but then when I went back for another visit, it looked like a truck had sideswiped it and knocked it down. I was told efforts were being made to put the sign up again. Perhaps the Rudisill Mine just can't get the respect it deserves.

Charlotte's gold mines and expanding population of gold seekers in the 1800s led local leaders, with the support of President Andrew Jackson, to put pressure on Congress to place a branch mint in Charlotte. In 1835, Congress passed an act to establish branch mints in Charlotte; Dahlonega, Georgia, and New Orleans, Louisiana. Charlotte's mint was the first branch to open in 1837 and was located where the federal courthouse sits on Trade Street today.

On March 28, 1837, the mint struck its first coin, a half-eagle, followed by the quarter eagle. An eagle was worth ten dollars, so the quarter-eagle was two-fifty and the half eagle was five dollars. And to make you remember what they were making, they hung a gold eagle above the entrance, but more about that below.

Of the three denominations of gold coins made at the Charlotte Mint, the quarter eagle is the most difficult to collect and requires patience. Maybe that's why it took Penny Penman so long to compile his collection.

Operations at the Charlotte Mint continued until April 20, 1861, when production was halted with the seizure of the mint by Confederate troops.

For the next four years, the flag of the Confederacy flew over the golden eagle, but the inside was turned into a military headquarters, begging the question: what happened to the gold? As tempting as it was, I decided not to turn this into a Confederate gold treasure story.

When the mint reopened in 1869 after the Civil War, it never made another gold coin but instead operated as an assay office.

In 1895, a federal courthouse and post office were built next to the Charlotte Mint, and in 1913, the mint's assay office closed, and the US Treasury vacated the building, leading in 1930 to a plan to demolish it to make room for an expansion of the post office.

But when demolition began in 1933, the Charlotte Woman's Club undertook an effort to save the mint—or, at least, its structure. With the club's fundraising efforts, a donation of land by E.C. Griffith in the Eastover neighborhood, and construction done by Depression-era CWA workers, the Mint Museum of Art, North Carolina's first art museum, came to life in September 1936.

In December 1935, *The Charlotte Observer* reported that a committee of five local chapters of the Daughters of the American Revolution were working to recover the gold eagle that "formerly spread its wings above the entrance to the old mint building for presentation to the Mint Museum of Art." The old bird was found, bought, and readied for restoration—the paper reporting an on-again, off-again prognosis for the project over several months given its condition. Finally, the eagle made of oak that stood five feet tall with a fourteen-foot wingspan was restored. The August 23, 1936, *Charlotte News* showed a picture of the eagle under the headline "Mint Eagle Will Grace New Mint Museum."

Another article shared with me by Ellen Show, director of Library and Archives of the Mint Museum, gave me an idea for the novel. The October 14, 1936 headline commented on what the artist faced when he undertook to gild the eagle with gold leaf: "Bees Found in Eagle at Mint."

The gold eagle proudly protected the entrance to the Mint Museum until it began to fall apart in 1971. Once again, local women came together to save the mint's symbol. This time it was the Charlotte Debutante Club who raised the money, but instead of wood, the new eagle was built of fiberglass impregnated with polyester over a foam core to last longer.

A July 8, 1972, article in *The Charlotte Observer* featured a picture of the eagle being lifted with a crane to "its new nest" over the front door of the former US Mint and Assay Office with the headline "The Eagle Flies."

According to museum staff when I took my own tour, the bees have continued to be a problem. In *Deadly Gold Rush,* I used artistic license and turned the bees into hornets.

The museum expanded several times, first in 1967 and again in 1985, and there is a new entrance on the opposite side of the building from where the eagle flies. But still, the eagle flies.

Today, the Mint Museum of Art offers permanent and rotating exhibits, community and cultural programs, and they have on display a complete set of every coin minted at the Charlotte Mint. If you walk the halls and grounds and use your imagination, you can wander back in time to the Charlotte Gold Rush era.

In my research, I ran across many truth-is-stranger-than-fiction stories that fueled my creative juices, including:

- A story of a man who wrote a book containing clues for his readers to find a treasure he buried in different places in the US.
- A story about coins someone's ancestor buried in the walls of a house that led to litigation as to their ownership.
- A story about a couple stumbling across a hoard of 1,400 gold coins dating from 1847 worth ten million dollars.

- A story about the movement of the Confederacy's coinage near the end of the Civil War, questions about what happened to the haul, and the fact the last cabinet meeting of the Confederacy occurred in Charlotte.
- A story about coins being moved by mules from a bank in Charlotte to a place called Grasshopper Springs to hide them from approaching Union forces led by William Tecumseh Sherman.
- And yes, stories about gold being discovered in uptown Charlotte in the modern era, though in small fragments.

A 1990 *Charlotte Observer* article reported that while workers for a local construction company worked on a building site at Trade and Tryon Streets, they found "chunks of granite embedded with gold." The supervisor said, "Everybody kind of got in on it. You could look out at lunch time, and everybody would be out there with a hammer chipping."

Maybe Penny Penman wasn't that crazy to believe he could discover gold in the twenty-first century under the streets of uptown Charlotte.

Thank you for reading my novel and for indulging my ramblings about Charlotte's gold mining history.

ACKNOWLEDGMENTS

When my characters decided their next mystery would involve the Charlotte Gold Rush, I reached out to Charlotte experts, and they were kind to respond.

I am grateful to Sheila Bumgarner, longtime librarian with the Robinson-Spangler Carolina Room of the Charlotte Mecklenburg Library, for her Charlotte Gold Rush knowledge and pointing me in the right direction; to Tom Hanchett, Charlotte historian, for his insight on Charlotte's history during the period; to Dan Morrill, Charlotte historian, for sharing his papers and knowledge about Charlotte's gold rush, and in particular, his papers on the Rudisill Gold Mine; and to Brian Trietley, numismatist with Independence Coin, for his knowledge about rare gold coinage, their value, and forgeries.

For a modern look at what has been happening in South End and South End's gold history, I am grateful to Caren Wingate, president of the Gold District of Charlotte, Inc, and Michael Sullivan, commercial real estate agent and local historian, both of whom met with me, shared gold mine stories, and served as early readers. Thanks also to Page Carson Rogers, descendent of the Rudisill Gold Mine owners, for discussing their family's mine; to Jennifer Winford, Mint Museum librarian, for her knowledge of Charlotte Gold Rush resources that led me to the blueprints of the original Charlotte Mint; to the authors and writers whose source work is referenced in the next section of this book; and to Ellen Show, director of the Mint Museum Library and Archives, for her tours of the museum, her research about how the Charlotte Mint became the Mint Museum, and in particular, educating me on the history of the golden eagle on the building, which led me to what Penny Penman thought was the perfect hiding place.

During the writing process, I leaned on seven beta readers to give me early feedback on the story. I am grateful to my wife, Janet, who is always the first to read an early version of the manuscript, and to a talented group of writers and readers made up of Bud Schill, Jake Breeden, Sarah Archer, Hannah Larrew, Michael Sullivan, and Caren Wingate, whose smart insights helped make the manuscript better before the editors dug in with their sharp pencils.

As always, I appreciate the work of my editor, Nora Gaskin, who pushed me to add, subtract, reorder, and clarify, and for her suggestions to eliminate history to improve the flow. Thanks to my copyeditor, Kelly Lojk, who fixed the punctuation, caught errors, and made sure I didn't violate the style guide. And thanks to my daughter, Jordan Wade, who helped proof the book prior to publication, though any final mistakes are the work of the gremlins who snuck them into the manuscript later and my failure to catch them.

I am grateful to Jennipher Tripp for her formatting and technical assistance with the print and ebook and her work on the audiobook, Tim Barber with Dissect Designs for the front and back covers, and Jessie Cunniffe with Book Blurb Magic for the back cover description. And I am grateful to have Heather Setzler as the audiobook narrator. As you can tell, it takes a passel of people to put a novel into the world.

I am grateful to the wonderful authors who took time to read *Deadly Gold Rush* and offer their kind praise: Sarah Archer, Joy Callaway, Mark de Castrique, Molly Grantham, Halli Gomez, Sara E. Johnson, and Mark West.

And I appreciate Park Road Books, Charlotte Mecklenburg Library, and the independent book stores, libraries, and online sites that help readers find my books.

Finally, I am grateful once again to Janet, who puts up with my habit of disappearing into my hyper-focused cone of silence to write, especially when I should be tending to other matters. And I particularly appreciate her knowledge of plants, fashion, and food, because without her insight, I couldn't have planted or demolished Harriet's garden, dressed the characters, and prepared the delicious meals my fictional friends enjoyed.

SOURCES

In addition to my interviews of Sheila Bumgarner, Dan Morrill, Tom Hanchett, Brian Trietley, Caren Wingate, Michael Sullivan, Jennifer Winford, Page Carson Rogers, and Ellen Show, my research sources included:

- *The Carolina Gold Rush* by Bruce Roberts (McNally and Loftin, 1971).

- *Minutes of Court of Common Pleas, Mecklenburg County, NC*, Volume IV, 1831–1840, transcribed by Herman Ferguson, located in FamilySearch Center Library in Salt Lake, Utah

- *Gold Coins of the Charlotte Mint 1838–1861*, Third Edition, by Douglas Winter (Zyrus Press, 2008), courtesy of Charlotte Mint Museum Library.

- *The United States Branch Mint at Charlotte, North Carolina: Its History and Coinage* by Clair M. Birdsall (Southern Historical Press, 1988), courtesy of Charlotte Mint Museum Library.

- *The Establishment of the Charlotte Branch Mint: A Documented History* by Anthony Stautzenberger (1976), courtesy of Charlotte Mint Museum Library.

- Numerous articles on the Charlotte Mint, the Mint Museum, and the mint's eagle published in *The Charlotte Observer* and *The Charlotte News* and collected by Ellen Show, director of library and archives at the Mint Museum.

- *Numismatic Forgery: An Illustrated Guide to the Practice, Principles, Methods, and Techniques Employed in the Private Manufacture of Rare Coins* by Charles M. Larson (Zyrus Press, 2004).

- *Gold Mining in North Carolina: A Bicentennial History* by Richard F. Knapp and Brent D. Glass (North Carolina Office of Archives and History, 1999).

- "Gold Mining on the Rudisill Lode and the Development of Charlotte, NC," prepared by Henry S. Brown and Mary F Hoffman with Geological Resources, for the City of Charlotte (August 1978).

- "Location, Geologic Setting, and Probable Extent and Condition of the Rudisill and St. Catherine Gold Mines, Charlotte, NC," prepared by Henry S. Brown with Geological Resources, for the City of Charlotte.

- "Survey and Research Report on the Pump Shaft Head of the Rudisill Hill Gold Mine" by Dan L. Morrill (October 11, 2017). http://landmarkscommission.org/wp-content/uploads/2017/09/RudisillSROctober2017-EASedit-2.pdf

- *Charlotte-Mecklenburg History with Dan Morrill* podcast episode "There's Gold in Them There Hills" (2020). https://www.buzzsprout.com/826069/2729884

- *A History of Charlotte and Mecklenburg County,* by Dan L.

Morrill, University of North Carolina at Charlotte, chapter 4: Gold and Railroads

- *The Charlotte Mecklenburg Story*, a resource of the Charlotte Mecklenburg Library. www.cmstory.org

- *History of Mecklenburg County and the City of Charlotte (1740–1903)* by Daniel A. Tompkins (Observer Printing House, 1903).

- *Hornets' Nest: The Story of Charlotte and Mecklenburg County* by William LeGette Blythe and Charles R. Brockman (McNally and Loftin, 1961).

- "A Brief History of Gold Mining in Mecklenburg County" by Issac Naylor, published in *Queen City Nerve* (July 6, 2022).

- "Charlotte's Historical Heavyweights: The Italian Prospector with a Gold-Tipped Cane" by John Short, published online in *The Charlotte Ledger* (October 1, 2022).

- "A Tour of Charlotte's Public Art" by Virginia Brown, published online at *Charlotte's Got a Lot*.

- "A Guide to the Carolina Gold Rush" by Mikala Young, published online in *Charlotte Parent* magazine (June 25, 2014).

- "What's the Story Behind the Giant Statues Guarding the Four Corners of Charlotte's City Center?" by Andie Judson, published online at WNCN.com (June 20, 2017).

- 2030 Vision Plan for The Gold District of Charlotte.

- "Mine Shaft Found Under Charlotte House Could Be 150-Year-Old Tunnel to Gold" by Anna Douglas, published online at WBTV.com (February 21, 2019).

- "G-G-Gosh! A Goldmine, Bulldozer Operator Drives Into 'Bottomless Pit' Here," by Bill Godwin, published in *Charlotte News* (1961).

- "Diggers Strike Gold, Mine Local History," published in *Charlotte Observer* (February 24, 1990).

READING GROUP GUIDE

1. Did the novel make you think about how history reveals itself in today's world, through the Charlotte Gold Rush, or in other ways?
2. Did the novel evoke for you feelings or questions about relationships?
3. Did the novel evoke for you feelings or questions about the loss of a loved one?
4. Did the novel evoke for you feelings or questions about living in retirement?
5. Which characters in the novel did you like the best? The least?
6. Which places in the novel (real or fictional) would you like to visit?
7. What were your favorite scenes?
8. What lessons learned by the characters did you appreciate?
9. Did you enjoy spending time with the characters?
10. Did this novel remind you of other novels?

ABOUT THE AUTHOR

Landis Wade is a recovering trial lawyer who writes mysteries and legal thrillers and the founder of the popular Charlotte Readers Podcast (where he interviewed more than 500 authors). *Deadly Declarations*, his first novel in the Indie Retirement Mystery Series, won ten awards, including winner in the 2022 American Fiction Awards in the Cozy Mystery category. His novella *The Christmas Redemption* won the Holiday category of the Twelfth Annual National Indie Excellence Awards. With the help of his podcast co-hosts, Sarah Archer and Hannah Larrew, he published The Write Quotes Series, an eight-book collection that feature inspirational and practical quotes about writing and the writing life from authors in more than thirty-three US states and four countries. Landis co-wrote a novella with podcast co-host Sarah Archer titled *Death by Podcasting*, a comedic mystery (in the vein of the Netflix series *Only Murders in the Building*) about the danger of podcasting with author guests.

The Charlotte Writers Club awarded him their 2025 Adelia Kimball Founders Award for service to the club and the literary community. He won the 2016 North Carolina State Bar short-story contest for *The Deliberation* and received awards for his nonfiction pieces *The Cape Fear Debacle* and *First Dance*. His short works have appeared in *Writersdigest.com*, *The Charlotte Observer*, *Flying South*, *Fiction on the Web*, and in more than six anthologies.

He lives in North Carolina, where he grew up, went to school, practiced law, and learned to write.

Linktree: www.linktr.ee/landiswade
Author website: www.landiswade.com
Podcast website: www.charlottereaderspodcast.com
Facebook Author Page: www.facebook.com/authorlandiswade
Bookbub Author page: www.bookbub.com/authors/landis-wade

Contact: author@landiswade.com